Tom Tullett is one of the best-known crime reporters in Fleet Street. He is the Chief of the *Daily Mirror*'s Crime Bureau and the only journalist to have been a member of the Criminal Investigation Department at Scotland Yard. Since the War he has covered every major crime in this country and many in other parts of the world. He has an intimate knowledge of London's underworld and of police work.

Also by Tom Tullett

Portrait of a Bad Man
Inside Interpol
Inside Dartmoor
Bernard Spilsbury: His Life and Cases (with
Douglas G. Browne)
No Answer from Foxtrot Eleven

Tom Tullett

Murder Squad

Famous Cases of Scotland Yard's Murder Squad

A TRIAD PANTHER BOOK

GRANADA
London Toronto Sydney New York

Published by Triad/Granada in 1981

ISBN 0 586 05218 6

Triad Paperbacks Ltd is an imprint of
Chatto, Bodley Head & Jonathan Cape Ltd and
Granada Publishing Ltd

First published as *Strictly Murder* in Great Britain by
The Bodley Head Ltd 1979
Copyright © Tom Tullett 1979

Set, printed and bound in Great Britain by
Cox & Wyman Ltd, Reading
Set in Intertype Times

To Susie and Joanna,
my daughters

Contents

Acknowledgments

This book is about the men of Scotland Yard, and it is to the people of that legendary headquarters of the Metropolitan Police to whom I give my sincere thanks.

In particular my most cordial thanks are due to Sir David McNee, QPM, Commissioner of the Metropolitan Police, for permission to look into criminal records and to talk to detectives who have first-hand knowledge of murder investigation.

Many policemen still serving have given immense assistance. They are: Sir Colin Woods, KCVO, CBE, formerly Deputy Commissioner at Scotland Yard; Gilbert Kelland, CBE, QPM, Assistant Commissioner (Crime); John Wilson, CBE, OBE, Assistant Commissioner; H. D. Walton, QPM, Deputy Assistant Commissioner; Arthur Howard, Commander of the Murder Squad and his staff; Commanders Donald Neesham and James Sewell.

Miss Plank and the staff of the New Scotland Yard Reference Library have been wonderfully helpful and so have many of the detectives, now long retired, whose exploits are related in this book and who have contributed so much in recalling their investigations in minute detail.

Thanks are also due to the following for permission to reproduce photographs: the Commissioner of the Metropolitan Police, numbers 1, 8 and 19; the *Daily Mirror*, numbers 2, 3, 4, 5, 6, 7, 9, 10, 13, 14, 15, 16, 18, 20, 22, 23, 25, 26; the *Daily Mail*, number 11; Associated Press, number 12; West Midlands Police Force, number 21; Bedfordshire Police, number 17; *Royal Gazette*, Bermuda, number 24.

Introduction

This is the story of Scotland Yard's Murder Squad, told through case histories, some notorious, many freshly brought to light. The Squad's title was never officially given but thoroughly earned because its members have been the men who have investigated cases of sudden death. It was founded in 1907 and in its seventy-four years it has achieved a clear-up rate of more than ninety per cent, an unprecedented record.

At the time of its foundation there were a large number of unsolved crimes in the provinces of England and Wales, many of them cases of murder. There had long been a criminal investigation department at Scotland Yard, and the then Home Secretary, Herbert Gladstone, decided to utilize some of these men to assist local forces.

There were seven hundred detectives in London but few anywhere else and in 1907 a Home Office spokesman wrote: 'The County Police, excluding a few large provincial cities, have no detective forces. They deal well enough with the ordinary run of criminal cases, but when a case of special application arises, they almost invariably muddle it.

'Sometimes at a late stage they ask for skilled assistance from Scotland Yard, but by then the scent is cold and, moreover, a Scotland Yard detective gets very little help from the local men who regard his intrusion with great jealousy.

'In London we have many detectives of great experience who have, more or less, specialized in dealing with particular classes of cases. It would be a great advantage if the County Police could be induced to call in their services at an early stage, but we have no means of compelling them to do so.'

It was suggested that Scotland Yard should take over the investigation of serious crimes in country areas when they were asked to, and deal with them in the way they would deal with them in London, while working in consultation with the local force, which would receive a copy of all reports.

Mr Gladstone decided that a small number of officers belonging to the CID should be specially designated for Home Office service and asked that Chief Constables should be induced to take advantage of that service in difficult cases.

The new squad had no official name, but all the detectives were to come from Central Office of the CID at Scotland Yard, and before long their services were being sought out, mostly to investigate cases of murder. In a very short time they became known as the Murder Squad. Their first chief was Superintendent Frank Froest, the man with the mutton-chop whiskers whose photograph hangs on the wall today of the room occupied by the Squad's present leader, Commander Arthur Howard.

In those early days there was no Murder Squad tie as there is today, but there was great pride in being a member of this exclusive coterie. The detectives made mistakes, but they learned by experience and what experience they gained they shared with their fellows. It was then, and still is, the greatest honour for a detective to be posted to Central Office in the CID, for it handles all major crime, and that includes murder.

The Squad's success in solving these crimes has captured the public imagination and has led to the printing of newspaper placards naming the Murder Squad chief appointed to investigate a case. It has produced many outstanding personalities whose names became as well known as those of film and television stars, men like Edward Greeno, Jack Capstick, Frederick Cherrill, William Chapman, Reginald Spooner and Peter Beveridge. It is not possible to mention them all, but it is true to say that they passed on to their juniors what they learned in the field. So it has been that detectives who worked as sergeants with those great investigators have, in their turn, been promoted to the senior ranks of the Squad and carry on the tradition.

All these men have been dedicated to a point almost unheard of in any other profession. Once an investigation begins there is no time for anything else, and that includes family life. Wives need patience and tolerance beyond understanding. Summer holidays have to be cancelled, or taken alone with the children. A night at the theatre can be stopped at the last minute.

The history of the Murder Squad has been made up of the sum of innumerable cases, coupled with the social developments over a period in which life has changed faster than most of us could have dreamed. This book relates many of those cases which illustrate the methods used over the years and the use of new technology as it became available. It tells of the work of some remarkable men who by skill, patience and 'nose' have overcome incredible difficulties, all starting from the circumstance of sudden death, sometimes bizarre, frequently macabre and often, even to a seasoned detective, horrifying.

I have set out to trace a pattern of murder investigation as it is seen by the officers in charge of each case, and not in a neat chronological sequence. I have tried to show how advances in science have been put to use, the varying standpoints from which a murder inquiry begins, the sheer weight of experience which, handed down through the years, remains the Squad's most powerful weapon.

What I have not dealt with, except briefly, when motive is at the forefront of an investigation, is the darker side of murder – the psychological make-up of those who have killed. This endlessly absorbing facet has already been part of many other books of a very different kind. The fact is that motive is often the simplest matter in an investigation, and once again illustrates the gulf between a thriller, with its pages packed with likely suspects, and the real thing, where a detective is not so much seeking who dunnit but *proof* of who dunnit.

CHAPTER 1

The Early Days

Up to 1905 formal training for the police was scanty and detection aids were scantier. Two weeks on the drill square, two weeks in a police court, and an order to study an instruction manual were the basis of a recruit's training. The education test was rudimentary, consisting of reading and dictation and the simple rules of mathematics. Even so it was hard to qualify. In 1905 there were 17,718 candidates and only 935 were accepted for the Metropolitan Police. To make a mistake in one test usually meant failure.

In 1868 Detective Inspector Wicher of Scotland Yard was sent to help the local police at Rode, Somerset, where a three-year-old boy had been found with his throat cut. He was the first Yard man ever sent outside London on a case. Wicher arrested the boy's half-sister, Constance Kent, then aged sixteen. He had discovered that one of her three night-dresses was missing, and in his view she had destroyed it to avoid discovery of bloodstains. The case was not strongly presented in the magistrates' court and the accused aroused much public sympathy. The charge was dismissed.

Some people blamed the magistrates for weakness while others castigated Wicher for incompetence. He was convinced of the girl's guilt, but his superiors considered he had made a wrongful arrest and he retired prematurely. The Yard's reputation also suffered.

Four years later Constance Kent confessed to the crime and explained she had slit her half-brother's throat with a razor and had burned her nightdress because she was unable to remove the spots of blood on it. She later served twenty years of a life sentence. Her confession vindicated the unfortunate Wicher too late for him to benefit, but the Yard regained some of its lost credibility.

Before the turn of the century the Yard had introduced a

system of classification of criminals by their methods and peculiarities which became known as the *Modus Operandi*. Detectives also spent hours studying photographs of criminals so that they could recognize them again.

In 1901 Sir Edward Henry was made Assistant Commissioner of the Criminal Investigation Department, which had been formed in 1873. He introduced a system of fingerprint classification based on a mathematical formula, which he had invented while serving as Inspector General of Police in India. This system revolutionized the work of the detective in London, and in the first years of its operation 1,722 people were identified through its use, three times as many as in the previous year when the Bertillon system of identification by measurement[1] was still being used.

A successful inquiry in 1905 using the new method convinced any doubters of its value. An elderly couple called Farrow were found murdered in their chandler's shop in Deptford in South-East London. Detective Chief Inspector Fox went to the shop and found a thumbprint on the japanned surface of a cash box. This was finally traced to one of two brothers named Stratton, who had been arrested on charges of being drunk and disorderly. In the end, one betrayed the other and they subsequently confessed to the crime, were convicted and hanged.

By this time the CID had a growing reputation and Sir Edward Henry had been appointed Commissioner. Inside Scotland Yard the men worked by gas light. All reports were handwritten, there were few telephones and fewer typewriters. There was no transport except that available to the general public.

Superintendent Froest appointed as his first officers in the new Squad set up in 1907 Detective Chief Inspectors Fox,

[1] Alphonse Bertillon, a Frenchman, had been the first person to realize the advantage of being able to identify a criminal with absolute certainty as opposed to relying on the normal human capacity for recognition. His method was simple – measurement of the parts of the body that do not change like the head, and middle or little fingers.

Arrow, Dew and Kane. Their working day was elastic, day frequently turned into night, and a working week was seven days. In the same year the new Peel House training school for recruits opened, as did the Old Bailey, where the Central Criminal Court was in future to sit. The detectives continued to build up their knowledge in the street and the police court, learning the faces and habits of criminals, passing on their knowledge to each other. They had long cultivated informants, whom they sometimes paid. Thus they were able to keep abreast of most of the activity in the underworld of the capital. They were to find things somewhat different in the provinces.

Walter Dew, a big, wide-shouldered, beetle-browed man with white hair, who was later to receive immense publicity for his part in the Crippen case, found his first country murder very little to his liking when he discovered all the clues had been cleaned away.

In November 1908 he was sent to Salisbury, Wiltshire, where a one-legged boy of twelve had been found dead with his throat cut. Dew learnt that the victim, who had had his leg amputated as a result of a diseased hip, had been saving up to buy a new cork leg. He had saved £8 but after he had been found dead by his mother it was discovered that half the money was missing.

The boy's mother, Mrs Flora Haskell, a widow aged thirty-four, told Dew that on the previous evening she had been sitting in the kitchen and, hearing a noise, went towards the front door. As she walked into the passage a man had run past her, and had thrown a knife at her, spattering her clothes with blood. She had found Teddy, her only son, dead in his bed, had screamed and raised the alarm. Neighbours had run to help, but said they had seen no signs of a strange man running away.

Dew, with his sergeant, looked round the house and discovered that all traces of blood had been removed, and the house thoroughly cleaned. He did manage to elicit the information that the knife was one from the kitchen and had been recently sharpened, and that the drawer where the money had been kept had been forced open. After five days' investigation, during which he called in Professor A. J. Pepper, the Home Office pathologist, Dew charged Mrs Haskell with the murder of her son, following a verdict of wilful murder against her at the boy's inquest.

In the following February she was tried at Devizes Assizes before Mr Justice Ridley. When he heard that the blood in the passage where the knife had been thrown had been cleaned up before the Yard men had arrived, he said, 'I cannot imagine a greater act of folly. It is the one piece of evidence in this case. It is up to Mr Goddard.'

Mr Rayner Goddard, who thirty-seven years later was to become Lord Chief Justice of England, was Mrs Haskell's counsel, and he was able to put enough doubt in the minds of the jury so that they were unable to agree on a verdict. At the next trial Mrs Haskell was found not guilty and discharged amidst an outburst of cheering.

The fact that the scene of the crime had not been preserved by local police made a profound impression on Scotland Yard and led to a memorandum from the Home Office to all Chief Constables. It set out the facts of the Haskell case – that the murder had been committed by 9 p.m; the Yard called at 12.30 a.m. and that Dew had left London at 8.30 a.m. By the time he had arrived the doctor had been allowed to wash the body of the victim and rearrange the bedclothes, while Mrs Haskell's mother had been allowed to wash the oil-cloth in the passage and kitchen.

New instructions stressed the importance of a quick decision being made if Scotland Yard help was required and said that the request should be made direct rather than through an application to the Home Office. It stated that nothing should be done which was likely to destroy possible clues, pending the arrival of an officer from London, and that a policeman should be posted at the scene of a murder to prevent any unauthorized person encroaching. It was particularly important that nothing should be done to alter the position or the condition of the body and that no traces of the crime should be removed. It was also necessary to ensure that inmates of a house where a crime had occurred were denied any opportunity to remove or destroy articles which might have a bearing on the investigation. The Home Office suggested that the importance of these points should be impressed on local junior officers as they were likely to be first on the scene.

The Murder Squad's early days were studded with the problems of ignorance, and indeed one of its major triumphs started out with what was considered a somewhat doubtful report on a missing person.

The case of Dr Crippen has long cast a spell over readers interested in crime and has been written about many times. It has a particular fascination for Scotland Yard detectives since success came very near to being disaster, and despite the dramatic chase across the Atlantic, and the use of radio communication for the first time for the capture of a murderer, the Yard came in for some severe criticism. The publicity the case received and the weight of forensic evidence produced made it something of a turning point in Yard history.

CHAPTER 2

The Mild-mannered Poisoner

Hawley Harvey Crippen was born in Michigan, USA, in 1862. He was small and dapper, a man of apparently mild habits. He had studied some medicine at the Homoeopathic Hospital in Cleveland, Ohio, and at a medical college in New York. He had two diplomas, but it is doubtful whether these qualifications would have satisfied the British General Medical Council. Crippen was entitled to describe himself as a doctor but not to practise in Britain. He came to London first when he was twenty-one to obtain more medical knowledge, and it is not known how long he stayed then, but by 1890 he was back in the USA in Utah where his first wife died, leaving him with a three-year-old son whom he sent to live with his mother-in-law in California.

New York seems to have been a favourite place of his, for he stayed there frequently, and it was there he met the ill-fated Cora Turner. She was seventeen, half American, half Polish Jew, and she had already been the mistress of a stove manufacturer when Crippen married her. He got a job in Philadelphia with the Munyon Company, which traded in patent medicines, while Mrs Crippen, who had a small voice but ambitions to sing in grand opera, went to New York to have it trained. He returned to London in 1900 to manage Munyon's office in Shaftesbury Avenue and later that year Cora joined him. They lived in rooms in South Crescent, off Tottenham Court Road, in central London.

However, life was not going well for them and at one point Crippen took the grave risk of practising as a dentist and as a women's consultant. Cora changed her name to Belle Elmore for, at the time, she was seeking work on the music-hall stage with some slight success. Then Munyon's recalled Crippen to Philadelphia for six months. During his absence Belle sang at smoking concerts and met an American performer called Bruce Miller, with whom she lived in Guilford Street, Bloomsbury, which in those days had a dubious reputation.

Crippen returned to London and forsook Munyon's for a variety of jobs vaguely concerned with medicine, all of which failed. Then he found a job with the Yale Tooth Specialists and took on a typist he had met earlier at one of the firms which had failed. Her name was Ethel LeNeve.

He and Cora moved into 39 Hilldrop Crescent, a large gloomy house in Holloway, North London. They rented the two lower floors and, although Crippen earned only about £3 a week, they managed to entertain some of her theatrical friends and even save a little. Extra money probably came

18

from some of Crippen's side-lines – dispensing quack medicines – for he gave his wife ermine and a fox fur as well as jewellery and stylish dresses.

In January 1910 Crippen was overdrawn at the bank, but there was £600 on deposit, more than half of which was in his wife's name. In order to improve their financial situation they took in paying guests.

Mrs Crippen, still using the name of Belle Elmore, had little more success in obtaining engagements, but she became popular in off-stage theatrical circles. She was smartly dressed, vivacious and pleasant, with her New York accent and dark hair dyed auburn. Her popularity led to her being invited to be honorary treasurer of the Music Hall Ladies' Guild. She was a Roman Catholic and converted her husband to that faith.

But beneath the seeming calm of the Crippen household there were dangerous currents. Cora found out that her husband was having an affair with Ethel LeNeve, using the bedrooms of small hotels as their meeting places. She threatened to leave him. This might have suited him but for the fact that she declared she would take their joint savings, which she claimed to be hers.

Crippen had long endured her domination. He allowed her to control their money, to choose his suits and ties, his shirts and underwear. He was a domestic drudge. It was he who cleaned the boots of the paying guests and took up their breakfasts before he went to work. He was at breaking point when she threatened to give notice to the bank that she was withdrawing their savings.

In mid-January Crippen ordered five grains of hyoscin hydrobromide at Lewis & Burrows chemist's shop in New Oxford Street. He collected it on 19 January 1910.

For some days he endured his wife's bad-tempered outbursts – he must have known it was for a limited time. He had poison which he knew could kill, but his reason for buying it, he claimed later, was to dampen her sexual passions. He chose to administer it early on 1 February, after he and his wife had entertained their friends, Mr and

19

Mrs Paul Martinetti, retired music-hall acrobats. For some time Mr Martinetti had not been well but Crippen pressed him to keep this date and promised a game of whist. 'It will cheer you up,' he said.

Dinner was served in the semi-basement breakfast-room, on the same floor as the kitchen and the coal cellar. Afterwards they played whist in the upstairs parlour and, at about 1.30 a.m., the Martinettis left, walking into the deserted street lit only by pale yellow gas lamps. Mrs Crippen waved good-bye from the upstairs parlour window because she had a slight cold. It was the last time the Martinettis were to see her.

About midday the same morning Crippen called on Mr Martinetti to ask if he had enjoyed the evening and if he was in better spirits. Asked about his wife he replied, 'Oh, she's all right,' and promised to give her Mrs Martinetti's love.

The next day he pawned a diamond ring and some earrings for £80 and Ethel LeNeve slept at Hilldrop Crescent. Two days later the secretary of the Music Hall Ladies' Guild received two letters signed 'Belle Elmore'. One resigned her membership of the guild and the other explained she had been summoned urgently to America because of the illness of a close relative. The letters were not in her handwriting.

Gossip reached Mrs Martinetti and, next time she met Crippen, she reproached him for not telling her about his wife's departure. He explained he had been busy and all the night before his wife left they had been packing.

'Packing and crying, I suppose,' said Mrs Martinetti.

'Oh, we have got past that,' said Crippen.

By all accounts Crippen was supremely unworried. He pawned more rings and a brooch for £115 and, three weeks after his wife disappeared, took Ethel LeNeve to the annual ball of the Music Hall Ladies' Benevolent Fund. That night Ethel LeNeve was wearing another brooch which, he told friends, had belonged to his wife. He seemed impervious to the interested glances of the other dancers as they watched him with his new partner.

In another two weeks he had moved Ethel LeNeve into

Hilldrop Crescent. She had given up her job and all restraint was gone. His next move was to give his landlord notice but, after three months, he extended his departure until September. This was an over-elaboration, for just before Easter he told Mrs Martinetti and other friends that his wife was dangerously ill in America and not expected to live. He further explained that if she died he would take a week's holiday in France, a statement which caused great astonishment among his friends and neighbours.

They were even more astonished when, on 24 March, the day before Good Friday, they heard from Mrs Martinetti that she had received a telegram. It read: 'Belle died yesterday at six o'clock.' It had been sent from Victoria Station before Crippen and Ethel LeNeve left for Dieppe. While they were away, notice of Mrs Crippen's death was published in *Era*, a theatrical magazine.

This strange sequence of events caused a good deal of speculation among Belle Elmore's friends and it began to harden into suspicion. When Crippen returned he was asked many questions, particularly where messages of remembrance could be sent. He was courteous and patient but no address was forthcoming. She had died with relations in Los Angeles, he said, even his son had been there at the bedside of his stepmother. He said the ashes were coming to England and so there was no point in sending letters or flowers as they would arrive too late. He told a neat story and appeared to be under no strain. He was his usual mild self and led his normal life with quiet dignity, going to his office and visiting the Martinettis and others. Each evening he returned home to Ethel LeNeve, who was now openly wearing Mrs Crippen's furs and jewellery, an ostentation considered in poor taste and giving rise to much discussion.

Life in Holloway settled down for a month until a Mr Nash, an old friend of Cora Crippen, returned from a visit to America. While he was there he had tried unsuccessfully to get some news of her last days and he decided to call upon Dr Crippen with some awkward questions. Whatever his motives, whether he was seeking the truth or was just

21

inquisitive, he did not like the answers he received and he went to Scotland Yard.

Detective Superintendent Frank Froest had been put in charge of the new Serious Crimes squad from its inception and was a highly skilled officer. He was well known in London for his successful pursuit of the famous swindler Jabez Balfour, whom he had arrested in Buenos Aires. Mr Nash had met the detective socially and it was to him he went when his suspicions were aroused. Superintendent Froest at that time had a squad of five Detective Chief Inspectors, one of whom was Walter Dew, and it was to him he assigned the Crippen case. Dew by that time had twenty-nine years' service behind him. One of eleven children, he came from Northampton, and had left school at thirteen. His early links with the law were confined to calling the fire brigade when he saw the Old Bailey roof on fire, and he worked as a clerk in a solicitor's office near the Law Courts before joining the police. Most of his service had been as a detective and he had taken part in many murder investigations, including the hunt for Jack the Ripper.

The background to the Crippen case was pieced together over the weeks of the inquiry, but when Dew stepped into the picture for the first time the 'crime' appeared to add up to not much more than suspicion over a missing woman. Realizing this, Crippen tried to deceive Dew. He admitted he had been lying – as far as he knew, he said, his wife was alive. She had left him on 1 February, as she had often threatened to do. He believed she had gone to Chicago to join her friend of the Guilford Street days of illicit love, Bruce Miller. Crippen even showed Dew his wife's jewellery and three baskets and a trunk full of her clothes. He explained that his lies were designed to shield her and himself from any scandal. He cut a pitiful figure and the detective was sympathetic though not entirely persuaded. Dew obtained a search warrant and went through every room in the house at Hilldrop Crescent and into the coal cellar, but found nothing he considered suspicious. However, he did circulate a description of the missing woman.

Crippen might have been safe had his nerve not failed. But he was badly shaken by Dew's visit and he decided to flee, taking Ethel LeNeve with him.

They travelled to Brussels, then to Antwerp, and boarded the SS *Montrose* bound for Canada. The journey took two days and about the time the ship set sail Dew returned to Hilldrop Crescent, to verify a date with Crippen. He found the house empty and the signs of recent flight.

He immediately circulated pictures and descriptions of Crippen and his companion, and detectives began a systematic search of the house and garden.

The Crippens had lived in considerable disharmony, in an atmosphere of constant bickering and explosive quarrels. Their living-room was the kitchen, which the police found in their searches to be squalid in the extreme. The dresser was crammed with dirty crockery, bits of food, his stiff collars, her hair-pieces; the gas stove was rusty and grease-stained and every surface covered with pots and pans, flat irons and cups and saucers. And, thrown carelessly over a chair, was a glamorous, chiffon negligée.

The general untidiness of the house might have deceived Chief Inspector Dew into thinking such carelessness was not likely to be part of the make-up of a man intent on concealment, for it was only on the third day of the search that anything was found. On the third day, Dew went once more to the cellar with Sergeant Mitchell, this time armed with a poker. He searched among the coal, wood and rubbish, and then began to prise up the brick floor. Some bricks worked loose and, when they were removed, Dew found the remains of Cora Crippen, buried in lime. There were no legs, arms or head, only the trunk wrapped in a pyjama jacket.

By modern standards the pace of the investigation seems to have been incredibly slow. Why did it take three days to search a small house and garden? And why was the natural hiding-place, the cellar, left until last? Perhaps Crippen did convince Dew that the inquiry he was handling was merely that of a missing woman who had left of her own volition.

Four medical specialists were called to inspect the

remains. William Willcox (later Sir William) was the senior analyst and pathologist to the Home Office: Dr A. P. Luff was also analyst to the Home Office: Professor A. J. Pepper was pathologist to the Home Office and Dr Bernard Spilsbury his assistant. All four were on the staff of St Mary's Hospital, Paddington, at the time. Willcox and Luff analysed the organs and the pathologists Pepper and Spilsbury examined the pieces of skin.

The toxicologists found the presence of hyoscin in the organs and the pathologists found an operation scar on the lower abdomen. It was known that Mrs Crippen had had such an operation just before she married.

The Crippen case was to be the making of the renowned pathologist Bernard Spilsbury. After he had examined the remains in the cellar he noted: 'Human remains found July 13. Medical organs of chest and abdomen removed in one mass. Four large pieces of skin and muscle, one from lower abdomen with old operation scar 4 inches long broader at lower end. Impossible to identify sex. Hyoscin found 2·7 grains. Hair in Hinde's curler – roots present. Hair 6 inches long. Man's pyjama jacket, Jones Bros., Holloway, and odd pair of pyjama trousers. Skill in evisceration.'

The rest of the body was never found but what was in that cellar provided all the evidence that was necessary.

The news of the find was printed in every newspaper with an appeal to find the two missing people, for there were no clues as to where they had gone. However, it was one of those tricks of fate which catches murderers that Captain Kendall of the SS *Montrose* was no ordinary skipper. He had always kept a wary eye out on his ship for confidence tricksters and card sharpers. He had seen the first message sent out by Chief Inspector Dew and now he read a second which ended with the words: 'The pair may have left the country or will endeavour to leave the country. Please cause every inquiry at shipping offices and other likely places and cause ships to be watched.' There followed a full description of the couple.

The SS *Montrose* was two days out of Antwerp when

Captain Kendall first had his suspicions. They were directed to a couple who had boarded at Antwerp giving the names of Mr John Robinson and Master Robinson. They shared a double cabin, and the captain felt sure that Master Robinson was a woman. He engaged the couple in conversation and learned from Mr Robinson that his 'boy' was aged sixteen and was going to California for a health cure. But he had also noticed that the couple frequently held hands and that when they played ball Master Robinson always closed his knees, making a lap as women do. One day he had a look in their cabin, and found Master Robinson's hat stuffed with paper to make it fit, as well as the sleeves of a woman's bodice which had been used as a face flannel.

As the *Montrose* steamed on the captain noticed another strange thing about the boy's clothes. A sudden breeze caught his jacket to reveal that the trousers had been split at the back to allow them to wrap over and be held with a large safety pin. Another breeze two days later disturbed Mr Robinson's coat tails, revealing a revolver in his hip pocket.

Despite the fact that Mr Robinson was clean-shaven and the police description of Crippen said he wore a heavy moustache, Captain Kendall was convinced he had the fugitives on board. He sent the ship's owners in England a message and they passed on his suspicions to Scotland Yard.

Immediately Chief Inspector Dew set out in pursuit. He managed to catch a faster boat, the SS *Laurentic*, and reached Father Point, the pilot station on the St Lawrence River, two days ahead of his quarry. To his consternation there were hordes of newspapermen at this desolate spot, which boasted only a few shacks, a wireless station and a lighthouse. Dew was not happy with the situation, more particularly because of the high spirits of the reporters who, like all reporters scenting a good story and in full cry, tended to ignore bed and to amuse themselves with song and any musical instrument which came to hand. Their efforts, combined with the melancholy note of the lighthouse foghorn, made sleep impossible.

But at least the wireless station enabled him to communicate with Captain Kendall, who assured him that he was more than ever convinced the fugitives were on board. Still Dew had to wait and then he received another shock. He heard that one group of reporters and cameramen were rigging up a raft. The plan was to sail it down the river and get picked up by the *Montrose* as shipwrecked mariners, thus getting on board before Dew could make his arrest. Once on the ship they planned to interview and photograph the couple and 'scoop' their rivals.

The Chief Inspector decided to make a deal. He promised that if they abandoned their scheme, he would let them know if the couple on board were, in truth, Crippen and LeNeve. It was agreed.

Because Crippen knew him, Dew needed some disguise, so he borrowed the uniform of a pilot and was rowed out to the *Montrose* on the pilot's cutter. It was shortly before nine o'clock on a Sunday morning when the boat pulled alongside in midstream. A ladder was thrown over and the pilot climbed aboard. Dew was right behind him and was taken to Captain Kendall on the bridge.

Dew was impatient, but he courteously introduced himself and Kendall pointed out a lone man strolling round the deck. At first Dew was unsure. The man looked like Crippen, yet he was different. There was no heavy, sandy moustache and no glasses. The two men walked from the bridge and along the deck. Dew, only a few feet away, looked hard at the man he had crossed the Atlantic to arrest. He had to be certain. A pair of bulging eyes looked up and Dew knew he had found his man.

Crippen was handicapped without his glasses and the pilot's uniform was an effective disguise.

'Good morning, Dr Crippen,' said Dew. The little man gave a start of surprise. Doubt clouded his face and then, resignation. But he recovered his composure.

'Good morning, Mr Dew,' Crippen replied.

Other promenaders were looking, sensing something strange. Some were edging closer.

Dew, speaking quietly, said, 'Dr Crippen. You will be arrested for the murder and mutilation of your wife, Cora Crippen, in London, on or about February 1st this year.'

Crippen did not answer and he was handcuffed and taken to an empty cabin, guarded by a police officer.

Then Dew went to find Miss LeNeve. She was standing just inside the cabin, waiting for Crippen to return. She was still dressed as a boy and she recognized the detective from his first visit to Hilldrop Crescent, although he introduced himself formally. As soon as he mentioned his name she collapsed. When she recovered Dew arranged for her to be lent some female clothing and then she was arrested on the same charge.

When Crippen was searched two cards were found in his pockets. On one side was printed: 'E. Robinson and Co., Detroit, Mich. presented by Mr John Robinson' and, on the back of one, in Crippen's own pencilled handwriting was the following: 'I cannot stand the horror I go through every night any longer, and as I see nothing ahead and the money has come to an end, I have made up my mind to jump overboard tonight. I know I have spoiled your life but I'll hope some day you can learn to forgive me. Last words of love. Yours, H.'

On the back of the other card had been written: 'Shall we wait till tonight about 10 or 11? If not, what time?'

Also found, pinned to his vest, were a rising-sun brooch and a butterfly brooch in diamonds and four diamond rings.

Dew went to the wireless cabin and sent his now historic message, the first of its kind ever used in a Scotland Yard murder hunt. It was addressed to 'Handcuffs, London', the telegraphic address of the Yard, and read: 'Crippen and LeNeve arrested, Dew.'

It is possible that Crippen might have escaped had Dew not caught the ship he did. At his trial Crippen declared that the messages on the cards were part of a scheme for evading capture. He said he had bribed the quartermaster to hide him and smuggle him ashore at Montreal. Then, when the police, whom he had not expected to meet until the ship docked, came on board, Miss LeNeve could hand them the cards so that they would think their quarry had committed suicide.

Dew returned with his prisoners to a tumultuous welcome from the British public and he was lionized in the press. However, he was also strongly criticized by Mr Richard Muir, the Treasury counsel who had been chosen to lead the case for the prosecution, who said he was gravely dissatisfied with the police work. In his view Crippen should have been watched and arrested the moment he tried to flee, if not before.

One of the reasons for his view was that he and Travers Humphreys, who was his junior counsel in the case, had gone to visit 39 Hilldrop Crescent while Dew was still on board the SS *Montrose*. Travers Humphreys (later Sir Travers) wrote afterwards:

'To my intense surprise I found no attention had been paid to the fact that, according to Crippen, his wife had gone to America with no intention of returning, leaving behind her all her warm clothing, including several furs and similar garments, and most, if not all, of her jewellery.

'When in course of time Inspector Dew was asked to explain why those furs were left in the bedroom instead of being removed and made exhibits in the case, his answers were not satisfactory to me. I directed him to take the necessary steps since, to my mind, such supposed conduct on the part of a woman would be regarded by the ordinary common-sense juryman as almost conclusive proof that Crippen's story was untrue.

'Inquiries among Belle Elmore's many friends in London had already established that she had not communicated to any of them her intention of leaving the country.

'Richard Muir (later Sir Richard) was by no means satisfied that statements taken from employees of Jones Brothers about the pyjamas were complete. We made more than one attempt through Dew to obtain further information but without success. Muir described Inspector Dew as suffering from sleepy sickness. After the committal for trial we decided as a last effort to write out a series of questions to be put to a responsible representative of the company.

'In the result, the company's buyer was able to assure us he could prove that the pyjama jacket in which the remains were wrapped was part of an order from 39 Hilldrop Crescent for three suits of pyjamas in January 1909. In the house were found the other two suits and the trousers belonging to the jacket in question.'

This left Crippen stripped of any defence to the charge of murdering his wife unless the medical evidence called for the prosecution could be shaken.

The trial at the Old Bailey attracted large crowds and the court was packed for the five days. The murder charge against LeNeve had been dropped and Crippen stood in the dock alone, wearing a smart grey frock-coat. He pleaded not guilty, and appeared to be as calm and assured as ever.

The medical evidence was devastating for Crippen. Professor Pepper, Dr Spilsbury and Dr Marshall, the police surgeon, all said that, in their opinion, one piece of skin found in the cellar measuring eleven by nine inches came from the upper part of the abdomen and the lower part of the chest of a woman, young or middle-aged, while another piece of skin measuring seven by six inches came from the lower part of the front of the abdomen. The second piece had upon it a scar, corresponding to that left by an operation performed to remove the ovaries. Cora Crippen's sister testified that her sister had had such an operation.

The defence sought to prove that the so-called scar was in fact a fold in the skin caused after death. But Dr Spilsbury proved that it was a scar by sending for his microscope and, in a side room of the court, he demonstrated by the use of slides and a patient explanation, why he had reached his firm conclusion.

The defence also tried to cast doubt on Dr Willcox's evidence that the hyoscin found in the body was the cause of death, but they failed.

It was never discovered what Crippen had done with the

rest of the body – the head, legs, arms and most of the trunk. The only theory put forward was that he had thrown them overboard from the ship when he took Ethel LeNeve to Dieppe, which leaves the question: why did he not also dispose of the totally incriminating piece of skin from the lower abdomen?

Towards the end of the trial the prosecutor, Mr Richard Muir, played his final ace. He made an application to rebut Crippen's statement about the purchase of the pyjamas and the application was allowed.

Earlier, Crippen had said that the pyjamas were bought in 1905 or 1906. It was now that Muir's insistence on a minute investigation paid off, for, following the lawyer's criticism of Dew and his men, the missing link had been found.

A buyer for Jones Brothers of Holloway was able to prove that the pyjama material was not acquired by his firm until the end of 1908, and that three suits made from it were supplied to 39 Hilldrop Crescent in January 1909. Muir said, 'Who alone during the next twelve months could have buried the jacket in that house? Who was missing who could have been buried in it? Nobody but Belle Elmore.'

The jury took the same view. They were out for only half an hour. Crippen's appeal was dismissed and he was hanged in Pentonville Prison, less than a mile from where he committed murder. Miss LeNeve was found not guilty of being an accessory after the fact and was discharged.

Scotland Yard men learned a lot from the Crippen case. Had a watch been kept on the house the flight of Crippen and LeNeve would have been discovered sooner and the transatlantic pursuit have been unnecessary: it was only the keen observation of Captain Kendall that had saved the day. And an earlier and more thorough search of the house would almost certainly have revealed the remains of Mrs Crippen. As it was, far too much had been taken at face value. Inquiries among the Crippens' friends would most likely have revealed his close association with Ethel LeNeve and shown a powerful motive for murder. If Chief Inspector Dew had been a little more curious about the presence of

Miss LeNeve at the house he would have discovered that she had been living there for some time. But the Murder Squad has never been slow to recognize its faults, and they have seldom made the same mistakes twice.

The public, however, were unaware of the flaws in the investigation. Instead, they were completely gripped with the sensation of the romance and the chase across the Atlantic, the dramatic arrest at sea and the use of wireless to catch a criminal.

CHAPTER 3

The Daddy of Them All

In 1913 the first detective training school was established. However, then as now, each recruit to the CID had to start his life in uniform, walking the beat for a starting wage in those days of thirty shillings a week, the same as that of a postman. For the first time they had one day off duty a week. Fingerprint evidence was now fully accepted in the courts, and the Criminal Record Office had opened.

The mechanization of the police had begun – a limited number of cars were available and some men were allowed to ride bicycles. Following the siege of Sidney Street, certain police stations were given an armoury of automatic pistols.

Although right from the very first investigations a murder chief would take a sergeant with him as his right-hand man, it now became established practice to send young detectives out on cases to learn from and assist their senior officers. Thus they were helped to develop a new inquisitiveness, allied to a keen observation and a fine attention to detail.

Old hands stressed what they called 'smell', the capacity to spot a 'wrong 'un' by a sort of sixth sense.

Many of the great detectives have been men who have grown up in the country, and certainly the early theory was that recruits from rural areas would be less cocksure and keener to learn than city youths. The backbone of training relied on officers like Frederick Porter Wensley, who even now is sometimes referred to by detectives as 'the Daddy of them all'. Wensley, a West Country man, joined the Metropolitan Police in 1888, and was appointed to the CID in 1895. He retired at the end of July 1929 with the rank of Chief Constable of the CID. He was a tall, sardonic-looking man with a cool, almost off-hand manner set off by his high collar and shrewd eyes. He had no poses and his single object in life was to get at the truth of the case he was working on. This simplicity of outlook, combined with great resolution and a complete absence of fear, made him one of the great detectives. Yet he was probably one of the few men who never wanted to work at the Yard.

The simple reason for this was that he loved London's East End, where he spent many years of his service; he knew the area and its inhabitants as none of his predecessors had, and when he was promoted Detective Chief Inspector, a rank which had always meant a transfer to the Yard, in an unprecedented move he was allowed to stay where he was. He might have remained in the East End until he retired but for the death of Chief Inspector Alfred Ward, killed by a Zeppelin bomb in 1916. Wensley took his place as senior man on the Murder Squad.

By then he was no stranger to murder, but even so Wensley did not altogether believe in capital punishment. He once wrote, 'Many murderers have passed through my hands. Some of them have thoroughly deserved to hang but others have been really victims of circumstances – men or women who have killed under some sudden or over-mastering passion. The great majority of murders are crimes of impulse. The people who commit them do not stop to think of the consequences. If capital punishment were abolished tomorrow I do not believe crimes of this sort would either increase or decrease.' They were prophetic words.

London's East End was, in those days, a dangerous place to be on the streets after dark. The criminals were ruthless and violent, and Chief Inspector Wensley and his men were kept at full stretch to hold them in check. This chapter will trace some of Wensley's cases which began to clean up that notorious area.

Both Marks and Morris Reubens lived on the earnings of prostitutes, but not content with that income they robbed the clients as well. On a March night in 1909 two officers came ashore at London's docks from a merchant ship back from Australia. Mr McEachern and Mr Sproull each had about £5 in their pockets but also carried a number of silver threepenny pieces to give to the many dockside spongers who begged for a piece of silver.

Later that evening the officers met two girls in Whitechapel who invited them home. At about 2.30 in the morning Mr Sproull was found dead in the street. Apart from other wounds, he had been stabbed. A constable found Mr McEachern wandering around, very drunk, unable to remember how he had got there. He knew there had been a fight but that was all.

It was a bright moonlit night and patches of blood could be seen in the roadway, and between them the glint of silver. Closer inspection revealed they were threepenny pieces. The trail of blood and silver led to a lodging house in Rupert Street, Whitechapel. On a door panel there was the bloodstained impression of a man's right hand. Wensley, called to the scene, saw that the dead man had put up a desperate fight. There were many injuries other than the fatal stab wound. Both his trouser pockets had been turned out and still clinging to the folds of one was a threepenny piece. The other was stained as though a bloody hand had been thrust into it – proof that the robbery had taken place after the attack.

There were many rooms in the house and the police

searched until they came to Number 13, the room inside which murder had been done. There were blood marks and the signs of a fierce struggle. Lying on the bed in a drunken sleep was a pretty young girl who turned out to be only eighteen.

In another room Wensley found Morris Reubens, who agreed that he and his brother had been in a fight with the two men. Marks Reubens had already been arrested and had tried to get rid of a bloodstained handkerchief. When Morris was searched the watch and chain belonging to the dead man was found suspended from a hook sewn into the inside of his trousers. It was a trick of thieves of that time to have a series of such hooks on which to hide small pieces of jewellery.

At that point Morris Reubens blurted out, 'I did not stab him. If he was stabbed my brother must have done it.'

It was an illuminating remark since up to that time no mention had been made of stabbing.

All the four suspects were known to Wensley, the two girls as prostitutes, the two men as their pimps. All four were charged with murder, but it became clear later that the two women were unlikely to have taken part in planning the murder because they had been too drunk, and they became witnesses for the prosecution.

They told Wensley that they had picked up the two officers, taken them back to their room and begun drinking. After some time McEachern wanted to go back to the ship but Sproull refused and in the midst of the ensuing argument the Reubens brothers dashed in, Morris carrying a heavy stick of hippopotamus hide with which he had struck Sproull on the head. The officer had fought back and McEachern had tried to help him but was too drunk to be of much use. The two women had rushed from the room and McEachern had staggered into the street. Sproull fought on while Marks stabbed him repeatedly with a pocket knife. When he could fight no more the brothers pushed him through the street door. As he reeled through he put his hand on the

34

door to keep upright and had left the bloodstained imprint which had helped to identify the house of murder.

In the room detectives found Sproull's overcoat, a bottle of whisky still in one of its pockets. There was the broken walking-stick and McEachern's bowler hat. It took several hours to find the knife, but one of the women admitted eventually that she had dropped it down behind the gas stove.

Like many detectives, Wensley had a sense of drama, and he had the bloodstained door removed and taken to the Old Bailey as evidence in the trial. There was little defence, although many hysterical outbursts by the two prisoners, and the jury made up their minds in twelve minutes. On hearing their 'guilty' verdict Morris Reubens shrieked and collapsed, but then recovered to beg for mercy. Marks also asked for mercy. However, they were both hanged in May 1909.

The judge commended Detective Inspector Wensley and sometime later someone sent the detective a glass tumbler, on the bottom of which had been engraved a sketch of a scaffold with two men hanging. An inscription read: 'The Brothers Reubens. The last drop.'

Success in solving such cases gave Wensley his great name. There was little that happened east of Aldgate with its polyglot population that he did not know of. His knowledge of criminals was encyclopaedic and he could understand and talk Yiddish. It was perhaps for that reason he was nicknamed 'Mr Venzel'.

At the time the whole of that area of London was infested with powerful armed gangs who extorted protection money from tradesmen, publicans and billiard-hall owners, just as the Kray brothers did in the 1960s.

At the end of 1910 Wensley had been investigating the murder of three City policemen which led to the famous siege of Sidney Street. On New Year's Day, 1911, he was due for a day off when he was called up by Detective Chief Inspector Alfred Ward about a murder.

At first light that morning a policeman patrolling Clapham Common had found the body of a man lying among some bushes. He had been killed by a number of heavy blows to the head and his face had been slashed with a knife. The body had been dragged ten yards from a footpath where bloodstains marked the murder spot. Ward had searched the dead man's clothes and found a halfpenny, a rent-book, a tobacco pouch and two paper bags, one of which held part of a ham sandwich.

Such was Wensley's knowledge of Whitechapel and its population that he was able to identify the man as Leon Beron, a Russian Jew who, before coming to London, had lived in France. In spite of his injuries he was recognizable because, although he was a small man, he invariably wore a short overcoat heavily trimmed with astrakhan, the same coat in which he had been found. The local belief was that he was wealthy and that he carried expensive jewellery and large sums of money; he was reputed to be fond of the company of women and it was rumoured that he sometimes dabbled in stolen property. He was also believed to own some houses.

But Clapham Common was six miles from where Beron lived – an unusual journey for a man from Whitechapel unless he had been lured there on the pretext of buying a house or some stolen property. The other possibility was that he had gone there to meet a woman.

Wensley knew that Beron was not connected with any of the many foreign revolutionary organizations in Whitechapel. He was not a member of any of the secret societies which abounded in the area, neither was he an informer, though rumour was rife at the time that he was one or all of these things because of the notoriety of the Sidney Street siege in which the protagonists had had Russian names. These stories were given the more credence because the doctor who examined the body described the knife wounds on the dead man's face as resembling the letter S – which suggested the word 'spy'.

Chief Inspector Ward was in charge of the case but Wensley's knowledge and network of informants led him to play an important part in the investigation.

Ward discovered that Beron had been seen in Whitechapel early on New Year's Day by a Mrs Deitch. She had been returning from a party with her husband and had seen Beron with a tall, well-dressed stranger. Her description of the latter was vague but she remembered he had worn a long overcoat. Almost unbelievably Wensley remembered he had seen recently a man in a long coat, who had not long been out of prison and was a 'ticket of leave' man after serving a term of penal servitude. Wensley had seen him at his police station when the man was reporting, as he had to under the terms of his licence. The detective also recalled he was a handsome man who wore distinctive clothes topped by a wide-brimmed hat.

It was a long shot, but Wensley sent for the Convict Register. The name of the man he remembered was Morris Stein, alias Tagger, who had a record for burglary and theft and had been released in September 1910. He had first gone to Whitechapel but had since moved to Lavender Hill, Clapham Common, where he was an assistant to a baker. His place of work was only ten minutes' walk from the scene of the murder.

Morris Stein had not recently been seen around Whitechapel, and he had moved on from the bakery without leaving an address. At that stage there was no evidence against him for murder, but his failure to comply with the terms of his release had made him liable to summary arrest. Accordingly a notice went in to *Informations*, the police circular for wanted persons.

> 'Wanted for Petty Offences.
> CO (CSO) Licence holder Morris Stein,
> office No. 141,701, for failing to reside
> at his registered address. Caution: Carries
> firearms and may attempt to use them.'

Stein had lived at Newark Street, Whitechapel, in a room he rented from a Jewish family for three shillings a week. He had left there on New Year's Eve but was to call back some time for his laundry. For eight days detectives watched the house before Stein called. The detectives waited. When he came out again, they followed him to a telephone box where he made a call and then to a restaurant in Fieldgate Street, near Spitalfields. They watched him sit down at a table and then sent for Wensley.

Because of the possibility of Stein being armed Wensley took four detectives to the restaurant to make the arrest. It was peaceful, but Stein complained that they had made a mistake. He said he had been living in Whitfield Street, near Tottenham Court Road, and that he had also been living with a girl in York Road, Lambeth. Wensley sent for Ward, but before he could arrive Stein asked to see Wensley again and said, 'You have accused me of murder. I want to make a statement.'

Wensley replied that he had not mentioned murder, but he recorded the passage of words as an official record, and then Chief Inspector Ward took a formal statement. The man gave his name as Steinie Morrison and said that he was an Australian, born in Sydney but brought up in England. He was a baker but had saved £4 while working at Lavender Hill and had set up as a traveller in cheap jewellery. He had left Newark Street on New Year's Day and had been staying with a girl at York Road.

The detectives were soon able to prove that Morrison had been associating with Beron for some time and that they had frequently eaten out together. The last time was on New Year's Eve and before leaving the Warsaw Restaurant, Whitechapel, Morrison had collected from a waiter a long brown paper parcel. The waiter said it had felt like a bar of iron. In the inquiries another waiter claimed that he had seen Morrison with a pistol, and the same man had seen Morrison and Beron together in Whitechapel Road at a quarter to two next morning. Mrs Deitch had seen them in the Commercial Road, near by, at some time after two o'clock. Three cab drivers came forward to tell of the movements of Morrison on New Year's morning. One said that he had picked up Morrison and a man believed to be Beron at Sidney Street, Mile End, and driven them to Lavender Hill, Clapham Common, at about two o'clock. A second claimed to have driven Morrison some time later from Clapham Common to Kennington Church. Morrison was then alone. A third cab driver said he had picked up Morrison and another man at 3.30 a.m. at Kennington Church and driven them to Finsbury Gate, near Aldgate. This was important evidence. It established that soon after Mrs Deitch had seen Morrison with Beron the two men were together in a cab and taken to Clapham, where Beron was found murdered. Then Morrison had taken a cab from Clapham Common alone.

In the room at York Road, Lambeth, where Morrison had lived with his girl-friend, a cloakroom ticket for a parcel left at St Mary's railway station, Whitechapel, was found hidden in the lining of a bowler hat. That parcel contained a revolver and a box of cartridges. A railway clerk identified Morrison as the man who had deposited them there under a false name at eleven o'clock on the morning of New Year's Day.

Morrison was charged with the murder of Beron, and Sir Richard Muir was chosen as the leading counsel for the prosecution. As in the case against Crippen, he drove and directed the detectives to uncover as much evidence as possible.

Using the same cabs, the detectives tested the times taken on the journeys, including the walk from Lavender Hill to the scene of the murder. The only time unaccounted for was half an hour between the moment when Morrison and his companion were set down at Lavender Hill and the picking up of Morrison at Kennington.

Other facts came to light. There were small blood spots on the shirt and collar Morrison was wearing when arrested. More people were found who had seen Morrison and Beron together before the murder. Morrison had pawned a watch and chain two days before Christmas yet had £24 on him when he was arrested. On New Year's Day Morrison had cashed a cheque for £4 and he had tipped a girl two sovereigns. A woman said that Morrison had worn a five-guinea gold piece on his watch-chain on New Year's Day, similar to one worn previously by Beron, but she later retracted her statement.

The trial of Steinie Morrison began at the Old Bailey before Mr Justice Darling in March 1911, and bearing in mind that the murder was committed on 1 January, this showed how fast the police had worked. The trial was marked by the behaviour of the many volatile, often foreign, witnesses, who appeared not to be intimidated by English courtroom procedure.

The evidence against the accused was circumstantial but weighty. Morrison's counsel, Mr Edward Abinger, tried to prove that two of the witnesses for the prosecution were people of bad character. He imputed that Mrs Deitch had been running a brothel, and when five women who lodged in her house were brought into court, he suggested that they were prostitutes.

The move was not helpful to Morrison since the judge then ruled that the usual privileged position held by an accused person (non-disclosure of previous convictions and evidence of character) should not be allowed, and Morrison was cross-examined about his past. His offences of housebreaking and theft and the consequent prison sentences therefore became known and his reputation as a criminal was established.

The trial lasted ten days and the jury returned a verdict of guilty. After the passing of the death sentence, with the customary plea for God to have mercy on the prisoner's soul, there was a passionate outburst from Morrison, declining any such mercy. There were strenuous efforts to secure a reprieve for him and, eventually, they were successful. The death sentence was commuted to penal servitude for life, and he died in Parkhurst Prison in January 1921 after a prolonged hunger strike.

Wensley had an enviable record when he finally arrived at

the Yard in 1916, having solved every murder case with which he had been involved. He had been used to organizing and directing a considerable force of detectives to whom he was the 'Guv'nor', the title all junior detectives accord to the men of the rank of Detective Inspector and above. But at the Yard Wensley himself had a 'Guv'nor', Superintendent John McCarthy, and it was he who, in November 1917, sent Wensley to Regent Square, Bloomsbury.

There he was confronted with a three-part investigation. First he had to establish the identity of a murder victim, then find the murderer and, finally, prove his case. Wensley appears to have achieved it all with consummate ease and great speed! The first and potentially most difficult stage was achieved simply by tracing a laundry mark, the use of which had been established as part of the growing industry of commercial laundries, and which had proved invaluable in many subsequent cases.

A roadsweeper, known as Jack the Sweeper, had spotted a bundle done up in sacking inside the railings of the central garden of Regent Square, which it was his duty to tend. He untied the bundle and found inside, wrapped in a blood-stained sheet, the trunk and arms of a woman. There was no head, no legs or hands. The roadsweeper ran for a police-man.

The initial stages of the investigation were undertaken by the Divisional Detective Inspector, John Ashley, the local police chief. A search in the garden of Regent Square produced the missing legs, in a brown paper parcel. The sacking in which the torso was wrapped was in fact a meat sack, marked 'Argentina La Plata Cold Storage'. On the blood-stained cotton sheet was the laundry mark '11H', sewn in red cotton. With the trunk were some pieces of coarse muslin, delicate underclothes of silk and lace, and a scrap of brown paper on which the words 'Blodie Belgiam' had been scrawled.

It took only a few hours for the detectives to trace the laundry mark, which led them to 50 Munster Square, in the decaying area east of Regent's Park. A Frenchwoman,

Emilienne Gerard, whose husband, a chef, was in the French Army, occupied two rooms in the house. She had left the house during an air raid to take shelter and had not been seen for three days. Her absence had caused no particular interest.

A few inquiries revealed that Mme Gerard, who was thirty-two, had a lover and that she was frequently away in France, it was rumoured on missions for the British Government, though it was also thought she went to see her husband. Wensley made a close examination of her rooms and found a small number of bloodstains in the kitchen and bedroom. He also noticed the portrait of a man hanging over the mantelpiece, and, on a table, an IOU for £50 signed by one Louis Voisin.

Local inquiries established that the portrait was that of Voisin, who was known to be Gerard's lover and who had a key to her rooms. The police surgeon who had examined the remains was certain that the dismemberment of the still nameless body had been carried out with the skill of someone with a knowledge of anatomy, possibly a butcher. Voisin was a butcher and the muslin found with the trunk was of the type used by butchers.

Wensley decided to call on Voisin, who lived in a basement flat in Charlotte Street, less than half a mile from Munster Square, and half that distance from Regent Square. It was forty-eight hours after the discovery of the murder that the detectives walked into his flat to find Voisin sitting in the kitchen with a woman named Berthe Roche. At that stage there was nothing to connect her with the murder, but the general untidiness of the kitchen and the fact that neighbours had said that they had heard the voices of more than one woman in the basement the night before the body was discovered prompted Wensley to take her along with Voisin to Bow Street police station.

There were twenty or thirty other witnesses waiting to be interviewed but Voisin and Roche were seen first. Like Gerard, they were both French refugees living in England. Voisin was a short, thick-set man, powerfully built and heavy-jawed with dark upturned moustaches. He spoke aggressively in slightly broken English. Berthe Roche spoke little English and Wensley had the help of an officer who spoke French.

Voisin's attitude was one of complete ignorance. He admitted he knew Mme Gerard, having met her eighteen months before, and that she had at one time been his housekeeper. In all that time they had been on the most friendly terms. On 31 October he had met her and she had asked him to visit her rooms to feed the cat because she had told him that she was going to France with a woman friend called Marguerite. He said he had been to Munster Square once only, and that was all he knew.

Voisin and Roche were detained that night and Wensley continued his investigation. By going from house to house in Charlotte Street and Munster Square he found a man who said he had had dinner with Mme Gerard in a restaurant on the night of 31 October and that she had not mentioned going to France.

Next morning Wensley resumed his interrogation of Voisin and Roche and decided on a test which might show that Voisin had guilty knowledge of the crime. He asked him, through the interpreter, if he had any objection to writing the words 'Bloody Belgium'.

'Not at all,' said Voisin, and a sheet of paper and a pencil were handed to him.

He wrote laboriously and in an illiterate hand – but he wrote. The writing was smaller than that which had been found on the piece of paper near the body but the spelling was the same – 'Blodie Belgiam'.

Wensley was a perfectionist and he persuaded Voisin to write the same words four more times. Each time the spelling was the same. The detective was now convinced that he was on sure ground.

Voisin had been searched when he was arrested and among the objects found in his pockets was a key that opened the door of a cellar next to his basement kitchen at Charlotte Street. Detective Sergeant Collins searched the premises and found a cask of sawdust and, buried inside, he found the head and the hands of the murdered woman. The police not only had positive evidence that the victim was Mme Gerard, but also the manner of her death was now plain. She had been hit at least eight times on the face and head with a blunt weapon and there were bruises on her right hand that indicated she had tried to protect herself. Close examination of the ill-lit room revealed that there were bloodstains all over Voisin's kitchen, particularly on the inside of the door, and they were all of human blood.

Sir Bernard Spilsbury filled in the gaps of knowledge. He confirmed that dismemberment of the body had been done by a skilled hand with a butcher's knife, in contrast to the wild ferocity of the blows to the dead woman's head. He visited Mme Gerard's room in Munster Square and was able to assert that the murder was not committed there, although he found bloodstains in the kitchen, on the counterpane of the bed and on the neck of a water jug. There was a bucket of reddish-coloured water and tests on all these clues gave a positive reaction to human blood. However, the amount and the distribution were so small as to suggest the murder had taken place elsewhere.

The basement of 101 Charlotte Street told another story. In the kitchen, mingled with animal blood, there was human blood everywhere, on the floor, on the walls and even on the ceiling. There were more stains on the sink and draining-board, and on the gas stove. Spilsbury deduced that the attack on Mme Gerard began near the back door, possibly when she was trying to escape. He and the detectives came across more evidence in the cellar. There they found a man's shirt and woollen jacket, a towel, three pieces of cloth and a butcher's overall; from the kitchen came a chopping board and a butcher's knife. In the stable, at the rear of the yard, was a blood-soaked hearthrug, and, in the blood, hairs resembling those of Mme Gerard. There was also a bloody towel with one of the dead woman's earrings attached.

When Wensley charged Voisin and Berthe Roche with the

murder of Emilienne Gerard, Voisin was calm but the woman was furious and accused her lover of betrayal. Six weeks after their arrest Voisin and Roche stood together in the dock of the Old Bailey after one of the fastest investigations ever on record. Mr Justice Darling took the view that Berthe Roche could not be convicted of wilful murder and she was remanded to be charged at the next sessions as accessory after the fact.

The police evidence was slowly adduced and told the story of the butcher who had had two mistresses. Emilienne knew about Berthe but Berthe did not know about Emilienne. On the night of the air raid Emilienne had gone first for shelter and then had changed her mind and sought comfort from her lover. When she arrived she found Berthe Roche and Voisin asleep in bed. Both women had excitable temperaments and the strain of the night produced an instant quarrel. Emilienne was the senior mistress, but although she was wildly jealous it was Berthe who struck the first blows, probably with a poker. The frenzied screams of both women wakened Voisin, who silenced Emilienne by smothering her screams with a towel while Berthe continued to rain blows on her head, to the hideous accompaniment of gunfire and bomb explosions.

In the heavy silence that followed the air raid and the gunfire Mme Gerard lay dying on the floor of the kitchen. Voisin decided to cut the body into pieces and, as he did so, he wrapped them in the hearthrug. At dawn Berthe Roche had gone to the yard to draw water from the communal tap to clean up the blood and had volunteered to a neighbour the information that Voisin had killed a calf and had bloodstains on his clothes.

That same morning Voisin and Roche had made a plan to take the body to Mme Gerard's rooms and in the afternoon Voisin had gone to Munster Square and told the landlord that his tenant would be away for a week or two. Before she went, said Voisin, she had asked him to mention to the landlord that she was expecting a sack of potatoes which she would deal with on her return. It was then, presumably, that he had smeared blood he had somehow brought with him around the kitchen and bedroom and taken away the sheet from the bed. The purpose had been to lead the police to believe Mme Gerard had been killed in her own rooms. But then Voisin had had second thoughts and decided on a simpler form of disposal for the body. That night he had taken out his pony and trap and, with intent to mystify, written the words 'Blodie Belgiam' on a scrap of paper and put it in with the sacking-wrapped torso. Voisin had driven through the dark, silent streets with his grisly burden to Regent Square, with its church and garden.

His intention had been to postpone identification, but as Emilienne's face was still recognizable, and perhaps mindful of fingerprints, he had hidden the head and hands in the sawdust cask in his cellar. The couple obviously thought that by this time they had done enough to put the police off the scent, as they seemed to have made no attempt to clean up the blood in Charlotte Street.

At the Old Bailey the proceedings were translated into French. Voisin was found guilty and hanged shortly afterwards at Pentonville Prison. On the day before his execution Berthe Roche stood in the dock of the same court and during the trial the jury were taken to Charlotte Street to look at the scene of the crime. Wensley and Bernard Spilsbury went with them, the latter to point out the bloodstains and to demonstrate how the killing had been done. It was a macabre dumb-show, because the judge had decreed that no word was to be spoken. If anyone had been allowed to speak the trial might have been abortive.

Berthe Roche was found guilty as an accessory after the fact of murder and sentenced to seven years' penal servitude. Within a few months she went mad, and in two years she was dead.

Frederick Porter Wensley went on to reach the rank of Chief Constable, the first detective to do so. For five years he was to direct Scotland Yard's detectives with a brilliance that has seldom been surpassed, and with a friendliness which always gave him time to talk to younger colleagues who needed advice.

CHAPTER 4

The Brides in the Bath

Wensley's spectacular career may have spanned many of the Squad's early successes, but no case exposes the advantages and disadvantages detectives laboured under during the period more than the one that came to be known as the 'Brides in the Bath'.

The pluses included the steady development of forensic science – Bernard Spilsbury had been appointed honorary pathologist to the Home Office in 1911 – a smaller population in which to seek a villain, and a public whose sense of duty and powers of observation had not yet been blunted by television, with its accompaniment of a sometimes apathetic acceptance of violence.

Not least of the obstacles to successful prosecution in the first quarter of the century, though, was the slowness of communications and the relative lack of sophistication in any authority outside – and sometimes even inside – London. It is quite possible that George Joseph Smith would not have gone undetected for so long had there been more time between the deaths of his victims and the resulting coroners' inquests and burials. Not only was there no means of keeping bodies in mortuaries for any length of time, but, although it was general practice to appoint lawyers to the office of coroner, almost anyone with means could in fact serve. It was not until the Coroners (Amendment) Act of 1926 that it was laid down that coroners must be barristers, solicitors or legally qualified medical men of not less than five years' standing.

In the annals of crime, repetitive murder is no rarity, and in many cases it is simply numbers that have led to discovery. There can be little doubt that had George Smith been satisfied with one murder he would never have been found out. Instead, he became over-confident, committed bigamy in the same style no fewer than eight times, and murdered three of his 'wives' all by the same method. The pillars of his initial success were his original murder technique and poor communications.

For six years the extraordinary Smith got away with fraud, bigamy and murder until in December 1914 the boss of the Murder Squad, Detective Superintendent John McCarthy, later Wensley's 'Guv'nor', received a letter from a Mr Crossley who kept a boarding house in Blackpool.

Mr Crossley had written to Scotland Yard to say he had read a newspaper story about a woman called Mrs Lloyd who had drowned in her bath at Highgate. What had kindled his interest was the fact that he recalled an exactly similar tragedy which had occurred in his boarding house two years before. The maiden name of that woman had been Alice Burnham, and a few days before her death she had married a Mr Smith.

Alice's father, Mr Charles Burnham, a fruit grower from Aston Clinton, Buckinghamshire, had also read the newspaper account and his thoughts went back to his daughter, who had died in such similar circumstances. His suspicions revived, he contacted his solicitor who conveyed them to the Aylesbury police, who in turn informed the Yard.

Superintendent McCarthy sent for Chief Inspector Arthur Neil, always known as 'Drooper Neil' because he was round-shouldered and wore a permanently lugubrious expression. He was almost unknown to smile, but he was a good policeman and he started one of the most widespread investigations ever mounted in those early days. Before the case was over inquiries had been made in forty-five towns and statements taken from one hundred and fifty people.

First Chief Inspector Neil went to Highgate to see Miss Blatch, the landlady of the house in Bismarck Road where Mrs Lloyd had died. She told Neil that Mr Lloyd, the dead woman's husband, had already moved away and taken all their belongings with him. The couple had moved in only the day before the tragedy and on the afternoon in question Miss Blatch had heard sounds of a struggle in the bathroom and hands slapping the wet sides of the bath. A few minutes later she had heard the organ pealing from the sitting-room – John Lloyd was playing *Nearer my God to Thee*. Soon water began to leak through the ceiling of the room beneath the bathroom, and shortly afterwards Mr Lloyd had appeared at the front door, saying, 'I have bought some tomatoes for Mrs Lloyd's supper.'

Some time later Mr Lloyd called Miss Blatch to the bathroom. His wife was naked and dead in a bath half full of water. At the coroner's inquest a verdict of misadventure had been returned and the funeral had taken place the next day.

Inspector Neil and his men discovered that Mrs Lloyd's maiden name was Margaret Elizabeth Lofty. She was a clergyman's daughter and had been a lady's companion, and had married in Bath on 17 December 1914.

Neil then turned his attention to the death of Alice Burnham in Blackpool, who had married a man called George Joseph Smith. Not only did he find the two women had died in exactly the same way but that Lloyd and Smith were undoubtedly the same man. What was more, Smith had a considerable history in the files of the Criminal Record Office.

He was born in Bow in 1872, and when he was only nine years old he was sentenced to eight years in a reformatory for petty theft. Reform schools in those days were places of rough justice, where the birch and the cane were used freely, and certainly not conducive to reform. Further crimes earned him a six-month prison sentence but, on his release at the age of nineteen, he joined the Northamptonshire Regiment. In 1897, when he was twenty-five, he married

Catherine Thornhill in Leicester, where he had become a baker and confectioner. On that occasion he used the name of George Oliver Love and, under his influence, his wife became a maidservant in London and pilfered from her employers. Eventually she was caught, gave her husband away and he got a two-year gaol sentence.

But even before this he had already begun his lucrative business of exploiting women for profit. He had met and 'married' a middle-aged London boarding-house keeper, and it was to her he went when he was released from prison, his wife having already gone to Canada.

He fleeced the boarding-house keeper of her savings and then vanished. In the next six years he seems to have travelled all over the country without working. It has never been discovered just how many women he 'married' and swindled, but his technique, with odd artistic variations, was always the same. He was a man of exceptional nerve and his skill at picking his victims appears to have been unerring. In a very little time he was able to find out the state of their finances and, if their money was in the form of savings, induce the women to hand it over. Sometimes he had to go to the expense of a marriage licence to get his prospective victim into the right frame of mind. Next would come a walk in the park or a visit to some place of entertainment. Smith would then excuse himself on some pretext, dash to the victim's rooms, collect all her belongings and vanish.

In 1908 he met and 'married' Edith Mabel Pegler. She had originally gone to him as housekeeper and he appears to have had some genuine affection for her. At the time he was living in Bristol, working as an antique dealer. He went away frequently, saying he had to travel to buy antiques, and he always returned with quantities of clothes which, he said, he had bought second-hand.

Two years later Smith was in Clifton, Bristol, when he met Miss Bessie Mundy, a woman of thirty-one and the possessor of £2,500. This time he called himself Henry Williams. The courtship was swift and Smith's extraordinary powers led her into marriage within ten days. Then he had a setback, for he learned that Bessie Mundy's family had had no confidence in her handling of money, and had put it all in trust. She received only the income, but as that exceeded her monthly allowance a sum of £130 had accumulated. Smith persuaded her to obtain these arrears, and then disappeared with the money. On the same day he wrote her an abusive letter, complaining that she had infected him with disease.

Smith had already moved Miss Pegler to Southend, having bought a house with the money he had stolen from a woman whom he had abandoned in the National Gallery, and it was to Southend he returned. He stayed there for the next two years but, in 1912, he was back in Bristol and from there one day journeyed to Weston-super-Mare where, by ill-chance for her, he met Miss Bessie Mundy again. She was lonely and, astonishingly, appears to have been immediately forgiving of his earlier behaviour. This time, however, Smith tried a different tack and suggested that now they were re-united they should each make a will in favour of the other. By that time they had moved to Herne Bay and were living in a small house in the High Street. On 8 July 1912, mutual wills were executed and deposited with a local solicitor. Next day Smith bought a cheap, zinc bath and, because it had no taps, got the price reduced by half a crown.

Twenty-four hours later he took Bessie Mundy to a doctor with a story that she had had a fit, although she did not remember being ill. However she took her 'husband's' word and the doctor prescribed a sedative. Two days later the doctor was summoned and found the patient in bed, although she showed no symptoms of illness. As before, another sedative was prescribed. That night Smith got Miss Mundy to write a letter to her uncle, obediently describing her 'fit', praising her 'husband's' goodness and the marvellous medical treatment he had arranged for her.

The next day was Saturday 13 July. At 8 a.m. Smith sent the doctor a note which read: 'Can you come at once? I am afraid my wife is dead.' The doctor hurried round to find 'Mrs Williams' lying in the bath, her head under the water, her right hand clutching a piece of soap.

An inquest was fixed for the following Monday afternoon and, in the meantime, Smith sent telegrams to Bessie Mundy's uncle and brother. The latter wrote to the coroner demanding a post-mortem but the coroner was a lawyer without medical knowledge and all he did was to get 'Mr Williams' to sign a deposition. Smith was the only witness apart from the doctor and the jury's verdict was misadventure.

So a week after the mutual wills were signed Miss Bessie Mundy was buried – in a common grave, which was part of Smith's ruthless economy. The date of the funeral was unknown to the Mundy family until it was too late for them to attend. Neither uncle nor brother had attended the inquest, the sequence of events and the intervening week-end having given them little time.

As his investigation progressed, Chief Inspector Neil had carefully fed the press with sufficient information so that, despite the war news, space had been found for stories headlined 'Brides in the Bath Case', and the dossier on Smith grew daily.

For nearly a month Neil travelled the country, following leads to this man who had neither education, appearance nor manners yet was able to fascinate women of a better class than himself and persuade them to live with him, using their money. Neil discovered that after the death of Miss Mundy, Smith had obtained her money and rejoined Miss Pegler, then living at Margate. He explained his affluence by saying he had been on a profitable business trip to Canada. In fact he did buy seven houses in Bristol for £2,180, which gave him an income.

The trail led back to Bristol and again to Weston-super-Mare, where Smith had been accompanied by the faithful Miss Pegler. During 1913 Smith had met a governess and suggested she should insure her life for £500. Provisional arrangements were made, but, luckily for her, the governess grew suspicious and moved away. She was a fortunate woman for, in the space of three years he had met, married and murdered three times. First Miss Mundy, in 1912, then

Miss Burnham in 1913, and finally Miss Lofty in 1914. Each one had been found dead in her bath and in each case the inquest verdict was death by drowning by misadventure.

Smith had remained at liberty throughout the inquiry, although Neil had found out that he was living in Hammersmith and had a detective watching his every move. The evidence against him at that stage did not justify a charge of murder although Neil had no doubt that Smith was responsible for the deaths of Miss Mundy, Miss Burnham and Miss Lofty. In each case the method was exactly the same, even to the ritual of appearing with the supper immediately before the discovery of the sudden death. In Miss Mundy's case he had bought fish, for Miss Burnham he had bought eggs.

It is interesting to recall that Smith himself seldom took a bath. In fact his most faithful woman, Miss Pegler, told Chief Inspector Neil that he only took one bath in all the years of their association.

Neil had found out that Smith was due to call on his latest victim's solicitor at Shepherd's Bush to arrange to collect the insurance money she had left to him in her will. So on 4 February 1915, when he duly turned up, he was arrested and charged with causing a false entry to be made on the certificate of his bigamous marriage to Miss Lofty at Bath. That night he was taken to Bow Street police station and put up for identification. He was picked out by Mr Charles Burnham and several other witnesses and next day, at the magistrates' court, he was remanded in custody.

The Yard once again called in Dr Spilsbury and on the day of Smith's arrest he was at Finchley cemetery supervising the exhumation of Miss Lofty's body. Six days afterwards he was at Blackpool, at the grave of Miss Burnham and, later, he went to Herne Bay to attend the disinterment of Bessie Mundy, the earliest of Smith's known victims. Although no one disputed that all the women were drowned it was necessary to find out whether there was any other cause of death, like heart failure, a fit, suicide or accident.

Spilsbury carried out post-mortem examinations on all

three women and his report cemented Chief Inspector Neil's view that Smith was at least a triple murderer. Two months later this killer who hunted his victims wearing a top-hat and frock-coat was further charged with three murders. In June he appeared at the Old Bailey.

Chief Inspector Neil had done his work well. Of the 150 persons from whom he had taken statements, 112 appeared as witnesses. He had uncovered the fact that Smith was the same person as Oliver Love, John Lloyd, Henry Williams and Oliver James and, under these various names, he had 'married' seven times since 1898, the last being Miss Alice Reeval, at Woolwich, three months previously. From her he got £78, a piano, furniture and clothes. Neil had also traced Smith's complicated business dealings in connection with his three dead 'wives'. He had even found the three baths which had been used!

Spilsbury's evidence, which was supported by his fellow pathologist, William Willcox, proved that it was impossible for any of the victims to have drowned accidentally in baths of so small a size and that, in his opinion, all had died as a result of being suddenly immersed. During the trial the jury was taken out of court to witness an experiment by Chief Inspector Neil which ended in a frightening but convincing manner. A bath was half filled with water and a nurse in a bathing costume got in. Chief Inspector Neil grasped her feet and pulled her head under water. She immediately showed signs of distress, was quickly pulled out and had to be revived by artificial respiration.

The case lasted eight days and coincided with the Dardanelles campaign of the spring of 1915. Nearly all the news in the daily papers was about the battle front and the war effort at home. Crime received little or no attention from the press, but the case of 'The Brides in the Bath' was the exception. The public interest was centred on the character of the prisoner, an extraordinary and, apparently, uncouth man whose sex appeal had lured so many women first into his bed and some to their deaths. Such was his powerful attraction that the public gallery was always two-thirds full of women who wanted to see for themselves this 'monster' who loved poetry, could play the piano quite well and draw with some skill.

The jury returned a verdict of guilty after retiring for only twenty-one minutes. Smith's appeal failed and he was executed at Maidstone Prison on 13 August 1915. The whole investigation, arrest and execution took considerably longer than any one of Smith's courtships to murder.

CHAPTER 5

The Killer of Dandelions

The crime wave which followed the 1914–18 war was violent and it was significant in that criminals began to use cars for the first time. This resulted in the formation of the Flying Squad, so called not simply because it gave the detectives greater mobility but because they used vehicles which had been formerly used by the Royal Flying Corps.

Following the beginning of broadcasting on station 2LO, some police cars were fitted with wireless, transmitting in morse. In 1921 the first police telephone box was erected in Trafalgar Square – a sign of the willingness of the police to assist the public and to get the public to reciprocate. It was also a place for the man on the beat to communicate with his station, write reports and take his meal-break. In the same year there was another case of bungling by local police, this time at the scene of a murder in Redbourn, Hertfordshire. When Detective Inspector Alfred Crutchett arrived to investigate the killing of seventy-one-year-old Mrs Seabrook in her home, he found that kindly neighbours had been allowed to clean up the cottage, and wipe the blood off the murder weapon, a bent poker. Crutchett did in fact make an arrest – of a thirteen-year-old schoolboy who was later found guilty and ordered to be detained during His Majesty's pleasure.

In 1922 twenty women were sworn in as police constables with powers of arrest, and someone tried to murder the Commissioner of Police, with the anonymous gift of a box of poisoned chocolates. It was 9 November and he was expecting a box from a relative to mark his birthday. He was to attend the Lord Mayor's banquet that night, so ate only one or two, but promptly collapsed and only immediate medical attention saved his life. The postmark of Balham, South London, on the parcel led eventually to a man called Tatam, who had a history of insanity and who was later committed to Broadmoor.

It was recognized that newspaper publicity had greatly assisted the solving of some murders and that there was no faster method of recruiting the help of the public. So in 1927 the Press Bureau was formed at Scotland Yard to feed newspaper men with details of cases where public help was required.

The case of Major Armstrong shows what an advantage the expertise of the Yard men still had at that time over less experienced local police. Confronted merely by a suspicion of murder, which would not be easy to prove, possibly involving a well-known and respected member of a small community, the London detectives could keep their inquiries at a discreet level, and at the same time apply some relatively sophisticated methods of collecting evidence to pin down their quarry.

In December 1921 the Director of Public Prosecutions sent for Wensley, by now in charge of the Murder Squad, and consulted him about a suspected case of poisoning by arsenic in the little Welsh town of Hay. The suspect was an unlikely one: Major Herbert Rowse Armstrong, TD, MA, solicitor and clerk to the local magistrates. The intended victim was a fellow solicitor, Mr Oswald Martin.

Wensley decided to send Alfred Crutchett, by now Detective Chief Inspector, with Detective Sergeant Walter Sharp on the case. They had instructions to make their inquiries in absolute secrecy, and that on no account was Major Armstrong to hear of their presence in the town.

The men from Scotland Yard moved in at night, and Crutchett went first to see Dr Thomas Hincks, who had practised in the locality for twenty-three years and whose suspicions had brought the Yard on to the case. It was he who had been called in to see Oswald Martin when at the end of October he had been taken ill. Dr Hincks had found he was suffering from what appeared to be a severe bilious attack but with one addition – a very rapid pulse. Although the patient had improved with treatment his pulse rate had remained high and the doctor had become suspicious. Finally he had sent a sample of urine to the Clinical Research Association for analysis. A week later, when Mr Martin was quite recovered, the reply came back that one thirty-third of a grain of arsenic had been found in the sample – normally a fatal dose of arsenic is two to three grains.

The doctor's opinion was that Mr Martin's illness was caused by taking a considerable dose of arsenic, and since the doctor made up his own medicines and never used arsenic, the poison must have come from another source. He told Crutchett that he had questioned Mr Martin about meals taken immediately before his illness had developed. He had eaten lunch and dinner with his wife and the maid and they had remained perfectly well. But on the day he was taken ill during the evening, he had had tea with Major Armstrong at his house, Mayfield, in Cusop.

Dr Hincks suddenly realized that when Armstrong's wife had died earlier that year she had experienced similar symptoms to Mr Martin, although the cause of her death had been certified as heart disease. He had written to the Barnwood Asylum at Gloucester, where Mrs Armstrong had been treated, and told the doctors there of his suspicions. They agreed that they too might have been misled as to the cause of her illness and so Dr Hincks warned Martin not to accept any more hospitality from Armstrong and not to talk to anyone about the matter. Then the resolute doctor reported his suspicions to the Home Office.

Crutchett moved on to see Oswald Martin, who confirmed the recent events and also mentioned a box of chocolates which had arrived at his home, without any card or note as to who the sender was. Mrs Martin had eaten some and then put the box away. They had produced it a few days later when friends came to dinner and one of their guests was later taken ill. However, they had kept the chocolates and Crutchett removed them. In the laboratory some were found to contain arsenic which had been inserted through minute holes pierced in the base of the sweets.

Mr Martin also told the detective about a business deal concerning the sale of some land in which the two solicitors were representing opposing parties. Major Armstrong's client had not completed the contract. Mr Martin had had to press him and, after a year's delay, to threaten to declare the contract broken and demand the return of the deposits. Major Armstrong had continued to plead for more time but in October Mr Martin's client had refused to go on with the sale and insisted on the return of the deposits. This had caused considerable friction between the two solicitors.

It had also been the beginning of invitations to Mayfield for tea. Mr Martin had politely refused many times but had eventually felt obliged to accept. He described the meal – tea, bread and butter, currant bread and buttered scones. As soon as the tea was poured the Major had reached across and picked up a buttered scone, which he put on Mr Martin's plate with the words, 'Please excuse fingers.'

Martin had eaten the scone, then he had had some currant bread. After a cigarette and a talk he had returned home. That evening he was taken ill. During the time he was in bed and being treated he had been bombarded with more invitations to tea and dinner at Mayfield.

Chief Inspector Crutchett and his men quietly continued their inquiries and called at the local chemist's shop where Major Armstrong was a frequent visitor. He was a keen gardener, apparently hated weeds and, in particular, the dandelions which infested his lawn. He bought weed-killer and pure arsenic, sometimes as much as half a pound at a time. He also had a little squirt-gun with a tiny nozzle so that he could eradicate the dandelions singly without having to leave a hole in the grass.

Everyone in the village knew the major and that he was a widower, his wife having died a year before. He was quite popular and his wife had been respected, although it was also well known that she was something of a disciplinarian. She had been six inches taller than her husband and apparently he had given in to her when other men might have argued or refused her bidding. Chief Inspector Crutchett learned, for example, that when Mrs Armstrong had called her husband from tennis in the middle of a match he had simply apologized to his partner and left the court. He had appeared to take this rigorous domestic situation with good grace, and had treated his wife with consideration and affection. His eyes were a vivid blue, he was always neatly dressed, never without a flower in his buttonhole and wore gold-rimmed pince-nez. His wife had disapproved of smoking, so he enjoyed his pipe and cigars in secret. She had also been teetotal so he had drunk neither wine nor spirits in her presence.

Some months before his wife had died Armstrong had drawn up a new will for her, in which she left him everything she possessed. Soon afterwards he had bought some more weed-killer. On her death in February 1921, Dr Hincks had certified the cause as heart disease and three days afterwards the burial had taken place in the churchyard at Cusop. Then Major Armstrong had spent some weeks in London where he had been seen with a woman he had known in his Army days. At his home the restriction on drinking alcohol had been removed.

By Christmas time Armstrong was still busy trying to lure Oswald Martin to tea or dinner, with no success, while Chief Inspector Crutchett was at Scotland Yard reporting on what he had found out during his secret investigation. The Director of Public Prosecutions, mindful of the danger to Mr Martin, decided to have the solicitor arrested.

Back to Hay went Inspector Crutchett and his sergeant. It was New Year's Eve and the two Yard men had picked up the Deputy Chief Constable of Herefordshire, Superintendent Albert Weaver, on the way. They had watched Armstrong enter his office and, a few minutes later, they followed. Superintendent Weaver was in uniform and he knew that Armstrong's office was on the first floor. The three police officers walked up and entered Major Armstrong's office without knocking. Weaver introduced his companions and Crutchett told Armstrong of his inquiries about the illness of Oswald Norman Martin, the analysis of his urine and the presence of arsenic in it. He also mentioned the chocolates containing arsenic.

Armstrong appeared not to turn a hair. He said, 'This is a very serious matter and I will help you all I can. I was not aware that arsenic had been found in Mr Martin's urine, and I appreciate that the circumstances call for some explanation from me. I will make a statement and tell you all I know.'

A statement was then taken from Armstrong which Crutchett described as 'guarded'. In essence he agreed that he had invited Martin to tea but denied handing him a particular scone. He also denied having bought and sent the chocolates but admitted buying arsenic on several occasions. When he had signed the statement, after making a few alterations, Superintendent Weaver cautioned Armstrong and arrested him on a charge of administering arsenic to Mr Martin on 26 October 1921, at Mayfield, Cusop, with intent to murder him. In reply to the charge, Armstrong said, 'I am quite innocent.'

The prisoner was told to turn out his pockets and the contents were packed into a brown-paper parcel. When the parcel was examined later a tiny packet of white arsenic containing three and three-quarter grains was found caught in the flap of another envelope. And, later, another small packet of arsenic containing almost two ounces was found in a drawer in Armstrong's bureau.

Two days after the arrest, the body of Mrs Armstrong was exhumed from Cusop churchyard. After the post-mortem examination by Bernard Spilsbury, sixteen jars containing organs and other parts of the body, sawdust and wood-shavings from the coffin, and soil attached to it, were handed to the analyst, John Webster. He found the presence of arsenic in a quantity consistent with the poison having been given in a number of large doses over a period, probably of not less than a week, and said, 'It is the largest amount of arsenic I have found in any case of arsenical poisoning.' Spilsbury's opinion of the cause of Martin's illness was that it was also caused by acute arsenical poisoning.

At his trial it was inevitable that Armstrong would give evidence. After all, he was an intelligent, professional man, used to courts and court procedure, and it would have looked odd if he had elected not to do so. He was in the witness box for five hours and among the awkward questions he had to answer was to explain the presence of arsenic in the contents of his pockets and in the drawer of his bureau. He was a cool, competent witness until the judge took a hand and then his composure was less sure.

In his statement to the police he had said that he had no arsenic in his possession except in the diluted form of weed-killer. His story now was that after he had been charged he had discovered a little screw of paper containing white arsenic in his waistcoat pocket which he had forgotten. He had said nothing about it, knowing that the police would find it, as they did. He had transferred it into one of his letters when he had taken them from his pockets. The arsenic found in his pocket, he claimed, was the last and twentieth packet of a quantity he had divided into equal parts. Nineteen, he said, he had used to kill dandelions. The packet contained three and three-quarter grains – a fatal dose. The judge, Mr Justice Darling, inflicted a merciless cross-examination on Armstrong and demanded to know why he had not explained the last packet – and how could he have forgotten it? Penetrating questions followed as to why he had made up twenty packets of arsenic when he could have poured it straight into the ground to kill the weeds. Armstrong could only answer that it seemed the most convenient way of doing it.

Armstrong had remembered the packet of arsenic in his bureau drawer after his arrest and told his solicitor, Mr Matthews, who found it and handed it to the police. The judge wanted to know why Armstrong had not told the police earlier about that.

The jury at Hereford Assizes no doubt noted that Armstrong was arrested on the last day of December, a time when the dandelion season could hardly be said to be at its height. They found Armstrong guilty and he was executed at Gloucester Prison.

Detective Chief Inspector Crutchett was only disappointed in one phase of the investigation – he had failed to prove that Armstrong had bought and sent the poisoned chocolates. He had found the little squirt-gun with the tiny nozzle which fitted the puncture marks in the chocolates, but, despite widespread inquiries at thousands of shops and at Fullers factory where they had been made, he was unable to identify the purchaser.

CHAPTER 6

A Wife's Suspicions

On Thursday, 1 May 1924, a former detective inspector went to see Frederick Wensley, now Chief Constable of the CID. He told him that a woman he knew, a Mrs Mahon, had found a cloakroom ticket in one of her husband's pockets and, since she suspected him of being unfaithful, had asked the inspector to check on the bag's contents. He had presented the ticket at the left-luggage at Waterloo Station and a bag was handed to him. It was locked, but the ex-detective was able to ease it open on either side of the lock and look inside. He had seen some articles of women's silk underclothing, which appeared to be bloodstained, and a knife. He had returned the bag to the cloakroom and instructed Mrs Mahon to put the ticket back in her husband's pocket.

That call to Scotland Yard was the introduction to the discovery of a horrific murder in a bungalow on a desolate stretch of shingle known as The Crumbles, which extends from Eastbourne to Pevensey Bay. It was also a turning point in the history of Yard murder investigations, for it led to the introduction of the now famous Murder Bags.

Before that case a detective had to handle all the evidence he found with his naked hands. If he wanted to preserve clues, like a human hair on clothing, or specimens of dust or soil, he had to wrap them in a piece of paper, or an envelope. He had no tapes to measure distance, no compass to determine direction, nothing with which to take fingerprints, not even a magnifying glass.

Detective Chief Inspector Percy Savage was given charge of the case. His first task was to determine the contents of the locked Gladstone bag at Waterloo and he sent Detective Sergeants Frew and Thompson to watch the cloakroom and detain the man who came to collect it. Soon after six o'clock Patrick Mahon, using the name Waller, presented the ticket, and the detectives introduced themselves. At the Yard Mahon was taken in to meet Savage, who noted Mahon's well-made dark brown suit, his gloves and folded umbrella. He was well-spoken and calm, his brown curly hair tinged with grey, and he moved with athletic ease.

With the key the sergeants had found in Mahon's pocket Savage opened the bag and laid out the contents – a torn pair of silk bloomers, two pieces of new white silk, a blue silk scarf and a large cook's knife. The clothing was stained with blood and grease. There was also a brown canvas racquet bag, with the initials 'E.B.K.', and some disinfectant powder.

'How do you account for these things?' Savage asked.

'I'm fond of dogs,' Mahon replied. 'I suppose I've carried home meat for dogs in it.'

'You don't usually wrap dog's meat in silk. Your explanation does not satisfy me.'

As always, this was a delicate point in the investigation. At that time Savage had no knowledge of any crime having been committed and yet the contents of the bag had to be explained. The two men sat there in silence. Mahon declined a drink or a sandwich, and continued sitting, staring in front of him.

However, at about eleven o'clock that night Savage's patience was rewarded. Mahon began to talk. He was calm and composed, which was exactly how Savage wanted him. It is one of the main principles of interrogation, laid down by Dr Hans Gross, formerly Professor of Criminology at Prague University, and now part of the 'Yard Man's Bible', that too much reliance should not be placed upon testimony given when a witness is in a state of excitement.

Mahon began by saying he had met a woman in London about ten months before, when she was a clerk in the City. 'On April the twelfth,' he said, 'I met her at Eastbourne and we went to Langney bungalow and stayed until April the seventeenth. On the night of the sixteenth we quarrelled over certain things, and in a violent temper she threw an axe at me. It was a coal axe. It hit me a glancing blow. Then I saw red. We fought and struggled. She was a very big, strong girl. She appeared to be quite mad with anger and rage. During our struggle we overturned a chair, and her head fell on an iron coal-scuttle, and it appeared to stun her. This happened about twelve o'clock, midnight. I attempted to revive her, but found I could not.

'The reaction after the struggle having set in, the consequences to me came home with stunning force. I put the body in the spare bedroom and covered it up with her fur coat. I came up to London on the morning of April the seventeenth and returned to the bungalow fairly late, taking with me a knife I had bought in a shop in Victoria Street. I also bought at the same shop a small saw.

'When I got back to the bungalow I was still so upset and worried that I could not then carry out my intentions to decapitate the body. I did so on Good Friday. I severed the legs from the hips, the head, and left the arms on. I then put the various parts in a trunk in the bedroom and locked the door. On Saturday, April the nineteenth, and the twentieth I stayed at the bungalow and came back to London on Monday.

'I again went to the bungalow on Tuesday and on that day I burned the head in the sitting-room grate, and also the feet and legs. I came back to town late on Tuesday night or Wednesday morning and went down again on Friday night and stayed at a hotel, going to the bungalow in the morning. I had to cut up the trunk. I also cut off the arms. I burned portions of them. The smell was appalling and I had to think of some method of disposing of the portions. I then boiled some portions in a large pot in the bungalow, cut the portions up small, packed them in the brown bag, and I threw them out of the train between Waterloo and Richmond. These portions were not wrapped in anything. This was about ten o'clock on Sunday night.

'I went on to Reading and stayed at the Station Hotel in the name of Rees. Next morning I came to London and left the bag in the cloakroom at Waterloo Station. I had disposed of the remaining pieces between Waterloo and Reading on April the twenty-seventh. The bloodstained cloth that was in the bag was a pair of bloomers that I got out of the girl's trunk. I tore them up and used it to wrap up some of the flesh.'

There can hardly have been a more macabre statement ever made but it is interesting to note that while Mahon hadn't mentioned the name of the woman, he had made up a not unreasonable defence against premeditated murder. Finally he gave the woman's name as Emily Beilby Kaye who, he said, was single, aged twenty-nine and well educated.

Savage had Mahon's story, but was it true? He had to find that out. There was no sleep for him or his men that night. They went straight to the bungalow to confirm the details.

The bungalow stood only a short distance from the spot where four years before Irene Munro, a seventeen-year-old London typist, had been murdered by two men. It was known as Officer's House because it had formerly been the home of the officer in charge of the coastguard station. Savage and his men walked through the gate in the white stone wall, up to the porch overhung with climbing roses and entered the front door.

The stench that met them was no surprise. They knew a murder had been committed there, but even so they could not have imagined a more ghastly scene. The bungalow had four bedrooms, a sitting-room, dining-room, kitchen and scullery. There were burned bones in the grates of the dining-room and sitting-room. A saucepan and a bath in the scullery contained human remains that had been boiled. In a bedroom to the right of the passage was a bloodstained saw. In a trunk, marked with the initials 'E.B.K.' were dismembered portions of a woman's body and in a biscuit tin the heart and other internal organs. A trail of blood suggested the woman had been killed in the sitting-room, then the body dragged across the hall, through one bedroom and into the scullery.

When Bernard Spilsbury visited the bungalow he was astonished to find Savage handling pieces of putrid flesh, putting them into buckets. He pointed out the danger of infection and said, 'Are there no rubber gloves?' The answer was no, there never had been any, although the Murder Squad had been going away on murders for seventeen years. As a result of this, Detective Superintendent William Brown, then chief of the Squad, consulted with Spilsbury and other members of his team, and the first Murder Bag was planned. Since then they have been improved to the point where any clue can be safely preserved and any task undertaken with the correct apparatus.

Spilsbury, himself inured to horror, said the human remains found at the bungalow were the most gruesome he had ever seen. The atmosphere was so dreadful that he had a table erected in the garden and worked there while hundreds of local people tried to peer over the fence.

During that day the detectives and the pathologist found practically the whole body of the victim. In the fire grates alone, mixed with coal dust and ash, were found nearly one thousand fragments of calcined bone. Some even fitted together. An examination of the reconstructed body proved that there was nothing to account for natural death and that the woman was probably in an early state of pregnancy, between one and three months.

Savage took possession of a woman's brush and comb, a gold wrist-watch, some jewellery, six hats and other articles of clothing. He also took a leather kitbag, a hat-box, a big fibre trunk, an axe with a broken shaft and a carving knife.

Detective Sergeant Frew, who had been left at the Yard, had discovered a good deal about their prisoner. He was of Liverpool-Irish stock, with a quick intelligence and good looks, and in his early youth his behaviour had been exemplary. He had attended church regularly, was active in local social affairs and was good at games. But he had married a girl of eighteen in 1910 when he was only twenty, and, a year later, was taking another girl to the Isle of Man with money obtained by forged cheques. Bound over for this offence, he was soon sentenced to twelve months for embezzlement. He had moved to Wiltshire, and then got employment in Surrey where the notoriety of his love affairs cost him his job. He was constantly picking up women and, in 1916, he had broken into a bank and stunned a maidservant with a hammer. Such was his preoccupation with women that he had waited until she had recovered consciousness, had kissed and fondled her, and then asked forgiveness for the attack! For that offence he went to prison for five years.

Mahon's wife had stood by him and there were two children by the marriage, though the younger one, a boy, had died while his father was in prison. Mrs Mahon had then come to London and found a job at Sunbury. She was so well regarded, and so forgiving, that when he finished his sentence her recommendation got him a job as a salesman with the firm where she worked.

Mahon's victim – Emily Kaye – was thirty-four, and had worked as a shorthand-typist in the City, living at a residential club in Guilford Street, Bloomsbury. One of the partners in the firm where she worked had become the manager of the business in Sunbury-on-Thames where Mrs Mahon worked as a secretary. It was a strange trick of fate that this man introduced her husband to Miss Kaye at the City office. Emily Kaye quickly succumbed to Mahon's blandishments and they began going out together. Early in 1924 she knew she was pregnant.

Mahon had not hidden from her the fact that he was married – he had little option under the circumstances of their employment – but that did not stop him from giving Emily Kaye a diamond and sapphire engagement ring and promising to take her to South Africa. She told all her friends this news and, on 7 April, she gave up her room at Guilford Street.

Chief Inspector Savage began to put a different complexion on Mahon's version of the tragedy. He discovered that three days before the alleged quarrel in the bungalow Mahon had bought the cook's knife and saw from the shop in Victoria Street. He also found out that Emily Kaye had saved over £600. Her banking account showed that in the two months before her death she had drawn most of her money and given it to Mahon. She was left with a balance of only £70. In fact, she gave Mahon four separate £100 notes. Two were cashed by him at the Bank of England before her death, and one afterwards. On each occasion he endorsed the notes with a false name and address. The fourth note was never traced.

Mahon was in a hopeless predicament. He had fleeced the woman who loved him and he knew that if the child was born he would be exposed. So on 4 April he answered by telephone an advertisement for the letting of a furnished bungalow at Pevensey Bay, giving his name as Waller. He said he was living at a hotel in London, that he was connected with the British Empire Exhibition, and that he wanted a bungalow because his wife needed rest and quiet.

He arranged for Miss Kaye to stay at an Eastbourne hotel until the bungalow was ready. Meantime she had written to her sister saying she was going abroad with her fiancé, Pat Derek Patterson: 'We shall be off in ten days and will be married when we get there,' she wrote.

Miss Kaye left London on 7 April for the Eastbourne hotel and there she waited alone for her lover.

Mahon was then staying at home in Kew. Three days later he was walking in Richmond one evening when he met a young woman, Miss Ethel Duncan. He was adept at street meetings and they conversed while walking towards her home at Isleworth. Before parting he suggested dinner and she gave him her address which he noted in his diary. Mr Savage had seen this address when he searched Mahon and went through his papers. It was a detail Mahon had neglected to mention.

On 12 April, during the afternoon, Mahon had gone to the shop in Victoria Street and bought the knife and a meat saw, then had travelled to Eastbourne to meet Miss Kaye. After dinner they had taken a taxi to the bungalow, arriving at midnight. Two days later Emily Kaye wrote her last letter. It was to a friend, telling of her future travels, of her happiness, and giving a forwarding address at Cape Town.

Exactly when Mahon killed her has never been discovered, but it must have been soon after that letter was sent. It is also not known how long his grisly task took him. But the day after the letter was posted he sent a telegram to Miss Duncan: 'Charing Cross seven tomorrow; Sure. Pat.' He came to London on that day and kept the appointment, giving her dinner at a restaurant in Victoria. Over the meal he told her he had the use of a friend's bungalow at Eastbourne and invited her to spend the Easter holiday with him.

She agreed and on the seventeenth she received from

Mahon a telegraphic money order for four pounds and the message: 'Meet the train as arranged. Waller.' It was post-marked Eastbourne. On Good Friday morning she caught the train to Eastbourne, and was met by Mahon who took her to lunch. Then they went on a motoring tour, had dinner in the evening and went to the bungalow. That night they shared the bedroom which only two or three nights before Mahon had shared with Miss Kaye, whose dismembered body was now hidden in a trunk in the room next door. Miss Duncan later told Savage that Mahon seemed to be quite normal and in good spirits. She did know that another woman had been there because she saw a tortoiseshell hair-brush and some cosmetics, and a pair of high-heeled shoes. Mahon had told her he was married and said these things belonged to his wife. She had also caught a fleeting glimpse of the cabin trunk, while Mahon had been fastening the door with screws. His excuse was that his friend, who owned the bungalow, had some valuable books he wanted to safeguard.

Next day Mahon took Miss Duncan to Eastbourne. He left her to spend the day alone there, while he himself went to Plumpton races. Savage was sure, but was never able to prove, that it was there he changed the fourth £100 note he had received from Miss Kaye. Mahon had decided that Miss Duncan had outlived her usefulness and he also sent himself a telegram at the bungalow saying: 'Important see you Tuesday morning. Lee.' That excuse was on the doormat when they arrived home after another evening in East-bourne, so he and Miss Duncan went to London on the morning of the Bank Holiday so that he could answer his bogus summons to the office.

Mahon said afterwards that he would have gone 'stark raving mad' if Miss Duncan had not been at the bungalow with him. It was not exactly the romantic idyll she had thought.

From that time on Mahon was busy trying to dispose of the body. He worked at it all that week and, on Sunday 28 April, he deposited the locked bag with its incriminating contents in the left-luggage cloakroom at Waterloo Station. But for the suspicions of his long-suffering wife, who had guessed correctly that he was once again caught up with another woman, his crime might never have been discovered. There would have been nothing to connect Waller of the bungalow with Mahon of Kew, and Miss Kaye would never have been reported missing because her friends would have assumed she was happily in South Africa.

Percy Savage was of the opinion, shared by the forensic experts, that Mahon had killed Emily Kaye by hitting her on the head with the axe which was found with the broken shaft, and that he had then burned her head. Savage and Spilsbury made an experiment and put a sheep's head on a burning coal fire in the sitting-room of the bungalow. Within four hours it was reduced to charred fragments.

Percy Savage, whose father was a policeman, was born in a room over the cells in Acton police station. As a baby he had played with handcuffs and a police whistle. He had joined the force in 1900 and his twenty-four years' experience told him that he should not necessarily believe Mahon's story of accidental death leading to disposal of the body. He was eventually able to prove that the crime was in fact premeditated murder.

At the trial the abundant panache of Mahon had another airing. In the dock he wore a stylish blue suit, which had been specially ordered from his own tailor at a cost of seven guineas, a smart collar and tie, and his hands were carefully manicured. His face was tanned but his complexion, like most other things about him, was a sham. Rumour said he had used tobacco juice. Whatever it was, it helped to bolster his confidence and, at the close of the prosecution case, he went into the witness box. His composure was remarkable until towards the end, when after a merciless cross-examination by Sir Henry Curtis Bennett, who led for the Crown, he sobbed and wiped his eyes with a silk pocket handkerchief.

There had been another dramatic moment earlier, when Mahon was answering questions put to him by J. D. Cassels, his own counsel. He had got to the point of telling how he had broken Miss Kaye's skull with blows from a poker and had put it on the roaring fire. The July weather outside the Old Bailey was dark and sultry, and as he described his gruesome activity in the bungalow a thunderclap reverberated through the courtroom and lightning flashed. Mahon went white despite the tan on his face – it reminded him of another storm, many months before. He told Cassels that when he had put the girl's head on the fire, her hair had blazed, her eyes had opened and at that moment there came a fearful clap of thunder and lightning played around the room. He had fled in terror.

Savage and his men proved Mahon to be a liar whose many mistakes had put him in the dock. Savage had said from the beginning that he did not believe Emily Kaye had died by striking her head on the coal-scuttle. It was a cheap and insubstantial piece with thin metal legs that buckled. His view was confirmed by Sir Bernard Spilsbury who, when asked if she could have died that way, replied, 'No, in my opinion, she could not.'

On 9 September Mahon was hanged at Wandsworth Prison for what the Director of Public Prosecutions described as 'one of the foulest crimes which has been committed in recent years'.

And the next team which left the Yard on a case carried a Murder Bag.

CHAPTER 7

The Charing Cross Trunk Murder

The Charing Cross Station trunk murder of 1927 was another three-stage investigation in which an unidentified victim had to be married to a name, then linked to a killer, and evidence found to prove guilt. Laundry marks were again instrumental in completing identification, but in the event final proof rested largely on the chief investigator's 'nose'.

The whole inquiry from discovery of the body to the execution of the murderer took only three months and two days, but it took the team, without the help of a special police laboratory, more than a week to link the clue of a bloodstained duster wrapped round the head of the victim with her name, by the simple process of washing the duster out in a cloakroom washbasin!

Balanced against this lack of facilities was the far smaller caseload confronting each detective, enabling him to concentrate on a single investigation almost exclusively, with plenty of manpower to assist him.

10 May 1927 dawned in London with the promise of a warm day, so much so that the evening papers carried optimistic headlines announcing that midsummer had arrived. There were photographs of office workers strolling in the parks. One place where the weather was not so welcome was in the left-luggage cloakroom in Charing Cross railway station. A horrible smell met the nostrils of the attendants, and one of them traced it to a trunk which had been brought in several days before.

It was a large, round-topped wickerwork affair, popular in those days, covered with black cloth, and fastened with a broad strap. It was clearly far from air-tight. A police constable was brought from his beat and the trunk was opened. In it, under some brown paper, was the body of a woman divided into five parts by amputation at each shoulder and hip joint. The constable, a stickler for the rules, refused to allow the grisly remains to be removed to the mortuary until a police surgeon certified the woman was dead, and, more importantly, a detective from the Murder Squad was present.

This was Detective Sergeant Leonard Burt, who went on to become famous as chief of the Special Branch. He wrote later: 'It was ghastly enough to be unforgettable! The head was still joined to the body, but the arms and legs had been hacked off and an attempt had been made to cut one leg in half at the knee. Perhaps the most ghastly touch of all was that each limb was wrapped separately in brown paper and neatly tied with string. The woman's clothing was packed into the trunk with the body, making it a tight fit.'

The trunk had the letter 'A' painted on each end of it and 'I.F.A.' painted on the lid. Attached to it with string was a label addressed to 'F. Austin, St Leonards'.

Burt had the trunk and the remains removed to the Westminster coroner's court in Horseferry Road. The Divisional Surgeon unpacked the trunk, watched by Detective Chief Inspector George Cornish, who had been sent from the Yard to take over the investigation.

First the surgeon took out a pair of black shoes, size five, and a handbag, which contained four pieces of chewing gum. The limbs were wrapped in brown paper reinforced with two towels and a pair of grey knickers, which had the name 'P. Holt' worked on a white tab in blue cotton. One leg was wrapped in a jacket and the other in the matching skirt and another towel. The head was contained in a duster and the body wrapped in a pale blue jumper and other underclothes. On a pair of white knickers were two laundry marks.

The doctor decided the woman had not died from natural causes. He was of the opinion that death had been caused by a heavy blow to her forehead and that, when unconscious, she had been suffocated. She was reckoned to be aged about thirty-five to forty, about five feet in height with brown bobbed hair.

There were several good clues to work on. Inspector McBride, the senior Yard photographer, took pictures of the trunk, clothes, shoes, handbag, and of the laundry marks – 447 and 581. One was in black cotton and the other in black ink. All the photographs were sent to the newspapers and appeared for the first time that evening.

Results came in swiftly. A second-hand dealer in Brixton recognized the trunk as one he had sold early in May. He described the man who had bought it as aged about thirty-six, dark with a slight moustache, of medium build and good looking, and wearing a dark suit.

The attendants at Charing Cross left-luggage cloakroom had no recollection of the trunk's depositor, which was not surprising as they handled hundreds of pieces of luggage every day. The porter was found who had fetched the trunk from a taxi, but it was the luggage he remembered, not its owner. He said it had been left between half past one and a quarter to two on 6 May, and that it was very heavy. Meanwhile the Home Office pathologist, Sir Bernard Spilsbury, had examined the body. His diagnosis of death agreed with that of the Divisional Surgeon and, in his view, the woman had died about a week before the discovery of the body. In describing the amputations Spilsbury at first suggested they might have been made by an experienced slaughterman. This was one of his rare errors of judgment and he corrected it, following a second examination, saying the murderer was not skilled. But his correction came much later and, at the time, was of no help to Cornish.

By now the newspapers were carrying banner headlines which sparked the memory of a shoe-black who had his pitch in the station yard at Charing Cross. He claimed he had seen a small, rolled-up piece of paper thrown from a taxi window and had picked it up. When he looked at it five days after the discovery of the body he realized it was a cloakroom ticket and he took it to the police. It was the receipt for the black trunk.

Next came the news that the laundry marks had been traced to a laundry in Shepherd's Bush. Cornish hurried down to see the manageress who told him the number 447 was the mark used on the linen of a Mrs Holt of South Kensington. The name on the knickers and the laundry mark fitted together. He also learned that the laundry marked the customers' linen in red, and that of their servants in black. The white knickers, therefore, probably belonged to one of Mrs Holt's servants.

Mrs Holt did not recognize them, but she did know the grey knickers. They were her own and she had sewn on the name tab herself. Cornish asked her to describe her staff and one, Mrs Rolls, whom she had employed some time before as a temporary cook, sounded very like the dead woman. She confirmed this when she saw the body at the mortuary.

A parlour-maid, Frances Askey, had been friendly with Mrs Rolls and Mrs Holt recalled that the two had been thinking of sharing a room together. A servants' agency produced an address for Miss Askey and she provided some valuable information. The real name of Mrs Rolls, she said, was Bonati, and she had a husband living in Marylebone, but she had been living with a Mr Rolls, and he often passed as her husband. There were times when she had also used her maiden name of Budd.

Mr Rolls was traced and agreed that he had lived with Mrs Bonati, whose first name was Minnie. He said he had not seen her recently but that the description of the body he had read about in the newspapers did sound rather like his former lover.

Three people were found who had seen Mrs Bonati alive on 4 May, but there was no evidence that she had been seen since then, which suggested she had been murdered on that day or soon after.

Mr Bonati, an Italian waiter, was found and was able to satisfy Inspector Cornish he was innocent of any connection with the murder. He positively identified the body, particularly from a crooked finger his wife had had from birth.

By now a good deal was known about Minnie Bonati and her way of life. She was thirty-six and was obviously highly promiscuous. She knew a chauffeur named Jim, who had written her postcards, a bricklayer called Tom and a butcher. The last was of particular interest because Spilsbury had said the murderer had a knowledge of anatomy and no little skill with a knife. It took some days to trace all these men, but they were all able to prove they had had nothing to do with the murder.

Police had also been searching for the man whose name was on the label on the trunk, F. Austin of St Leonards, but he, too, was quite innocent – the police never discovered why it should have been addressed to him.

The investigation was now six days old and slowing down. Then a taxi-driver came to Scotland Yard who said he had taken a man with a similar trunk from Rochester Row, in Westminster, to Charing Cross Station where the trunk was carried in by a porter. His story was that on 6 May, or thereabouts, he had taken two young men from the Royal Automobile Club in Pall Mall to Westminster Police Court. When they had paid him he saw a man on the opposite side of the road, beckoning him across. He turned his taxi round and stopped. The man asked him to take a black trunk to Charing Cross. He took one handle, the man the other, and they carried it to the taxi. The driver said it was heavy and he jokingly inquired if it was full of money. The man laughed and said it wasn't money but books.

The two young men who had taken the taxi from the Royal Automobile Club were traced. They confirmed they had arrived at the police court at 1.35 p.m. to face a charge of dangerous driving. The story began to fit together and it checked with the porter who said he had handled the trunk at the station between half past one and a quarter to two. The taxi-driver and the porter did not recognize each other, but that would have been too much to expect in the fore-court of a busy station. The trail led back to Rochester Row, to the place where the trunk was picked up, a point which slightly aggrieved the local constabulary. They felt they should have noticed something which happened exactly opposite Rochester Row police station!

Detectives went to the office building outside which the man had been standing with the trunk. The ground floor was used as a shop, while the first and second floors were let to a solicitor who had sub-let two furnished front rooms to a man named J. Robinson who ran a business under the name of 'Edwards and Co., Business Transfer Agents'. The third floor was let to a number of different societies who used the large single room for meetings.

All the people in the building were interviewed and asked if they had seen anything of a trunk. The solicitor's clerk did remember seeing a trunk standing in the street doorway at about half past one one day, and he thought the date would have been about 6 May. He had good reason for remembering this because he had been inconvenienced, having to step round it to get into the building. There was no one with the trunk at the time and he had wondered how it got there. Shown the trunk at Scotland Yard, he said it looked very like the same one. None of the people in the building had much recollection of Mr Robinson and their efforts at a description bore no relation to that of the Brixton second-hand dealer.

Mr Robinson was not in his office and did not seem to have been there recently. He had rented the offices on 22 March, paying a month's rent in advance. He paid again on 22 April but had not been seen since 9 May. Inside his office was proof that he did not intend to return.

On the desk was a note saying he was not coming back as he was 'broke', even though he could have stayed on until 22 May. There was no home address anywhere to be seen but there was one interesting clue in the room. This was an official letter from the Post Office to Robinson saying that a telegram addressed to Robinson, Greyhound Hotel, Hammersmith, had not been delivered as the addressee was not known there.

Robinson's wife was found to be working at the hotel as a barmaid, and the reason she had not received the telegram

78

was that it had been handed to a new barmaid who did not know the names of the staff and had handed it back to the delivery boy. The girl could not have known at the time that she had done the police a kindness.

Mrs Robinson told Cornish that she was meeting her husband at the Elephant and Castle that evening at six o'clock and she gave them his address. Robinson was not there when the police called, and so when he arrived that evening to meet his wife he found her accompanied by two detectives. He readily went with them to Scotland Yard and spoke freely about himself, his career, his various jobs and his movements on 4, 5 and 6 May. It all seemed quite innocuous. He knew nothing of any trunk and had never heard of Mrs Bonati until he saw her name in the newspapers. He was put up for identification, but although the trunk dealer's description was not inaccurate he, the taxi-driver and the porter all failed to recognize him, and Cornish had, unwillingly, to let him go. Robinson strolled away from the Yard as though he hadn't a care in the world.

George Cornish, a tenacious policeman from Wiltshire, watched him leave and felt more than ever certain Robinson was his man. But he still had to prove it.

He held a conference at the Yard with all the detectives, junior and senior, who were engaged on the case. Every aspect of the murder was discussed and all the evidence was scrutinized again. One article was the dirty, yellowish blood-stained duster which had been wrapped round the dead woman's head. It was just possible there might be some name or laundry mark on it. Cornish took it to the nearest cloakroom and washed it out with ordinary soap and water, which revealed the word 'Greyhound' printed on a white tab that was sewn in one corner.

There were thirty-seven people employed at the Greyhound Hotel, Hammersmith, and they all used similar dusters. One barmaid remembered this duster, which was the same in make and pattern as the rest, but its colour was unusual. The reason for this was that she had washed it in the same water in which she had previously washed a yellow polishing cloth. She had hung it up to dry outside a bedroom she shared with Mrs Robinson who had, most probably, taken it home.

Then came a further search of Robinson's office, a much more thorough search than before. Sergeants Clarke and Burt went there and turned it upside down, and the waste-paper basket revealed something that had been overlooked before – a bloodstained matchstick. Robinson was known to be a heavy smoker. There were scores of matches, but only one saturated with blood.

Robinson was brought back to Scotland Yard, no doubt thinking as so many have done before and since that the police knew far more than they did. There is something about a policeman's demeanour when he is poised for the kill that communicates to the person who knows he is guilty. Robinson made a statement beginning, 'I'll tell you all about it. I done it and cut her up.'

Robinson's story was that on the afternoon of 4 May he was accosted at Victoria Station by Minnie Bonati, and had taken her to his office. When she asked for money in ex-change for sexual favours and he said he couldn't give her any, she became abusive and violent. She tried to strike him, he struck back, and she fell. He insisted he had thought she was shaken and dazed and he left the office, expecting her to go home when she recovered. He returned next morning and found her still lying there, dead.

'I didn't know what to do,' he said. 'I sat down and de-cided to cut the body up in pieces and cart it away in parcels. I went to a big stationer's shop in Victoria Street and bought six sheets of brown paper and a ball of string. Then I went to a shop in the same street and bought a chef's knife.' It was the very same shop where three years before Patrick Mahon had bought a similar knife to dismember the body of Emily Kaye near Eastbourne.

One wonders about Robinson's thoughts and emotions when he faced the gruesome task ahead of him. There was nothing to suggest he was a ruthless, hardened criminal. Although he was a shiftless, rolling stone who was far from scrupulous it is doubtful if he ever planned murder.

In any event, he told Chief Inspector Cornish the whole story, most of which the detective knew from his own investigations. Robinson filled in the few gaps that were missing. He had carried the trunk from the shop at Brixton, boarded a bus at Kennington Church and carried it up to his office. After he had dropped the trunk at Charing Cross he had buried the knife under a tree on Clapham Common. In between the murder and the macabre operations to dispose of the body he had met frequently with his wife, although they were not living together, perhaps for the solace of being with someone he knew instead of being alone with his thoughts.

All his statements were checked and they were all true. His typist verified that the yellow duster had been in use at the office, and Robinson showed Cornish where he had buried the knife. The shops where he had bought the paper and string and knife confirmed his purchases.

His trial at the Old Bailey before Mr Justice Swift opened on 11 July and lasted only two days. Nearly thirty witnesses testified to the thorough spadework of the police, but they were scarcely needed. Robinson elected to go into the witness box and admit almost everything except any intention to murder. The prosecution case ended with medical evidence which proved to the satisfaction of the court that Minnie Bonati had been first knocked unconscious and then suffocated by someone covering her nose or nostrils. The defence suggested that the police had obtained Robinson's statement under duress, but when this was denied the matter was not pressed.

The verdict of guilty surprised no one, least of all the prisoner. The only real surprise in the case was that a murder and all the actions to keep it secret happened in an office not twenty-five yards from a busy police station and yet nothing suspicious was seen. Robinson himself did not seem to have been in the least inhibited by the close proximity of a large number of policemen. However, there is the possibility that Minnie Bonati threatened to scream on that fateful afternoon and that Robinson had felt impelled to silence her in case the police heard and came running.

John Robinson went to the gallows on 12 August 1927. The bloodstained match, the clue that was so important, went to Scotland Yard's Black Museum.

CHAPTER 8

A Ray of Sunlight Unmasks a Killer

By the end of the Twenties, investigations had gained some sense of order, and the countrywide search for the killer of a man who had been dead for more than two months when his body was found shows how the use of technical aids and methods of record-keeping were paying off.

At 6.45 on the evening of 10 January 1929 a telegram from Mr McCormac, Chief Constable of Southampton, was received at Scotland Yard. It read: 'A case of murder has occurred here. A man has been found shot dead in a room the door of which was padlocked. The body was found today and has probably been in the room for some eight or nine weeks. Will you please send an officer down to investigate the matter.'

Detective Chief Inspector John Prothero was tall and commanding and his colleagues called him 'Gentleman John'. He was always immaculately dressed, and spoke in an accent thought then to be the mark of a university education. He wore spats and had his shirt cuffs showing, at that time a rich man's luxury. But he was not rich, nor had he been to university. He was a great detective, who decided he wanted to be better dressed than the rest of his colleagues.

He never raised his voice, never appeared to be angry, but his quiet insistence got the facts he required.

Prothero took with him to Southampton Sergeant Hugh Young, a Scot from the Black Isle in Ross and Cromarty. Like others before him he was a country boy who rose to command the Squad, and the experience he gained on this particular case was a great stepping-stone in his distinguished career.

The detectives went first to the Southampton mortuary to see the body of the victim, Vivian Messiter. The local police surgeon said that the murder had taken place some weeks before, and Messiter had last been seen alive on 30 October 1928. The body was in a bad state of decomposition and the rats had been busy, so that the features of the dead man were unrecognizable.

Vivian Messiter had been found in a lock-up garage-cum-storeroom at 42 Grove Street, Southampton, where he carried on business as a local agent of the Wolf's Head Oil Company, whose head offices were in London. He had not been seen alive since he left his lodgings at 3 Carlton Road on the morning of 30 October. He was a quiet man of regular habits, and when he failed to return home as usual his landlord, Mr Parrott, an ex-policeman, informed the police he was missing.

An officer went to the garage, but on finding the place securely padlocked from the outside, concluded that wherever Messiter was, he was not in the garage.

Mr Parrott wrote to Messiter's employers, reporting his lodger's absence. They asked him to visit the garage and, by breaking a window and peering through the aperture with the help of a candle, he could see that Messiter's car was safe and that nothing appeared to be amiss. It was concluded that Messiter had simply walked out of his job and had, perhaps, returned to the United States, where he had spent many years of his life. The subsequent lack of interest in his whereabouts was one of the striking features of the case.

Messiter was a member of an old Somersetshire family, educated at a minor public school. As a young man he had

83

gone to the States with his brother Edgar and together they started a horse-breeding ranch in New Mexico. When Edgar drifted into mining operations in Colorado, Vivian went into business in Denver. Later he went to New York City, where the new subway railroad under the Hudson River was in course of construction. Such was his energy and ability to handle men that he rose from a subordinate position to the office of Chief Engineering Constructor. He became so well-known in this capacity that engineers from England were invited to meet him.

At the outbreak of the First World War he was wealthy and generally prosperous. He came home and enlisted, was commissioned in the Northumberland Fusiliers and went to fight in France. He was shot through both thighs and he remained slightly lame for the rest of his life. In 1928 he was fifty-seven, a reserved, solitary man, divorced from his wife, and he returned to England that year from another long absence in the United States and Mexico. Yet he had relatives in this country, and he had a job, and the fact that he was lost to sight and knowledge for more than two months without any serious efforts being made to discover what had become of him throws a curious light on the casual attitude of his friends and family and of the firm which not only employed him, but had recently made him a director.

Messiter's job was that of local agent for the Wolf's Head Oil Company and the garage in Grove Street was his head-quarters. It was not until 10 January that this firm sent a Mr Passmore to take over the agency. With a friend Passmore gained access to the outer yard of the garage via the roof of the Royal Exchange public house next door. The garage was a long, narrow building with white-washed walls. Along the right-hand side was a double row of oil drums upon which boxes were piled. More boxes were stacked at the end, and in a recess was the body of Messiter lying face upwards.

After moving the body to the mortuary local police searched the garage. On the back seat of Messiter's car they found a duplicate order book and a memorandum book, from both of which a number of pages had been torn out.

On one page of the memorandum book was a receipt signed by a Mr H. H. Galton for 2s. 6d. commission on the sale of five gallons of oil, dated 30 October, the last day Messiter was seen alive. The next page had been torn out, but on the following page were the words: 'Cromer & Bartlett, 25 Bold Street, 5 gallons heavy'. In the duplicate order book there was no writing of any kind, but, tucked away at the end of it, were two sheets of carbon paper on which could be just seen some names and addresses. The first was 'Cromer & Bartlett' of Bold Street, Southampton. Then there was a note, 'Sold to Ben Baskerfield, Clayton Farm, Bentley Road, near Winchester' and a third entry, 'Ben Jervis, Crescent Bassett, 5 gallons number 8 at 5s. 6d'.

When the Yard men went to the garage they were given these items by the local police and then began their own search for any clues which might help. But first, since nothing had been moved apart from the body, they decided to reconstruct the crime. The local detective inspector persuaded Mr Hall, the licensee of the pub next door, to play the part of the corpse and he was placed in the same position as the body was found. A trilby hat had been found near Messiter's head, and to give a touch of realism for photographic purposes, Sergeant Young placed his own hat beside the recumbent figure of Mr Hall. The detectives noted the position of several bloodstained boxes in relation to the body, some of which had been splashed to a height of several feet, an almost sure indication of blows by a heavy weapon used as a club.

John Prothero then ordered all the boxes to be moved. 'Search every nook and cranny,' he commanded. During this search three clues were found which played a vital part in the investigation.

The first was a rolled-up ball of paper, stained and begrimed with oil and dirt, lying between two oil drums near the garage door. It was a receipt for rent dated 20 October and bore the name 'Horne' of Cranbury Avenue. On the back of this scrap of paper were some faint words which obviously referred to an order for '35 or 36 gals, Tuesday' and there was a signature – 'W. F. Thomas' – the small 'O' being crossed out.

A second piece of paper was found behind another oil drum and on that was a written message. It read: 'Mr W. F. Thomas. I shall be at 42 Grove Street at 10 a.m. but not at noon. V. Messiter.'

The third clue found in the garage was a hammer, lying at the back of more oil drums against the side wall. Both the shaft and the head of the hammer were stained with blood, and stuck in the blood there was a single eyebrow hair. This last discovery changed the whole complex of the killing, for the hammer was without doubt the murder weapon. Vivian Messiter had not been shot, as had at first been suspected, but battered to death, and the small wound in the dead man's forehead had not been caused by a bullet but by a ferocious blow from the pointed side of the hammer head.

The pathologist Sir Bernard Spilsbury was called in, and while the Yard men waited for him to arrive, they began to make inquiries about the other things they had found.

The landlady at Cranbury Avenue, Mrs Horne, established that she had recently had a quiet, well-behaved couple staying there for about two weeks. Their names were Mr and Mrs Thomas and they had left on 3 November, leaving an address care of Allied Transport Co., 38 High Road, Chiswick.

The Chiswick police checked and found there was no firm of that name and, moreover, there was no house in the High Road bearing that number. Further checks relating to names and addresses on the other scraps of paper found in the garage revealed there was no Bold Street in Southampton, nor any firm bearing the name Cromer & Bartlett. There was no such place as Clayton Farm anywhere near Winchester, while Ben Jervis had never been heard of at Crescent Bassett.

It began to look as though Mr W. F. Thomas was at least a liar and it did prove he had some connection with the murdered man. The only thing so far proved genuine was the signature of H. H. Galton, and it looked as though it had

86

been deliberately left in the memorandum book to make him a suspect, for Mr Galton was traced and proved to be a genuine customer.

Messiter's lodgings were in Carlton Road, and among the papers he had left behind was a letter bearing the address of Cranbury Avenue and signed 'W. F. Thomas'. The writer was applying for an agency with Messiter in reply to an advertisement which the latter had inserted in the *Southern Daily Echo*. This was another link between Thomas and Messiter, but where was Thomas?

Prothero issued a full description of Thomas to the press, mentioning a small scar on his face. Newspapers always like a dramatic headline and so the hunt for Thomas became 'Hunt for Man with a Scar.'

Five days after the discovery of the crime Bernard Spilsbury went to Southampton and examined the body of the victim. He described his findings: 'At least three blows on the head, any one producing immediate unconsciousness. The head of a large hammer, used with great violence, would account for injuries. Those across base and on right side produced when the head was on a hard surface. Position of injuries at back suggest that desceased was bending forwards. Puncture wounds on top of head – striking edge of tin box in fall.'

The Yard men went over the information they had and came to the conclusion that the man they wanted was cunning enough to be no stranger to crime, as evinced by his inventing bogus orders to get commission; his flight from one place to another; the tearing out of what were probably incriminating pages from the books found in the garage; and the adroit way he had tried to cover his tracks. Sergeant Young suggested to his chief that the man might have a record.

'Send for Battley,' Prothero said. A call to the Yard brought Detective Inspector Harry Battley, then head of the Fingerprint Bureau, to Southampton and with him he brought all the files in the name of Thomas. There were eighty-three dossiers.

Battley examined the hammer and the shaft and all the other finds but there were no useful fingerprints. All the files holding the photographs of men called Thomas were shown to the landlady, Mrs Horne, and to various other people who might have recognized him. But not one person was able to pair up a photograph and the missing man.

The investigation seemed to be running down when luck took a hand. The Wiltshire police, who had seen the circulated description of W. F. Thomas, sent a message that they were looking for a man with the same name. This man had worked for a building contractor named Mitchell at Downton, near Salisbury. Thomas had entered the employ of Mr Mitchell on 3 November 1928 (the day Thomas had left his Cranbury Avenue lodgings) and had disappeared with more than £130 of his employer's money on 21 December. He had given as his previous employers the Allied Transport Road Association, Bold Street, Southampton.

A landlady in Downton told the police that a Mr and Mrs Thomas had lodged with her and, in a vase in the room they had occupied, was found yet another scrap of paper. It was a docket from an order book, headed: 'A & R S'.

Underneath was an address – 85 London Road, Manchester.

The piece of paper left at Downton was one piece of paper too many – it began to provide leads.

A swift inquiry was made to the Manchester police. They did not know a W. F. Thomas, but they did know Auto & Radio Services at London Road. A detective said, 'We are looking for a man named Podmore who used to work for them. We want him for conversion of money he received for a car. His picture was in the *Police Gazette*.'

Criminal Records now came into their own. William Henry Podmore had a file, and there was no question that he and Thomas were the same person. A check on his history was revealing and began to fill in the gaps. He was well known to the Staffordshire police, having been first arrested by them when he was only eleven. He was married but parted from his wife and had been living with a young woman in various parts of the country.

At one time he had lived with his parents at Greenly Road, Abbey Milton, Stoke-on-Trent. Near his home was Bold Street, the street name which kept cropping up in the Messiter case. He had known a Mr Baskeyfield whom he always called Baskerfield, the name of the person mentioned as living at the Clayton Farm address, while a Mr Albert Machen, who actually lived at Clayton Farm, Newcastle, Staffordshire, used to deliver milk to the Podmore family. He also knew a Mrs Lucy Jervis, although not personally.

Podmore had made the mistake common to petty criminals, that of mixing up familiar names and places in the faint hope of appearing to be honest. It is an error that has helped to trap many people. It began to look very much as though Podmore, alias Thomas, was the man who had murdered Vivian Messiter. But proof was still lacking. Prothero decided to concentrate his search for the woman companion who was called 'Lil'.

Inquiries at Podmore's home revealed that he had stayed there over Christmas and had left early in the New Year to take a job as a garage hand at the Stonebridge Hotel, Solihull, near Birmingham. He had arrived there on 5 January 1929 with his 'wife', Lil, who was to work as a cook. Six days later, when the evening paper printed the reports of the Southampton garage murder, Podmore handed in his notice, saying he wanted to leave at once. Next day Podmore and Lil departed without even asking for their wages. Podmore obviously thought that Lil, called 'Golden-haired Lil' in the press, was an embarrassment, and that it was no longer safe for them to be seen together. The first signs of panic had set in, and he sent her back to her home at Stoke-on-Trent. There she was interviewed by the local detective inspector, Mr Diggle, who had been making all the inquiries in Staffordshire. She told him she thought it likely that Podmore would have gone to the Leicester Hotel in Vauxhall Bridge Road, near Victoria in London.

Two telephone calls, one to Southampton and one from

there to the Yard, had Detective Charles Simmons with a sergeant casually leaning against the reception desk of the Leicester Hotel asking quietly for 'Mr Thomas' or 'Mr Podmore'. He was in his room and agreed to accompany the officers to Southampton. Under the circumstances refusal would have been difficult although, in truth, there was little evidence of murder against him at the time.

On 18 January, just eight days after the finding of Messiter's body, Podmore met for the first time the two men who had been hunting him, Detective Chief Inspector John Prothero and Detective Sergeant Hugh Young. Podmore was nonchalant, almost cocksure. Prothero was his usual calm, gentlemanly self, and Young sat at a table, pen in hand and a pad of statement forms in front of him, the classic reception for all suspects.

It was clear that Podmore had been through this routine before and was fairly confident. It was also clear that he was not going to give in without a struggle. He admitted he was in trouble in Manchester and in Downton and that he had worked for Messiter. He had seen the report of the finding of Messiter's body. He was completely frank about using the names of Thomas and Podmore. He said he went to see Messiter on the morning of 30 October and that also there was an agent named Maxton or Baxton, a subtle suggestion that this was the man who had killed Messiter. He had only seen him once but he did not need pressing to give a description. Details of the man's height, build, hair, complexion and clothing rolled off his tongue in almost indecent haste.

Podmore said he had left Messiter's employ for a better job with Mr Mitchell at Salisbury. He admitted taking Messiter's car to go for the interview at Downton on 30 October, the last day on which Messiter was seen alive, and said that he had returned at 4.30 p.m. that day, parked the car in the garage and gone to his lodgings.

In its way this was a helpful admission. Unless someone else could be found who had seen Messiter later, Podmore was the last person to have seen him alive.

There was one obvious motive for the murder in Podmore's case – the bogus orders in equally bogus names and addresses – an easy way to get commission on non-existent sales of oil. And if Messiter had found out and challenged Podmore, what then?

Podmore was held in custody. This caused no problems to the Yard men, since he was already wanted for other offences. Meanwhile luck again turned in favour of the detectives. They had circulated a description of the hammer to the newspapers and a Mr Marsh came forward to say the hammer was his. He had bought it in France and was able to recognize it because it had been 'touched up and filed down' by him. He remembered that at some time around 29 October a man with a scar on his face, who looked like a mechanic, had come to the motor works in Southampton where Marsh worked and asked to borrow a hammer. It was never returned.

Podmore blandly denied he had ever borrowed a hammer.

The case looked like breaking. Podmore was put up for identification with several other men of similar age, build and appearance and Mr Marsh walked quietly along the line. It is one of the nightmare moments in the life of a suspect. The parade was held in the yard of Bathgate police station with a uniformed inspector in charge. The Yard men stood well away. It was explained to Podmore, before the men formed themselves into line, that he could stand anywhere he chose.

It is a time for the mind to race. Which is the best place? Which of these men looks most like me? Which is wearing similar clothes? For the policemen it is slow, inexorable and ordinary. To the suspect it is mounting panic. 'Will the expression on my face reveal my guilty knowledge?'

Mr Marsh tried hard. Three times he walked up and down the line and, in the end, shook his head.

'The man is not there,' he said.

The volunteers departed and a relieved Podmore went back to the cells. Soon afterwards he was arrested by the Manchester police for the theft of a car and he was sentenced to six months' imprisonment. For a while he was away from the attention of the Yard men, but he was not far away and not for long. Two months later he was brought from prison to attend the resumed inquest on Messiter, which had been formally opened and adjourned. He sat between two prison officers but was able to smile and wave at 'Golden-haired Lil' who was also in court.

Only one red herring was trailed across the path of justice, when a man serving a sentence in Winchester prison was called as a witness. He had previously made a statement that a woman he knew had returned home at 2.30 p.m. on 30 October in Southampton with blood all over her face. But before the coroner he admitted his story was pure invention.

During the inquest the exercise book containing the receipt from Mr Galton for 2s. 6d. was produced and handed to the jury, as were the two sheets of carbon paper found in the duplicate order book. The jury returned an open verdict, Podmore went back to prison to serve the rest of his sentence, and the Yard men took away the exhibits to carry on the investigation. They went back to the Murder Room at Scotland Yard and analysed every bit of information they had collected. Prothero, Young and Battley debated the case for hours. Then Prothero picked up the exercise book and sauntered across to the window overlooking the Thames. They had nothing in mind but it was as though they were willing this tatty, torn book to yield up its secret. They looked again at the pages they had scrutinized so many times before. Then, as Prothero held the book up in the light, a ray of sunlight, striking the paper slantwise, threw up in relief the shadowy outline of some writing. It was not the actual writing itself, only the faint impression left on the page underneath the one which had been torn out, and on which the message had been written.

When photographed the shadowy words read: 'October 28, 1928. Received from Wolf Head Oil Company commission on Cromer and Bartlett, 5 gals 5/6 commission 2/6. W.F.T.'

Comparison handwriting tests proved that this message had been written by Thomas, alias Podmore.

This now proved, beyond doubt, that Podmore had been swindling his employer, Mr Messiter. And it proved that the page from the exercise book had been torn out with Podmore's own hand. If he was the murderer he would have had good reason to destroy every bit of written evidence which connected him with Messiter. If, on the other hand, somebody other than Podmore was the murderer, what possible motive could he have had in tearing out the pages showing details of the transaction between himself and Messiter?

Still the authorities hesitated to bring a charge of murder and still Podmore remained in prison. When he finished the first sentence for the Manchester offence he received another six months for stealing money from Downton. This rather Micawberish attitude may have been influenced by the verdict of the coroner's jury. What would have happened had not Podmore been safely in custody is an interesting conjecture. But something more did turn up; two of Podmore's fellow-prisoners in Wandsworth reported statements made by him, and one of these amounted to a confession. The man's name was Cummings and he gave a statement to Prothero and Young. That was in October, and, on 17 December 1929, the Yard men were waiting outside the gates of Wandsworth Prison.

In accordance with regulations, a prisoner must first be released and the new arrest made outside the prison gates. Podmore walked out with his usual jaunty air. Perhaps he felt confident he had covered all his tracks and that he had nothing to fear. Then a handcuff was locked round one of his wrists. The other handcuff was already round the wrist of Sergeant Young and Podmore was taken back to Southampton to be charged with murder.

He was tried at Winchester Assizes in March 1930, fifteen months after the crime, before the Lord Chief Justice, Lord Hewart. He was convicted, and his appeal against conviction was dismissed. An attempt to take the case to the House of Lords failed and Podmore was hanged on 22 April.

There was some agitation by well-meaning people to alter the course of the law because of the delay in bringing to trial and because two convicted criminals had been called to give evidence. They shared the common misunderstanding of the value of circumstantial evidence. In the volume on the case in the 'Famous Trials' series the authors, one of them a lawyer, pointed out that the case against Podmore rested not only on what was found, but on what was not found.

Had the books been unmutilated, had the missing invoice and the missing receipt been there, they would have established a case of swindling against the prisoner, but it is more than doubtful whether any jury would have held that they established more – it is a very long step from false pretence to wilful murder. But they were not there, and there could have been but one hand that removed them – the hand of the man who had fabricated the orders and signed the receipt. And that removal must have taken place after Messiter's death, for before it would have been useless. That was the evidence that really convicted Podmore.

There can be no doubt that Messiter discovered the swindle and taxed Podmore with it, threatening to call the police. If it had been Podmore's first offence he would have had no cause for undue concern. But he was already wanted by the police in Manchester. Podmore, who had never before used violence, lost his temper. The hammer was there, maybe in Podmore's pocket, certainly to hand, and Messiter was struck down. The worst feature of the attack was that while the unconscious man lay on the concrete floor his assailant rained more blows on him. That callous behaviour must have told on the jury, and so must his actions immediately afterwards. For Podmore admitted that he had locked the garage and taken Messiter's car to give his lady friend, 'Golden-haired Lil', a drive and 'some fresh air'.

CHAPTER 9

Careless Words Lead to the Scaffold

One of the most difficult types of murder inquiry involves making a link between victim and killer where murder has been committed in the course of pursuing some other kind of crime. Each time a detective has to start from the most basic principles he has learnt, including the methods and habits of criminals.

John Horwell was born in Hackney, East London, where his parents kept a small shop. He went to the local board school and left at the age of thirteen. He ended his career in the Metropolitan Police in 1940 as Chief Constable of the CID. In the following stories from his casebook one can see how a good detective puts principles into action, and how experience from one case can be overlaid on another. In both instances the killers had criminal records. Their method was to knock on a door and take what opportunity offered: it is doubtful if murder was in their minds at the time.

In February 1928 Horwell was a Divisional Detective Inspector in charge of Paddington, covering a large area of West London. A constable telephoned to say that a Mr Webb had been found unconscious outside his luxury flat in Pembridge Square, Kensington. He had a bullet wound in his head, and had died shortly after.

It was soon apparent to Horwell that the crime was the work of an expert afternoon flat-breaker. A glass panel in the door had been smashed from outside – the glass was on the carpet inside the door – and the thief had got in by putting his hand through the door and turning the key. The mortice lock had not been used by the occupier.

The flat had been thoroughly ransacked. Drawers had been pulled out and the contents turned out on the floor, jewel cases were on the carpet, empty. On the inside door mat was a letter, facing downwards, marked with blood, and there were particles of skin on the jagged edges of the broken glass panel. It was obvious the thief had cut himself, possibly on the left hand because of the position of the lock. It was the first clue – look for a man with an injured hand, possibly the left.

The son of the victim told Horwell all he knew of the tragedy. He said he and his father had returned home at about 6 p.m. and they saw the flat had been entered. Mr Webb had tried to turn the Yale key but could not, so he had told his son to run for a policeman. The son had run down the stairs but when he reached the street he had heard the sound of a shot.

He told the police he was frightened. It was a foggy night but he remembered glancing backwards, seeing a short dark man run out of the house and disappear into the gloom. A lady in the crowd which had gathered outside the house also mentioned seeing a short dark man run out of the house. She added that she had seen his right hand shoot out as though he was throwing something away a few doorways away in Pembridge Square. A detective went to search and found a small automatic pistol which had recently been fired.

Horwell had no doubt that this was the work of a 'drummer', a thief who knocks at a door to find out if the occupier is in. If the door is opened the thief is ready with an innocent inquiry, such as 'Does Mr Jones live here?' In this case silence had satisfied the thief it was safe to enter. Once inside he had pushed down the catch on the lock and proceeded to search for what he could find. He was obviously disturbed by the return of Mr Webb and heard his instruction to his son to get a policeman. He was trapped, for the only way out was through the front door. If he was caught he faced a heavy prison sentence. He saw Mr Webb peering through the broken glass and decided to shoot his way out. The shot, fired point-blank, had caused Mr Webb to fall backwards down the stairs. Then the killer had unlocked the door, stepped over the body of his victim and fled the house.

That was a simple reconstruction but not of great assistance. The gun proved to be Spanish – it fired a small bullet which would usually inflict only a nasty wound unless it found a vital spot. But when it was closely examined it was found that a second bullet had jammed in the breech. It was evident, therefore, that the murderer had not fired to frighten or maim but to kill, and the second shot had been meant to reinforce the first.

Next morning the newspapers carried big stories of the crime, but all Horwell had was the gun and a sketchy description of the killer. Since he was fairly certain the man was a 'drummer' he organized a house-to-house visit of the whole area in the hope of finding a householder who had answered the door to an unexpected knock.

While that was going on other detectives were rounding up local crooks who might have been responsible. All these men had cast-iron alibis for the time in question.

A list of the missing jewellery was circulated to all pawnbrokers as a long-shot, for thieves involved in murder seldom dispose of their loot locally or quickly.

Every murder investigation has a slow period when all inquiries seem to come to nothing, and this was Horwell's. Six days had passed and then one of the men visiting houses on a routine inquiry interviewed a woman who remembered that on the day of the murder, at about 5 p.m., she had answered the door to a short stocky man. She had asked him whom he wished to see and he had replied, 'I would like to see the chauffeur, madam.'

'Where do you come from?' she had asked and he had replied with a slight hesitation, 'Warwick Garage.' She had told him she was not expecting anyone from that garage and suggested the man had mistaken the address. He had apologized and gone away.

The lady gave a good description of the man, which was circulated to every police force in Britain. However, Criminal Records were unable to produce anyone matching the description and the whole of London was combed for a Warwick Garage without success.

Even so Horwell was convinced that Warwick Garage

held the vital clue. He assembled his men and told them what he knew and asked for their thoughts. One of his sergeants recalled a flat-breaker named Stewart who used to frequent Warwick Mews. It was a possibility. Many people when asked for an address unexpectedly blurt out a name they know, and, in the following split second, recover sufficiently to lie about the next word to cover the truth.

Stewart had disappeared from his usual haunts but inquiries revealed that he was a keen racing man, going to racecourses in the afternoon, when he was not flat-breaking, and dog tracks in the evening. There was no flat racing in February but there was dog-racing. Horwell argued that a man on the run would keep away from the London tracks but might try a place like Southend, conveniently near London but far enough away to be thought safe. Horwell sent two detectives to Southend, both of them able to recognize Stewart on sight. It was the twelfth day of the investigation.

That evening one of the officers in Southend telephoned to say Stewart had been located in a public house near the greyhound track, had been arrested and was in a cell at Southend police station.

Stewart had a scar on his left hand, which he later admitted had been caused when he broke into the flat in Pembridge Square. Horwell was an expert in interrogation and the woman who remembered the words 'Warwick Garage' also remembered the face of the man who spoke them. She picked him out in an identification parade before he confessed.

Stewart was prepared to admit he had broken into the flat but said his pistol had gone off accidentally. He had seen a man looking at him through the front door, and with his jemmy under his left arm and his gun in his right hand he had made a dash for it. As he did so the man outside the door struck him a blow on the back of the neck which sent him reeling backwards and the gun went off.

It was a story easily disproved. The jemmy was never found in or near the flat. A pathologist said that the bullet

98

had entered Mr Webb's head through the left eyebrow and must have been fired from inside the flat when Mr Webb was peering through the broken glass door. If Stewart had been knocked backwards his head would have hit the door or the landing, yet no marks were found.

Stewart's landlady was a nurse and she told Horwell he had come home that night in an agitated state and appeared to be frightened every time there was a knock on the front door. In his bedroom police found a fully loaded Colt revolver.

At the Old Bailey Stewart pleaded not guilty but the jury found for the prosecution and he was sentenced to death.

Stewart was a regular racegoer and had not missed a Derby for many years. He missed it that year, for he was hanged at Pentonville Prison on the day of the race. He actually asked for his hanging to be postponed for one day so that he could be told who the winner was. His request was refused but, as he was led to the scaffold he gave a last tip: 'Have a bet on Felstead.' It won at 33 to 1.

Nearly three years later John Horwell had been promoted and was on the Murder Squad, one of the seven Chief Inspectors on call. On August Bank Holiday, 1931, he was the first on the list and the call came from the Chief Constable of the Oxford City police asking for assistance to solve the murder of a highly respectable widow. She had been killed in cold blood in her own house.

The call had come at 10 p.m. and Horwell was on the midnight train from Paddington with Detective Sergeant Rees. The City of Oxford was awash with torrential rain as the detectives, with the Chief Constable, drove to the scene of the crime, a small semi-detached villa on the outskirts of the city. The scene left an indelible mark on Horwell, who described it in his memoirs. 'There, lying on the floor, was the body of the occupant of the house, a Mrs Louisa Kempson, a widow aged fifty-four, neatly covered up with a rug and a cushion. We lifted the rug and at once saw she had been the victim of unbridled ferocity. There was a round wound in the centre of her forehead which had penetrated the brain, and which had probably been inflicted with a hammer. There was a similar wound at the back of the head. But even worse was to come, for we quickly saw that a sharp instrument, such as a chisel, had been thrust clean through her throat, entering below the left ear and coming out of the right.'

Despite the phlegmatic reputation of senior detectives who see death in all its violent forms, they still react to horror as the average person does. Horwell and the others were sickened at the sight – only training masked emotion. It appeared by the dreadful wounds that the murderer had thought the head wounds had not at once caused death so he had made sure with a second attack. This gave rise to the thought that the dead woman might have been able to recognize her killer.

The room and all the other rooms had been ransacked in haste, and several small articles had fallen from the sideboards. In different parts of the house police found three purses, all empty. There were no visible clues or weapons.

Back-tracking on the recent movements of the victim revealed she planned to spend a short holiday in London with relatives, leaving Oxford on the Sunday. She had not arrived on schedule so the relatives had telegraphed her and, when no reply was received, had telephoned other relatives in Oxford asking them to go to the house. One of them, getting no reply, had climbed through an upstairs window and discovered the crime. By then it was the afternoon of the Bank Holiday Monday.

While inquiries were being made with neighbours, who were unable to help, Sir Bernard Spilsbury was called in to conduct a post-mortem, with Horwell present. The pathologist was of the opinion that the head wounds had been caused by a hammer and the throat wounds by a dagger or some other sharp instrument. The first hammer blow had been delivered from behind, and the victim had not attempted to defend herself. Other blows had followed as she lay stunned. In Spilsbury's view she was then moved from

the entrance hall, where the attack had taken place, to the dining-room, and there, as she was still alive, the murderer had used another weapon, a sharp cutting instrument, which he had driven through her neck, severing the carotid artery.

A detailed search of the house was rewarding. In the kitchen were the remains of breakfast, a cup and saucer which had been used, a portion of a small loaf and a little butter still in its original wrapping, and the remains of a custard. Neighbours and relatives said that Mrs Kempson was a house-proud woman and was unlikely to have left the table uncleared for more than about ten minutes after finishing her meal. Was she then killed before she could clear away? And on which day? Soon afterwards Spilsbury was able to help further by telling Horwell that her last meal was bread, butter and egg and that, therefore, she had almost certainly been killed on the Saturday morning.

The search of the house continued and behind a mirror were found a number of old and stained visiting cards. Every one of the names and addresses on them was verified both in Oxford and elsewhere in case they gave a lead. Horwell had every article of furniture moved into the garden so that he could search them in daylight. The reason for this intensive hunt was that Mrs Kempson's husband, who had died ten years earlier, had left her a number of shops and houses and it would be reasonable to suppose that she might have money or valuables hidden in the house that would tempt a thief.

On a chest of drawers taken from her bedroom was a small work-box which was covered with a piece of orna-mental crochet-work and, standing on the box, was a large china crucifix – the two objects appeared to be all one piece. But in fact the box opened and inside was more than £100 in £5 gold pieces, obviously the haul the intruder was after.

One other clue, a written receipt for an electric cleaner, was found in a desk and, although it meant nothing at the time, Horwell put it in his pocket. Many of the householders said they'd remembered a suspicious-looking man but nothing more specific, and Horwell ordered a house-to-

house investigation within a quarter of a mile of the scene of the crime. He and his men meanwhile made another search of the house to make sure they had missed nothing. He still wanted to find the murder weapon, and extended the search to the houses and gardens further afield, first to half, then to three-quarters of a mile, then the full mile. The case was nine days old and no further forward.

There had been little time for sleep and tempers were getting short when a constable telephoned to say he had been talking to a widow who lived at the foot of Headington Hill and he thought she had the lead they had so far missed.

Her name was Mrs Alice Mary Andrews and she told them that two years previously she had bought an electric cleaner from a man named Seymour. He had called several times afterwards to check that the cleaner was satisfactory and had then stopped coming. But she had remembered that on the Friday before the Bank Holiday, at 7.30 in the evening, she had answered a knock on the door to find Seymour. She had recognized him and he told a long hard-luck story of how he had been bathing in the Thames and some youths had stolen all his money. To convince her, he had turned out his pockets. All the widow had in the house was 5s. 6d. She lent him 4s. 6d. and off he'd gone.

Three hours later he was back and this time said he had missed the last bus and could he stay for the night. She let him sleep in the spare room. Next morning the old lady was first up and noticed a brown-paper parcel, open at both ends, by the hall stand. More importantly she saw what the parcel contained – a new hammer and carpenter's chisel.

Seymour came downstairs at 8 a.m., went out for a shave, came back for breakfast and finally left at about 9.30 a.m., giving profuse thanks for her kindness. Before going she had seen him put the hammer and chisel into his mackintosh pocket.

Mrs Andrews's house was a ten-minute walk from the scene of the crime but the widow did not see which way he'd gone. She produced a letter which she had received from Seymour on the following Thursday containing a postal

order for 10s. 6d. with thanks for her kindness. He added that he hoped to see her in about ten days' time, when he would be visiting Oxford again. The letter had no address but was headed 'Hove, Wednesday' and was postmarked 'Hove' for the 1.45 p.m. collection on 5 August.

It transpired that Mrs Andrews knew the victim had bought an electric cleaner about the same time as her own transaction. That checked with the receipt found in Mrs Kempson's desk. Inquiries at local ironmongers' shops produced a salesman who remembered selling a hammer and chisel for four shillings on the Friday night. He described the man but was too vague to be useful.

More and more people were coming to light who had bought Mr Seymour's cleaners and one of them, a Mrs Collins, had talked to him on the morning of the murder at Headington bus stop. He told her he was going to London and then to Brighton. She thought he seemed nervous and agitated and not his usual smooth-salesman self. While bus conductors, hoteliers and pub landlords were being questioned Horwell tried the Criminal Record Office. The answer was dramatic.

Seymour had several convictions for serious crime. About a year previously he had been charged with attempting to murder by strangulation a woman in Paignton, Devon. The charge was reduced to manslaughter and he was bound over for two years on condition that he paid her £10 compensation within one year for a throat injury he had inflicted. That year expired on the day of the Oxford murder and Seymour had not paid the money.

The search radius for Seymour had grown to thirty miles and a publican was found who had served Seymour with two gins and gingerbeers at about 11 a.m. on the morning of the murder. The police knew that when he'd left Mrs Andrews's house he had had no money at all. He had borrowed 4s. 6d., spent four shillings on the hammer and chisel and had a sixpenny shave. Yet within three hours of Mrs Kempson being murdered he was miles away, having paid a bus fare, and was spending money on drink.

103

A witness came forward to disprove Seymour's story of bathing in the Thames because he told police he had been at the spot Seymour had mentioned all day and would have warned anyone against swimming there because the river was in spate.

The Buckinghamshire Constabulary, like the police all over the country, had been hunting Seymour and had traced him to a hotel in Aylesbury. On Friday 31 July he left without paying his bill and it was that evening he had called on Mrs Andrews in Oxford. He had returned to the hotel on the afternoon of 1 August and crept up to his bedroom, when he was seen by the landlord. Seymour asked for his shaving kit but the landlord refused unless he paid his bill. Seymour left for lunch, promising to return, but never did. His suitcase was handed over to the police and was later sent to Horwell.

It provided many clues, the first one being the hammer. It had been well washed, scraped and soaked, especially where the maker's label should have been. All marks of identification had been removed. If Seymour was innocent why go to such trouble? Next Horwell went to the hotel, hoping to find a lead to Seymour's whereabouts. In the Commercial Room he saw a green blotting-pad and held it up to the mirror. In the reflection he saw a name and address at Brighton. Seymour had written to Mrs Andrews from Hove and so he might live there, reasoned Horwell. The address was sent to the Brighton police and Seymour was found and detained. While that was happening Horwell gave the suitcase another microscopic search. He found fluff, old pins, cigarette ends, matches and some tiny particles which looked like breadcrumbs. There seemed to be no good reason for their presence so he put one in a saucer of water. It slowly uncurled and proved to be a portion of the label from the hammer. Fortunately Horwell, when he discovered the shop where the hammer had been purchased, had bought an exactly similar one himself so he was able to check the design on the label. Piece by piece he gave the rest of the crumbs the water test and finally put together the whole label. It was Exhibit 14 at the trial.

Horwell considered that Seymour had gone back to his hotel room on 1 August after killing Mrs Kempson to remove the identity marks from the hammer and had forgotten that the shreds of the label were dropping into the suitcase.

Using the name of Harvey, Seymour had been living at Brighton with yet another widow for a landlady, and he had returned there on the day after the crime at Oxford. He was given a room above his landlady's bedroom, where, as he may have known, she kept her ready money at night. When he had paid her £2 6s. he was almost penniless. She had already discovered two eyeholes bored through the floor of his room giving a good view of her bedroom below. There can be little doubt that once Seymour had found his landlady's hiding-place for her money he would have taken it and disappeared. Instead he went for trial at Oxford Assizes before Mr Justice Rugby Swift.

Seymour was an assured confident man and when questioned by the police as to what he had done between leaving Mrs Andrews at 9.30 a.m. and meeting Mrs Collins at 11.30 a.m. the same morning he gave a long detailed statement of his movements. The trouble was that none of the witnesses he named supported him.

Things looked grim for the door-knocker salesman, who only a month before had left his wife and ten-year-old son to see if he could fare better on his own.

Although Horwell was confident, his case was far from water-tight, for he could not prove that Seymour had been in Mrs Kempson's house and had committed the crime. On the other hand, the chain of circumstantial evidence was overwhelming and could not be broken down. It all stood or fell on the hour and a half of the Saturday morning when the prosecution said Mrs Kempson was killed.

The Home office pathologist made four separate examinations of the body and finally confirmed that death had indeed occurred on the morning of Saturday. The hour and a half, neatly bracketed by two witnesses, left Henry Daniel Seymour with his movements unaccounted for. He did badly in the witness box. His confidence had left him and as the history of his lies and deceptions tumbled out he became a crumpled figure. After a five-day trial the jury took thirty-eight minutes to bring in a 'guilty' verdict and on 10 December 1931 he was hanged at Oxford Prison.

CHAPTER 10

The Anonymous Letter

Lord Trenchard had taken over as Commissioner in 1931 and in 1934 he opened not only the Officer Training College at Hendon but also the Forensic Science Laboratory which was to give detectives in the field the close support they needed.

The underlying principle of forensic science is attributed to Dr Edmond Locard, the French criminologist, who said, 'Every contact leaves a trace.' Until 1934 all forensic work had been done by pathologists appointed by the Home Office working in their own laboratories, and in the field of ballistics, Mr Robert Churchill, a gunsmith of renown, had been the police expert.

The new laboratory was divided into five sections: biology, chemistry, photography, documents and firearms. It was staffed by men of the CID and included people like Cyril Cuthbert, who had studied forensic medicine and science in his spare time. He had got to know a number of doctors and chemists who also had an interest in criminology, and eventually he was able to carry out such simple techniques as deciphering erased writing. Detective colleagues often sought his help, his reputation grew and he was asked to set up the new support service. Two other early

106

members of its staff were Superintendent George Salter, who had worked in the photographic section at the Yard, and John McCafferty, who is still one of the leading experts in the world of ballistics.

Progress was slow because there was so much to learn and equipment was in short supply, and for some time it was still necessary to call in outside pathologists, as for example in the case of Ethel Major. One feature of this fascinating case is the increased speed with which the police had begun to move. The anonymous letter which sparked off the investigation resulted in a funeral being stopped as the mourners were gathering at the bereaved family's home!

It is doubtful if anyone would have thought there was anything amiss about the death of forty-four-year-old lorry driver Arthur Major but for the anonymous letter sent to the local police on 26 May 1934. A death certificate had already been issued giving the cause of death as epilepsy; the funeral arrangements had been made and the grave dug, when Inspector Dodson of Horncastle police in Lincolnshire received the following note:

'Sir, have you ever heard of a wife poisoning her husband? Look further into the death (by heart failure) of Mr Major of Kirkby-on-Bain. Why did he complain of his food tasting nasty and throw it to a neighbour's dog, which has since died? Why did it stiffen so quickly? Why was he so jerky when dying? I myself have heard her threaten to poison him years ago. In the name of the law I beg you to analyse the contents of his stomach.'

The letter was signed 'Fairplay'. It bore no address and the identity of the writer was never discovered. In general everyone abhors anonymous letters, but the police cannot afford to ignore anything which suggests a murder has been committed, and an inquiry was set up.

First Inspector Dodson found out from the doctor who had attended Arthur Major that the man had been taken suddenly ill with violent spasms and painful muscular contractions on the night of 22 May, and had died two nights later from an epileptic fit. The doctor had not attended Major before and was, therefore, entirely reliant on what Mrs Major told him of the medical history of her husband. She said that he had suffered from fits over a period of years, and the doctor had no reason to suspect any other cause of death. His diagnosis turned out to be woefully wrong.

The inspector then went to the little house in the peaceful village where Arthur Major had died. He saw the wife, Ethel, and he saw the body. As he was leaving Mrs Major came to the door and asked, 'I am not suspicioned? I haven't done anything wrong.'

The policeman thought this a strange remark because she could not possibly know of the anonymous letter or that he had been to see the doctor.

Inspector Dodson now looked at the question of the dog referred to in the letter. The Majors had no dog, but on the night of 23 May the wire-haired terrier of Mr Maltby, a next-door neighbour, had been seized with a sudden stiffness and had died during the night, following severe muscular contractions. Mr Maltby was mystified but had buried the dog in the garden.

Arthur Major had died from the very same symptoms and there was an obvious way to check this grim co-incidence. In the gathering twilight of the same evening the body of the dog was exhumed from its shallow grave.

Next day the coroner, Dr Walker, was acquainted of the facts and at once issued an order stopping the funeral and ordering a post-mortem examination on both the dead man and the dog. Both sets of organs were sent to Dr Roche Lynch, a famous Home Office analyst at St Mary's Hospital, Paddington.

The dramatic news leaked out and caused a sensation among the two hundred village inhabitants whose tranquil lives had never before been so disturbed. The Major family was well known in the district where they had lived for many years. Speculation was rife as Roche Lynch patiently carried out his analysis, and his final report left little doubt that this was a case of murder.

He detected the presence of alkaloid strychnine in every organ he examined. Altogether there was a total of 1·27 grains. By far the greater quantity, more than half a grain, was found in Mr Major's stomach.

'Strychnine is extremely bitter,' he wrote in his report. 'A poisonous dose is anything from half a grain to two grains. Usually death takes place in three hours. If a recovery takes place the fits become less severe. The symptoms in this case inevitably lead one to the conclusion that the victim received a dose of strychnine on the evening of 22 May, probably at tea time. But he did not die as a result of that administration. There can be no doubt that somewhere about seven o'clock on the evening of 24 May he received another dose and that dose caused death.'

He emphasized that it was unlikely that the poison was self-administered because no one, except a madman, would take a second dose after suffering the dreadful agony of the first. That discounted the possibility of suicide and pointed clearly to murder.

Dr Roche Lynch also found a fatal dose of strychnine in the unfortunate dog.

Armed with this report the Chief Constable of Lincoln did not hesitate. He called in Scotland Yard and Detective Chief Inspector Hugh Young, who as a sergeant had been with Chief Inspector Prothero on the Messiter case in Southampton.

Hugh Young, a tall, lean Scot, was better educated than most policemen of that time, and had been brought up strictly in the Nonconformist tradition. When he joined the force he had been given a six-week training course and by 1934 he had served twenty-four years.

When he arrived at Horncastle, on a bright sunny day in July, he began to learn about the married life of Arthur Major and his wife, which had been punctuated by quarrels far beyond the ordinary squabbles of most married couples.

At the time of his death the marriage had almost reached breaking point. During that week Arthur Major had arranged to put a notice in the local newspaper repudiating responsibility for his wife's debts. They were not large but they were numerous, mostly bills from local tradesmen left unpaid.

Local people described Ethel Major as a quarrelsome, cantankerous woman, bossy and boastful. In their view she was extremely vain and had more clothes than any woman in the area. When Young searched her house later he found her wardrobe full of new dresses, and she had more than twenty pairs of high-quality shoes.

Like most villages, Kirkby-on-Bain was a hot-bed of gossip, and the tall stranger had little difficulty in piecing together the stormy life of the Majors. Mrs Major had made many unfounded complaints against her husband, accusing him of being a drunkard and an idler, and of having affairs with other women. She had also complained, on 19 May – three days before he was taken ill – that her husband had 'put something in her tea'. She had gone even further, suggesting that her husband had been trying to poison her and had hinted darkly that her neighbour, a Mrs Rose Kettleboro, had written letters to her husband couched in the most affectionate terms.

When Chief Inspector Young called on her she handed him two letters which she said she had found in the bedroom addressed to her husband. One letter began 'The dearest sweetheart in the world' and the other 'To my dearest sweetheart'. Mrs Major said they had been written by the woman next door, although this was denied. Another letter, which Mrs Major said had reached her earlier in May, contained the following passage: 'Don't you know how your husband spends his week-end? He has got a bit of fluff now. You could get rid of him easy if you had him watched . . .'

About two weeks later, she said, she had received a post-card on which was written: 'Meet me same place, same time. Baby got prize.' That puzzled Young because he could not imagine any woman engaged in an affair with a married man sending such incriminating evidence through the post to the home of her lover.

Nearer the time of the death, on 12 May, yet another

110

anonymous letter had been received, this time by the Chief Constable of Lincoln. The writer alleged that 'Arthur Major is *allways* drunk in charge and not safe on the road. It is my duty to inform you of the above for the safety of the *peopel* in the village.' Mr Young made a special note of the spelling.

The notice repudiating Mrs Major's debts was due to appear in the *Horncastle News* on 26 May. Arthur Major died on 24 May and on the following morning Mrs Major sent a letter to the paper cancelling the notice. Obviously she had been aware of his intentions and that knowledge might have made his death imperative by a certain date. The publication of such a notice would have been an irrevocable blow to her pride.

Slowly the little details were woven into a web of suspicion, but suspicion is never enough, particularly in a case of murder. Certainly there were now many things which Mrs Major had to explain. A long interview with her was essential, but Yard men seldom hurry.

First Mr Young interviewed the Majors' fifteen-year-old son, Lawrence, who told how his parents had quarrelled and said that on the night his father had died his mother had sent him out to buy some corned beef. In the last weeks of his father's life the quarrels had become so bitter that he and his mother had moved to his grandfather's house in Horncastle. However, they were still within walking distance, and Mrs Major still provided some of the meals in the family home, although she no longer slept there.

He described the scene on 24 May, after his father had eaten corned beef for tea. The boy said, 'My father sat trembling in the chair. My mother said she thought the corned beef had upset him. He started foaming at the mouth and said "Don't leave me yet. You have been good to me. I am going to die." He lifted his arms and dropped them on his chest. He died at twenty minutes to eleven.'

The canny, softly-spoken Scot now wanted to hear the story from Mrs Major herself of those forty-eight hours which had preceded the agonizing death of her husband.

111

Young was already suspicious and he was a careful detective. He worked 'by the book' as less meticulous officers would have said, so he gave her the usual caution in the well-known words: 'You need not say anything but anything you do say will be written down and may be given in evidence.' She was not in the least disturbed and seemed to be suffering from no pangs of sorrow. She even told Inspector Young that she had felt much better in health since her husband had died.

In her opinion her husband had died through eating corned beef and she was eager to insist that she had nothing to do with preparing his meals. She explained that she and her son had for the two weeks before stayed with her father in Horncastle. 'We dared not sleep at home because me and Arthur were on bad terms,' she said. 'My husband bought this tinned meat himself. I know I never bought any. I hate corned beef and I think it is a waste of money to buy such rubbish.'

There was an obvious desire to dissociate herself with any provision or purchase of corned beef and this was important because corned beef was the last meal eaten by Arthur Major before he was seized with his attack on the night of 22 May.

It was also important that she and her son had been staying with her father, Mr Tom Brown, for the two weeks preceding her husband's death. Young had already discovered that Mr Brown was a renowned gamekeeper and was in the habit of using poison for destroying vermin. Young asked her if she was aware of that.

'I did not know where he kept the poison,' she said. 'I never had any poison in my house and I did not know my husband died of strychnine poisoning.'

Young was a taciturn man and his face registered nothing at this staggering admission. But he knew that only he, Roche Lynch and some other high-ranking officers on the inquiry knew the cause of death. Yet, clearly, Mrs Major did.

'I never mentioned strychnine,' said Young. 'How do you

know your husband died from poisoning by strychnine?'

She was as cool as the detective.

'Oh, I'm sorry,' she said, 'I must have made a mistake. I didn't understand what you said. I am still of the opinion that he died from poison from the corned beef.'

It seemed to Young that she was always returning to the corned beef. It was obviously a strong factor in her mind and it was becoming more and more important in the detective's mind. It was being forced upon him. She went on to say that on the day her husband was taken ill she saw the corned beef, which he later ate for tea, standing on the pantry shelf. 'It was quite black,' she said. 'I thought at the time it was bad but I did not tell my husband.'

It was a remarkable admission, but she seemed unaware of how she was talking herself into a point of no return. Her callous indifference to her husband's health and safety was incredible, as was her next remark.

'You look tired,' she said, 'let me make you a cup of tea.'

The suggestion had no appeal for the detective. 'It is very kind of you,' he said, 'but no thank you.'

Without the least trace of embarrassment she smiled and said, 'You needn't be afraid of me. I won't put anything in it.'

Inspector Young smiled back. 'As a matter of fact, Mrs Major, I never drink tea,' he said, and she did not press any further.

That hurdle safely over, she told of the night of the 22nd when her husband was taken ill after the corned beef meal. She had not sent for the doctor and it was not until her father called at about 11 p.m. that he sent the son for the doctor who gave him some medicine to ease the agony.

The treatment was effective for on the following day Mr Major was somewhat recovered. But that night he had a relapse and was very ill.

'Did you send for the doctor?' Young asked.

'No,' she said. There was no other explanation.

By the morning of 24 May Arthur Major was much weaker, and at times could hardly speak. He did, however,

113

have more corned beef for tea. About ten o'clock that evening, she said, her husband managed to gasp he wanted a drink. Both the son and Mrs Major's father were present.

She got a glass of water and they sat him up and supported him while he drank it. He whispered, 'I'm going to have another fit . . . I'm going to die. Don't leave me yet . . . you have been good to me.'

An hour later, his whole body stiff and contorted, Arthur Major died.

Chief Inspector Young left her. He really had enough evidence, but he wanted more. He learned that after her husband's death she was feverishly busy, making arrangements for a hasty burial. She called on the doctor for a death certificate and got it, although he had inquired why she had not called him again to see her husband before he died. She made some glib excuse and then called on the local undertaker. She wanted her husband buried in three days and the funeral was fixed for 27 May. Some of the mourners were already assembled at the cottage when the coroner stopped the funeral.

Now the Yard man had to see young Lawrence Major again. It was one of his more unpleasant duties but it was necessary. The interview was conducted in the presence of the boy's mother and related to the purchase of the corned beef – now proved to have been purchased earlier than he had at first thought. The boy told how a day or two before his father died his mother sent him out for a tin of corned beef. He remembered that it was late, after the shops had closed.

Mrs Major denied this. 'I didn't send you. It was your father.'

But the boy was insistent and pointed out that his father was not at home at the time. Inspector Young mentioned that the woman in the shop recalled the purchase because it was after the shop had closed.

At this Mrs Major raged and shouted, 'Every woman in this village is a liar. If any woman says I sent my son she is a liar.' It was a significant outburst.

114

Mrs Major seemed obsessed with the corned beef. She had mentioned it to the doctor, to Inspector Dodson and to Inspector Young. There was also a desperate anxiety to conceal her connection with the purchase. It was the sort of slip which had proved the downfall of many a criminal.

Young had one more unpleasant duty to perform. He had to see Mrs Major's father, who was seventy years old. Mrs Major had revealed that she knew her father kept poison in a box in his bedroom. Now the Yard man had to ask this sad-eyed, erect old countryman about his poison box and his daughter.

Despite the painful situation Inspector Young went straight to the point. He asked, 'Did your daughter know the whereabouts of the box in which you kept the strychnine?'

'Yes, mister,' Mr Brown replied.

The old man showed Young the box, which was locked.

'Would your daughter be able to open this box?'

'No, mister.'

He took from his cloth belt a small key. 'I always carry the key of that box about with me in this pocket. It has never left me day or night.'

Young was baffled. He had made exhaustive inquiries at chemists for miles around and at all places where poisons could be obtained but had found no evidence which had led to Mrs Major. He read the letters again and came to the conclusion that Mrs Major had written them herself. He got samples of her handwriting and asked her to write the words 'people' and 'always'. She spelt them as they had been in the anonymous letters, 'peopel' and 'allways'.

He was still missing the final link but on 9 July, one week after arriving on the scene, he went once more to the cottage at Kirkby-on-Bain. Mrs Major opened the door and again he cautioned her and then arrested her for the murder of her husband.

'I didn't do it,' she exclaimed. 'I am as innocent as the day is long. If I have given my husband poison, it is Mrs Kettleboro or someone else who came to my house and put it

115

there. It is wicked for people to accuse me, I loved my husband, and I am his lawful wedded wife.'

This protestation of love for the man she had so recently vilified was in character. When she was charged she said simply, 'Not guilty.'

Hugh Young then took his men to search the cottage, and in the bedroom he found a brown suitcase containing some clothing and a small purse. Inside the purse was found a crunched-up piece of paper bearing the words 'Mother's Penny' and inside that was a penny and a key. There was also a number of documents bearing recent dates which proved that the purse had been used recently.

Young was interested only in the key. It looked remarkably similar to the one Mr Brown had produced from the pocket of his cloth belt. There was a difference. This key was worn down on one side.

He drove off to see Mrs Major's father and asked him if he had another key to the poison trunk.

'What have you found now?' he asked. 'I am an old man, mister, I will tell you nothing but the truth. I did have another key, but I lost it years ago. It was the one I got with the trunk and it was worn down on one side. I never knew the going of it.'

Here was the answer to how Mrs Major had got the poison, the last bit of the jigsaw. She must have found the key years before and kept it. Hugh Young had added it to his own bunch and he produced them and held them up, one by one. There was no hesitation.

'That's her, mister,' said Mrs Major's father, pointing to the small key.

Young made a final check. He tried the key in the lock of the trunk. It worked perfectly – the final link in the evidence.

On a cold November morning in 1934 the closing scene in the village poison case was enacted at Lincoln Assizes where Mrs Major stood her trial. The jury, after an absence of one hour and ten minutes, found her guilty, adding a strong recommendation to mercy. Mr Justice Charles pronounced sentence of death.

Mrs Major sobbed quietly, her frail figure drooped against a woman police officer. She was carried from the dock, her cries echoing through the crowded court.

The recommendation to mercy was passed forward to the Home Office but she was hanged at Hull Prison on 19 December 1934.

CHAPTER 11

Death for an Unpaid Debt

Inevitably, as crime increased in the Thirties, so developments at Scotland Yard speeded up to keep pace. Communications improved with the advent of the Information Room at the Yard, a control centre to direct and feed information to the rapidly increasing numbers of cars fitted with wireless.

In 1934 the public were invited to telephone the police if they could be of any help – the number issued was Whitehall 1212. The police force received this development with rather more enthusiasm than on the occasion of the first telephone being installed in New Scotland Yard in 1901, when an old sergeant had said, 'I don't know what we're coming to – if this sort of thing goes on, we'll have the public ringing us up direct.'

Detective Superintendent Harry Battley had worked for three years between 1927 and 1930 devising a system of classifying single fingerprints in such a way that they could be readily produced for comparison with single impressions found at the scene of a crime. This saved an immense amount of time, since previously prints had had to be compared with sets of ten prints, five for each hand.

Calling in the Yard had become something of a habit for county forces, even though in some cases there was little need, local officers being considerably better versed by now. There was certainly a need, however, when a murder was discovered at St Albans in 1936, because London turned out to be where the victim met his death and the trail then led even further afield. Murders in the Thirties tended to be sensational, and none was more bizarre than the Max Kassel case.

At ten o'clock on a cold morning in January 1936 a carpenter called Henry Sayer found the body of a heavily-built man lying in the grass beside Cell Barnes Lane on the southern outskirts of St Albans in Hertfordshire.

The local police were called and found in what had become a suburban area a murder victim whose dress marked him as a stranger. His clothes were distinctly flashy, and his pointed, polished shoes and manicured hands smacked of a city dresser. The man had been shot six times in the chest, back and side. His face, which was scarred with old injuries, appeared to have been battered by a fist.

Hertfordshire Police asked for Yard assistance, and one of the most colourful men ever to grace the CID was chosen, the redoubtable Frederick Dew Sharpe, known as 'Nutty' after the famous toffee. Before joining the Murder Squad he had already spent a long career in the Flying Squad, the guerrillas of the police force, and knew the underworld as Frederick Wensley had known it before him.

Within an hour he was at the scene with Detective Inspector Fred Cherrill of Fingerprints and Sergeant Tasker. There had been a sharp frost in the night and the ground had thawed. The detectives were soon ankle-deep in mud.

There were no tyre marks or any other indication of how the body had got there and nothing on the body to identify the man. In his shirt was a pair of heavy gold cuff-links and in a pocket the key of a safe on a split-ring on which were engraved some words in French. On one finger he wore a heavy signet ring bearing the letter 'W' or 'M' in blue enamel. He looked like a prosperous bookmaker and, as there was nothing in his pockets, robbery seemed a possible motive. A description was circulated – the dead man was about sixty, five feet nine inches tall, heavily built, with a pale complexion, hair auburn turning grey, clean shaven, false teeth in upper jaw. He was wearing a grey suit, mauve shirt (silk), underclothes marked with initials in red cotton.

A trickle of information began. Two men and a woman had called at the Spot Café near by as it was closing the previous night. They had demanded to be served and drank coffee. The proprietor thought the description of the dead man sounded like one of the two men who, he said, appeared to have been drinking. This witness was quickly taken to the mortuary, saw the naked body on the slab, and said he thought it was the same man. He described the man's companions: a man aged about twenty-eight, smartly dressed, slim and athletic; the woman, a platinum blonde with rouged lips, scarlet fingernails, wearing a leopard-skin coat. After their coffee they had played on the fruit machines and then driven off towards St Albans.

In the mud outside the café Sharpe found some footprints and an officer went off to get some fresh plaster of Paris. The dead man was wearing shoes with a similar pattern of small circles in a rubber sole, and the lead looked promising. The thick mud made it difficult to get good impressions and the situation was not improved when a huge Airedale dog, finding men on their hands and knees, thought he might join a new game. But after the casts were made they proved useless. The shoes were the wrong size.

Sharpe and his men went to where the body had been discovered. Sharpe was fairly sure the man had not been shot there, because his trousers were high up his calves, suggesting he had been dragged feet first. But he was also tolerably certain he had been shot not far away. A nurse living nearby confirmed this when she reported having heard a shot. However, no spent bullets or bullet marks were found.

Descriptions of the man at the Spot Café and his woman companion in the leopard-skin coat were also circulated. This got a tremendous reaction from the public. Women

119

wrote about their neighbours who had leopard-skin coats, saying what unsavoury characters they were and that they had always had their suspicions of them. Half the prostitutes in London seemed to be wearing leopard-skin coats that year, and a good many of them were taken in for questioning. One woman said she had picked up a man that night who had driven her in the direction of St Albans, but then they had quarrelled and at Barnet he had dumped her. She had had to walk back to London, but had noted the number of the car. The driver was traced but was clearly innocent. In fact, the two in the café were never found and as it transpired had nothing in any case to do with the murder.

Meanwhile Sir Bernard Spilsbury had taken four bullets from the body. Two of them could have been fatal but the immediate cause of death was haemorrhage.

Identification of the murdered man looked as though it could be difficult. Days later Sharpe learned through one of his underworld informants that there had been a tremendous fight in a flat in Soho where a prostitute had taken a male client who had attacked her. Her ponce was in a back room and he came to her rescue. When Sharpe got there the walls were spattered with blood, furniture was smashed and it certainly looked as if a murder had been committed. The three people involved were traced and a gun was found in the home of one of them, but tests proved it to be the wrong gun. All three were released, and another lead fizzled out.

The case was full of promising information like this, but nothing lasted for long until a man, who had read in a newspaper about the body, identified it as that of Emile Allard whom he had known for about two years. He told police Allard had had a room in James Street, off Oxford Street, and that he dealt in cheap jewellery. The witness was carrying a knife up his sleeve and some of the detectives thought the hunt was at an end, but that was yet another red herring. However, at least Sharpe now had a start with a positive identification.

Inquiries suggested that Allard was a French Canadian and Soho was scoured for information from Frenchmen and women in the vice trade. Chief Inspector Sharpe, describing the investigation afterwards, said of one typical police call, 'We visited a house where a Frenchman was living and the door was answered by a pretty Frenchwoman, who said she was alone and invited us to her room. I noticed a glass door covered with paper and asked, "What's in there?"

"Oh, that's the bathroom."

"Well, open it up."

"It's empty."

"Never mind, open it up."

"It's locked."

"Well, get the key."

'She went off up the stairs and did not come back. So I banged on the door and shouted "Come out of there" and out he came.'

That kind of dialogue was repeated many times as the detectives moved through the thousands of flats in Soho occupied by prostitutes. At that time Soho was a more fascinating and certainly more dangerous area than it is today. Respectable and fashionable restaurants there were still, but this was also the era of rough clubs, illegal gambling and hundreds of prostitutes, most of them smartly dressed, foreign born, and almost all controlled by ponces who had arranged for them to marry Englishmen they had never met before to get British nationality. There was nothing the public liked more than a glimpse of this underbelly of London, and the newspapers gave developments in the case ample space.

Police had taken a set of fingerprints from the dead man. As a result Allard was further identified by the alias Max Kassel, but he had no police record in England. Even so pressure from the police persuaded people to talk. Informants revealed that Kassel had moved in the underworld of the West End and that he had travelled extensively in the white slave traffic, that he was a Latvian, born in Riga in 1879, and that he had roamed the world with false passports. It was discovered that he had actually been present in a house in Conduit Street, Mayfair, when a number of French ponces had been arrested, but he had hoodwinked the police officers by producing a forged passport. Step by step Kassel's movements were traced and the last time he had been seen alive by anyone the detectives could find was at 7.30 p.m. on 23 January in Charing Cross Road, near Soho. He had been alone.

As a result of this steady trickle of rumour and whispered information, Sharpe became interested in Pierre Henri Alexandre, who lived in Mayfair but owned a garage in Soho and was the lessor of a number of flats occupied by Frenchwomen. Sharpe had him brought to Scotland Yard and Alexandre admitted he knew a man called Max the Red and had heard that he ran a number of women. He also said he had heard of a man called 'Joe the Terror', a man mentioned in connection with a recent international forgery scandal, but swore he had not been near St Albans in the past week. Alexandre concluded by saying, 'I don't know anybody who can tell you anything about Ginger Max or his friends.'

Then on 30 January, six days after the body had been found, things began to move.

The local CID of the West End, who in those days dealt with vice in the area, discovered that Alexandre was the lessor of a maisonnette consisting of the second and third floors of a house in Little Newport Street, which runs off Charing Cross Road. The tenant of the flat was a Frenchwoman named Suzanne Naylor. She had contracted a marriage of convenience with a British subject in 1933 and had been living in the maisonnette with a Frenchman known as Mr George. When Inspector Benson of Vine Street police station had made inquiries he had heard that on 23 January there had been a smashing of glass on the pavement outside.

Inspector Sharpe and his squad went to the flat but found it locked and deserted. They broke in, but there was no sign of any disturbance. However, they did find that two panes of glass in a window on the third floor and one pane in the window of the bathroom on the second floor had recently been renewed. They also noticed that a curtain in the sitting-room had been neatly shortened with a pair of scissors. On the chairs in the sitting-room and on the floor of the bathroom were some tiny, hardly discernible spots. Forensic tests showed these to be human bloodstains. They had found the scene of the murder.

In the intensive search of the flat which followed they found whips and instruments of torture and a large collection of obscene pictures, the accoutrements of the prostitute. Despite the seriousness of the investigation, there was laughter when Sharpe walked into a bedroom and saw between the pillows on the bed a large dildo, dressed with a collar and tie and surrounded by teddy-bears. And then came the great find. Underneath a chest of drawers was a Ministry of Health insurance card. It bore the name and address of Marcelle Aubin, Newnham Terrace, Hercules Road, London, SE.

Shortly afterwards she was sitting in front of Sharpe at Scotland Yard. She looked distraught although her manner was composed.

At first she told many lies mixed with a few truths. She had worked for Madame Naylor since Easter 1935 as a maid but she knew nothing of a man called Red Max or Emile Allard. She had broken the windows by slipping against them and hitting them with her elbow. As far as she could remember, Madame Naylor told her on 25 January she had received a telegram from her mother, who was very ill, and she was going to her at once. She had taken some clean underclothes in a case and left by train from Victoria.

That evening Sharpe sent for Alexandre and interviewed him again. He admitted he was the lessor of the maisonnette, but nothing else. Sharpe let him go but kept his Chrysler car and sent it to the new police laboratory at Hendon, where they found a number of bloodstains on the back seat. Once Sharpe heard this he had Alexandre brought back, and this time his witness decided to tell the truth.

Alexandre said that George Lacroix, who had lived at the Little Newport Street flat with Suzanne Naylor, telephoned him on the night of 23 January and asked him to come over. He gave him some whisky and asked for his help. At this point Alexandre was cautioned and then his statement was written down. It was an amazing story. Lacroix had claimed he was owed money by Max Kassel and that because Kassel had insulted him repeatedly, he had come to London and asked Kassel to call at his flat. He had come, there was an argument about money and about Kassel's insulting Lacroix's girl and threatening to break his neck. Lacroix told Alexandre, 'He jumped on me and I pulled a gun and shot him. I shot once or twice, the window got broken and I shot again. He's in the bathroom.'

Lacroix had then shown Alexandre the body in the bathroom and they had arranged to meet at 4 a.m. and take the body away by car. It was wrapped in a blanket.

Alexandre went on: 'We drove north and dragged him through a gap in the hedge feet first, because he was very heavy. We left him on the grass, took the blanket off and I drove George home. It was about seven o'clock, just before it was light. Max's overcoat collar was turned up and I did not see whether he was wearing a collar or tie. I asked about his papers and George said, "I burnt everything, including the letter I sent asking him to call." He said that Max had ten shillings on him. He did not say what he had done with it, but he said he had left him his ring and his cuff-links. When I left George he said he was going to Paris.'

Two French-speaking detectives were sent to Paris to arrest Lacroix and Naylor, and Sharpe sent for Marcelle Aubin. This time she told him the whole story. It was really amazingly simple – a small debt had led to a brutal murder. Red Max had owed Lacroix £25 but he had refused to pay it back. After waiting a year Lacroix had asked Suzanne Naylor to write, inviting Kassel to call. He had come and had seen her in the bedroom while Lacroix stayed in the upstairs sitting-room. Red Max had been rude to her and again refused to pay. She had refused to let Lacroix come down because of his quick temper, but later Lacroix had called Marcelle and asked her to write to Kassel, inviting him to call on Thursday 23 January between 6.30 and 7 p.m. The letter was signed 'Suzanne Naylor' and addressed to 'Mr Emile Allard, Rathbone Place, London, W.' This was an accommodation address where Kassel picked up his mail. The next night was the night of the murder and this is how Marcelle described it:

'Sometime between 6.30 and 7 p.m. Mr George (Lacroix) came into the kitchen and said, "You and Madame go down to the bedroom and stop there. When you hear the bell, Marcelle, answer the door and let him in. You'll know him, he speaks with a gruff voice. Show him upstairs and shut the door behind him and stop in the bedroom." I went to the bedroom with Mrs Naylor. At about ten minutes to seven the door-bell rang and I answered the door and a man was standing there whose photograph I have seen in the newspapers – the photograph of Emile Allard [the name by which she knew Kassel]. I asked him to go upstairs. I followed him and shut the door of the sitting-room behind him. Mr George called out "Come in." The wireless was on in the sitting-room and playing loudly. Soon after Allard went into the room I heard high words and they were quarrelling. After three or four minutes I heard footsteps back and forwards and while the high words were being spoken I heard some shots. There were several, I cannot say how many, in quick succession. Immediately after this I heard a scuffle and then Mr George shouted, "Marcelle." I ran upstairs and saw Mr George and Mr Allard fighting. Allard said, "Oh, mademoiselle, he's shot me." I pushed him back into the sitting-room and when he got near the window he swung half round and hit a deliberate blow, smashing two panes. Mrs Naylor and I pulled him away from the window. He said, "Take me to the hospital." Mr George pushed Allard into the bathroom. He kept saying, "Take me to the hospital. I won't say anything. I'll say I did it myself."

'I sat him on the chair in the bathroom and he said, "I am going to die, give me some water." He took his overcoat and jacket off. I thought he was going to fall off the chair and put my right arm behind his shoulders to steady him. My right hand was on the upper part of his right arm and became covered with blood. I held a glass of water to his lips. He held it as well. His hand was trembling and so was mine. Some of the water spilled down the front of his shirt. He kept saying, "Air, air, air." Then he opened the front of his trousers and showed two bleeding wounds in his stomach.

'Mr George during this time did nothing except push the man back as he tried to get up. He pulled down the bathroom window when Allard kept saying, "Air, air." Allard made a loud groaning noise repeatedly and George kept saying, "*Tais-toi!*" When I saw the blood on the shirt I went outside the bathroom with Mrs Naylor. I was shaking from head to foot and after a little while I went back into the bathroom. I think Mrs Naylor came with me.

'I pushed up the bottom of the window. Allard jumped up, pushed up the window and leaned over the ledge groaning. Mr George pulled him back and slammed the window down. I walked out as I was nearing collapse. Mrs Naylor was with me in the bathroom. She was trembling and we both cried.

'Mr George came into the bedroom and Mrs Naylor said, "Marcelle wants to go home." He said, "All right, don't upset yourself. You stop here, you speak good English. If anyone comes to the door you can speak to them."

'The last I saw of Allard he was kneeling facing the bath with his head hanging over it and his arms inside.

'I sat by the fire in the bedroom. I still heard groaning for a time. Then it stopped and just afterwards Mr George came into my bedroom. I said I didn't want to hear any more groaning and he replied, "It's all right, you won't hear him any more, he's gone." '

That was the real story of the murder in all its ruthlessness. After the body had been taken away and dumped the two women had cleaned up the flat, washing away the bloodstains, collecting the spent cartridges and cutting off the bloodstained section of the curtain, which they burnt together with the blanket used for wrapping the body. They had the broken window panes replaced but did not spot the insurance card, the vital clue.

Next day Lacroix left London for Paris and sent a telegram to Suzanne Naylor. It was in French and contained the words 'Perfect health, thousands of kisses', a code for her to leave. She left for Paris at once and joined Lacroix.

With the co-operation of the French police the two Yard men who had gone to Paris arrested Lacroix and Naylor, but they had not had time to get warrants before they left. Under French law the couple could be detained for only twenty-four hours without warrants. The Bow Street magistrate was brought from his home early on the Sunday morning, Sharpe swore the necessary information and the warrants were issued charging the man with the wilful murder of Red Max Kassel and the woman with being an accessory after the fact of murder.

Then began a controversy about their extradition. It had been supposed that Lacroix was a British subject born in Canada, but the French police said his real name was Roger Marcel Vernon, that he was a native of Paris and an escaped convict from Devil's Island. Naylor was really Suzanne Bertron, lawful wife of Emil Bertron, a Frenchman she had married eight years previously and by whom she had one child. Her English marriage to a sailor called Naylor – a marriage of convenience – was therefore bigamous. Finally the French refused extradition, which was fortunate for Lacroix, for in England he would doubtless have hanged.

The trial took place at the Assizes de la Seine, a building much larger than the Old Bailey. The defence was that Red Max was shot in self-defence, and the three judges decided on a sentence for Lacroix of ten years' imprisonment with hard labour followed by twenty years' expulsion from France. Suzanne Bertron was acquitted.

Marcelle Aubin, the vital witness, had died on her way to France. She was already a sick woman and police believed she had been terrorized by friends of Lacroix. Her evidence might have persuaded the judges to grant extradition, and then the story could well have ended differently.

During the case the sordid history of George Lacroix was revealed. He had been convicted of stealing at the age of nineteen and two years later of armed robbery. Later, for a similar offence, he had been sent to Devil's Island for seven years and banished from France for ten years. He escaped from the penitentiary in 1928 and went to Venezuela where he met Esther Odde, a Frenchwoman from Marseilles, who became his mistress. He lived with her in Caracas, Haiti, the USA and had finally settled in Montreal. There he had earned a living by selling cars and white-slave trading and had met Red Max Kassel, who had been expelled from France and Belgium, and had then lived in London, Buenos Aires and Canada as a ponce.

By means of false identity papers obtained in the United States, Vernon had assumed the name of George Lacroix and had returned to France where his mistress' mother ran a wine-shop in the rue du Port, Marseilles. For a while he had lived in Paris and Fontenay-sous-Bois, where he stayed with his family, and then, with Esther Odde, he had gone to London where they married. Lacroix dealt in motor cars and frequently visited Paris, where one day he met Suzanne Bertron in a café. She was twenty-one and already a prostitute, having deserted her violin-maker husband. Lacroix had a brother, whose mistress was Simone Ferrero, and her birth certificate was used to obtain a passport in her name for Suzanne Bertron. Armed with that she followed Lacroix to London and married an English seaman, William Naylor, on 18 March 1935. She never saw him again. This was a common loophole in the law then and it allowed her to continue her trade in London without being troubled by British legislation affecting her alien origin.

Lacroix went into the motor trade with Pierre Alexandre, and soon afterwards Red Max Kassel, also known as Emile Allard, or Kasserberg, or Max the Red, turned up in London. He was still in the white-slave trade and it was inevitable the three men should meet. Not long after Kassel borrowed £25 from Lacroix and a year later he had not repaid it. The stage was set for murder.

128

London in the Thirties had become one of the European centres of foreign prostitution, the women being brought over by *soutenirs* or pimps and having a 'marriage of convenience' arranged to give them British citizenship. The Messina brothers, from Malta, were running scores of Frenchwomen, who they had set up in flats all over the West End, and there were many other such organizations. Many years later the Messinas went to jail and were later deported. Scotland Yard knew that the prostitutes were prepared to help the underworld by looking after stolen property or helping men on the run, while pimps were making fortunes and keeping the women in submission by threats of violence. Prostitutes could only be prosecuted for soliciting and fined £2, and the chances of prosecuting a pimp for living on the immoral earnings of a prostitute were slight, for the women were frightened to talk.

The Kassel case caused a resurgence of interest in the problem and the authorities tried to clean up London, because it was realized that the heart of the Red Max murder was centred in that world of prostitution. It took another fourteen years for the Street Offenders Act to be passed, which made an effort to control the exploitation of foreign women.

CHAPTER 12

The Man Who Was Freed and Confessed

One of the early police laboratory triumphs was a case to which the Murder Squad had been summoned in 1935. Detective Chief Inspector Alec Bell and Detective Sergeant Albert Tapsell went to Sherborne, Dorset, to investigate an alleged poisoning. An illiterate thirty-three-year-old Irishwoman, Charlotte Bryant, was thought to have murdered her husband. Tapsell bought three new paint brushes and with them swept the dust from every cupboard and shelf in the Bryants' cottage. Analysis at the laboratory revealed the presence of arsenic, and at the post-mortem four grains of arsenic were found in Frederick Bryant's body. It was later proved that Mrs Bryant had bought weed-killer containing arsenic and had given it to her husband in his food for more than a year. His agonizing stomach pains had been diagnozed by the local doctor as gastro-enteritis.

The laboratory was again helpful in the case of Ruby Anne Keen, a factory worker at Leighton Buzzard, in Bedfordshire. She was twenty-three when she was found murdered in 1937. She had been strangled and almost all her clothes had been ripped off. The Yard was called in immediately, possibly because Ruby had been about to marry a local police officer.

Sir Bernard Spilsbury was also called in and he decided that the girl had been knocked down by a blow on the chin and then strangled with her own scarf. Chief Inspector William Barker of the Murder Squad noted that at the scene there were footprints made by a man's shoe and two clear indentations made by the knees of the killer as he had knelt by his victim. He took a sample of the sandy soil and plaster casts of all the prints and indentations.

Later Barker found out that Ruby had been in various pubs the night of her death with a man called Leslie Stone, whom she had known for some years. Stone admitted having been with the dead girl on the night of the murder, and Barker took away his suit and shoes for forensic examination.

The laboratory men found that the shoes roughly fitted the plaster casts and were also able to discern the weave of Stone's suit in the casts of the knee impressions. The suit was a mass-produced one, so this identification could do no more than establish that the knee impressions could have been made by Stone. However, although the knees of the trousers had been well brushed, under the microscope traces of the sandy soil showed up on them. And on the jacket was a minute silken thread of similar material to the dress the dead girl had been wearing.

Even so in 1939, when Hendon Police College was closed down, at the outbreak of war, the Yard laboratory was still so embryonic that historic tests on human saliva to help establish the identity of a killer had to be made with outside help. The tests were made purely on the basis of a detective's hunch, but the denouement to the case made history for very different reasons.

On 21 May Walter Dinivan, a wealthy retired garage owner, was found dead in his sizeable villa in Branksome, Bournemouth, where a garden with trees and shrubs screened the house from the main Poole road.

The house had been divided into two flats, and Mr Dinivan lived with his granddaughter on the lower floor, two elderly ladies occupying the upper flat. Dinivan, a widower, also had a grandson, a telegraphist in the Royal Navy, who had just returned from several years' service in China. He had visited his grandfather twice and on the night of 21 May had arranged to stay in the house, sleeping in the second bed in his grandfather's room.

The two grandchildren had been out and returned home just before midnight to find all the doors locked. They could get no answer by knocking so the grandson smashed the glass in the front door and went in, to find his grandfather lying in a great pool of blood in front of the fire in the drawing-room. Young Dinivan called the police who brought an ambulance, but Walter Dinivan died in hospital on 22 May without regaining consciousness.

The attack on him was marked by terrible violence. Not only were there ten wounds on his head and face but someone had tried to strangle him. The ferocity of the blows had driven bits of the old man's skull into his brain and the bones of his nose had been cracked. There was no indication that he had tried to defend himself and it seemed that the attack had taken him completely unawares. It also seemed possible that Mr Dinivan had been murdered by someone he knew and trusted, for there was no sign of a forced entry to the house.

The Dorset police called in Scotland Yard, and Hampshire-born Detective Chief Inspector Leonard Burt took the case with his sergeant, Leonard Dyke.

When the two Yard men walked into the room where the murder had taken place it appeared that Dinivan had been entertaining someone, for, on a small table near the body, was a bottle of beer and two tumblers. One tumbler had been overturned and had soaked the tablecloth with beer. There was also a small green glass containing whisky, the dead man's usual drink. It was discovered later that Dinivan always used that glass.

The table yielded the first clue. On the glass which had contained the beer was a thumbprint. It had been put there recently by a dry hand on a wet glass.

There were several cork-tipped cigarette ends on the beer-stained cloth, some more on the floor and one on a silk cushion on the settee. None of them appeared to have been stubbed out where they were found as there was no singeing of the cushion or the carpet. Burt wondered if they had been placed there deliberately to mislead and, if so, for what purpose? Whatever the reason, Burt's thoughts switched to the possibility of having saliva tests done on the cigarette ends. He had heard that all saliva has secreted in it the essential substance that determines a blood group, and that it might be possible to find out the blood group of a person from traces of his or her saliva. Accurate grouping was not then the exact science it later became and the use of saliva for that purpose was still in its infancy. It had certainly never been accepted as evidence in a court of law, but Burt thought it worth a try. He ordered that all the cigarette ends were to be taken to Dr Roche Lynch, the Home Office analyst.

There were more clues, all carefully collected. One was a woman's hair-curler, suggesting the presence of a female, which opened up some interesting possibilities. It didn't belong to the granddaughter, so who *was* the owner?

Near the pool of blood was a paper bag. From its creases and folds it looked as though it might have been used to wrap a hammer, which might have been the murder weapon.

The safe in the drawing-room had been opened and rifled, and the keys – which the dead man usually carried – were found inside. It was established that Dinivan would have had about fifteen pounds in notes in his jacket. They were missing. His watch and chain had gone, as had the rings from his fingers.

Fingerprints of all the people who normally had access to the house were taken but none of them matched the print on the glass.

First investigations were at laundries to find bloodstained clothing, with taxi-drivers to ask if they had taken anyone to the house, and bus conductors to see if they had noticed any obvious strangers near by. These inquiries yielded nothing.

On the day of the murder Dinivan with his grandchildren and a friend had visited Lulworth Cove. After tea they had dropped the friend off, and later his grandchildren had left Dinivan at his home at 7.15 p.m. and gone off to a dance together. Dinivan had planned to spend a quiet evening at home, and was expecting no guests. They left him sitting in the same chair he always used in the ground-floor drawing-room, with the windows latched.

Local detectives discovered that Dinivan sometimes had women visitors but nobody seemed to know who they were. A number of Bournemouth prostitutes were interviewed but they all denied knowing Dinivan. However, some local men came forward with an interesting lead about a male friend of Dinivan's who had been spending money freely on the day following the murder. Since he had been pleading poverty immediately before, Chief Inspector Burt decided to pay him a visit.

The man's name was Joseph Williams, a sixty-nine-year-old former soldier who had served in India. He had no job, his house was heavily mortgaged and he lived in unbelievable squalor. Chief Inspector Burt recalls that first meeting in his memoirs. 'He was a tall, gaunt creature and crazy with anger at my visit. There was a chair, a table and a sword from his soldiering days. He picked up the sword and swung it round his head, and shouted, "Busybody Burt, I'll show you the way to go home. I know you. I know what you're after. But you shan't bloody well get it." '

Williams was thoroughly unco-operative. He refused to give his fingerprints, perhaps because the local newspaper had published the fact that prints had been found on the glass. He accounted for his movements on the day of the murder with some innocuous detail, and he agreed that he had seen Dinivan on the Sunday before he died, and again on the seventeenth. He said that on the last occasion they had met in the street outside Dinivan's house and gone inside for a drink. Williams had asked to borrow some money but Dinivan would lend him only five pounds and he had taken the notes from his safe.

In the meantime Dr Roche Lynch had succeeded in finding the blood group from the saliva on the cigarette ends. The smoker was of a blood group found in only three per cent of the population.

The evening these findings came through Sergeant Dyke was given a mission – to find the public house used by Williams. Later he and Chief Inspector Burt strolled to the bar, to find their quarry without his sword and in rather better humour. He readily agreed to have a drink and took one of Dyke's cigarettes without hesitation. When he threw away the stub Dyke moved a step while, to keep Williams occupied, Burt argued with him about the relative merits of a number of racehorses. Dyke picked up the stub, retreated to the lavatory, and tucked it into an envelope. He need not have bothered to be so careful. Williams smoked continuously, and by the end of the evening there was ample evidence, a reward for Len Burt who was no great specialist on racing form!

Later that night all these cigarette stubs were delivered to Dr Roche Lynch and the following day he reported that the smoker belonged to the same three per cent group as the person who had smoked in Dinivan's drawing-room on the night of the murder.

The next call on Williams found him once again in truculent mood, with a greeting of 'What the hell do you want?' But he calmed down under the patience of the urbane Mr Burt, whose policy was never to raise his voice above normal conversational level. In the end Williams offered to show the detectives round his house.

In a pitch-dark, disused coal shed, Dyke switched on his torch to reveal a pile of old paper bags. Williams explained that he had been a greengrocer and also a fishmonger. The bags were part of his stock from those days. Dyke picked them up and put them in his brief-case, thinking of the bag found at the murder scene.

While the calm remained Burt asked Williams to produce his wallet. It was bulging with money, the result, he said, of backing Blue Peter in the Derby. He went on to explain why he had made the bet – Jack Jarvis was a good trainer and Eph Smith a good rider. Burt, having talked lengthily about a subject on which he was ill-versed with Williams in the public house, had got one of his men to check on whether Williams had really backed Blue Peter. The detectives took the money away with them.

The paper bags were sent to the Yard's forensic laboratory and compared with the one found near the body. They were photographed under ultra-violet rays and enlargements showed that the texture of the paper in both cases was identical. All the bags had been made by a firm in the South of England. The identification was strengthened by a member of the firm who said that the bags had been made on an obsolete machine. Even more, he was able to say that the irregular serrated edges on the folds of two of the bags indicated that they had come off the machine consecutively.

Then came the report on the hair-curler, a clue Burt had put into the 'machine' without really believing it would come up in his favour. On the other hand, like most policemen, he was not entirely surprised, simply because it is routine to try everything. The curler was of ancient make and out of production, but the bonus information was that Joseph Williams had been married and his wife had used that type of hair-curler when they had lived together. She had left him many years before but Burt was able to find her and she told him that she had used those curlers then, and was still using them. So Williams had probably found one she had left behind.

This fitted with one of Burt's original theories that the hair-curler had been planted to suggest that a woman had committed the murder or that a man, working with a woman, had trapped Dinivan into a blackmail situation.

As the pace quickened, another useful part of the initial search paid off. The notes found in Williams's wallet had been circulated through the Bank of England and one of their cashiers telephoned to say the numbers on the notes had been passed to Lloyds Bank head office and that they had sent them to their branch in Bournemouth. It happened to be the branch at which Dinivan banked, drawing bearer cheques for his weekly expenses.

Burt was by now fairly certain he had enough evidence to obtain a conviction, but he wanted one more thing to clinch it. So with Sergeant Dyke he went again to the squalid, smelly house where Williams lived. As soon as they arrived Williams began to shout, 'What a hope you've got! Innocent, that's what I am, innocent, and even you can't pin it on me! How's that for confidence, mate!'

So confident was he that when Burt asked quietly if he would have his fingerprints taken, he agreed.

The glass tumbler with the thumbprint on it had already been sent to Detective Superintendent Fred Cherrill at Scotland Yard and, within an hour of receiving the prints taken from Williams, Cherrill was on the telephone to Burt. He said that the thumbprint he had just received was identical with the one on the tumbler.

It was four months after the discovery of the body that Burt was satisfied that he had enough evidence. The blood group, the bank notes, the hair-curler, the paper bag and the thumbprint. In Cockney parlance, Williams was 'bang to rights'. That night he was charged with the murder of Walter Alfred Dinivan.

All through the hearings at the magistrates' court and throughout his trial at the Dorset Assizes Williams protested his innocence. He made so many interruptions that he had to be admonished, but he did get a great deal of press coverage.

In October 1939, to the astonishment of everyone in the court, the jury found him not guilty and he was acquitted. He stepped jauntily from the dock, a free man.

Both the Scotland Yard men were convinced Williams was guilty and they could only surmise that the jury had not fully understood the strength of the fingerprint evidence, to say nothing of the rest of the evidence. Perhaps they had been impressed with Williams's frequent protestations of innocence from the dock. There was no way of knowing.

However, Chief Inspector Burt was finally proved right. In March 1951 Joseph Williams died in his sleep and was buried just outside Nottingham. The following Sunday the *News of the World* carried a story by Norman Rae, a top Fleet Street crime reporter. He wrote the story he had got on the night of Williams's acquittal and which he had been unable to use because of the laws of libel.

He wrote that Williams had told him later that night that the jury was wrong. 'I did it. The jury was wrong. It was me.'

Norman Rae went on to tell how he had driven Williams from the court back to Poole, where, over a large whisky, Williams drank a toast. He said, 'To the hangman who has been cheated of his victim.'

Later that night, in a highly nervous state, he made a full confession to Rae. It was too late for anything to be done – he had already been tried on a charge of murder and acquitted by a jury, and could not be tried again on the same charge.

CHAPTER 13

A Tea Party that Turned to Murder

The 1939–45 war not only proved to be one of the Flying Squad's busiest periods, but it presented special problems of its own. Under cover of the emergency criminals had a field day – the blackout and the black market being just two factors in their favour.

For the Squad there were fewer men available to back up investigations, while transport and travel were restricted. Patrol cars had to use dimmed lights and frequently there was enforced radio silence, which meant crews had to work independently and could not be contacted from headquarters. There was also a plentiful and extraordinarily varied caseload.

In 1940 Detective Chief Inspector Peter Beveridge was running the Flying Squad and working an average of fifteen hours a day, so when he was transferred to the Murder Squad he hoped for a quieter life. On his first day, at 11 p.m. on 9 July when he and his close friend Inspector Ted Greeno were having a drink before signing off duty, he was given a message from the Chief Constable of Kent. It read, 'Request assistance in a murder inquiry. Three people, all female, killed by shooting at Matfield, near Tonbridge.'

Beveridge telephoned the CID chief of Kent, then Inspector Fred Smeed, who told him the murders had been discovered that afternoon about eight hours earlier. Three bodies had been found in the grounds of a cottage, and it was thought that two of the women were mother and daughter. They had been shot in the back, apparently with a revolver. The third woman, believed to be a maid, had been bludgeoned about the head.

The victims were Mrs Dorothy Fisher, her nineteen-year-old daughter Freda and their maid, Charlotte Saunders, aged about forty-eight. They had lived together in a pretty cottage set in a rose-scented garden at Matfield. Mrs Fisher's husband Walter lived at a farm at Piddington, near Bicester in Oxfordshire.

Smeed told Beveridge that the Fishers were known to the police because they had recently sought permission for a male friend of Mrs Fisher, an alien, to visit the cottage and that their request had been turned down. The reason for the refusal was the wartime regulation which made that part of Kent a protected area and therefore out of bounds to certain civilians and open only to Service personnel. At that time the German Air Force was particularly active over Kent, and dog-fights between British and Nazi fighters high above the orchards took place every day. On the ground thousands of soldiers were digging slit-trenches and preparing for the expected German invasion.

Beveridge sent for his sergeant, Bert Tansill, a tubby, fat-jowled man of great confidence, and they drove away from the Yard with a Murder Bag, but not in the direction of Kent. Beveridge had decided to change the usual routine and, instead of going to the scene, which seemed pointless in the blackout, he decided first to visit the alien, a Dane, and then to see Mr Fisher.

The Dane lived in a comfortable flat in West London and Beveridge broke the news of the murders to him. He was satisfied, and so was Sergeant Tansill, that the shock and upset shown by the man were genuine. Once he had recovered he was able to give a complete account of his movements during the day. Even so, the detectives searched the flat for firearms but found none.

On the way back from seeing the Dane, Beveridge picked up a bag with a change of clothing and made a bold, domestic decision – he decided to use his own official car and his driver, Jack Frost, on the investigation, although he knew he was breaking the rule which said that officers should travel by train and then use the cars of the police force they were serving. Beveridge was a Scot and a stern disciplinarian, but he could see no point in being handicapped with the blackout problem and a strange driver in unknown territory. Jack

Frost was the top driver of the Flying Squad and reckoned to be the best driver in the force.

Before anyone in authority knew about it, Beveridge was off with Sergeant Tansill to see Mr Fisher at his farm near Bicester. There he had a disappointment, for Mr Fisher had left for London where he had business to transact. Beveridge waited until he returned, met Mr Fisher on his arrival and told him of the tragedy. He was badly shaken but agreed to go with Beveridge to Matfield to identify the bodies. But first the Yard man wanted to see and search his farmhouse.

During the search the detectives inspected the shotguns owned by Walter Fisher. None of them had been recently fired. They went through the house, room by room, and in Mr Fisher's bedroom, where there were two beds, they found one was occupied by a woman. Mr Fisher explained that she was a Mrs Ransom, a friend of his, who was not feeling well and was resting. However, it was clear to the detectives that the woman was used to sharing Mr Fisher's bedroom.

Beveridge left Sergeant Tansill to talk to Mr Fisher and Mrs Ransom and walked round the farm to see what he could discover. He found one of the servants who expressed a solid dislike of the woman he called Mrs Fisher. He said she was domineering and dictatorial. A few questions established that he was talking about the woman Beveridge had seen in bed, and that she had been living there for some time. The man went on to say that she had been learning to fire a shotgun for the previous two weeks and that her tutor was the cowman. He had also been teaching her to ride a bicycle.

When Beveridge returned to the farm he was surprised to see that the woman he had so recently seen in bed was up and with Mr Fisher and Sergeant Tansill. She was dressed in blue slacks and a multi-coloured jersey, and was heavily made up, her fingernails bright red and her hair bright auburn.

Mr Fisher made the formal introductions and they talked pleasantly about the weather and the progress of the war. Nobody mentioned the murders at Matfield. The detectives

shook hands with her and they left to drive to the scene of
the murders with Mr Fisher.

As they got into the car Tansill whispered to Beveridge,
'I'll raise the subject of the family. Very interesting.' A few
moments after, as the car was humming along the road,
Tansill said to Mr Fisher, 'Can you tell us about the Danish
gentleman? I understand that he has been refused permission to visit Mrs Fisher at Matfield because it is a restricted area.'

Mr Fisher rose to the bait and explained the
extraordinary life he had led with his wife. He said they had
lived at Twickenham with their two daughters but before the
outbreak of the war they had parted and, without seriously
thinking of divorce, had each taken a lover. Mrs Fisher had
met the Dane and he himself had fallen in love with a young
widow called Florence Iris Ouida Ransom, whom he called
Julia. Both the Dane and Mrs Ransom went frequently to the
house at Twickenham and for a while the Fisher *ménage*
remained tranquil. Then Walter Fisher took Crittenden, the
cottage at Matfield, and spent week-ends there with Julia.

When the elder Miss Fisher married and left Twickenham
the home broke up, although everyone remained on extremely friendly terms. Fisher went to the farm in Oxfordshire and Mrs Fisher with their younger daughter,
Freda, went to live in the cottage at Matfield. They had
engaged Charlotte Saunders as a housekeeper.

Mr Fisher was at some pains to point out that throughout
all the domestic upsets the whole family had remained on
pleasant terms and that there was no bad feeling.

It had been a ninety-mile drive and the Yard men had
gathered some interesting and vital information. Before they
went to the scene of the murders Beveridge had a chance to
talk to Tansill. 'Bert,' he said, 'what do you make of Mrs
Ransom?'

'A good-looker but tough. Her eyes are a bit queer – sort
of vacant.'

They saw the body of Charlotte Saunders lying on the
path at the side of the cottage. She had been shot in the head,

not bludgeoned as first thought. About two hundred yards away, in a corner of the orchard, was the body of Freda, who had been killed by a shotgun blast in the back. In the opposite corner of the field was the body of the third woman, Mrs Fisher. She too had been shot in the back. Both women found in the orchard were wearing gum-boots.

The fact that they all died from gunshot wounds made Beveridge think back to the conversation he had had with the servant at Bicester. The phrase he recalled was: 'Mrs Fisher has been learning to use a shotgun owned by the cowman.' The attractive lady with the auburn hair, whose real name was Florence Ransom, was in the forefront of his mind as he walked into the cottage.

He noted all the obvious signs of breaking and entering; clothing and paper strewn all over the floors, desks and cupboards opened and the contents pulled out and left where they fell. All the rooms were in disorder and in some of them pieces of jewellery and money had been thrown on the floor. It was obvious that the murderer had intended it to appear that robbery was the motive for the crime. In the kitchen on the floor was a tea-tray and a quantity of broken crockery. Beveridge had it all collected and pieced together and the result was four cups, four saucers and four plates.

It seemed evident that Miss Saunders had prepared tea for four people, and that while she was carrying the tray she had been frightened and had dropped it. Beveridge's construction of the events was that someone, well known to the three women, had arrived at the cottage that afternoon with a shotgun and, as Mrs Fisher and her daughter were wearing gum-boots when they were found, he presumed they had gone into the orchard to shoot rabbits, or shoot something. The murderer, having got the Fishers into the orchard and at a reasonable distance from the cottage, had first shot the daughter in the back; the mother had seen her daughter fall and tried to escape by running to the other side of the orchard, which was up a slight incline. The murderer must have followed her, reloading the gun, and shot her in the back.

For the murderer there still remained Miss Saunders, the only possible witness, and she had to be disposed of. Beveridge theorized that Miss Saunders might have come face to face with her killer in the kitchen, which made her drop the tea-tray and run for her life. In his opinion she had intended to run to the main road for help. In any event, she had been intercepted by the murderer, who doubtless had guessed her intention, and had fired the gun at fairly close range.

There were two other clues found in the orchard, the first a lady's bicycle in the ditch only a short distance from the cottage door. It had been slightly damaged and was identified as belonging to Mrs Fisher. The second was found between the bodies of Mrs Fisher and her daughter. It was a lady's white hogskin glove. Beveridge had to find the hand that fitted the glove and, when he did, he reasoned he would have found the killer, now almost certainly a woman.

The Chief Inspector sent for the Yard fingerprint chief, Superintendent Fred Cherrill, and Sergeant Percy Law, one of the great Yard photographers. They worked in the cottage until dusk, Cherrill finding the prints and Law photographing them. Meanwhile Beveridge was establishing the extraordinary family history which Walter Fisher had outlined.

He discovered that in Oxfordshire Mrs Ransom, now calling herself Mrs Fisher, had taken over the management of the farm and that she had taken on as staff a Mrs Guilford and her son Fred. However, she had concealed from Walter Fisher that they were in fact her mother and brother.

Beveridge decided to call on Mrs Ransom at the farm and, like everyone else, she was asked to account for her movements on the day of the murders. She said she had not left the farm and she referred the detective to Mrs Guilford for confirmation. She agreed she had visited Mrs Fisher and her daughter in the past, but not on that day. Beveridge pulled the white hogskin glove from his pocket and said casually, 'I wonder if you'd mind trying this on?'

'Certainly,' she said, 'but I think it's too small.'

She pulled on the glove, showed it to the detective and

carefully pulled it off again and returned it. She made no demur and did not ask any questions.

Beveridge thought it was a perfect fit, but he said nothing and returned the glove to his pocket.

Before he left he questioned Mrs Guilford, confirmed that she was Mrs Ransom's mother and discovered that she was not entirely certain that her daughter had been home all day.

The Yard team motored back to Matfield to meet Sir Bernard Spilsbury, who had conducted the post-mortem examinations on the three victims. The pathologist said that they had all been shot at close range and was of the opinion that the person responsible was well known to the others because of the closeness of the gun when fired at the bodies. He went further and said that he was certain the killer had fired twice more into Mrs Fisher's back as she lay dying, and then walked back to where the daughter lay and fired once more into her back.

Beveridge had asked the local police to make inquiries, and they produced some interesting facts. A fourteen-year-old boy reported that on the day of the murders he had been on the road outside the cottage and on three occasions had seen a woman peering from the road through the hedge into the orchard. He remembered she was wearing blue slacks and a coloured jumper, that her fingernails were painted bright red and that she had a shock of red hair. There was also a taxi-driver and the ticket collector at Tonbridge railway station who said a woman of the same description had carried a long, narrow-shaped parcel under her arm. The ticket collector recalled the woman getting off a train at Tonbridge, about seven miles away from Matfield, at around noon, and the same woman had boarded at Tonbridge the 4.25 p.m. train for London.

At dawn the next morning Beveridge and Tansill, accompanied by Detective Inspector Smeed and his wife, drove up to interview Mrs Ransom. Mrs Smeed was taken in case of emergency and because there were no policewomen available. But Mrs Ransom had already left. She had been driven to Aylesbury railway station to catch a train for

London. The farmhand who had taken her told the police he thought she was going to see Mr Fisher, who had not been at the farm the previous day.

Sergeant Tansill stayed at the farm to take statements while Beveridge telephoned the Yard to warn them that Mrs Ransom was likely to get in touch with Mr Fisher at his City office. Detective Inspector John Black, who was supervising the London end of the inquiry, was able to confirm that an arrangement had been made for the two to meet at 1.30 p.m. in London at York Road underground station at the far end of Waterloo Bridge. Beveridge went back to the farm, picked up his colleagues, and was driven fast to London. He arrived before the appointed time and was met by Black who told him the time of the meeting had been changed to four o'clock in the same place. Later it was changed to a solicitor's office in High Holborn at six o'clock. When Beveridge arrived he found Mr Fisher there but Mrs Ransom had gone to do some shopping. He decided to wait, wondering whether she would return. But within a few minutes she walked up and Beveridge, towering over her, politely raised his hat and said, 'Mrs Ransom, I believe?'

One photographer, Stanley Sherman, took a classic picture of that arrest, but when Beveridge escorted Mrs Ransom to Scotland Yard there were dozens of other photographers waiting for them. Since it was essential that Mrs Ransom was put on an identification parade Beveridge could not afford to have the picture published before then, and the newspapers agreed to hold publication until after the parade had taken place.

Beveridge took Mrs Ransom back to Tonbridge where she made a statement. She claimed that she had been at the farm all day on 9 July and asserted that her servants could prove it – a complete alibi in fact. But what she did not know was that Beveridge knew the cowman was her brother and that his wife had admitted as much. Mrs Ransom continued to deny it.

Later, the detectives went back to the farm at Bicester and the cowman told them he had recently taught Mrs Ransom to ride a bicycle and also fire a shotgun. She had borrowed the shotgun from him on 8 July and had returned it on 10 July, saying it was dirty and wanted cleaning.

Six days after the investigation had begun Beveridge held an identification parade. Eight women, as much like Mrs Ransom as was possible, all dressed in slacks and a jumper, stood in line. Mrs Ransom, who was similarly dressed, was allowed to stand wherever she wanted.

She was picked out by several of the witnesses as the woman they had seen on the day of the murders.

After the parade Beveridge asked Mrs Ransom to try on the glove once again and, although she said it wasn't hers he could see it fitted her perfectly. The most meticulous search failed to turn up the other glove, and Beveridge suspected she had realized its importance and had disposed of it.

Beveridge was satisfied that Mrs Ransom had taken the shotgun, wrapped in paper, and caught the 8.56 a.m. train from Bicester to London on 9 July, reaching Tonbridge at 12.8 p.m. Then she had taken a taxi to Matfield, had used Mrs Fisher's bicycle to circle the cottage and make a reconnaissance and had fallen off. The local police doctor had examined Mrs Ransom and he had found a graze on one of her knees, the sort of injury one might expect in a fall from a bicycle. A lorry driver testified that he had given her a lift to Tonbridge where she had caught the 4.25 p.m. train and she had got home about 7 p.m. Several witnesses said they had seen her wearing white hogskin gloves that day. Beveridge had no hesitation and charged her with the three murders.

Mrs Ransom was tried at the Old Bailey in November before Mr Justice Tucker. The trial had been postponed so that she could be kept under medical observation. She said that her mind was a little blank about all events on 9 July and that she did not know what she was doing. She was convicted and sentenced to death. Her appeal failed but she was later certified insane, although insanity had been no part of her defence. In fact she had a history of mental disorders and was ordered to be detained in Broadmoor.

It was a deliberate crime. Peter Beveridge believed that

Mrs Ransom had telephoned the other Fisher household and invited herself to tea. The murder weapon was a single-barrelled, single-loader shotgun, heavy with a stiff pull. She had fired and reloaded at least six times and had remembered to collect all the used cartridge cases, which were never found. The only possible motive appeared to be jealousy caused by Walter Fisher's frequent visits to the cottage at Matfield, although she had never made any objection to them.

Many years later the London *Evening Standard* reviewed a play called *The Earl and the Girl* which was produced at Broadmoor. The last paragraph read: 'One of the most outstanding performances of the night was given by Daphne Brent. She played the part of a fairground dog-trainer's girl friend and did so with an aplomb that would have startled many experienced actors and actresses.'

Because prisoners cannot be identified to the public, Daphne Brent was a pseudonym. Her real name was Florence Iris Ouida Ransom.

CHAPTER 14

The Clue of the Remembrance Day Poppy

It is fortunate for detectives that most murders do have a motive, however obscure, but the relatively rare cases when it appears to have been committed purely for the sake of killing all too frequently involve children. Regardless of the psychological background, the principal difficulty in these cases usually lies in *proving* the link between killer and victim. A case in November 1941 had this extraordinary quality. The circumstances surrounding the deaths of two little girls in Buckinghamshire were completely negative, and the crime was seemingly motiveless. However, Murder Squad detectives were helped once again by the presence of a laundry mark, and by the very thorough documentation of all Service personnel and their movements at that time.

At ten o'clock on the night of Wednesday, 22 November, Detective Chief Inspector George Hatherill was at home in Surrey when he was told by the Yard's central office to report to the Buckinghamshire police headquarters at Chesham. He telephoned to say he would be coming and asked that in the meantime nothing be touched at the scene of the crime.

He was given the brief details: the bodies of two girls, Doreen Hearne, aged eight, and Kathleen Trendle, aged six, had been found in a copse called Rough Wood. Both girls had been stabbed several times in the throat.

There had been heavy rain since the beginning of the month and it was obvious from the dampness of their clothes and the dryness of the ground under their bodies that they had been lying there for some time. On the previous Wednesday the two girls had left school in the village of Penn at 3.30 p.m. and set off for their homes about half a mile away. They had not arrived, and next day searches were organized by the local police, volunteers from the village and the Boy Scouts. It was three days before the bodies were found.

Meanwhile Buckinghamshire police had questioned other children from the school and some of them said that Doreen and Kathleen had gone for a ride in an Army lorry.

When Hatherill and his sergeant arrived they were joined by Sir Bernard Spilsbury. The local inspector told them that a number of people had come forward to say the two girls had been seen sitting in the front of a lorry with a driver. The bodies had been found at a spot eighty-one feet from the south edge of the path which led through the wood. Both girls had their clothing pulled up under their arms, but their underclothes had not been interfered with in any way. Doreen Hearne's left shoe had been found lying near her feet and her overcoat was rolled up on the ground near the body. Kathleen Trendle's left shoe and stocking were missing. Before the bodies had been removed they were photographed exactly as they had been found.

Hatherill, a tall, broad-shouldered man well over six feet in height, was a stickler for examining the scene with minute thoroughness. He led the search, stooping low, looking hard for a yard ahead so as not to step on a clue and obliterate it. Barely twenty-five feet from where Kathleen's body had been found there was a khaki handkerchief and on it a laundry mark – RA 1019. Fifty-six feet from where Doreen had been found was a fawn sock, later identified as Kathleen's. It was hanging on the branch of a fir tree about four feet from the ground. Nearby was her red leather gas-mask case and a few feet away her missing shoe. In another part of the wood was found a hair ribbon, later identified as belonging to Doreen.

The heavy rain had made the path through the wood fairly soft and deep tyre marks showed that a motor vehicle had been driven along it. The marks showed that after a certain distance the vehicle had turned round, crushing the growth on both sides of the path, and had then stopped at a point between the two bodies, which were lying six feet apart from each other on either side of the path. The tyre marks were deeper there and a large area was stained with oil. Hatherill suspected that this was where the vehicle had stopped while the murderer carried the bodies to where they were found. It was clear that the vehicle must have had a bad oil leak which, from the position of the track marks, appeared to have come either from the back axle or one of the rear wheels.

A yard or so from the oil patch, eight feet from the path, Hatherill found a patch of ground stained with blood and another blood patch four feet farther on. Two feet beyond there was a bloodstained leaf. This succession of blood marks suggested to Hatherill that the murderer had paused there while he was carrying the bodies, putting them on the ground while he rested.

Where each article had been found detectives put markers, and then photographs were taken in case reference was required later. Hatherill also ordered plaster casts to be made of the tyre marks, and a large square of the oil-stained earth was dug up and sent off to the Yard laboratory for chemical analysis.

Sir Bernard Spilsbury performed the post-mortem examinations on both bodies. The elder girl, Doreen, had three stab wounds in the neck, one of them a large wound, which looked as though the killer had turned the weapon before pulling it out. She also had six small puncture wounds in her chest, three of which had penetrated one lung, and a fourth which had fractured her third left rib. Her clothes were soaked in blood, saturated with rain and infested with insects.

Kathleen had eleven stab wounds in her throat, each about five-eighths of an inch wide. One had penetrated her spinal column. Spilsbury was sure that the same weapon had been used on both girls and he thought it probably had a blunt point and a single cutting edge which was also blunt. There were no signs of any sexual interference in either case.

The atmosphere of any mortuary in the world is cold and impersonal, but Sir Bernard's next remarks were painful to the big detective, a gentle man who loved children. He said it looked as though both girls had been partially strangled before being stabbed and that they had died slowly, the cause of death being haemorrhage from the wounds. Doreen had lost about six pints of blood and Kathleen about four pints. Samples of their blood were taken for grouping and the detective cut some hair from their heads in case it was needed for comparison later.

Spilsbury's examination also showed that Doreen had last eaten meat with potato and green vegetables and that Kathleen had had a similar meal. It was confirmed by their mothers that the meal was the lunch on the day they disappeared, and that the clothes the children were wearing when they were found murdered were the same as those they had worn when they left home. Mrs Hearne also told Hatherill that Doreen was carrying her gas mask in a black tin case.

Spilsbury's analysis of the stomach contents and the position the food had reached in the intestines, coupled with the facts given by the two mothers, established that the girls had been killed on the afternoon they were taken away.

Since no blood stains had been found at the place where the bodies were discovered, and since the post-mortem examination showed that both girls had lost large quantities of blood, it was obvious that they must have been killed elsewhere. Hatherill immediately ordered an extended search to be made in the wood and of near-by coppices and open spaces to find any spot which was heavily stained with blood. The searchers were also told to look for Doreen's gas mask and warned that it must not be touched in case it had any fingerprints.

As soon as the new search had begun Hatherill and his sergeant interviewed the children who had last seen the two girls. Among a large number of children interviewed were three schoolgirls all aged eleven, who had seen Doreen and Kathleen after they left school. They told of seeing them talking to a lorry driver at the crossroads and they described him as aged about twenty-six with medium-coloured hair, a reddish complexion and wearing steel-rimmed spectacles and a Service cap. The girls were unable to help much about the lorry, whereas the boys who were interviewed were able to describe it in some detail but had hardly noticed the driver. One boy, Edward Page, aged twelve, had cycled past the lorry while it was stationary and another boy, aged ten, had walked past it. They both agreed that it was a fifteen-hundredweight Fordson, camouflaged to look like a wireless truck but without an aerial, and that it had a canvas hood which was lower than the top of the driver's cabin. They remembered that on the nearside front mudguard the figure 43 was painted in white on a red and blue square and on the offside front mudguard were the letters JP in blue, on a red circle. Edward Page mentioned that in the right-hand top corner of the radiator mesh was a Remembrance Day poppy and that there was a figure 5 on the offside front lamp.

Hatherill needed to know which unit of the Royal Artillery used the markings described by the boys and the War Office quickly identified it as 86th Field Regiment, which had been in the West Country until 16 November. It had then moved by stages to the East Coast and from 18–21 November it had been at Hazlemere, Buckinghamshire, a few miles from Rough Wood where the bodies had been found. It had then moved on to Yoxford, in Suffolk.

That night a message was sent to the Yard and all Home Counties' forces, requesting an inquiry to be made at every laundry to find the name of the person to whom the number RA 1019, found on the khaki handkerchief, was allotted. And, later, the detectives discovered that steel-rimmed spectacles were an official issue to men in the armed forces and that the blade of an official issue Army knife had a blade five-eighths of an inch wide.

The day had begun at seven o'clock in the morning and now stopped at midnight. There had been no break for food or rest, which was, and still is, a fairly average day on a murder inquiry.

The next move was to establish the route the lorry had taken after it left the crossroads. A number of people were found who had seen the girls riding in the front of the lorry on the day they had disappeared and police were able to pinpoint the places. The last time it was seen on that day was on the main road leading to the wood. Hatherill then called for a car and went over the route and was then driven by the most direct route to Hazlemere, where the artillery unit had camped, and then back to the crossroads. The speedometer reading showed a distance of fourteen miles.

George Hatherill was a thorough man. Some of his colleagues found his insistence on detail infuriating but he was a determined investigator who left nothing to chance. So he had a local surveyor make two scale maps, one showing the school, the crossroads and the route taken by the lorry; the other was Rough Wood showing the exact position of the various articles found. He was thinking ahead. It might be necessary to point them out to a judge and jury.

The searchers in the wood had found nothing, but the inquiries made at laundries bore fruit. The mark RA 1019 had been allotted by the Royal Standard Laundry at Chiswick to a Harold Hill, who was in the Army.

When the Yard men arrived at Yoxford, Suffolk, where the 86th Field Regiment had moved, they told the colonel the details of the murders and what their inquiries had established. The four battery commanders were called in and, after Hatherill had repeated his story, one of them told of one lorry that was giving trouble with a bad oil leak from the rear axle.

'What is the name of the driver?' inquired Hatherill.

'Hill,' said the officer. The description he gave of the man fitted well except that the officer thought Hill wore tortoiseshell-framed spectacles. Then the detectives were taken to a barn five miles away and there they saw the lorry. Underneath it was a large patch of oil near the back nearside wheel.

The lorry was searched. There were large reddish-black stains on the tarpaulin which, after an elementary test, proved to be human blood. What was astonishing to Hatherill was the amazing accuracy of the twelve-year-old Edward Page's observation. His description was complete in every detail, including the unit number and the poppy. Hatherill was particularly pleased about the poppy, for there had been no other reports of an Army lorry showing a similar decoration. A sample of oil was taken from the lorry for comparison with that found in the wood and then the Yard man compared the tyres with the plaster casts he had brought with him. They fitted exactly.

I don't know what Chief Inspector Hatherill said then, in his deep, rather growly voice, but I fancy it was something like, 'Now, perhaps, we can see Master Hill.'

Gunner Harold Hill was brought in, wearing tortoiseshell-framed spectacles. Hatherill told him he was investigating a murder and wanted to examine his belongings. The uniform he was wearing appeared to be without suspicion but in his kit-bag was a spare uniform which was very damp. Hill

153

explained it by saying he had been out in the rain, but the trouser pockets and the lining of the tunic were far too damp to have been caused by rain. It was obvious that the uniform had been soaked in water and the reason was equally obvious for, on the front and back of the tunic, on the sleeves and on the trousers were spots that looked like blood – the spots were where they could be expected if the wearer had carried a badly bleeding child over his shoulder for some distance. There were also some shirts and handkerchiefs in the kit-bag which carried the laundry mark RA 1019.

There was yet another piece of evidence which was to contribute to Hill's undoing. All army drivers had to keep a log book of their journeys, entering the speedometer reading at the beginning and end of each day. By pure chance the battery commander had inspected the log books on 20 November. The entry in Hill's log book for the previous day, the day of the murder, recorded 4,420 miles at the beginning and 4,429 at the end. Yet his speedometer reading when the check was made the next day showed 4,472. Hill had made an authorized journey of nine miles on 19 November and on the next day two authorized journeys, totalling twenty-nine miles in all. He could not account for the extra fourteen miles. Hatherill was sure he could – he had travelled the route and checked the mileage.

Hill was a shadowy character, an average soldier who obeyed most orders, and the sort of man who would be least suspected of the murder of two small girls. He made a statement at the police station, mostly about his routine duties. He said that on the day of the nineteenth he had eaten sausages and mash in the canteen, but had seen no one there he knew. He had no idea how a handkerchief with his laundry mark had been found near the bodies. He claimed he had lost his knife months before, and refused to admit the tarpaulin came from his lorry.

The detectives also learned that Hill had been issued with a pair of steel-rimmed spectacles when he joined the regiment. Hill's clothing and the tarpaulin were sent to the laboratory and the oil sample taken from his lorry to the same analyst who was working on the oil-stained earth from Rough Wood. They matched. The blood on the tarpaulin was the same group as that of the victims; some hairs which had been found on Hill's clothes were similar to those taken from the bodies in the mortuary.

Hatherill charged Hill with the murders but he still continued his inquiries. The detective liked to extract the last ounce of evidence.

He found out that Hill had never suffered an injury that had caused haemorrhage, that up to the morning of 20 November, the day after the murder, Hill had always worn steel-rimmed spectacles but afterwards had worn tortoiseshell, that he had lent his knife to other soldiers at the end of October and that the menu on 19 November had not included sausages and mash.

At his trial Hill pleaded not guilty but the jury did not believe him and he was hanged in April 1942. It was a totally senseless crime with no motive anyone could determine. Hatherill later claimed it was not a very difficult case to solve, but his meticulous investigation left absolutely no loopholes and no reason for doubt.

CHAPTER 15

The Killer of Prostitutes

Following a case in April 1942 a library of palmprints came into being at the Yard. The proprietor of a pawnbroker's shop in Shoreditch, East London, was hit over the head with the butt of a revolver. He died eight days later. Detectives searching the shop for clues had found no fingerprints but inside a safe door they came upon a palmprint. The inquiry led to two men being arrested – George Silverosa and Samuel Dashwood. Both had records and the palmprint was traced to Silverosa.

However, palmprints were unlikely to supersede fingerprints as important evidence, and in this field there is one remarkable man who in 1942 was in the prime of a career spanning more than thirty years.

Frederick Cherrill was part of the back-up team which every murder investigation now relies on and which had increased in importance dramatically since the beginning of the 1930s. Such men worked away from the glare of publicity surrounding the two men at the centre, but in many cases their specialist experience, built up continuously over years, was essential to 'Guv'nors' coming in from more generalized crime outside. Fred Cherrill, who did the brilliant fingerprint work on the Williams case (page 136) and who was always amazed at the 'not guilty' verdict, joined the Fingerprint Department as a constable in 1923 and rose to command it as a Detective Chief Superintendent. He was Oxfordshire born and always wore a bowler hat. It was seldom he did not visit a murder scene, and he was probably one of the most photographed Yard men ever. He was popular with newspaper cameramen because, while he would never pose, he would make sure he was in a position to be seen easily and would allow time for pictures to be taken. In his day Cherrill could read a fingerprint better than anyone else, and any detective investigating a case of murder was pleased to see him. Out of his hundreds of cases few are more telling than some of his wartime successes.

Detective Chief Inspector William Salisbury particularly welcomed Cherrill in 1941 when he was assigned to investigate the killing of Mrs Theodora Greenhill, widow of an Army officer, who lived in a flat in Kensington.

Her body had been found by one of her daughters who, when she could get no reply from ringing the doorbell, let herself in. In the drawing-room her mother was lying on the floor, dead, with a handkerchief over her face.

It was obvious that Mrs Greenhill had been attacked while sitting at her desk, for Salisbury found a sheet of note-paper on which was written in a bold hand: 'Received from Dr H. D. Trevor the s . . .' The handwriting finished with a fluttering line running down the page from the end of the 's'. Mrs Greenhill had been writing when she had been struck from behind. The pen she had been holding had marked the page as she had fallen to the floor. The murderer had then tied a ligature tightly round her neck and strangled her.

When Cherrill arrived the body was still in the same position. From the lack of disorder in the room he deduced there had been no struggle on the part of the victim, but the drawers of the bureau were open and had been ransacked.

The murderer had smashed a beer bottle on his victim's head and there were fragments of glass on the floor and many more in a waste-paper basket near by. In all, Cherrill collected ninety-four fragments. On four of them were un-mistakable finger marks. On top of a small table near the body was a thumb mark in blood and there was also a mark on the underside of the table where the murderer had gripped it momentarily. In the bedroom was a small tin money box, which had been forced open with a nail-file. The nail-file had been thrown to the floor and the money box was empty, but there was another fingerprint on its surface.

Then Cherrill studied the receipt and saw the name Trevor. The name was familiar and Cherrill was certain his prints were in the Criminal Record Office. He sent for the records of all men using the name Trevor, and when they arrived Cherrill, using a magnifying glass he always carried, compared them with the prints found on the four pieces of glass on the cash box and on the table. A few minutes later, still in the room where Mrs Greenhill lay dead, Cherrill told Chief Inspector Salisbury that the man he wanted was Harold Dorian Trevor.

Salisbury and his team were incredulous at the speed of the identification but happy to act on the opinion of Fred Cherrill. Within twenty-four hours Trevor was arrested in

Rhyl, Wales, as he was leaving a telephone box and, in due course, he appeared at the Old Bailey.

Despite his style Trevor had always been an unsuccessful crook. His lack of success is revealed by the fact that he had spent forty of his sixty-two years in prison. The style came from a good education, a solid, comfortable background and a good appearance. He possessed great charm, wore a monocle and used a remarkable number of names in the course of his criminal career – 'Lord Reginald Hubert', 'Sir Francis Ford' and 'Commander Crichton' were examples. His exploits were petty but he appears to have loved the drama of the courtroom. Every time he was found guilty by a jury he could not resist making an impassioned plea from the dock.

In this case he had called on Mrs Greenhill and told her he had come from an estate agent and understood she wanted to let her flat furnished. It was while she was writing a receipt for his first instalment of rent that he had hit her on the head. When he was found guilty of her murder he stayed true to form. In loud, ringing tones, he cried, 'If I am called upon to take my stand in the cold, grey dawn of the early morning I pray that God in His mercy will gently turn my mother's face away as I pass into the shadows. No fear touches my heart. My heart is dead. It died when my mother left me.'

Fred Cherrill used to recall that while Trevor was in the death cell awaiting execution he wrote a dramatic document, part of which read: 'I have lived my life not as I would have liked to have lived it, but as it was forced upon me by fate. I was educated at a first-class school in Birmingham, and was the friend and playmate of men who are bishops today. Some of them are sitting in the Episcopal Chairs, while I am waiting the short walk from the condemned cell to the scaffold.'

Trevor's aim had always been to live in comfort without working by means of the spell cast upon credulous women by his charm, his eyeglass and his stories of money always coming, but never there. The last time he had been released from prison a friendly policeman had given him a warning. He pointed out that as Trevor grew old his attractions would fade; he would become desperate and turn to more serious crime, perhaps to murder. Trevor was amused. He had never resorted to violence.

The case of Trevor was only remarkable for the speed of Cherrill's work on the fingerprints, although I doubt if he would have considered it so. But, within a few months, he was part of the team investigating a series of 'Ripper' murders, which, because they all occurred in blacked-out London in February 1942, struck as much terror in five days as Hitler's rain of bombs.

The first was on 9 February, when the body of Miss Evelyn Hamilton was found in an air-raid shelter in Montague Place, Marylebone. She had been strangled. The shelter was one of the kind that lined the streets – brick-built with a seat along one side. The body was found by an electrician and the local police were called. Miss Hamilton was a highly respectable woman of forty, a chemist's assistant who had moved from Hornchurch, Essex, to London. Her body lay on the floor near the door, face upward. The woman's own silk scarf had been wound round her face, like a gag, and her clothes were disarranged. At her side were a matchbox and a powder compact which appeared to have fallen out of her handbag. Near by was an electric torch, an aid carried by most people at that time.

In the dim light of the shelter Cherrill noticed some marks on the victim's neck and, from their position, he deduced that the murderer was left-handed. When he looked again with a powerful light and his hand-lens he confirmed that opinion, but he could not find any helpful clues. The marks were bruises caused by fingers at strong pressure. There were no prints on the handbag except Miss Hamilton's own.

Early next morning Cherrill was called to a flat in Wardour Street, Soho, where a Mrs Evelyn Oatley had been found murdered. She was lying across a bed on a flock mattress and she was practically naked, the victim of a sadistic attack reminiscent of the Jack the Ripper murders.

Evelyn Oatley was a prostitute – also known as Nina Ward. There was little sign of disorder in the room. Stockings hung on a rail and the room looked almost peaceful apart from what was on the bed. Near the body was a pair of curling tongs and a heavily bloodstained tin-opener, and that was the weapon used in the mutilation of the victim's body. At one side of the room was a couch and there the woman's handbag was found. It was open, as if the contents had fallen out, but inside was a piece of a mirror. Cherrill took the tin-opener and the piece of mirror and then, as he had done with the earlier victim, he took the woman's fingerprints.

There were many fingerprints on the mirror which belonged to the dead woman. But there was one alien thumbprint. There were also faint finger impressions on the tin-opener. Cherrill was certain that they had been made by a left hand. They were so arranged that it looked as though the utensil had been grasped by the murderer during his attack on the woman – certainly they were not in a position for the innocent use of opening a tin. And some aspects of the thumbprint on the mirror indicated that it too had been made by a left hand.

Had any corresponding prints been in the files at the Yard, swift indentification would have been made, but there were none. The killer of these two women, if it was the same man, had never been in the hands of the police.

Margaret Lowe was the third woman to be murdered in the West End of London within a week. She was found strangled in her small room. The discovery had been made by a neighbour who noticed an uncollected parcel outside the door and called the police. They could get no reply so they broke down the door.

The flat was scantily furnished except for a single bed, a table, a small carpet and a rug. Mrs Margaret Florence Lowe was a handsome, finely-built woman, known locally as 'Pearl'. On the black eiderdown near the foot of the bed lay a woman's skirt, coat and jumper which looked as though they had been dropped when the wearer undressed. The

Above 'A group of Scotland Yard detectives in various disguises. Photographed before setting out on a special observation mission which resulted in the important capture of a cunning gang of thieves.' From the Scotland Yard archives c.1922.

Left Crippen and LeNeve coming off *SS Montrose* at Liverpool after their arrest.

The cellar where Voisin hid the remains of Emilienne Gerard's body.

Major Armstrong in the dock at his trial.

George Joseph Smith in 1912 with one of his victims, Bessie Mundy.

Patrick Mahon.

Opposite One of today's 'Murder Bags'. These were first developed after the Mahon case.

Sir Bernard Spilsbury in his laboratory.

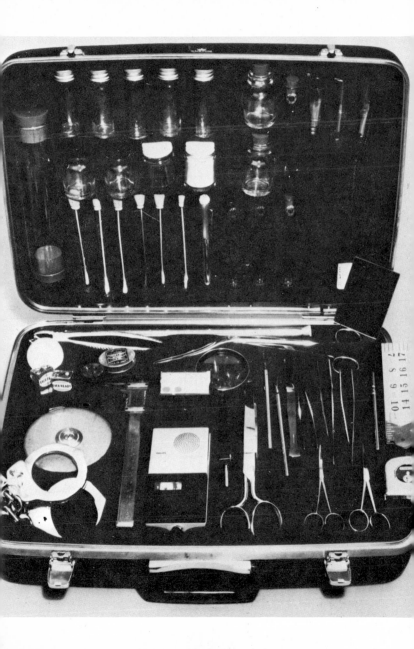

The trunk and some of Minnie
Bonati's belongings.

Minnie Bonati, victim of the
Charing Cross trunk murder.

The Max Kassel case: the victim.

The Max Kassel case: the accused, Roger Vernon, at his trial in Paris.

Mrs Fisher and her daughter Freda, victims of Mrs Ouida Ransom.

Joan Pearl Wolfe, victim of August Sangret.

Peter Griffiths, murderer of June Anne Devaney in Blackburn.

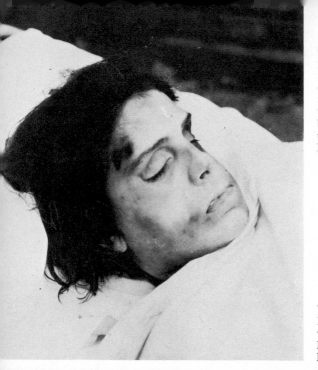

One of the
pictures shown in
Luton shops and
cinemas to seek
identification of
the woman's
body found in
the River Lea in
November 1943.

The body of
Keith Arthur,
victim of the
Dunstable
Murder.

Leslie Green, ex-chauffeur of Mrs Wiltshaw.

George Salter, scientific guide and mentor to many murder investigations, at work.

The death scene in Braybrook Street, Shepherd's Bush, 12 August 1966.

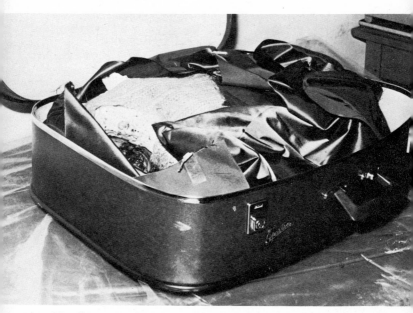

The olive-green suitcase containing the upper torso of Sarabjit Kaur, found on a train in 1968.

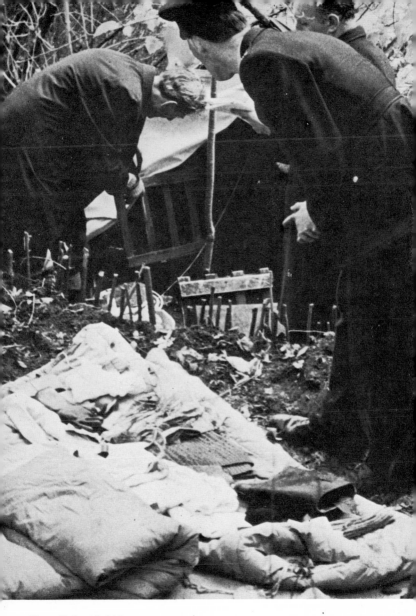
Harry Roberts's hideout.

Reginald, Charles and Ronald Kray.

Erskine Durrant Burrows after his arrest in Bermuda.

The drainage inspection shaft in which Lesley Whittle's body was found.

The Black Panther's working gear.

eiderdown was removed to reveal the body, naked, with a much darned silk stocking tied tightly round her neck. The injuries to the lower part of her stomach were even more hideous than those inflicted upon Mrs Oatley. By the body were a number of bloodstained weapons.

Detective Chief Inspector Edward Greeno had been sent from the Murder Squad to take over this series of murders and, while he was talking to Sir Bernard Spilsbury, the pathologist, about the first three he received a message from the Yard. Another woman had been found murdered in Sussex Gardens in Paddington.

The fourth victim lived in a two-room ground-floor flat. She was Doris Jouannet, the thirty-two-year-old wife of an hotelier aged seventy. Her extra-marital career had ended only one hour before. The body was still warm. She also had been strangled with a silk stocking and mutilated like the others. The murderer had held up a breast and almost sliced off a nipple with a razor blade. Spilsbury examined the wound and said, 'When you catch him I'd like to know if he is left-handed.'

Meanwhile Cherrill was searching for clues in the room where Mrs Lowe had died. He saw that a candle had been wrenched from a glass candlestick on the mantelpiece. The candle was lying on the bed by the body and Cherrill found fingerprints on the candlestick. In the kitchen he found a half-empty bottle of stout. There were fingermarks on it and on a tumbler in the bedroom. The marks on the candlestick were made by a right hand and Cherrill made a quick experiment. He placed himself in the position of the murderer. He was satisfied that a right-handed person, in snatching the candle, would place his left hand on the base of the candlestick. The process would be reversed in the case of a left-handed person. Once again, the work of a left-handed killer.

Chief Inspector Greeno had by now discovered that the man he wanted was a murderer for gain, for in each case the women's handbags had been rifled. It was common ground that he was also a sex maniac. Two of the victims were prostitutes, and one was a part-time prostitute. Greeno set

161

up his headquarters at Tottenham Court Road police station, roughly in the centre of the area where the murders had occurred, and then had his detectives make a systematic tour of Paddington and Soho, asking every street girl if they knew of a Jack the Ripper type, or anyone who was particularly violent.

Fred Cherrill went to the Sussex Gardens address of Doris Jouannet and, in the dust on the mantelpiece, saw faint outlines as though some articles had been removed. One mark suggested a fountain pen and the other possibly a pocket comb. And in a drawer of the dressing-table was a roll of Elastoplast from which someone had cut a narrow strip.

The murderer had now struck on Sunday, Monday, Tuesday and Thursday. Greeno was interested as to why the killer took a night off on Wednesday.

While he was puzzling over the problem dramatic news reached him that while he was still in the room with the corpse of Doris Jouannet, another girl had been attacked in the West End by a young airman. He had picked her up and persuaded her, somewhat against her will, to join him in a drink and a sandwich at the Trocadero, then an old-fashioned restaurant near Piccadilly Circus. Then he had walked with her across Piccadilly to a side street near a popular public house called the Captain's Cabin. There he had suddenly kissed her and grabbed her throat. A young man delivering bottle-party drinks from an off-licence saw the girl's torch go out, saw the flash of silk stockings as her legs shot from under her and heard her scream. Something dropped on the pavement and there was the sound of footsteps, running away. The young man picked up from the street a service gas mask and then he helped the woman to her feet and took her to West End Central police station.

She described her attacker as about five feet seven inches tall and said he wore the white flash in his forage cap of an officer cadet. She also remembered he had wide-set green eyes. Inside the gas-mask case was the service number of its owner, 525987. A quick check with RAF Records identified the number as that allotted to Gordon Frederick Cummins, a twenty-eighty-year-old cadet. He was soon located at a billet in St John's Wood.

Chief Inspector Greeno records that a mistake was made then in that somebody telephoned the billet asking the duty corporal to inform the police when Cummins returned. He also mentioned that a girl had been attacked and a gas mask found. At 3.30 that morning Cummins got that message and disappeared. But the dragnet was out and he was arrested in ninety minutes, charged with assault with intent to commit grievous bodily harm and remanded in custody.

Inquiries about Cummins and his recent movements were at first discouraging. He could not have murdered Evelyn Hamilton, Evelyn Oatley or Margaret Lowe because he was in billets at the time. The billet pass-book proved the times he was there. His room-mates said they saw him go to bed and he was certainly in bed when they woke in the morning.

Greeno went back to questioning the street girls but none of them were able, or inclined, to assist the police. However, Greeno was not easily put off and he chased anything which looked like a likely lead. One telephone call got him to Brixton on the promise of some information and he went to meet the person in the Effra Arms. While he was in there his police car vanished, although it had been immobilized. Greeno said afterwards: 'It only needed that to get into the papers to make me look very bright indeed, and some smart manoeuvring was called for in the underworld to trace the car. That didn't take long, but the thieves sent a message back: "We know the Guv'nor always uses his Wolseley or a Railton. This is an Austin, so what's the game?" We convinced them that the stolen Austin was in fact a police car used by me and it was returned within three days to the forecourt at Scotland Yard.'

Despite that embarrassing episode Greeno continued questioning prostitutes and, at last, he was successful. Two of them remembered that a woman called Phyllis O'Dwyer had told them of an encounter she had had with a customer on the Thursday night between the time Mrs Jouannet was murdered and when the girl was attacked near the Captain's

163

Cabin. Greeno found Mrs O'Dwyer and she told him of how she had met an RAF cadet wearing the white flash outside Oddenino's Restaurant in Regent Street and had taken him home. It had been snowing and was freezing cold and her room was chilly, even with a gas-fire, so she kept on her boots and a necklace. The necklace nearly cost her her life, and the boots saved it, for he tried to strangle her with the former and she kicked him off the bed with the latter. She ordered him out and he paid her ten pounds. Luckily she still had the money.

Cummins was on remand in Brixton gaol and he made a statement denying everything. He signed it with his left hand. And there was another helpful sign. Doris Jouannet had owned a wrist-watch like one found in Cummins's possession. The one he had was padded at the back with a strip of Elastoplast that fitted exactly into the cut roll found at her flat. He also had a comb that fitted the outline in the dust found at Doris Jouannet's flat. And in his best uniform at his billet was found a fountain pen which fitted another dusty outline in the Sussex Gardens flat. Greeno showed these things to old Mr Jouannet and he remembered he had bought the pen for his wife's birthday and the comb had been the subject of a slight squabble. He had noticed it had some teeth missing and had offered to buy her a new one. She had spoken sharply and told him to mind his own business.

A search of Cummins's billet yielded a green pencil that Evelyn Hamilton had borrowed from a friend. It had been discarded in the dustbin. And a check on the last pay parade attended by Cummins, working out where he had stood in order of payment, gave the numbers of the notes which matched those given to Mrs O'Dwyer.

His alibi of being in his billet at the times of the murders was smashed when police found an airman who had checked back one night and asked the corporal to check Cummins in as well. And then another airman admitted that although he had seen Cummins go to bed, he had also seen him get up again and go down the fire-escape. He knew that because they had gone out together!

The evidence was now coming in fast. On the night Evelyn Hamilton died Cummins had had little money in the early evening yet the next day he had been able to treat a friend to a night out in the West End. Evelyn Hamilton, who had planned a trip north, had about £80 in her handbag. It was empty when it was found by her body.

Greeno discovered that Cummins had gone home with another prostitute before he had murdered Evelyn Oatley. He traced her to a room in Frith Street, Soho. Greeno wrote: 'It was just one room divided into two by a partition that was a blanket on a clothes line. While I talked to her, I suddenly felt we were not alone. There were two peepholes in the blanket and behind those holes was a pair of eyes. While she was telling me how Cummins had brought her home, given her a couple of pounds and then leapt to his feet and vanished I also leapt to my feet and tore down the blanket. Behind it was a Negro.'

He had been there on the night the airman was in the room, and but for those eyes staring through the blanket, which Cummins must have seen and taken fright at, that girl too might have died.

When Cummins was first formally charged at Bow Street Cherrill took his fingerprints and compared them with the prints on the tin-opener found on the bed where Mrs Oatley was killed. The clearest mark was made by the left little finger of the accused man. The mark on the mirror taken from her handbag was made by his left thumb. The finger-marks on the base of the candlestick taken from the flat of Mrs Lowe were made by the fingers of the right hand of Cummins, as were the marks on the beer bottle and the tumbler.

Cummins was brought to his trial at the Old Bailey in April 1942. He was tried for only one murder, that of Mrs Evelyn Oatley – normal practice when a person had been committed for trial on more than one murder charge.

Obviously, if a jury knew there were other charges their verdict might be prejudiced and, in this case, it nearly was.

Cherrill was in the witness box, about to give his evidence, when he noticed the jury had been given copies of the fingerprints of another case on which Cummins had been indicted but was not being tried. Even at that distance he could read the difference in the prints. He told the court what he had seen and, after a slight delay for legal discussion, Mr Justice Asquith discharged the jury. A new jury was sworn and the trial reopened. It closed when Cummins was sentenced to death.

Cummins had come from a good family and was well educated. He had been married to the daughter of a theatrical producer, and his companions accused him of being a 'Walter Mitty' character, and of talking with an assumed Oxford accent. He told them he was entitled to use 'Honourable' before his name because he was the illegitimate son of a peer, and they called him 'the Duke'. Doctors found no sign or history of insanity. He had been dismissed from countless jobs for dishonesty and had any of those cases been reported to the police Cummins would have been registered at the Criminal Record Office with his fingerprints. In that case the left-handed strangler might have been caught earlier.

CHAPTER 16

The Blade Like a Parrot's Beak

The body was partly skeleton and some of it was mummified. It might never have been discovered at all but for Marine William Moore crawling through the scrubland of Hankley Common, Surrey, on an army exercise. It was the army who had, unwittingly, made a nearly perfect hiding place for a corpse. Bulldozers had pushed earth into great mounds to make a training ground for tracked fighting vehicles and someone had used a deep rut for a grave. He had covered the body and the heather had grown over it again. But on the morning in October 1942, a half-track vehicle had moved the earth again and, like a signpost, an outstretched arm appeared above the ground.

Marine Moore was taking part in a mock battle, but as soon as it was over he reported his strange find and later that afternoon one of the Yard's toughest detectives, Chief Inspector Edward Greeno, was at the spot. He was a remarkable man with an enviable record of success.

In his career this man with powerful shoulders and deceptively sleepy eyes had cleaned up the racecourse gangs and cleared the London streets of gangs of pickpockets.

During the First World War he served as a radio operator on an ammunition ship. It was a highly dangerous pastime but it suited Greeno, for while the ship was being loaded at night he was able to ride his big motor-cycle to London for a few hectic hours of pleasure. He was a great racing man and always calculated the odds in anything he did. He took chances, but they were deliberate and were reasoned. His sergeant always had strict instructions to include a bottle of whisky in the Murder Bag, which was certainly not on the official list of contents. But bitter experience had taught Greeno that investigations frequently take place in areas like open fields where there are no creature comforts.

Hankley Common near Godalming was such a place and the nip in the air prompted Greeno's sergeant, Fred Hodge, to mention that the whisky was present in case of emergency.

The detective saw that the earth which covered the corpse was four inches at its deepest. The body was that of a young woman. She had worn a green flowered dress, now dank and rotten. The body was lying face down, with legs apart, the right arm pushed out, the left bent under the trunk. Apart

167

from the dress, with its cheap lace collar, the dead woman had worn a brassière and a pair of French knickers, a vest and a slip. Her shoes were missing and she had worn red-striped blue woollen socks which were torn in places. Round her neck was a kerchief, quite loose as though she had worn it as a head scarf and it had slipped down.

Her skull had disintegrated into twenty pieces, leaving only a tuft of short-cropped bleached hair and scraps of shrivelled scalp. That was all there was to identify the body in an area teeming with soldiers, English, Canadian and American. Nearby was Jasper Camp, where illiterates from the Canadian backwoods were given courses in English. There was another camp where Americans who had joined the Canadian Army were allowed to transfer to one of their own units, staying only two weeks, and there was also a camp for British marines where they were trained for battle fitness. In all more than a hundred thousand men had been in the area during the past three months.

Dr Keith Simpson, the pathologist at Guy's Hospital, London, visited the scene with Dr Eric Gardner, the Surrey police pathologist. Simpson took the body to Guy's Hospital so that it could be cleaned, since rodents had feasted on the buried flesh and maggots abounded.

Greeno organized a dragnet of sixty policemen and strung them out across the countryside at two-yard intervals, looking for clues. He told them to march slowly, looking only at the ground immediately in front. They started that day and carried on for many weeks.

The soil was raked and sifted. Hundreds of bits of bone were found and some teeth. Dr Gardner, in his surgery at Weybridge, gradually built up the dead woman's skull with one large piece missing at the back which was thought to have been caused by a smashing blow which probably caused her death.

But the rebuilding of the skull did not tell Greeno who the woman was or for how long she had been dead. At first the doctors thought she might have been dead for many weeks but then, after more experiments and noting the rate of growth of the heather, they decided that she had died about one month previously.

Meanwhile Greeno's meticulous search was paying dividends. The woman's right shoe was found three hundred and thirty yards from the body and the left shoe twenty-five yards further away. Close by, on the bank of a small stream, was found a canvas bag containing a rosary and some soap. Between the shoes police found a heavy birch stake. It was slightly over a yard long, five inches thick and weighed two and a half pounds. About six inches from the thicker end of the stake, where the bark was bared, were a number of fine hairs caught in the splintered bark. Microscopy showed these to be identical with the hairs taken from the dead woman's scalp. The scientists were in no doubt that the stake was the weapon which had killed her.

A personal problem intervened for the detectives – there was no room at the local inn and although they were to see little of bed they needed sleep sometimes. Greeno guessed, correctly, that the presence of policemen would have the locals thinking their late-night drinking might be inhibited. He instructed Hodge to let it be known that the regular pattern of drinking would not be disturbed and, he added, 'Let them know that I'm not a teetotaller either.' Rooms were quickly made available.

Dr Keith Simpson had deduced from his post-mortem examination that the dead girl was aged about twenty and he also reported to Greeno the presence of a number of stab wounds. There were three wounds to the left side of the top of the head as though in an assault by a right-handed person from the front. There were seven protective wounds of the same kind on the right forearm and hand. The wounds showed one character in common – they had been caused by a sharp pointed weapon like a knife or a marlinspike. In two of the protective injuries there had been a hooking out of tissues which suggested the weapon was curved or hooked at the end.

An injury to her mouth, which had dislodged the two upper front teeth, suggested a heavy blow there or that she

169

had fallen heavily on her face. And there was the heavy blow on the back of her head, possibly inflicted while she was on the ground. The fact that the right cheek-bone was fractured supported this theory as it suggested that it was caused by counter pressure from the ground as her head took the impact of the blow.

There were also wounds on her right lower leg which had been sustained after death. The tears in her skin corresponded with the tears in the woollen sock. The injuries were ragged and looked as though they had been caused by dragging the body across rough ground studded with stones and tree stumps.

While the search on the common continued Greeno started to make inquiries among the illiterates in Jasper Camp. Many of them were half-breeds and some swarthy Cree Indians. A Canadian brigadier told Greeno, 'They are good men, great fighters. Sometimes a bit sullen, though, and sometimes with a streak of real savage.' Since the savagery of the murder was clearly apparent Greeno began to concentrate on the Cree Indians, but the men themselves were not helpful. Suspicious of authority and, in particular, of policemen, they spoke little, but their dark, brooding eyes, fixed immovably on the face of the questioner, implied their mood of non-co-operation.

Greeno then turned to the local policemen, and there he found a gem. Constable Tim Halloran, stationed at Godalming, remembered a woman who looked as though she had been living rough and, in July, he had taken her to the police station for questioning together with her boyfriend.

Halloran recalled that the man had been an Indian type and in his note-book he had written his name. It was August Sangret, aged twenty-eight, of the Regina Rifles, stationed at Jasper Camp. He had also made a note of the woman's name, Joan Pearl Wolfe. He described her as five feet four inches tall with big breasts and big uneven teeth. She had dressed like a tramp but had a good speaking voice and she had worn a crucifix.

At Jasper Camp Greeno talked to the commanding officer about Sangret. The major remembered a young woman who had looked as though she was living rough, so much so that he had given her £1 for food and shelter. He also knew that Sangret had lived with her on the camp-site in wigwams that he built Red Indian style by binding down a growing sapling to make a frame which he thatched with heather and bracken. He had been disciplined for not sleeping in barracks. The major knew the name of Joan Pearl Wolfe because Sangret had talked of marrying her, though he had never asked for official permission.

Greeno had a suspect for the murder but he did not want to talk to Sangret too early. He wanted more evidence, and he ran into an unexpected snag. The course at Jasper Camp was ending and Sangret qualified for a fortnight's leave, which began on the following Monday. Few details of the case had leaked to the press and, in any event, the newspapers were full of news of the war, but if a story appeared while Sangret was away he was not likely to return. Greeno asked the major if he would postpone Sangret's leave to give him more time before the confrontation and he agreed to try. He also said he would mention Joan Pearl Wolfe and ask Sangret if he still thought of marrying her.

The major reported back to Greeno over the week-end. Sangret had told him that the woman had gone away and that he was no longer interested in her. Under those circumstances he was unable to postpone the man's leave. Sangret was due to draw his pay and pick up his travel warrant next Monday and travel to Glasgow.

It was then that Greeno had to take one of his biggest gambles. He decided to postpone Sangret's leave himself. 'I'll have to see him today,' he said. 'I didn't want to but I must.'

He recalled the occasion later when he wrote: 'While the man paraded for pay I waited in the major's office with Sergeant Hodge and the local Superintendent Webb. Nobody else knew we were there except the provost sergeant, a wily old warrior called Wade who had been in the

171

Coldstreams in World War One, and who figured that Scotland Yard would not be there unless something serious was afoot. When Sangret had checked in his kit and blankets, drawn his pay and warrants and was heading for the camp gate, one of Wade's men called him back. "Hey, soldier, you're wanted in the guard room." '

Sangret waited in the guard room and went on waiting. He was nervous and drumming his fingers on the wooden tables. He asked Corporal Stiles for permission to go to the shower-room to wash his hands but when he got there he found the water was cut off. He stayed there for a few minutes and then was taken to see Chief Inspector Greeno, who recalled the first sight of his suspect.

'He was a handsome brute,' he wrote, 'stocky, not more than about five feet seven inches tall, with a deep chest and massive shoulders tapering to a ballet dancer's waist. His hair was oily black and his face lean and swarthy.'

Greeno asked him about his friendship with Joan Pearl Wolfe, but he did not mention she was dead. In fact, he was still not sure of the identity of the victim. After a while Greeno suggested the talk should continue in the police station and Sangret agreed. Sergeant Fred Hodge wrote fifty-eight pages of statement, more than seventeen thousand words, in which Sangret described his association with the woman and how they had lived on intimate terms in various shacks in the woods and in wigwams near his camp from July until September. On the fourteenth of the month, he said, she had failed to keep an appointment and he had never seen her again. He had never reported her missing to the civilian police, but had mentioned to a military policeman that she had gone away.

He claimed he had met her in a Godalming public house after her boy-friend, a Canadian called Francis, had been sent home. She was bedraggled and dirty but that evening they had made love. After that he built wigwams where they stayed and later they had moved into a derelict cricket pavilion until an air-raid warden turned them out. He suggested that after 14 September, when he claimed he had last seen her, she had gone off with a Sudetan Czech soldier in the Canadian Army, or with an American soldier.

When the statement was finished and Sangret had signed it Greeno showed him the rosary found on the common, the cheap red and blue socks, a piece cut from her dress and her shoes – one with the wedge sole hanging off.

Sangret said, 'I guess you have found her. Everything points to me. I guess I shall get the blame.'

Greeno said, 'Yes, she is dead.'

'She might have killed herself,' Sangret said.

Nothing had emerged from that long interview to enable Greeno to make a charge and he had to let Sangret proceed on his leave to Glasgow where he had a woman waiting to greet him.

While the statement was being taken, Sangret's kit was taken from the quartermaster at the camp. One of his blankets had been washed not long before but there were still three small stains that looked as though they might be blood, although an analyst was unable to say so positively. Nevertheless Greeno thought the marks appeared where he would expect to find them if a victim about five feet four inches high were stabbed and wrapped in the blanket. He found a policewoman of the same height and wrapped her in the blanket – the marks were in the same places as the wounds on the body.

The dragnet on the common had brought in some more finds. Behind the derelict cricket pavilion was found a pair of stockings and a black elastic garter, a knitting book and four pieces of sacking. Not far away police found a little white elephant charm and a letter which Joan Pearl Wolfe had written to Sangret when she had been in hospital for a few days. They also found an identity card, mildewed and illegible until Scotland Yard's laboratory deciphered the name – Joan Pearl Wolfe. The last find was the crucifix Constable Halloran had seen her wearing. It was twisted round a straggling branch as though it had been torn from her neck when she was running through the woods.

It was now beyond doubt that the dead woman was Joan

Pearl Wolfe. To make absolutely certain Greeno went to Tunbridge Wells and found the dead woman's mother. He showed her the white elephant charm and she remembered bringing it home two years before after a holiday in Hastings and giving it to her daughter.

But there was still no proof that Sangret had killed her. Greeno had the stake which had been used but he wanted the weapon with which she was stabbed. For a few days there was little progress until Greeno discovered there was a period when Sangret, who rarely spoke to anyone, had suddenly become talkative. It had been after the night of 13 September when he had told one Canadian soldier that the girl had gone to hospital and another that he had sent her away because she was too scruffy. To yet another he had confided that she had left him, although two days before he had told the same man that he was thinking of marrying her. He even told one man that she might have killed herself.

To Greeno, Sunday 13 September was becoming a significant date. He began to believe that that was the day of the murder.

The man named Francis, the Canadian soldier who had lived with Joan Pearl Wolfe before she met Sangret, was traced in Canada, but he had been there long before the murder. In his statement Sangret had referred to an American GI who had been friendly with the woman for a time. He had only a description and no name, but Greeno went to US Army headquarters and went through thousands of photographs. There he found the man, who was traced to Ireland. He was brought back to the murder headquarters, and told Greeno that he had three times urged Joan Pearl Wolfe to leave Sangret. He told the Yard man, 'I told Sangret to stop using her like a goddam squaw.'

The investigation had been going on for seven weeks and on Monday 27 November there was a telephone call to Greeno from Provost Sergeant Wade at Jasper Camp. The information had the bulky Chief Inspector running from his office to jump into his car. At the camp Wade showed him a jack-knife with a strangely hooked end. It looked as though the tip had been snapped off and re-ground into a shape like a parrot's beak.

Greeno asked where it had been found and was told that somebody had put it down the waste-pipe in the shower-room behind the guard room at Jasper Camp – but whoever it was did not know the pipe was blocked. Greeno thought back to the morning he had decided to see Sangret. While he had been waiting in the major's office Sangret had been in the same guard room and had asked permission to visit the shower-room.

Dr Gardner was given the knife. He found it fitted exactly into the wounds in the skull of the dead woman. Someone had to be found who could testify the knife belonged to Sangret. A military policeman who discovered him and Joan Pearl Wolfe in their wigwam on 20 August had seen the knife sticking in a tree there. And a provost corporal was able to swear that when Sangret was released on that occasion from the guard room he had handed the knife back to him.

Greeno and Hodge returned to Hankley Common with Dr Simpson and Dr Gardner and they reconstructed the crime. They worked it out that an attack with a knife was made on the woman near a shack in the woodland at the top of the steep slope where the identity card had earlier been found. Wounded and terrified, she ran away down the hillside, losing her crucifix on the way and falling across a military trip-wire laid along the side of the stream, when she smashed her front teeth. As she lay there, only partly conscious and close to where the shoes and canvas bag were found, she was murdered by blows on the back of the head from the stake. The murder weapon had been thrown a short distance away and that was where it had been found. The body had then been dragged back into the wood. One shoe had come off; the other one almost parted from its sole before it too came off.

Greeno had all the evidence he needed but Sangret had left Glasgow by this time and had been posted to Aldershot.

He was sick with some slight illness but a few days later Ted Greeno and Fred Hodge collected him and took him back to Hankley Common in case he wished to make any explanation. Greeno pointed out the spot where Joan Pearl Wolfe had died.

'I don't want to go there,' Sangret told him.

When he was charged with the murder, on 6 December, he said, 'I didn't do it. Someone did, but I'll have to take the rap.'

The trial took place at Kingston Assizes and after two hours' retirement the jury returned a verdict of guilty and Sangret was hanged at Wandsworth Prison in April 1943.

Detective Chief Inspector Greeno said later that Sangret confessed to the murder before he died – he certainly gave no help to the detective while the investigation was on. One small doubt remained – a motive was never really established. It is possible that he thought Joan Pearl Wolfe was pregnant, but the doctors had no hope of establishing that for her body had deteriorated too much.

She was a strange, unhappy character who had been educated at a convent and at the age of nineteen had taken to wandering through the countryside. In this vagrant life she always carried a Bible and she read it frequently. In the old cricket pavilion where she had spent so many hours with her lover she had pencilled a prayer in girlish writing. It read: 'O holy virgin, in the midst of all thy glory we implore thee not to forget the sorrows of this world.'

CHAPTER 17

A Stray Dog Finds a Clue

In all murder cases the establishing of the identity of the victim is of paramount importance, and because most killers seek to deny the police as much information as possible the task is sometimes long and difficult. In the following case the murderer nearly succeeded in preventing the investigators establishing who the victim was and for three months must have felt secure as he watched the detectives working away, trying to name the woman whose naked body had been found in a shallow stream in Luton, Bedfordshire.

One foggy afternoon in November 1943 two sewer-men were walking along the bank of the River Lea when they noticed a roughly tied bundle of sacking lying in about six inches of water. When they looked closer they realized that the bundle contained a human body and they called the police.

Detective Inspector Thomas removed the sacking to find a woman absolutely naked, with a face so battered as to make recognition almost impossible. Her ankles and wrists were tied together with string, there were no rings on her fingers and no necklace. Even her teeth had been removed.

Inspector Finch of the Luton CID came to the conclusion from his local knowledge that the crime must have taken place elsewhere and the body somehow taken to the river. There was a footpath alongside the river, four feet higher than the water, used daily by scores of people, and near by was the Vauxhall motor works. He scented a murder of more than usual difficulty and asked his Chief Constable, Mr G. E. Scott, to call in Scotland Yard.

Detective Chief Inspector William Chapman, who because of his plump, pink complexion was nicknamed 'the Cherub', was ordered to Luton with his sergeant William

Judge, and there, using powerful lights, they examined the scene.

The body was that of a young, well-proportioned woman, aged between thirty and thirty-five with dark bobbed hair, brown eyes and about five feet three inches tall. Scars on her lower abdomen indicated she had had at least one child and it was clear she was about five months' pregnant. She also had an appendix scar. Otherwise there was nothing to help identify her – no tatoos, no deformities.

Inspector Finch had taken her fingerprints and sent them to the Criminal Record Office and had preserved the only track marks found near the scene. That night and at first light on the following morning the area and the river were searched for clues, but nothing was found. Chapman sent for the assistance of Dr Keith Simpson, the Home Office pathologist. He looked at the place where the woman had been found and then examined her body at the Luton and Dunstable Hospital.

The sacks wrapped round the body had been used to contain variously soda, sugar and, two of them, potatoes. One of them was marked 'M.F.D.' and the other bore the name of a local dealer who distributed hundreds of them without individual records. They led nowhere at that stage. The string round her ankles and wrists was of a common type and equally uninformative.

Track marks which Inspector Finch had found were traced to a milk-van which passed the spot daily and appeared to have no connection with the crime.

The two sewer-men had gone to the river to test the water level of the stream. They had been at the same spot on the day before at four o'clock and they were certain the body had not been there then. It could have been put there at any time after that and been hidden from view by heavy mist.

Dr Simpson reported to Chapman that the victim was killed by a violent blow from a blunt and heavy weapon which had fractured her jaw, split her ear and resulted in haemorrhage of the brain, the actual cause of death. He also mentioned that there was a slight thickening and chafing of the gums which suggested the woman had worn dentures. Before her features were further disturbed by decomposition, swelling or staining, the police took full-face and profile pictures of her and Chapman asked for a plaster cast of her jaws to be made by a local dental surgeon, in the hope that a dentist might be found with records of her dentures.

The not very beautiful photographs of the dead woman were shown on the screens at local cinemas and displayed in shop windows, but no one was able to identify her. Samples of head and pubic hair were taken in case they were needed for later checks. Scrapings from her nails proved uninformative and there were no foreign human hairs or fibres on her body or on the sacking.

All the newpapers carried her picture, but there was no response. Detectives went from house to house showing the pictures and asking, 'Do you recognize this woman?' but each time the answer was negative. Street by street, house by house, they plodded on. Local dentists were also visited. As the weeks lengthened into months and the publicity grew, distracted soldiers serving overseas who were receiving no letters from home wrote of their fears that the unknown woman might be their wife.

Inquiries were made at factories over a wide area to see if any woman had failed to attend work. Shops were visited to find out if a woman's ration card had been withdrawn. More than four hundred missing women were traced and eliminated. Nearly seven hundred addresses of women were traced through *postes restantes* and letters addressed to women which had not been delivered for one reason or another. Thirty-nine people paid visits to the mortuary and nine of them identified the body in genuine error as that of four other women. Laundries and cleaners' records were searched in case some woman had failed to collect clothing she had deposited. Hundreds of lorry drivers who had called at the Vauxhall works at about the time of the murder were traced and interviewed. Statements were taken from a large number of people who had heard screams or seen someone

179

acting suspiciously before the body was found. Streets, refuse dumps, dustbins and open spaces were searched for any clothing the killer might have thrown away and great piles had accumulated in one of the police station garages.

Even Bill Chapman, the most optimistic of men, was beginning to think his luck was running out. He had tried everything, even having the photographs shown at local football matches, but the woman's identity continued to elude him. He became a familiar figure, broad and stockily built, wearing a bowler hat and a long coat and puffing at his pipe, walking around areas of abandoned land, looking for the one clue that might help.

On a chilly February day in 1944, three months after the body had been found in its sacking shroud, his luck turned. He noticed a black and white mongrel dog nosing and scratching on a piece of waste ground littered with old tins and rubbish. He saw the dog had a tattered piece of cloth in its mouth and Chapman called to the little girl who was playing with it. He asked if she could get the rag from the dog's mouth, and eventually she handed it to him. It was torn, dirty and slimy but he could see it had on it a tab from a cleaner and dyer's shop. He tucked it away in his pocket and walked back to the police station where he had set up his incident room. That same night a police scientist was able to decipher what was on the tab – the letter and figures 'V 12247'.

Cleaners' shops were checked again, and at one of them the mark on the tab was recognized. The piece of cloth was part of a coat which had been sent to them to be dyed black by a Mrs Manton of Regent Street, Luton.

It was an amazing turn in the investigation, but Chapman, like most other good policemen, held the theory that luck comes to the persevering. Even so he moved slowly. A quick check with his records told him that Regent Street had been visited by his detectives and the photographs of the dead woman shown to all the residents, who had failed to recognize her. The woman in the house next door, who knew Mrs

Manton well, had not seen any likeness. In any event, she said when she was interviewed a second time she knew Mrs Manton was away because Mr Manton had said his wife was visiting her mother.

Chief Inspector Chapman and Sergeant Judge called at the Mantons' house and the door was opened by a girl who, Chapman said later, was the image of the dead woman. In fact it was her daughter. She told detectives that her father was working as a National Fire Service lorry driver in Luton. His full name was Bertie Horace William Manton, and he had once been a light-weight boxer of some repute. Chapman asked him the whereabouts of his wife and was told she had left some months ago and was living in London. Then he produced a bundle of letters from his pocket. They were creased and looked as though they had been read frequently, then re-folded and put back in the envelopes.

'You can see,' he said, 'she still writes to me.'

Chapman examined the letters and noted the dates and the postmarks. They had been posted from Hampstead, and they covered a period from December 1943 to February 1944. One of them was dated only a few days before. Manton was cool and glib but polite. If the letters were genuine then she was obviously still alive and the body found in the River Lea could not be hers. But by now Chapman had seen a photograph of Mrs Manton taken while she was alive and he remembered the incredible likeness to the daughter who had answered the door.

He asked Manton to make a statement to clarify matters and he readily agreed. He said that his wife and he had not got on well together for some time, mostly because she was too friendly with soldiers in the locality and because of his habit of spending his off-duty hours in a public house where he was on good terms with a barmaid. After a quarrel on 25 November, he said, she had 'slung her hook'. He could remember the date because it was the last day of a four-day leave he had taken.

Chapman showed him the identity photographs and he

181

said, 'No, that's nothing like my wife. I wouldn't do a thing like that. She's alive.'

While the interview went on Chapman had a message sent to Scotland Yard asking for Superintendent Fred Cherrill, the fingerprint expert, to come to the house. He did not need to be told what Chapman wanted – a good fingerprint from Mrs Manton to prove identity positively. Cherrill began work in the kitchen as being the most likely place.

Every piece of crockery, glass, pots and pans, cutlery, chopping boards, ornaments and even pictures on the wall were carefully scrutinized. There was not a fingerprint anywhere. Every single article in that kitchen had been carefully cleaned and polished. It looked as though a legion of house-proud women had been at work. Slowly Cherrill went right through the house, using every test he knew until, at last, he arrived at the cupboard under the stairs.

The walls were grimed with dust, yet one shelf was crammed with empty bottles of every description and every one was clean and gleaming. They had all been cleaned and polished with the same scrupulous care as the articles in the kitchen.

One by one Cherrill tested the bottles and jars, but there were no prints. Then he came to the last bottle of all, tucked away almost out of sight at the end of the shelf. It was covered in dust and Cherrill removed it with the delicacy of a connoisseur handling rare porcelain. It was a pickle bottle and it had not been cleaned like the others. On its sloping shoulders, in a fine film of dust, was a thumb print and it compared exactly with the set Inspector Finch had taken from the dead body.

There was no longer any doubt that the body in the sacks was that of Mrs Caroline Manton and Bertie Manton was arrested and charged.

Chapman had previously questioned Manton about the letters allegedly written by his wife and asked him to write the word Hampstead. He had written the word without the 'p', which was exactly the same spelling as in the letters. Chapman had also ascertained that Manton's leave, which he said ended on 25 November had, in fact, ended on 18 November.

Faced with this powerful evidence, Manton broke down and, after being cautioned, admitted killing his wife on the day his leave finished. He made another statement, the principal point of which was as follows: 'I am sorry to have told you lies about my wife ... I killed her but it was only because I lost my temper. I didn't intend to.'

He told the detective how they had quarrelled about her going out with soldiers and his going to the local public house and that in 1942 she had gone to live with her parents. She had returned four months later but the reunion had not been satisfactory and the quarrels had resumed. On the afternoon of 18 November, when the children were out, they had had another quarrel while they were having a cup of tea. He was sitting at the table when, according to his statement, she had thrown a cup of hot tea in his face. The statement went on:

'I lost my temper, picked up a very heavy wooden stool which was near my feet under the table, and hit her about the head and face several times. She fell backwards towards the wall and then on to the floor. When I came to and got my sense again I see what I'd done. I saw she was dead and decided I had to do something to keep her away from the children. I then undressed her and got four sacks from the cellar, cut them open and tied her up in them. I then carried her down to the cellar and left her there. I had washed the blood up before the children came home to tea. I hid the bloodstained clothing in a corner near the copper.'

After the children had come home and had tea they went out again and so after dark Manton had brought his wife up from the cellar and laid her body across the handlebars of his bicycle and wheeled her down to the river. He said, 'I laid her on the edge of the bank and she rolled into the river.'

Chapman was tolerably sure that Manton had told most of the truth but certainly not all. He remembered the report of Dr Keith Simpson who wrote that the woman's injuries were caused by her being gripped across the neck by a right hand from in front; struggling to free herself but being pinned on her back to a wall or a floor; sustaining a most violent single blow across the left side of the face from chin to ear from the edge of some blunt weapon, such as a rifle stock or some similar heavy object; being felled by that and striking her head in falling; having her legs tied as death was supervening.

Simpson said that it was reasonable to suppose that her injuries took place in that order, for no struggle could have taken place after such a blow to the head.

This point was revealed when Manton was tried for the murder of his wife at Bedford Assizes. The counsel for the prosecution, Mr Richard O'Sullivan, KC, cross-examined Manton.

'She was quite a small woman?' queried counsel.

'About my size, sir; a little shade bigger.'

'No match for your strength?'

'No, sir.'

'Did you hear Dr Keith Simpson tell the jury that there were marks upon the neck of application of a hand and reapplication of a hand?'

'Yes, sir. I remember taking hold of her throat and pushing her against the wall.'

'And that the marks showed that the hand had been applied with considerable force?'

'I may have grabbed her twice, but that was in my temper.'

'You said nothing about that in your statement to the police?'

'No, sir.'

It was a deadly admission and completely at variance with his statement. He had been compelled to admit an act which told heavily against his story of a sudden blow with a stool in a fit of temper.

The loose ends of the case were neatly tied in the end when Chapman found bloodstains in the house, and also envelopes and notepaper similar to those used in the letters which Manton had posted to himself. He also found Manton's dismantled bicycle. The sacks were traced to another fire officer, Manton having bought them to take potatoes home. And the black coat, which had yielded the vital clue from the rubbish dump, was proved to have once belonged to Mrs Manton who had had it dyed in March 1943, to go to a funeral. It had been thrown away after her death by her husband.

Manton was convicted and sentenced to death. Later he was reprieved and given a life sentence but died in Parkhurst Prison in 1947.

He very nearly got away with his crime. He had been thorough in making his wife's face unrecognizable – so much so that when her own daughter saw the face flashed on to a cinema screen she had failed to notice any likeness. Two of her other children had seen the photograph in a shop window and told their father it looked like their mother, but he had put them off by saying it could not be because she had called in several days after the murder to collect some clothes.

The only other person who expressed suspicion about the true identity of the woman was a man, a close neighbour, who, when he told his wife what he thought, was told 'Don't be a damn fool!'

CHAPTER 18

One Fingerprint in 46,000

John Capstick was certainly something of a legend in his own lifetime, for he was phenomenally successful in every aspect of criminal investigation. He had an amazing flair for 'smelling' criminals and for cultivating informants to put him on the right track, and he is a supreme example of the continued importance of a detective's 'hunch'.

He himself didn't find his success altogether surprising – he used to tell the story of how a professor of phrenology forecast his future when he was sixteen. The occasion was a house-warming party given by his parents at Aintree, Liverpool. Professor Best, famous for his 'bumps reading' tent on Blackpool sands at half a crown a head, was a neighbour. The Capstick parents were keenly interested, for John had already deserted the family milk round to run away to sea. His one trip as a deck boy in a cattle boat to the Argentine had cured him of sea-going ambitions but they hoped the professor might suggest a suitable career. At last the phrenologist spoke: 'Madam, your son will be either a great detective or a great thief.'

It was not the answer his mother had hoped for but it was completely satisfactory for Jack Capstick who had long been on friendly terms with local policemen and admired their way of life. The fact that he was only five feet nine inches tall left him with little alternative in 1925 but to join the Metropolitan Police – most forces then demanded a higher minimum height. He was posted to Bow Street where he soon established his individuality, partly born of his scorn for what he considered unnecessary regulations. He had been ordered to buy boots to wear with his uniform but they were stolen on the eve of his first day of duty, so he wore shoes and kept his braces slack so that his trousers were long enough to defy detection.

In one year he had caught so many thieves that he was transferred to the CID, a record in those days. He notched another record seven years later when he was promoted to Sergeant. Later he became a Chief Inspector on the Murder Squad. He had developed a remarkable ability for getting his man and he had a great capacity for work and play. In private life he delighted in growing roses and playing bowls and his keen sense of fun made him vastly popular. He was an expert in all the tricks of his trade, quickwitted and a

186

match for the most cunning of criminals, so much so that he was known as 'Charlie Artful'. Yet to see him strolling down the street, with a rose in his button-hole, puffing contentedly at his pipe, with his curly grey hair neatly combed and his tubby waistline, he could have been anyone's next door neighbour.

His first case at the Yard was one that detectives call 'sticky', when every move seems to fail. For two months he had been working ceaselessly to find the person who had stabbed and battered to death Jack Quentin Smith, an eleven-year-old schoolboy. His body had been found on a railway embankment in Farnworth, Lancashire.

He had a description of the killer, given by Jack's companion, nine-year-old David Lee, who had managed to stagger home with knife wounds in his chest and stomach. They had been attacked, he said, by a thin, tall, youngish man with deep-set eyes and a spotty face. There were no other clues. The killer had vanished into the sprawling mass of smoke-grimed factories and terraced houses of the area.

Farnworth had become a town of frightened people. Four years earlier six-year-old Sheila Fox had disappeared on her way home from school and had never been seen again, and eighteen months later Patricia McKeon, aged nine, had been attacked by a tall, thin man with deep-set eyes.

At the end of two months Capstick and his sergeant John Stoneman returned to London for a conference with their chiefs at the Yard. First, however, they went to their homes for a night's sleep.

At four o'clock the telephone aroused Capstick. It was the Chief Constable of Blackburn, Mr C. G. Looms, asking him to return to Lancashire at once to investigate another murder, this time of June Anne Devaney, aged three years and eleven months. She had been snatched from her cot in the Queen's Park Hospital and her body found in the grounds.

Capstick telephoned Sergeant Stoneman and they met at Euston for the 6.20 a.m. train. Since Capstick had to pass

Scotland Yard he picked up a Murder Bag. Unshaven and bleary-eyed, the two detectives slept most of the way to Preston and a fast car got them to Blackburn around lunchtime. The Chief Constable rapidly outlined the facts of the case.

June Anne Devaney had been admitted to the hospital on 5 May suffering from mild pneumonia, and had been placed in Ward CH. 3. It was a twelve-bed ward but there were only six patients, all younger than June Anne, who was the only one who could talk. She was large for her age and could have been mistaken for a child of six or seven years. She had made a good recovery from her illness and had been due to go home on the morning of 15 May.

Shortly after midnight on 14 May, Staff Nurse Gwendoline Humphreys had heard a baby crying in the ward. She had changed the child's clothing, and then walked down the ward with him, soothing him to sleep. She had put him in the next cot to the one occupied by June Anne, who was asleep. The time was twenty minutes past twelve.

Ten minutes later Nurse Humphreys had heard a girl's voice. She thought another nurse might be playing a joke on her, and after a quick glance into the grounds, seeing nobody, she returned to her work. At one o'clock she had gone back to the ward to look at the patients. The inner and outer doors giving access to the ward from the hospital grounds were open, with a strong wind blowing through. Nurse Humphreys knew that the catches of the doors were faulty, so she thought nothing of the incident. She had closed the doors and continued her round.

It was then she saw that June Anne's cot was empty and she had looked in adjoining wards and toilets. When she could not find her, she had told the night sister. Together they had searched the ward again. Nurse Humphreys noticed that a Winchester bottle containing sterile water stood on the floor beneath June Anne's cot but at half past twelve, she remembered, it had been in its usual place on the trolley some yards away. Then, on the highly-polished floor of the ward, they saw a line of footprints which seemed to have been made with bare feet. One of the clearest impressions was by June Anne Devaney's cot. The night sister reported the child missing and the police were called.

At seventeen minutes past three the little girl's body was found near the boundary wall of the hospital grounds. She had frightful head wounds and it was clear the killer had a sexual motive.

Queen's Park Hospital stands about a mile from the centre of Blackburn in extensive grounds covering many acres, and is bounded by an eight-foot sandstone wall. At the furthest end from the road a chestnut paling fence cuts off the hospital from a large park and a disused quarry known as 'the dell'. A thin drizzle was falling as Capstick and Stoneman got out of the car and waited for the white protective sheeting to be removed.

Of that moment Capstick wrote: 'I am not ashamed to say that I saw it through a mist of tears. Years of detective service had hardened me to many terrible things; but this tiny, pathetic body, in its nightdress soaked in blood and mud, was something no man could see unmoved, and it haunts me to this day.'

The body was removed and Capstick went to the ward. Detective Inspector Colin Campbell, chief of the Lancashire Fingerprint Bureau, was already at work among the white cots, taking pictures of the footprints. He pointed to the Winchester bottle, on which he had found more than twenty finger and palm impressions. Some had been made recently and others were fairly old. Among the recent ones were some much larger than the rest.

Campbell had been at the hospital since five o'clock and had examined both the outside and inside of the ward and every item of furniture and apparatus. The footprints were troublesome to record. Several kinds of powder were applied to the floor to make them more easily seen, but as none of them had any effect each print was circled in white chalk and photographed with a fifteen-inch ruler placed alongside. They began at the door at the north end of the ward, led to the cots and then towards the south door and then back to the north door. There were footprints by the side of June

Anne Devaney's cot, which suggested the killer had been stationary there for some moments. Closer examination proved that the prints had not been made by bare feet but by stockinged feet, and one print showed the texture of the woven fabric quite clearly.

The fingerprints of all the staff who attended the ward were taken and checked against the marks on the bottle. The fresh impressions had not been made by any of them. Campbell was positive that the fingerprints and the footprints had been made by the murderer. By two o'clock next morning it was found that, with the exception of ten finger and palm impressions on the bottle, all the other fingerprints found outside and inside the ward were eliminated as having been made by persons with legitimate access there.

Another Murder Squad team consisting of Chief Inspector Wilfred Daws, known as 'Flaps' because of his big ears, and Sergeant Millen had arrived, and the Lancashire force made a huge squad available. Capstick ordered a search of every lodging house, hotel, public house and dosshouse in Blackburn for any likely suspects. He ran checks on the railway station and sent men to all the dyers, cleaners, and laundries to find any bloodstained clothing. One team of detectives was detailed to take the fingerprints of every male aged between fourteen and ninety who lived in the streets around the hospital.

The work was non-stop. More than one thousand sets of prints were taken from people who had worked or had any business in the hospital in the previous two years. Noel Jones, the biologist at the Forensic Laboratory, Preston, had obtained hair from bloodstained grass at the scene of the crime; samples of the bloodstained grass; hair and fibres from the wall near which the body was found; samples of June Anne's hair, blood and clothing; fibres, fingernail scrapings and other substances. He determined the child's blood group was A, a fact which played its part in convicting the killer.

Capstick had delegated Detective Chief Inspector Bob McCartney of the local force to take statements from everyone who worked in the hospital and he got what seemed at first a lead. Two nurses said they had been accosted by a man in the hospital grounds on the night of the murder. He had insisted on walking with them to the Nurses' Home, and later they had seen his face pressed against their bedroom window. They were able to describe him, and to say they thought he appeared to be unbalanced. Capstick ordered that he be found.

Accompanied by the nurses, detectives combed the cinemas, theatres, dog tracks and football grounds of Blackburn, but not a trace of the man could be found. And then came an extraordinary coincidence. One of the nurses spotted him sitting beside a woman patient's bed and he was brought to Capstick for questioning. He admitted he had been in the grounds within hours of the murder, but he was there playing Peeping Tom among the nurses. He was released but kept under observation until the real killer was arrested.

More research into the footprints and fingerprints revealed that only a tall man could have lifted June Anne clearly over the raised side of her cot. The span of the fingerprints suggested he had large hands. Their condition indicated that he was probably young and not a manual worker. The size of the footprints, which were ten inches long, fitted the theory that the man was about six feet tall. The detectives knew he must be a local man, for no stranger would have found his way around the hospital and its grounds so well.

Capstick was growing impatient. He did not want the trail to go cold or the public to lose interest. At a conference with the Chief Constable he announced his bold decision: 'We are going to fingerprint every male in Blackburn and district between the age of fourteen and ninety. Every male, no matter how unlikely, who is not actually bed-ridden.'

It was a staggering idea. It was explained to him that there were 123,000 people in the town and that they might not co-operate. But the wily Capstick had an answer and he could be extremely persuasive.

'It may take years,' he said, 'but it is certain. Those fingerprints are something our man will never lose, even after he's dead. He can't escape from them. As for co-operation, I don't believe there's a decent man or woman in Blackburn who would not go with us one hundred per cent.'

And then he played his trump card. 'I'm going to ask the Mayor to set the lead by giving his own prints first,' he said.

That master-stroke won the day. Backed to the hilt by the Mayor, who gave his personal word that all prints would be destroyed after scrutiny, Capstick made his appeal public and it was acclaimed. The Mayor was the first volunteer.

The town was divided into twelve sections, like a clock dial, with the police station as the focal point. Thirty officers worked a fourteen-hour day, from eight in the morning until ten at night, visiting every house. They carried a specially designed card three and three-eighths inches square with spaces for the name and address, National Registration Number, and imprints of the left thumb and index finger. The completed cards were filed systematically in wooden trays and checked by a team of five male and five female police officers against the electoral rolls. Then they were sent off to the Fingerprint Bureau.

Meanwhile photographed copies of the murder prints had been sent to every police force in Britain which had a fingerprint bureau, as well as police forces all over the world. Capstick alerted every branch of the British armed forces and every base of the United States Army, Navy and Air Force in Britain. There were more than three thousand male displaced persons working and living in the Blackburn district and they, too, were questioned and fingerprinted. So was every mental patient known to have been on licence from any institution on the night of the crime. Tramps in casual wards, schizophrenics, known sufferers from social diseases, all came into the net.

The fingerprints came pouring in by the thousand and then came a setback – the traditional Wakes Week, when the whole of Blackburn and district took a holiday. More importantly, because of the hold-up the Yard insisted on Capstick and Millen taking their summer holidays, which had been booked long before. Their protests were vigorous but superior counsel prevailed. On the eve of his departure for Pevensey Bay Capstick was visited by Inspector Bill Barton, a local uniformed inspector who had been in charge of checking the files against the electoral rolls. He was of the opinion that the murderer had somehow slipped through the fingerprint net. He argued that if the man was young, he could be a serviceman in which case he would not be on the electoral roll. He suggested that as there was a new issue of ration books due they should be checked against the fingerprint index in case there were any odd men out.

Capstick gave him the go-ahead and travelled south.

About two hundred males, many of them servicemen, were involved in this new check and Capstick had been with his wife and family but an hour when the telephone rang and the exultant voice of the Chief Constable of Blackburn, Mr Looms, said, 'Get here quickly. We've got him at last.'

A detective's life is hard, particularly on wives and families: equally no detective likes not to be in at the kill. Capstick rang Millen, who was at Herne Bay, and they joined forces in London and travelled north.

Two constables, Calvert and Lamb, had gone to a house in Birley Street, Blackburn, and had taken the prints of a man named Peter Griffiths, a six-foot-tall ex-Guardsman aged twenty-two. About three o'clock in the afternoon on 12 August Detective Inspector Campbell and his men were checking the latest batch of cards and one of the experts spotted the long-sought prints. He shouted, 'I've got him! It's here!'

Shortly before nine o'clock that evening Capstick, Millen and Barton were taken by car to Birley Street, a drab terrace of red-brick houses in one of Blackburn's poorest districts. Even in triumph Capstick's cunning did not desert him. His younger officers wanted to arrest Griffiths in the house but 'Charlie Artful' wanted to take him in the street. 'He can't do himself any damage there,' said Capstick. Then he added a phrase he often used, 'Softly, softly, catchee monkey.'

Fifteen minutes later the front door of the house opened and a tall, slim man came out and walked up the street. He was wearing dungarees and an open-necked shirt, like any other man bound for work on the night-shift. Capstick grabbed his arm and allowed the local man to say the words of arrest. Inspector Barton said, 'We are police officers and I am going to arrest you for the murder of June Anne Devaney at Queen's Park Hospital on the night of the 14–15 of May this year. I must warn you that anything you say may be taken down in writing and given in evidence.'

The police car rolled in to the kerb. Capstick sat in the back seat with Griffiths who, when they arrived at the police station, said, 'Is it my fingerprints why you've come to me?'

Capstick cautioned him again and said, 'Yes.'

'Well, if they're my fingerprints on the bottle I'll tell you all about it.' Then he made a statement, and admitted everything including how he had banged the child's head against the wall because she had cried.

After the statement was taken, Sergeant Millen writing and Capstick asking the questions the two detectives went to see Griffiths' parents. They were honest, hard-working, elderly people who were heartbroken by the tragedy which had shattered their lives. They stood silently while the detectives took possession of their son's clothes and, as they left, his mother handed them a pawn ticket. It was for a suit he had pawned for thirty shillings and eightpence. That ticket sealed his fate, for when the suit was recovered from the pawnbroker the forensic scientists were able to prove that fibres from it were exactly the same as those found on June Anne Devaney's body, and the bloodstains on the suit were proved to be her blood.

Peter Griffiths was a solitary, indifferent person who had a poor record in the Army, having once deserted. He was a heavy drinker and unable to make lasting friendships with people of either sex.

The jury took only twenty minutes to return a verdict of guilty and he was hanged at Walton Prison, Liverpool, not far from where John Capstick was born. Capstick always suspected that Griffiths might have been responsible for the murder of Jack Quentin Smith, although he had no evidence and no proof. However, he pointed out later that it was interesting that there were no more murders of small children in the area.

On one occasion, while he was remanded in Walton Prison, Griffiths tried to cheat the hangman. Sergeant Ernest Millen was deputed by Capstick to travel with Griffiths in the car that took him back to his cell after each court appearance. On one trip Griffiths asked for a glass of water and the driver, a kindly man, stopped and got him one and handed it to him. Sergeant Millen dashed it from the prisoner's hand and the glass fell into the car.

Thirty years later Mr Millen, who retired as Deputy Assistant Commissioner at Scotland Yard, told me that story. He said, 'I couldn't tell you why I did it. It was a hunch that something was wrong. But I knew later I had done the right thing for Griffiths told me he had planned to break the glass and cut his own throat.'

CHAPTER 19

Mosaic of Murder

The late 1940s and 1950s were to prove some of the greatest years for the Murder Squad. It was also the period in which the campaign for the abolition of capital punishment received partial success: in 1957 the Homicide Act was passed, giving only five categories of murder for which a person could be executed. Human nature being what it is, this inevitably took the edge off the public's keen interest in murder and its prosecution. Nevertheless the names of detectives were well known to the public, and placards featured items like 'Capstick called in to murder' or 'Yard man probes poisoning'. The public was also served with minute details of investigations and their help was regularly sought.

Pathologists were able to estimate time of death more accurately; scientists had discovered how to classify human blood into smaller groups. Infra-red photography helped detect writing on charred documents and was used to bring up faded or washed-out laundry marks. The science of ballistics had also improved, which made it possible to decide with absolute certainty if a killing bullet had been fired from a suspect's gun. No two weapons can produce identical bullet markings, so the bullet which kills is examined against a test bullet fired from the suspect weapon. Under a double microscope with a single eyepiece they are rotated groove by groove. If they are from the same weapon there is a perfect sequence of exact comparison, so that a cartridge case can be identified as surely as a fingerprint.

One of the most notorious murder trials of those years was that of John George Haigh.

Haigh was the Yorkshire-born son of a colliery foreman. He was soft-voiced, charming and immaculately dressed. He had won a scholarship to a grammar school, sung in the choir at Wakefield Cathedral and had become a persistent criminal at the age of twenty, which led to frequent spells in prison. Soon after serving a sentence in 1943 he settled at the Onslow Court Hotel in South Kensington and embarked on a planned course of murder.

He got on well with the other residents of the hotel, often talking to them of things he invented for the commercial world. One of the guests was a wealthy widow, Mrs Olivia Durand-Deacon, and in February 1949 she had interested Haigh in the manufacture of cosmetic fingernails, with the result that he invited her to his workshop at Crawley, Sussex. In truth it was a borrowed storeroom but it suited

196

his purpose. On the afternoon of 18 February Haigh drove her there, shot her through the back of the head, and removed all valuables from her body. Then he dropped the body into a previously prepared vat of sulphuric acid where it disintegrated.

Haigh was short of money at the time and on the same day pawned his victim's wrist-watch for ten pounds and left the other jewellery she had worn for a valuation. After taking a tea of poached eggs on toast in Crawley and afterwards dining at the George Hotel, he returned to the Onslow Court Hotel and went to bed. At breakfast the next morning he inquired for Mrs Durand-Deacon, telling other residents that she had failed to keep an appointment with him the previous day at the Army and Navy Stores in Victoria.

Another guest, Mrs Constance Lane, suggested to Haigh that they should report Mrs Durand-Deacon's disappearance to the police, and they went together to Chelsea police station. Woman Police Sergeant Lambourne was given the inquiry and she did not like the look of Haigh. She conveyed her distrust to Detective Inspector Albert Webb and he made a check on Haigh at the Criminal Record Office, which disclosed the details of his misspent career. It was not long before police searched the Crawley storeroom and found a cleaner's ticket dated 19 February in receipt of a Persian lamb coat, later identified as the one Mrs Durand-Deacon had worn on the day she disappeared. Then the sale of the jewellery came to light; traces of blood were found on the storeroom walls and a ·38 Webley revolver, recently fired, was found in a hat-box there.

Haigh was arrested and in his statement blurted out, 'Mrs Durand-Deacon no longer exists. I've destroyed her with acid. You can't prove murder without a body.' Then he inquired of the chances of being released from Broadmoor (the criminal lunatic asylum), an illuminating remark from a murder suspect!

Haigh was charged with Mrs Durand-Deacon's murder, and then unfolded the horrific story of his earlier murders, which police were able to prove by documents found in his room at the Onslow Court Hotel.

First he had killed a young man called William Donald McSwann, who had confided to Haigh that he wanted to 'disappear' to avoid war service. He was killed in a workshop Haigh rented in Gloucester Road, Kensington, in 1943, where McSwann had brought a pin-table for repair. Haigh killed him with a blow to the head and then put the body in an acid bath. In the following year Haigh traced the parents of the young man, Donald and Amy McSwann. He told them their son had disappeared to avoid military service and then he killed them in the same way. Having murdered the whole family, he forged a power of attorney and got possession of everything they had possessed, collecting about £4,000. No suspicions were aroused and the disappearance of the McSwann family was never reported to the police.

Haigh then began negotiations for the purchase of a house in Ladbroke Grove, Notting Hill, West London. The owners of the house were Dr Archibald Henderson, a Scotsman invalided out of the RAMC, and his wife, Rosalie. The sale fell through but Haigh became friendly with the Hendersons and in December 1947 he ordered large quantities of sulphuric acid and two forty-gallon oil drums for delivery to the storeroom at Crawley. In the following February Haigh persuaded Dr Henderson to accompany him to Crawley and there shot him in the head. Mrs Henderson was living at Brighton and Haigh took her to Crawley on the pretext that her husband had been taken ill there. She followed the fate of her husband and Haigh melted down both bodies in the sulphuric acid.

Haigh sold the doctor's car and forged deeds, by which he acquired the house – which he afterwards sold – and finished up being the richer by more than £7,000. But by 1949 he was heavily in debt and Mrs Durand-Deacon was sitting at the next table in the hotel dining-room ...

When the investigation into her death was over police found some evidence which suggested Haigh was planning to dispose of yet another victim, for they found countless

198

sheets of paper covered with the signature of 'Cyril Armstrong'. He was found to be the Reverend Cyril Armstrong, the vicar of St Bride's Church in Fleet Street, and one-time Chaplain to the Royal Household. He told me that he had known Haigh when he was curate at Wakefield Cathedral and that when Haigh came out from one of his prison sentences he had asked the vicar for a helping hand. 'I was able to help financially and help him towards employment. I remembered him as a choirboy with a lovely voice but I had no idea he was practising my signature and I would hate to think of the reason.'

Haigh was hanged at Wandsworth Prison on 6 August 1949.

One of the best known Murder Squad names of the Fifties was that of Reginald William Lockerby Spooner, who for most of the war had been seconded to British Security from the CID and who had served as a major in the Intelligence Corps. There he worked with his old chief and colleague, Lieutenant Colonel Len Burt; before the war Burt had been a Chief Inspector to Spooner's sergeant and they had made a formidable team.

They added to their laurels during the war, Burt being involved in bringing William Joyce – Lord Haw-Haw – to justice among many others. Spooner investigated sabotage all over Britain, and had helped to hoodwink the enemy by organizing harmless explosions in places where the Germans expected them to have been made by one of their agents who had been captured. Spooner had flown to Sweden to trap a British traitor, and had also hunted Paul Cole, who had betrayed scores of British agents and was shot dead in the course of being arrested. Spooner had led the hunt because he had known Cole in London's East End when he was a young detective and Cole a thief.

Most senior men of the Murder Squad had previously worked in it as sergeants, and Reginald Spooner was no exception. Afterwards he had been promoted to the rank of Divisional Detective Inspector (a rank which no longer exists), and was for a time in charge of a large area of West

London. It was there that he took charge of two sensational murders, both of young women and both killed by the same hand. The case is not in the Murder Squad records but it made Spooner's name a household word.

The victims were Margery Gardner and Doreen Marshall. The first of the two girls was killed and terribly mutilated in a London hotel on 21 June 1946, and Spooner was called in. The second murder took place a few days later in Bournemouth, and that victim also had been mutilated.

The killer was later proved to be George Clevely Heath, a handsome, arrogant RAF pilot. He walked into a police station at Bournemouth saying he thought the description of the man wanted for the killing of Doreen Marshall fitted him, although he hastened to add that he was completely innocent. The policeman who interviewed him had his doubts and telephoned Spooner at his Hammersmith headquarters. Spooner had a series of questions about Heath's physical appearance, finally asking if the man had a small mark on the bridge of his nose. He did, and Spooner ordered that he should be detained. He was later found guilty of murder and executed in October 1946.

Spooner talked to me about some of his cases when I was covering his investigation of the murder of Mrs Alice Wiltshaw, sixty-two-year-old wife of a wealthy pottery manufacturer, who lived in a fourteen-roomed house in the village of Barlaston, Staffordshire. It was the summer of 1952 when, during a lull in his inquiries, we chatted over a drink. He used to say that talking of things other than the current problem gave him fresh impetus.

Mr Cuthbert Wiltshaw had found his wife dead at 6.20 on the evening of 16 July. They lived alone, their four daughters having married, and two daily maids were employed who went off duty at teatime. Mrs Wiltshaw liked to prepare the evening meal herself.

He had entered the house, as always, through the kitchen door, and was frightened by what he saw. On the floor was a saucepan with a broken handle, two heavy logs and his wife's spectacles. Water and raw vegetables had been spilled

200

over the tiled kitchen floor. In the hallway he found his wife. She had been beaten to death by repeated blows. The top of her head had been smashed in, her nose flattened and both jaws shattered. There were two large gaping wounds on her face, her left arm was badly bruised and there were stab wounds in her stomach and right shoulder. Near the body lay an old-fashioned poker, normally in the sitting-room fireplace, a bloodstained brass bowl and a bloodstained fragment of a china vase which had stood on the hall table.

Mr Wiltshaw called a neighbour, Dr Harold Browne, who telephoned the police and gently guided Mr Wiltshaw into the garden, to get him away from the ghastly scene in the hall. They walked along a path which led through a market garden and, underneath a tree, Dr Browne spotted a pair of bloodstained light cream wash-leather gloves. He marked the spot in his mind but walked on.

The Yard Murder Squad was called and Detective Superintendent Spooner took a most astute detective sergeant, Ernest Millen, to the murder scene. Millen, who was to rise to command the whole of the Yard CID, had already been blooded in murder and had experience unusual in a young officer. He had taken part in the massive fingerprinting exercise in Blackburn to find the brutal killer of June Anne Devaney (see Chapter 18), and had also been to Australia to investigate a gold fraud. He was a big man with a large imperious nose, a feature which, behind his back, led to his being nicknamed 'Hooter'.

At Barlaston the detectives met Mr Wiltshaw and examined the scene. On the bloodstained tiled floor of the kitchen were several footprints, including one made by a shoe with a rubber sole. Spooner grunted with suppressed fury when he saw so many footmarks, for he was a great believer in preserving the scene. 'Careless buggers,' he muttered to Millen.

It soon became clear that robbery was the motive for the killing. A purple leather case containing jewellery worth more than £3,000 had been taken from a drawer in which it was always hidden. Also missing was a gold cigarette case, and from Mrs Wiltshaw's handbag a wallet and a purse. The two rings she wore, a baguette ring and an eternity ring, had been torn from her fingers. The safety catch of an RAF brooch she wore on her blouse was twisted as though someone had tried to unclasp it. Whoever had killed her was probably wearing gloves as there were no alien fingerprints anywhere. A pearl button had been found under the body.

Dr Browne had mentioned seeing the gloves on the footpath. They were quite heavily bloodstained and forensic examination proved the blood to be the same category as that of Mrs Wiltshaw. On the thumb of the left glove was a recent tear. Missing from one of the gloves was a pearl button – the button found underneath Mrs Wiltshaw's body.

Millen, who despite his stern looks could be gentle in questioning, took Mr Wiltshaw through the day of the tragedy. He was, inevitably, a suspect, if only because he had easy access to the house, but the sergeant was quickly satisfied of the truth of his answers. There was no sign of anyone having broken into the house and it appeared that the murderer must have been someone who knew it well. Mr Wiltshaw had come home at his usual time of 6.20 after playing bridge with some friends. He had a precise memory for detail and was able to describe the jewellery and all the other missing items in detail.

Millen asked, 'Is there anything else gone?'

'No. Only a . . . but that's not important.'

'What is it?' Millen asked.

'I can hardly think it's anything worth stealing. It isn't worth anything. It's probably been misplaced.'

'What has been misplaced?' queried Millen.

Mr Wiltshaw said he had noticed his old RAF raincoat, which he occasionally wore in the garden, was missing from its usual place in the lobby.

'Can you identify it?' came the question.

Not only could he identify it, he said, but he could remember three spots on it where he had burned it with cigarettes.

Spooner decided in his reconstruction that the first attack

202

on Mrs Wiltshaw had been made in the kitchen when she was preparing the evening meal. The murderer had picked up the two logs of wood on his way through the scullery and struck her down. As she fell the saucepan full of water and vegetables had fallen to the floor. The murderer had then come down to rifle Mrs Wiltshaw's handbag. She had recovered consciousness and had seen the intruder, then staggered into the hall, perhaps to telephone the police. At that moment the intruder decided on murder. He had picked up the poker with a barbed end and stabbed her in the body. He also hit her with a brass bowl and a china vase. Then he had grabbed the raincoat, probably to cover his bloodstained clothing, and escaped through the back garden and down the path towards Barlaston railway station. On the way he had discarded the gloves.

Spooner had to find someone who had a knowledge of the house and someone whose shoe matched the print left on the tiled floor. He also wanted to find the raincoat. He and Millen had compiled a list of twenty-one people who knew the daily routine of the house, and detectives were sent to find them and check their movements. Police called at youth hostels and boarding houses to inquire about any strangers in the neighbourhood and all the villagers were questioned. One detective sifted through the essays of the children at the local school, who had been asked to write about anything unusual they had seen on their way home from school on 16 July. The school essay was Spooner's idea. He had a great regard for the observation powers of children.

Above all, Spooner reckoned the man he wanted must have been short of money for he believed that initially the murderer had planned only a robbery. Every person interviewed was asked specifically what he had been doing on the afternoon of the murder.

Previous staff at the house were traced one by one and the detectives were able to check on all of them but one, Leslie Green. His wife said that he had left home some time before and she did not know where he was. She knew he was short of money.

Spooner already knew that Green had been Mr Wilt-shaw's chauffeur until two months before the murder, when he had been dismissed for using his employer's car without permission. He had worked as a labourer and a van driver after that but early in July, said his wife, he had become unemployed. He was short of money because paying a mortgage had reduced their savings and he had been spending money freely with no income.

Sergeant Millen was worried about the missing raincoat. He considered it was a vital clue which, if found in the pos-session of the murderer, would be enough evidence to hang him. He argued, therefore, that he would have been foolish to keep it and had probably abandoned it somewhere on his escape route. At one of the many after-midnight conferences at the Crown Hotel in Stone, where the Yard men were stay-ing, Spooner agreed that the raincoat would be a major clue.

The after-midnight conferences sometimes went on until nearly dawn and sometimes, when the official work was done, the detectives relaxed with the crime reporters, for whom they both had a soft spot. The rules were strict, even in that friendly, attractive bar. If something was off the record then any mention of it was forbidden. And no one was allowed to buy a drink out of turn – Spooner was very snappy if anyone disobeyed his strict bar protocol. But in general he was relaxed and always surrounded by a haze of cigarette smoke. He had the odd habit of keeping a ciga-rette burning in his mouth so that the ash dropped down on to the lapels of his jacket. After a while he removed it by vigorously hand-brushing his suit.

Every day at noon, in the police court at Stone, Spooner held a press conference. If he could he also held one in the evening, and he sent word around when he was ready. Some-times it was at six o'clock and, occasionally, at midnight. He now wanted to see Green urgently, and he urged and got immense publicity for his hunt. He had plenty of evidence, though he could not give that away to the greedy newsmen. Green's picture had appeared in the newspapers and so had descriptions of the stolen property.

Unbeknown to Spooner, Green was a worried man. He had seen the papers and he was being pressured by his new girl-friend, whom he had promised to marry. He was aware that the net of suspicion was tightening and he resolved on a desperate step. He walked into the police station at Longton, not far from Barlaston, and told the policewoman at the reception desk, 'I'm the man you're shouting for. I'm *the* Leslie Green.'

Spooner and Millen arrived with the local CID Superintendent, Tom Lockley, twenty minutes later. After assuring himself that this was the man he wanted, Spooner told him, 'We now propose to question you as to your movements on 16 July when Mrs Wiltshaw was murdered at Barlaston. We think you might be able to help.'

Green was casual. 'All right,' he said.

Spooner decided to let Millen take the first statement. He knew his sergeant was a skilled interrogator and he thought a junior approach might get more in the beginning.

It was obvious from the first that Green had concocted an alibi, but Millen was content to write down anything he said. He addressed Green as 'Chummy', less intimate than using a Christian name but less formal than a surname. It is a term that has long been used by the Yard and it tends to produce a more favourable atmosphere than that of hunter and hunted.

Green said that on 16 July he was at Stafford, ten miles away. He had fallen in love with a nurse at Leeds and, after visiting London, he had decided to return home to try to get a separation from his wife. On the way he had stopped at Stafford and gone to the Station Hotel, where he had stayed drinking with four men he met in the bar. They had lunch, which finished about 4.30, and then had more drinks until five o'clock. He felt then he had drunk too much and had gone across the road to a park, where he fell asleep. When he woke he had gone to the left-luggage office, picked up his bag and gone back to the hotel, where he had met the manager in the hall. It was then a quarter to six. He had washed, changed his shirt, had dinner and caught a train for Leeds which left Stafford a few minutes after seven o'clock. He had arrived in Leeds after midnight and, after booking in at the Metropole Hotel, had gone to see his girl-friend at the nursing home where she worked. He had arrived at one o'clock in the morning and found his girl-friend had gone to bed, so he had coffee and something to eat with one of her fellow nurses who was on duty.

While Sergeant Millen was still taking the statement Superintendent Spooner left the police station to start checking on Green's alibi. It did not stand up, but it did not totally collapse. The waitress who had served Green at the Stafford Station Hotel said he had finished lunch at 3.15 or 3.30 at the latest. The hotel manager said that when he had seen Green for the second time it was 6.30 and not a quarter to six. Green had asked him for an early dinner and he had said they did not start serving dinner until seven o'clock. Green had had dinner, so he could not have left the hotel until a quarter past seven at the earliest. But all the times were approximate and, because of the time-lapse, they could not be more precise.

Spooner studied the timetables and discovered that if Green had caught the 5.10 train from Stafford to Barlaston and returned on the 6.05, he would have had fifteen minutes to commit the crime. That was the vital time, the period Green said he was sleeping.

Millen was on the first train the next day to Stafford, and there he met a sixteen-stone giant of the Railway Police, Harry Grimley, a detective with a capacity for untiring work.

Ernie Millen told me later of that meeting and why he wanted to find the raincoat.

'I'll do it,' said Harry Grimley. 'Anything to help a sergeant. I wouldn't do it for a Super, though.'

'Why ever not?'

'I've no time for Supers. It's people like you and me who do all the work. I'll find your raincoat.'

Grimley decided he would have each side of the permanent way searched between Stafford and Holyhead, and all the luggage and lost property offices at each station. The bargain struck, Grimley took Millen off for a drink and Millen left the Stafford Station Hotel in a more cheerful frame of mind than he had been in for some days.

Spooner was mildly amused at Millen's preoccupation about the raincoat and gently chided him about his hangover after the Stafford visit and the time taken on the inquiry. But, within a week, the telephone rang and it was Harry Grimley.

'Are you sure it's the one?' asked Millen.

'Of course it's yours. It's got three burns. And it's bloodstained.'

It had been found on the Stafford–Holyhead train, which stopped at Barlaston, on the night of the murder by the porter clearing the train. He had put it in the lost property office at Holyhead. Harry Grimley had also unearthed a ticket to Leeds bought at Barlaston and handed in at Leeds on the evening of the murder.

Reg Spooner was delighted and agreed to have Grimley over for a drink. Millen warned him Grimley would not want to have much to do with a Super but he agreed to come if the Super paid for all the drinks. It was an amicable occasion and Grimley left Spooner with a higher regard for Supers than previously.

Mr Wiltshaw identified the raincoat, and the analysis of the blood on the sleeve showed it was the same group as Mrs Wiltshaw's. The railway ticket was also important, but why had the murderer chosen Leeds? Obviously it was an easy escape route since Barlaston station was near the scene of the murder.

During the weeks that followed the Yard men had built up a picture of Green's movements. It took more than a thousand telephone calls and hundreds of personal inquiries.

After Green had been sacked by Mr Wiltshaw he had worked for two weeks as a builder's labourer and had then taken a job as a chauffeur again. During that time he had met a woman and become involved with her, though nobody then knew her name.

Spooner now knew more about Leslie Green than Mr Wiltshaw had ever done. He had been convicted four times for theft. His parents had parted when he was six and his first job had been as a pageboy in a luxury hotel. He had joined the Army as a regular soldier in 1937 and had served in the RAF until being demobilized in 1949. It was shortly after that he had gone to work at Barlaston.

The girl-friend in Leeds was sent for and Spooner saw her at Barlaston. For the first time he heard about two rings which Green had given her on the day after the murder. She described them, and her description fitted that of the two rings wrenched from the fingers of Mrs Wiltshaw.

Detective Chief Superintendent Tom Lockley went to see Green and told him that he had evidence to show that he, Green, had given two rings to an Irish girl and that they sounded like the two missing from Mrs Wiltshaw.

Green agreed he had given her two rings but said he had bought them for £15 from two men called Lorenzo and Charlie. Lockley nodded, called in Spooner and told him, 'Green says he didn't do the murder, but he knows he's involved in it.'

'Do you want to make a statement then?' asked Spooner.

'Yes,' replied Green.

He told them that when he arrived in Leeds he went to the Metropole Hotel, where he had booked a room by letter. Next morning he had breakfast and read the papers. About eleven o'clock he went out and met friends Lorenzo and Charlie who he knew were fellow criminals. Some time before he had asked Lorenzo to get him two rings and Lorenzo produced them. He did not charge him for the rings because Green told him he had no money. Lorenzo also gave him a gold cigarette case and a chain and lent him £15. He pawned the cigarette case and gave the two rings to his girl-friend. When she returned them to him later he threw them into the River Aire in the centre of Leeds. He did that, he said, because he had seen the newspapers and thought they might have something to do with the murder of Mrs Wiltshaw.

To expect seasoned detectives to believe such a tale was the act of a desperate man, and was accepted as such. Even so it is a foolish policeman who does not search for evidence which will clear a suspect as well as convict him. The River Aire was dredged and Spooner and his men looked for Lorenzo and Charlie. They found many Charlies and even a Lorenzo, but none of them had anything to do with the murder.

But they found an unexpected bonus. The hotel manager at Stafford remembered that when Green returned to the hotel at 6.30 he was carrying a blue RAF type raincoat, the coat which was already in the possession of the police and which had been taken from Barlaston on 16 July.

Green was then asked to try on the gloves which had been found in the garden of the Wiltshaw home. They were a perfect fit and the cut in the left thumb, caused by a fragment of the china from the vase which had been crashed on Mrs Wiltshaw's head, corresponded exactly with a newly-healed cut in Green's thumb.

The blood on the inside of the left sleeve of the raincoat was Green's. It had come from a recent abrasion on his arm. On the day of the murder Green had worn a short-sleeved shirt.

In Green's luggage was a pair of rubber-soled shoes which he claimed he had bought in Majorca. They were compared with the print found on the tiled kitchen floor, which Spooner had had removed. They were a perfect match, although the ridges on the tiles were slightly curved and those on the shoes straight.

'Why is that,' asked Spooner.

'Because the wearer was running,' answered the forensic scientist.

Only one other piece of evidence was needed to clinch the case – what had happened to the two rings?

Spooner and Millen saw Green's girl-friend again. She said that when he had called to see her in the early hours of 17 July she had been asleep and he had taken coffee with another nurse. That nurse told Spooner that Green had shown her two rings, one in diamonds, the other a baguette. Spooner produced replicas of the rings which he had had made by a jeweller in Birmingham, a brilliant touch of foresight. The nurse was positive in her identification.

Her evidence meant that Green had had those rings in his possession ten hours before he claimed to have received them from Lorenzo and Charlie.

Spooner still wanted to find them, but he had enough to prove his case and he charged Green with the murder of Alice Wiltshaw. Green had been in custody for two weeks on a charge of stealing a dress shirt and some other articles worth £2 15s. while the murder inquiry went on.

The girl-friend in Leeds was interviewed again. Spooner felt sure that Green would have hidden the rings after she had returned them to him and he checked all the possible places. One was the flat of another nurse where Green had stayed the night with his girl-friend. Detectives took up every board in the flat, they searched water-pipes and electrical fittings. They caused damage which cost £50 to repair, but they found no rings. The last place they searched was the coal-house building. Three policemen on their knees sifted through three hundredweight of coal with their fingers and found nothing. Then they examined the coal-house wall and their perseverance was rewarded. They found a loose brick and, behind it, the two rings. It was the final piece in the mosaic.

The evidence at Green's trial at Staffordshire Assizes took three days to unfold and when Millen went into the witness box Green whispered to the policeman guarding him, 'If Ernie Millen gives evidence which hangs me I'll come back and haunt him.' Spooner's comment when the remark was reported to him was typical. 'He'll have to get into the queue,' he said.

Leslie Green was executed two days before Christmas in 1952. The case was, and is still, considered one of the Yard's greatest triumphs. There could be no defence against such complete and devastating evidence.

CHAPTER 20

The Man Who Talked Too Much

In only two murder cases in the annals of Scotland Yard has a suspect who claimed to have 'heard voices' at about the time of a killing been proved guilty of the murder itself. The first was eighteen-year-old Henry Julius Jacoby who, in 1922, was a pantry-boy at a fashionable hotel in London's Mayfair. In the early hours of the morning of 14 March he told the night porter that he had heard 'whisperings' in the basement where he slept. The two men searched the basement but found nothing amiss. At eight o'clock that morning a chambermaid took a can of hot water to Room 14, a large double-bedded room on the first floor occupied by Lady Alice White, a wealthy widow of about sixty. She was lying in bed with her skull crushed in, her pillow soaked in blood.

When Jacoby was arrested the prosecution was able to prove that he had first murdered the old lady with a hammer and then told the porter of the mysterious voices, hoping that when the crime was discovered burglars would be blamed. The case caused a sensation because of the savage and brutal nature of the attack and the youth of the accused.

It was 1953 before another murderer sought to confuse the investigators by claiming he had heard mysterious voices, this time coming from the basement of a church. But when the Yard's Murder Squad was called in it was not yet a case of murder, but the fact that a pretty six-year-old girl called Mary Hackett was missing from her home in Halifax, Yorkshire.

For two weeks the local police had been searching the old town, tramping round the cobbled streets, searching some of the old woollen mills, shops and houses. Reservoirs had been dragged, derelict cemeteries scoured, tombstones lifted. When the Chief Constable, Mr G. Goodman, had exhausted every line of inquiry he travelled down to Scotland Yard and asked for help from William Rudkin, now a Detective Chief Superintendent and Chief of the Murder Squad. He agreed to send two of his men to help the local force and chose Detective Superintendent John Ball. He was then the latest recruit to the squad although no stranger to murder.

Ball was then fifty-one, a Londoner, immaculate from his slightly tilted homburg hat to his highly-polished shoes. When he left for the bustling West Riding cloth manufacturing town, he took with him Sergeant Dennis Hawkins, who had already accompanied five different superintendents on murder cases.

The officers were told that the last time Mary Hackett had been seen was at 12.55 p.m. on 12 August. Her mother had been out shopping then and her father was mending a lawnmower. The child had told her aunt, who was staying with the family, that she was going to play in some sand only a few yards from her home. Nothing more was heard of her. Her disappearance was reported to police an hour later and then the hunt began. In the next two weeks troops, men of the Special Constabulary and Boy Scouts had searched everywhere for the little girl in the green dress and, in the end, the baffled Chief Constable had gone to the Yard.

Ball and Hawkins went to the Hackett family home in Lister Lane and saw the parents. They told the detectives that the child was not given to wandering away and always played close to the house, as she had done on the day she disappeared. Since not one single person among the many thousands interviewed had seen Mary the Superintendent was convinced that she had been murdered and his theory was that if that was so her body was still in the district. And so too, he thought, was the murderer. Why, he argued, should a stranger delay his escape by stopping to hide the body so thoroughly?

Across the road from the Hackett home was the Congregational church. The crypt there was a huge place which had once been used as an air-raid shelter to accommodate nearly a thousand people. It was honeycombed with extensive tunnels and had already been searched several times. Superintendent Ball decided to have it searched again and for the first time he met the caretaker, Mr George Albert Hall, who mentioned that on the day the child disappeared he had been in the church and heard 'whisperings' from the region of the crypt. It did not mean much, but Superintendent Ball recalls he said to Hawkins, 'I think we shall keep an eye on Mr Hall.'

The search was done by the same officers who had been there before and, although they did not find anything new, they did notice that instead of the pews and chairs being strewn all around the crypt quite a number had been stacked in one corner.

Next day the Superintendent and Sergeant Hawkins dropped in on Mr Hall and he greeted them effusively, inviting them to stay to tea. They accepted and, during the conversation, Mr Hall mentioned casually that he remembered seeing a strange man in the church grounds some time before. He gave an elaborate description of him. It seemed strange that he should have omitted to mention the matter earlier, the detectives thought.

From that time on Albert Hall was under police surveillance wherever he went, a different policeman being given the task each day so that his suspicions were not aroused. Superintendent Ball continued with his occasional visits and got the impression that Hall was feeling confident. He referred to the detectives as 'my friends' and Ball in his turn invited the suspect to visit the police station and have a cup of tea. So sure of himself was Hall by now that he walked into the station and was directed to the Murder Room, where he expressed great interest in the filing cabinets and the organization of a murder investigation.

Then the Yard man decided to have another search of the crypt, but he went only with Hawkins and a few men. The furniture stacked in the corner had now been joined by two pots of paint with the lids removed. Why? Were the paint fumes intended to smother another, more sinister smell?

When the search party came out Hall was waiting for

them and the detectives expressed their dismay at not finding anything new. The caretaker was sympathetic, saying what a difficult job it must be trying to find a missing person.

By now John Ball was certain that Hall considered himself in the clear and was brimming with self-confidence. He therefore reasoned that yet another search of the crypt was due, and he determined it was going to be the last. He assembled a force of policemen as well as some firemen. He also asked for arc-lights, as all previous searches had been only by torchlight, and a good many of the searchers carried picks and shovels. On the morning of 21 September, when Mary Hackett had been missing for forty days, Superintendent Ball led his men to the church.

As they arrived Hall gave his customary friendly greeting, but when he saw the size of the party and the lights and equipment, he became angry and shouted, 'You have no right to come digging and I am not going to let you in.' But in they went and started digging in the corner where the furniture had been piled up and the open paint tins placed. Digging slowly and carefully so as not to disturb any evidence, brushing away soil, the detectives suddenly exposed a few inches of flesh. That was at 12.30 p.m. and Superintendent Ball ordered his men to stop digging and sent for the Home Office pathologist, Dr Price, who arrived at 2.00 p.m. The officers then continued with the task of lifting stones away and brushing gently, and in little over an hour the body of the missing Mary Hackett was exposed. She had been buried face down, still wearing the green dress. The little piece of flesh the policemen had first exposed was the back of her right leg. Whoever had buried her had made a little recess and piled up stones over the top of it. Bloodstains were also found on the wall and on the soil.

Her body was taken away to the mortuary and the clothing was removed. The child's parents had to identify the body from the clothes as her face was unrecognizable. The post-mortem examination revealed that she had seven small wounds on her scalp and a big hole on the back of her skull on the left-hand side, measuring about six inches by four inches. Her skull had been beaten in so that the bones round the edges were broken up into thirty-two fragments. The pathologist's opinion was that the child had either been hit from behind by some blunt instrument over and over again with great violence or that her head had been taken and beaten repeatedly against a wall or a floor. There had been no sexual interference.

The caretaker was still trying to be helpful and when he was asked if he knew anything that would assist the investigation he replied, 'No, nothing.' But, on the very next day, he was followed to a mental hospital at Scalebor Park, at Burley-in-Wharfdale, where, it was discovered, he had once been a patient. When he left, the detectives went in to see the resident medical superintendent, Dr Valentine, who had talked to Hall for more than an hour. The doctor reported that Hall had told him that the body of Mary Hackett had been found in the church where he was employed. He had gone on to say that his memory of 12 August was quite clear and that he had nothing whatsoever to do with the death of the child. Then he had said that Detective Sergeant Dennis Hawkins had told him at the police station at one o'clock on the day her body was found that the little girl had died from severe injuries to the back of the head.

Superintendent Ball found that interesting, for when the small piece of flesh of the leg had been uncovered Sergeant Hawkins had been sent away from the church to make an inquiry elsewhere and did not know of the injuries which had caused death. Indeed, nobody knew until Dr Price had concluded his examination at 3.15 p.m.

Ball continued to play his man like a fish, and let out some more line. Three days later Hall told him that on 12 August, the day Mary disappeared, he had heard a child screaming. Why had he not remembered such an important fact before? A policeman had told him on 13 August about the missing girl and the search. Why had he not mentioned the screaming child then?

Then he talked to Sergeant Foster who was on duty at the

church, guarding the spot where the body was found. Hall said he had just remembered during the night that he had been in the church on 12 August and had heard noises coming from beneath. He said he had remembered it again that very morning when he had gone there with his wife to pray.

It was significant to the Yard man that it had taken from 12 August to 24 September for Hall to remember a child's screams at 1.30 p.m. on the day she vanished from a spot ten yards from the church where he worked, but he let the man go on talking. Hall said again that he had seen a strange man and then gave an elaborate description, even to the fact that he was wearing a blue tie. Later he corrected that and said the man was wearing a blue scarf.

In all Hall had made more than thirty voluntary statements, not one admitting any guilt. But the Superintendent by now had enough evidence. He charged him with wilful murder and cautioned him. Hall replied, 'Very well. I have been expecting this.'

At his trial at Leeds Assizes before Mr Justice Pearson Hall pleaded not guilty and, in the course of four days, the prosecution continually made the point that Hall was 'a glib liar'. His efforts to cover up his crime by talking to police officers had finally led to his undoing, for the jury of two women and ten men found him guilty after a retirement of six and a half hours.

George Albert Hall had talked too long and too often and the Yard men had listened patiently, waiting for him to make the vital mistake. He did that when he revealed to a doctor the knowledge that Mary Hackett had been battered to death before the fact had been announced. And, when he had been asked how he got the information, he told a lie. He said he got it from a detective but, at that time, the detective himself did not know of the injuries which had killed the child.

To the last Hall declared his innocence and before he was sentenced to death he said, 'I am not guilty of this terrible crime. It is a terrible crime I admit, but I am not guilty of it.'

I just thank you, my lord, for conducting this trial in the best of . . .' Then, for once, he ran out of words.

The white-haired, forty-eight-year-old church caretaker was hanged at Leeds Prison in April 1954. The man who solved the case has long retired. He still lives in Fulham and is often seen, immaculate as ever – in white – playing bowls on the local green. Of all his cases he remembers the Halifax investigation best of all.

'The longer we were there,' he recalls, 'the more Hall wanted to be near us. It made me suspicious, for most people would rather be at a distance from a Yard man working on a murder. The other important thing was that, despite the work done by the Halifax police and the appeals to the public, not one single person had ever seen the child from the time she ran away from home to play. And it was only five minutes later that she was called for lunch. I was sure that the man was close by, and Hall was only yards away. I still have no positive idea of the motive, but I always suspected he did something which frightened her sufficiently that if she had told her parents he would have been vulnerable. It's always been a good motive to silence your only witness.'

CHAPTER 21

A Paint Trail Leads to a Killer

Throughout the Sixties violence escalated: guns, knives and coshes were used more and more. Case loads increased, manpower decreased. In 1966 capital punishment was abolished. The Stephen Ward trial, the Great Train Robbery, the escape of master spy George Blake, the shooting of three

London policemen in Shepherd's Bush were landmarks. It was also a period when there were so many murders that officers had to be borrowed from other branches.

There was hardly a murder in those days which was not attended by Detective Superintendent George Salter, who by this time was the senior liaison officer at the Yard laboratory. He had been to so many scenes of sudden death, first as a photographer, later advising on the scientific side, that he could 'read' a scene rather like an Indian scout on the trail. I remember being with him when he explained to Detective Chief Superintendent Richard Lewis the route a man had taken across Yately Common, in Hampshire, when he had dumped the body of twelve-year-old Brenda Nash, a Girl Guide who had vanished from home some weeks previously. Later Arthur Jones was convicted of murder in the course of rape and was sentenced to life imprisonment, with fourteen years for rape to run consecutively.

Salter, now retired, later became Commander in charge of the Detective Training School and it is the men who studied under him who are leading today's murder hunts.

A new idea from Los Angeles was introduced to the Murder Squad at a lunch I arranged in 1959 with Peter Pitchess, Sheriff of Los Angeles County, and Sir Richard Jackson, who was the Assistant Commissioner (Crime) at the Yard. It was a folder of interchangeable transparencies, each bearing a drawing of one facial characteristic, hairline, eyes, nose, and so on. It was designed to be handled by a skilled operator who would interview witnesses to a crime and make up a useful picture of a wanted man. It was called Identikit, the forerunner to Photofit which uses photographs instead of drawings, and it took nearly two years for it to be finally accepted.

In 1961 the Identikit system got its first 'victim'. Mrs Elsie Batten had been stabbed to death in the antique shop where she worked in Cecil Court, off Charing Cross Road in central London. There was no apparent motive and the owner of the shop was unable to say if anything was missing. He did recall seeing a man of Indian appearance in the shop on the previous day who had asked the price of a certain dress sword, which he had quoted at £15. He gave a description of this man, but could not say if any of the dress swords were missing.

Opposite the antique shop was that of a gunsmith, whose son had been there on the morning of the murder. He remembered that a young Indian had come into his shop and tried to sell him a dress sword, saying he had paid £15 for it but would sell it for £10. The gunsmith's son had asked him to come back later when his father would be there. The young man had agreed and had left the sword, but did not return. The gunsmith himself recalled that on the previous day a young man had inquired if he bought swords and he had said he might but would have to see the article.

Police identified the sword as having been part of the stock of the antique shop and it was sent to the Yard for a fingerprint test. Meanwhile Detective Sergeant Ray Dagg (who later rose to be a Chief Superintendent) had been on the Identikit course, and he interviewed the owner of the antique shop and the gunsmith's son and built up pictures matching the descriptions they gave him. The two results were strikingly alike except for the hair style.

They were circulated to all police forces and to the press and television. Four days later in the early afternoon PC Cole was on duty in Soho, close to where the murder had happened, when he spotted a man who looked like the circulated picture. He took him to Bow Street police station where he denied any involvement with the crime.

However, the murderer had also left at the shop some partial impressions of the soles and heels of his shoes and these matched with those worn by the young man, a twenty-one-year-old half-caste Indian called Edwin Bush. He was put into an identification parade, where he was picked out by witnesses, and finally admitted the murder and stealing the sword. There was other evidence, too – blood on his clothes, and a palmprint and two fingerprints on the brown paper in which the sword had been wrapped. Edwin Bush was found guilty and executed.

The first course for a new department called Scenes of Crime was held in 1963. Detectives had always been told of the importance of finding clues at the scene of a crime, but in future they were to be supported by a Scenes of Crime Officer whose sole job would be to deal with this aspect, leaving the investigator free to follow up other leads.

In the following year explosives experts were appointed to the Yard laboratory for the first time. In 1965 the Special Patrol Group was set up. It had two hundred men and transport to carry them quickly to a scene of crime, or any other urgent situation. It is a mobile unit which is self-sufficient, carries arms and other equipment, like drags for searching rivers, and it can do a number of tasks like searching for clues – or people – maintaining a road block or marshalling an unruly demonstration.

In 1968 the Murder Squad chief, Commander Frederick Gerrard, reorganized the Murder Room at the Yard and streamlined all the operations. There had always been a man to look after the London end of provincial murder inquiries, but now there was a whole team, equipped with railway timetables and reference books of all kinds – information on rivers, times of high and low tides, extensive road maps, locations of airports, lists of useful telephone numbers. In short, they had up-to-date data on everything and anything a detective in the field might need.

However, an investigation in the early part of the decade owed its success not so much to sophisticated aids as an astonishing piece of luck, as the man in charge readily concedes. By 1960 Dennis Hawkins, who had 'carried the bag' – assisted a senior officer – on so many other murders, found himself a Detective Superintendent and in charge of an inquiry into the death of a man whose body was found under some sacks in a farm shed outside Dunstable in Bedfordshire. He took with him Detective Sergeant Roy Habershon, who was later to lead the Yard's Anti-Terrorist Squad.

The murder in August had come to light when farmer Tony Sinfield and his wife Enid were driving a tractor each to one of the fields on the outskirts of the town to bale hay.

Mrs Sinfield noticed a man's jacket lying in a bed of nettles near a shed and jumped off her tractor to look at it. She found it was heavily bloodstained and called her husband. He looked at the jacket and then went to the old farm shed and saw a leather shoe sticking out from under a sack. He felt the shoe and realized there was a foot inside. He pulled away more sacks and exposed the body of a man lying on his back. In the pocket of the jacket he found an Army pay book in the name of 'Arthur'. He called the police and within hours the Bedfordshire police had called in the Yard.

Dr Francis Camps, the Home Office pathologist, was also called in to examine the body. He said that the man had been shot but had not died where he had been found, and suggested that he had been taken there in a motor vehicle, dumped in the shed and covered up.

Local police told Hawkins that Mr Keith Arthur had been working as a machine operator in a local factory and that he also bought and sold second-hand cars. Hawkins learnt that the victim had been married with two children, was a heavy drinker and something of a braggart.

Hawkins took the view that the murderer was probably a local man because of his choice of hiding place for the body. The old corrugated-iron shed could not be seen from the road, being well screened by thick hedges, and was unlikely to have been chosen by a stranger to the neighbourhood. He also thought the body must have been dumped in a hurry, without any careful thought about covering up the crime. The existence of the identifying pay book backed up this theory.

There was no sign of any weapon in the shed or near the body and Hawkins called for police dogs to make a search. Policemen in their shirtsleeves began to cut the barley in a near-by field in the hope of finding the gun.

That night, when the Yard men returned to the police station in Dunstable itself, a young policewoman told them that she had seen a trail of blood in Regent Street in the centre of town and she wondered if it had anything to do with the murder. To Hawkins it seemed unlikely, but he reasoned that the killing had obviously not taken place in the shed and agreed to go out at first light with the police-woman, a photographer and Detective Superintendent George Salter from the Yard laboratory, to see where the trail of blood led.

The next morning the policewoman showed the blood-stains to the team and they followed them for some distance to a public lavatory, inside which was a considerable amount of blood. As the detectives came out they were called to a near-by house and a woman asked if they were detectives. When she was told that they were and were inves-tigating the murder on the Downs, she smiled and said, 'Don't waste your time on bloodstains you find round here. I'm a dentist and most of my male patients go straight to the lavatory after extractions to spit away blood.'

Hawkins laughed, and so did the others, except the police-woman, who had thought she was on to something. She then told the Superintendent that there was another blood trail leading in a different direction. Good humouredly, they went back to where she indicated and followed some more blood spots that led up an incline to Edward Street, about two hundred yards away. The police photographer had been recording shots of the blood marks and as they reached the end of the trail a woman came out of a house and asked the detectives if they were investigating the murder. They asked why she was interested, and she said her daughter had told her that she had witnessed the killing.

She pointed out to Superintendent Hawkins and Sergeant Habershon the house where she said she was sure that Keith Arthur had been shot, and where a man called Jack Day and his wife and children lived. They then talked to her daughter, Patricia, who was on holiday from school. The girl told them that she had seen the murder, and Hawkins sent her to the police station to be interviewed first by a policewoman. He himself went to the house opposite and asked for Mr Day, but he was told he was at work. Hawkins left, saying he would return later.

Back at the police station, he interviewed Patricia. She

told a fantastic story, but, providing it could be proved, it practically solved the murder case.

She said she often visited Mrs Margaret Day to play with her two children and sometimes baby-sit. On the last occasion she had been there she had been accompanied by a school friend, Marie Davies, and, although she could not remember the day, she knew it was about nine o'clock in the evening. Mrs Day had asked her to run an errand and the two girls had gone out. Marie had continued on home but Patricia had returned to the Days' shortly afterwards. The front door was ajar. She went in and walked into the living-room where Mrs Day was talking to a man she did not know.

'He was talking about a gold identity bracelet,' she said. 'The man showed it to me and after a while I saw Jack Day come round the back. I saw him through the window.

'Jack Day came into the room and I think the other man said, "Are you going to buy me a drink?" and Jack said, "What are you doing here?"'

Patricia did not think it was a friendly meeting because of the tone of the men's voices, and she was sure there was going to be a fight.

She went on, 'I edged over towards the door. Jack Day said to the other man, "It depends what you want to go with it," or something like that. Then I saw he had a gun in his hand and heard a bang and saw a big flash. Then I saw the man go down, shaking his head. The men were standing close to each other. I went out of the door and ran straight home.'

Few Yard men have ever had such luck early in an investigation. It was even more remarkable when Superintendent Salter analysed the 'blood marks' they had followed. He reported that they were, in fact, spots of red paint. It was never discovered from whence they came.

Witnesses were found to support the fact that the murder had taken place at the Days' house. One man and two women were traced who had seen on the night of 23 August at about 9.30 p.m. two men walking, sometimes staggering, along Regent Street from Edward Street. One of the men seemed injured and was bleeding heavily. There was blood on his face and chest and he was being helped along by the second man. Another witness had seen the couple later, and this time they were staggering back towards Edward Street.

All inquiries then centred on Jack Day. It was found that he was an enthusiastic collector of antique guns, but was believed to own a ·38 revolver as well, and that he was a jealous man, particularly concerning his wife. It was also discovered that Keith Arthur frequently boasted of his successes with women.

A neighbour told the police that Day had thought his wife was carrying on an affair with someone else and had said in front of his wife that he would shoot anyone he caught with her. She added that it might have been meant as a joke, but she was not sure. Another neighbour said that she had seen Keith Arthur on the evening of the murder and that he had been wearing his distinctive gold bracelet.

A witness was found who had seen bloodstains in Edward Street which had stopped outside Number 64, the house of Jack Day. When analysed these were found to be genuine bloodstains, although they were on the other side of the road from the trail of paint followed by the detectives. It was a case where the wrong trail led to the right place, a coincidence unique in murder investigation.

Day worked at Stansbridge Motors as a salesman and in July of the previous year a corporal in the RAF police had gone there to look at a car with a view to buying it. In one of the cars he looked at he saw a gun holster and the butt of a revolver protruding from it. It was a Service type, he thought a ·38. He said he had been approached by Day, who shouted, 'That car is mine. It's not for sale.'

The corporal had reported this encounter to the local police at the time, and they had sent a man to the garage to tell Day that information they had received suggested he was in possession of a gun for which he had no licence. Day refused to open his car and the policeman left.

Thirty hours after arriving in Dunstable Hawkins and

Habershon took a team of detectives to the Horse and Jockey public house and arrested Day for the murder of Keith Arthur.

Day said, 'What, me? It is ridiculous. You have got the wrong man.' But Hawkins thought differently and he lodged Day in a cell at the police station. Then he went to the house in Edward Street. In the back room he noticed that a fresh piece of wallpaper had been pasted over the old. He lifted the strip of paper to reveal a hole in the wall, but although he probed it there was no bullet in it.

The detective took from the house a brown suede jacket, a pair of brown shoes and a pair of trousers which Day had been wearing on the day of the murder, and they were sent to Dr Louis Charles Nickolls, the chief of the Yard laboratory. He already had a sample of the victim's blood, which was Group A, and he found blood on Day's clothing to be of the same group. On the shoes were found traces of straw, soil, plant debris and fertilizer which matched with samples taken from the shed where the body was found.

In the jacket of the dead man was a bullet hole on the right side of the collar and there was a corresponding hole in his shirt. The distribution of blood on the garments indicated that he had been standing up or sitting for some time after being wounded and before he died. On the trousers Dr Nickolls found some coarse bright red woollen fibres. He found similar fibres on the rear seat of Day's motorcar and on Day's brown shoes. The suit that Arthur had been wearing consisted of grey wool and grey rayon fibres. Similar grey wool and rayon fibres were found on the car seat.

The garage where Day worked had been searched, and found hidden in the store-room was a Lee Enfield ·38 revolver. Dr Nickolls examined it and found it in good working order and not liable to go off on its own. The trigger pull was five pounds cocked and fourteen pounds uncocked, normal for that type of gun. Using some of the thirteen spare rounds found with it, Dr Nickolls test-fired the gun into a piece of pig-skin, from different distances. The pattern he obtained he compared with a photograph taken of the wound in the dead man's neck, and he was able to prove that the gun had been fired from a distance of two inches. He was able to state positively that the killing bullet had been fired from the same revolver – Day had hidden the spent bullet among the thirteen unfired bullets found in the garage. The bullet was also scratched, as though it had had impact with the gritty plaster of a wall.

Superintendent Hawkins already had a wealth of evidence when, on the morning following his arrest, Jack Day asked to see him. He made a statement which read:

'I should like to tell you how it happened. I came home from the Horse and Jockey, parked my car and went indoors. Keith was there. I hadn't seen him for some time. I said "Hello" to him, like you know. I went to take my clothes off as I got indoors. The wife and the baby-sitter were there. That is why I cannot understand how it happened. I took my gun out of my pocket. It was in a handkerchief. I always kept it in a handkerchief.

'I went to take the handkerchief off and put the gun down on the settee as I always do. The next thing I knew the damn thing went off. Keith was sort of standing there. It went off. I said, "Blimey, sorry it happened." He said, "It has got me in the throat." It looked as if it had scratched like. I gave him my handkerchief to put on it. I had two handkerchiefs, one on the gun and another in my pocket.

'Then we went to see if we could find a doctor in the town. We got as far as the milk bar and Keith collapsed. No one came to give us a hand and he was choking, you know, and coughing blood out of his mouth. I got my arms round him and we rushed home.

'I ran all the way down to the Square to get my car, that is the Square near the public conveniences. When I got back Keith was lying in a pool of blood in the kitchen. I picked him up and took him through to put him in the car. He was dead when I got him in the car.

'I just panicked then, and did not know what to do. I don't know how I got him into the car. I did not know what to do with him so I dropped him in the old shed at the top there. I just grabbed any old thing. I knew they would find him. It was dark. I expected to find you when I got back.

'The wife told me to give myself up but I daren't. I wrapped my gun and hid it the following day with the ammunition at Stansbridge Motors. That is what happened exactly.'

Further inquiries revealed that Day had never held a licence for a gun and also the reason he knew of the shed where he had hidden the body. He was related to the farmer who had found it and often visited him.

At his trial at Bedford Assizes, Jack Day was in the witness box for three hours. He told the court that he used his revolver to shoot pigeons and that was why he carried it. He explained how he had sometimes played Russian Roulette and that he had twice been fined for not having a gun licence. He claimed the shooting was an accident and that when he had said, 'It depends what you want to go with it' he was referring to a joke between them, as to whether he could afford to buy Keith Arthur a beer and a whisky chaser as well.

Day said after he had realized Arthur was dead he had driven him to the shed. 'I went mad then,' he told the court, 'and dragged everything from all over the floor. When I got home I told the wife that Keith was dead and she gave me the bullet which I put back into the cartridge case and hid with the rest of the ammunition.

'I wanted to give myself up but I couldn't. I hadn't the courage.'

The jury believed that Day shot Arthur because he thought he was having an affair with his wife and he was found guilty and sentenced to death. He refused to allow his lawyers to apply for a reprieve on the grounds that he did not commit murder and should not need to appeal. Then, strangely, while he was in the condemned cell, he issued a writ for libel just forty-eight hours before he was to be hanged. The grounds for the writ was a letter in the *Spectator* magazine, dated 24 January, and written by Harvey Cole, a campaigner for the abolition of capital punishment. In the letter

Cole had listed a series of murder cases and one referred to Jack Day. It read: 'On 20 January 1961, Jack Day was found guilty of the capital murder by shooting of Keith Arthur, and subsequently executed.'

It was on 26 January that Jack Day issued the writ but the action died with him, for the Home Secretary refused a stay of execution.

Dennis Hawkins, now retired to be landlord at the Maplin Hotel, Frinton-on-Sea, recalls the Dunstable Downs murder well.

'It was the most quickly solved case of my career and yet, as in all cases, the evidence had to be collected and proved. But it began with a fantastically lucky break due to a young policewoman.

'She had spotted a blood trail which ended in a lavatory. She insisted there was another blood trail which turned out to be red paint, but it led us to the vital witness, and only twenty yards away was a real blood trail which led to the house of the murderer.

'Murder investigation is a difficult science. There are many basic and useful rules which have been passed on through the years. But if the luck is on your side, as it was in this case, then follow it. I did that and the necessary evidence was found and proved the case.

'I think we would have solved the murder in any event but it would have taken longer.'

CHAPTER 22

The 'Q' Car That Died

For the men of the Murder Squad the killing of three policemen in Shepherd's Bush, West London, in 1966 provided a
unique set of circumstances. They knew the names of the
three men responsible for gunning down their colleagues,
and they could prove that responsibility, but could they find
the leader, a man armed, desperate, trained to hide and kill?
There is an element of primitive violence about a hunt of
this kind, but in this case public interest and the offer of a
reward helped the Squad get its man without further blood-
shed; and they were backed up by the Special Patrol Group
on one of its early operations.

On 12 August 1966, a day of warm, sunny spells, a rapid
succession of pistol shots shattered the quiet of Braybrook
Street, in the Shepherd's Bush area of West London, and
silenced the cries of children playing. Within thirty seconds
the crew of 'Q' car Foxtrot 11 were dead.

Detective Sergeant Christopher Head was in charge of the
'Q' car, so named after the armed 'Q' ships of the First
World War which hunted U-boats disguised as innocent
merchant vessels. The police car had a roving commission to
hunt criminals in West London. It was equipped with radio
and had a three-man crew. The second-in-command was
Detective Constable David Wombwell and the third
member was the driver, Police Constable Geoffrey Fox, a
comparative veteran uniformed constable, who, because of
his enthusiasm and expert knowledge of thieves, was always
in demand for work with the CID.

They had been working together since July and on that
day had been on the early shift of 9 a.m. to 5 p.m. They had
lunched together in the Beaumont Arms, only a few hundred yards from Shepherd's Bush police station. When they

resumed patrol, Sergeant Head reported by radio to Scotland Yard that the car was back on the air. Geoffrey Fox swung the car into the traffic.

Fox drove at normal speed along Western Avenue, past the BBC Television Centre to Acton where, at three o'clock, they received a radio message from their operational chief, Detective Inspector Kenneth Coote, who was at Marylebone Magistrates' Court. At the time Sergeant Head was out of the car, following a suspect bicycle thief. When he had dealt with the man, who had been able to prove his innocence, Head telephoned Inspector Coote to say he would pick him up in twenty minutes. That was at 3.10 p.m. and the last communication with Foxtrot 11.

Sergeant Head was sitting in the front with the driver and Wombwell was in the back of the car, when it arrived at the T-junction of Braybrook Street near Wormwood Scrubs Prison and stopped before turning into it. At that moment a blue Vanguard passed and Head decided to stop it. Fox drove alongside and forced it into the kerb. Fox stayed at the wheel while Head and Wombwell got out to talk to the occupants of the other car. Guns blazed and the three policemen died. The blue Vanguard was put swiftly into reverse, then turned and disappeared.

Many local residents dialled 999, and Commander Ernest Millen, the operational chief of the CID, was given the news. He knew the local CID chief, William Marchant, was on holiday, and he appointed Detective Superintendent Richard Chitty of the Murder Squad to take the case. Chitty, in fact, had returned only the day before from Gloucester Assizes, where he had been giving evidence in a murder case he had solved, and he was only third 'in the frame' to take over a major crime. There are always three senior officers on call to take over a murder investigation. The names are pinned, in order, in a wooden frame. The first name is on one hour's notice, which means he must remain within easy reach. The second 'in the frame' has eight hours' notice and the third twenty-four hours. Chitty had looked forward to a few days of peace, having just moved house. He knew none

230

of the facts and mentioned to his superior that he had only just finished a murder job.

'Three coppers have been shot dead at Shepherd's Bush. I want you to do it,' said Millen. 'I'll see you later at the Bush.'

Policemen do not like cold-blooded killers at any time but, when one of their own is murdered, there is an extra edge to the investigation and Chitty needed no further bidding. He telephoned his wife, called for a car, and then this veteran of fourteen murder investigations was on his way.

The choice of Chitty was no idle one. He had served before in the Hammersmith area and his local knowledge was great. He was given Detective Chief Inspector John Hensley, known to everyone as 'Ginger' because of his hair, as his second-in-command. He too knew the area well. At Shepherd's Bush they organized a formidable team of detectives. Detective Inspector Jack Slipper was chosen from the Flying Squad and the rest of the team was Inspector Coote, Detective Sergeants Robert Berry, Sheila Acton and Ronald Lawrence from the forensic laboratory. A brilliant young detective, Clive Martin (who later resigned), was deputed to run the office.

Superintendent Chitty chose a code name for the hunt – Operation Shepherd – and he was given an open radio channel for transmitting and receiving both in cars and in his headquarters. Sergeant Berry was put in charge of all radio communications.

Chitty joined other detectives at the scene and met Dr Donald Teare, the Home Office pathologist. The 'Q' car had been searched for clues; the three bodies taken to the mortuary. One empty cartridge case had been found and was sent to the laboratory.

A local resident, Bryan Deacon, who had been driving home with his wife at the time of the shooting, reported that he had nearly collided with a blue Vanguard which had reversed across his path. Then he had seen the police car, the engine still running, and the bodies of its crew lying on the ground. He had shouted to his wife, 'Get the number,' and made a mental note of it himself. Then he drove to a telephone, remembered it was not working, and drove to a nearby butcher's shop and dialled 999. As he did so he tore off a piece of the butcher's wrapping paper and wrote down the registration number of the Vanguard.

That was a vital piece of evidence and the number PGT 726 went over the radio to all police cars and was repeated on teleprinters to all police stations. Deacon had handed over the written number to Police Constable David Owen, who had been sitting at the wheel of a patrol car in Braybrook Street. He broadcast the number immediately.

The hunt was on with one tangible clue, and Superintendent Chitty assigned a special team to find the car owner. There was a delay, however – at that time registered owners of cars were filed by individual counties instead of centrally at Swansea as they are now. Police knew this was a London number but County Hall closed at 5.00 p.m. However, they held a key to the offices, so they went and made the search themselves.

Meanwhile, the Flying Squad and the Regional Crime Squad men, the guerrillas of the police force, had drawn guns from the Shepherd's Bush police station and were out raiding in the labyrinth of the underworld, searching houses of known criminals and seeking information.

At around 8.30 p.m. the detectives traced the blue Vanguard to the registered owner, John Edward Witney, thirty-six years old and unemployed, of Fernhead Road, Paddington, where he lived with his wife, Lilian, in a basement flat. Detective Inspector Ronald Steventon (now a Deputy Assistant Commissioner) was sent there with a sergeant. Steventon told Witney, 'We are making inquiries concerning the owner of a blue Vanguard shooting brake PGT 726 which we understand is yours.'

Witney replied, 'Oh no, not that.'

Steventon asked him what he meant and Witney said, 'We have just seen the telly about the coppers being shot.'

Witney then told Steventon that he had sold the car that day to a man he had met outside a public house and that he had driven the buyer to Hayes, Middlesex, and had then just wandered around for the rest of the day. The detective did not believe him, particularly when he learned that Witney's wife had not been told of the sale.

Towards the end of the interview Witney became agitated. He was trembling and perspiring and continually mopped his face with a towel. Steventon said, 'I believe that men using your vehicle were concerned with the killing of police officers. I must ask you to come to Harrow Road police station for further inquiries.'

Witney's wife pleaded with her husband to tell the truth, but it would take him some time to do that.

Chief Inspector Hensley was sent to Harrow Road to see Witney and after a while he decided to take him to Shepherd's Bush, where he was locked in a cell. In the early hours of the morning Witney volunteered a statement. It lasted two hours and twenty minutes and it was written down by Detective Sergeant Begg. In it Witney stuck to his story of selling the car to a stranger for £15 and said that he had called at the Clay Pigeon public house at Eastcote, near Hayes, Middlesex, and had talked to a tobacco salesman. Otherwise, he said, he had been alone.

Inspector Slipper (now a Detective Chief Superintendent) was given the task of checking Witney's alibi. He found that Witney had been in the public house and so had the tobacco salesman, but Witney had been there with two other men, and the three had been drinking together. He got descriptions of the other two and sent them to the Criminal Record Office for checking.

That Saturday evening the saturation cover given by newspapers, radio and television on the index number PGT 726 was rewarded when a member of the public telephoned the police to say that on the previous day he had seen a blue Vanguard being driven up a cobbled cul-de-sac off Tinworth Street, near the Thames embankment. The speed of the car had attracted his attention and the driver had scratched the side along the wall.

Detective Sergeant Bernard Harvey and a squad of

officers found the car in a garage under a railway arch near Tinworth Street. It was parked alongside a lorry, an old jeep and a van. At midnight the men from the Murder Squad arrived and with them photographers, fingerprint experts and scientists from the laboratory.

There were fingerprints everywhere, and these were photographed and rushed to the Yard for comparison tests with those on file. In the back of the car were a pair of car number plates, the necessary equipment for a car thief, and three ·38 cartridges, all recently fired. There were also some overalls and part of a woman's nylon stocking, which most robbers use for a mask.

John Witney had now been at Shepherd's Bush for more than thirty hours and was still insisting he had sold the car at lunchtime on Friday, but Superintendent Chitty considered it highly unlikely that any man who had bought the car would then park it in a garage which turned out to be rented by Witney. In addition, the Yard's ballistics expert, John McCafferty, reported that the three cartridges found in the car had been fired from the same gun. Witney was charged with the murders.

Only a short time afterwards Witney pressed the bell in his cell, asked to see Superintendent Chitty and volunteered another statement which gave a very different story. He claimed to have had nothing to do with the shooting but agreed he was there with two other men, Harry Roberts and John Duddy. He said:

'I drove into Braybrook Street where a small car pulled up alongside. Two men got out and one asked if it was my car. I said it was and then he asked for my road fund licence. I told him I hadn't got one. The elder of the two policemen walked round to the other side of the car and said, "Let's have a look in here." Without anything further Roberts leant across and shot the young officer in the face. The sound of the shot deafened and dazed me.

'The other officer ran to the front and Roberts, followed by Duddy, gave chase, still shooting. I saw the second officer stumble and fall. Roberts fired again, I don't know how many times. Duddy ran alongside and shot through the window of the police car. Then they ran back to my car, jumped in, and Roberts shouted "Drive!" '

A check at the Criminal Record Office revealed that the full names of the two men were Harry Maurice Roberts and John Duddy. Both had previous convictions for robbery.

Witney had told the police a great deal but he could not remember the addresses of either of his confederates, although he knew where they lived. Soon after midnight he was smuggled into a police taxi – which looked like any other taxi – at the back door of the station while a Flying Squad car raced out of the front to divert the attention of the waiting reporters.

Witney navigated Chief Inspector Hensley to Wymering Mansions, a block of flats in Maida Vale, and pointed out where Roberts had been living. Then they drove to another block of flats, Treventon Towers, off Ladbroke Grove in West London. In the early hours of the morning Chitty and Hensley led armed teams of detectives to both addresses, reinforced by a strong team from the Flying Squad, four police dogs with their handlers and a constable with a tear-gas gun. Slowly and quietly they cordoned off Wymering Road, while the residents slept, and the chimneys were silhouetted against the dawning sky.

By now they were very weary but the possibility of catching Roberts acted as a stimulant. At five o'clock, the time policemen say of suspects 'They have the dew on them,' they burst into the flat in Wymering Mansions. Two women and two children were in bed in one room but there was no sign of Roberts. The raiders moved on to Treventon Towers where the same cordoning procedure was followed and again the detectives put their shoulders to the door. When they picked themselves up from the floor, they realized they need not have bothered. The door key was on a piece of string inside the letter box.

In the flat they found Duddy's two rather frightened teenage daughters alone and it took the detectives some time to quieten their fears and to prove their identity. The girls explained they were alone in the flat, their mother having left home some time before. They said they had not seen their father since the previous week and there was no sign of him.

That was on Monday, 15 August, and the nation, much of it on holiday in a heatwave, was still appalled at the enormity of the crime. Sympathy for the dead policemen's wives and families was expressed in spontaneous gifts of money to police stations all over the country.

On the Tuesday, four days after the shooting, police issued descriptions of the two men. Harry Roberts, born in Wanstead, Essex, on 21 July 1936, was described as five feet ten inches tall, with fresh complexion, brown hair, blue eyes, and a half-inch scar below the left eye and another on the base of his left thumb. When last seen he had been wearing a grey suit, white shirt, dark tie and brown suede boots. He had used two aliases – Ronald Ernest Hall and John O'Brien.

John Duddy, born in Glasgow on 27 December 1928, was described as five feet five inches, of medium build, slightly corpulent with a fresh complexion, light brown hair, blue eyes and scars on the top of his right forefinger and both knees. He had a tattoo on his right forearm of a pierced skull and heart with the words 'True to Death'. When last seen he had been wearing dark trousers and a dark patterned – probably striped – pullover.

Scotland Yard warned the public not to take any chances but to get in touch with the nearest policeman at once as the men were dangerous and known to be armed.

As these notices were being read in the morning's papers, the inquest on the three victims was opened at Hammersmith by Mr Cyril Baron, the West London Coroner. He said, 'This was an appalling and dreadful crime which has resulted in the deaths of three courageous police officers, officers who have been killed in the execution of their duty. They were officers whom the police and the public could ill afford to lose.' Detective Superintendent Chitty then told the court that one man had been arrested and would appear at West London Magistrates' Court and that two other men

236

were being sought. As he left the witness box Mr Baron said, 'I am sure the public are deeply grateful to you and the other officers who have been investigating this case, for what I am sure have been the very long hours, and the tireless efforts you have put into it. Thank you.'

Slightly embarrassed by the praise and the gratitude, Chitty replied, 'We have only done what was expected of us.'

Already, in the space of a few hours, the picture was changing. One of the two women the police had seen at Wymering Mansions had been living with Roberts and she told detectives that she had been with him until the Monday following the shootings and that on that day she had parted from him at the Wake Arms public house in Epping Forest. She knew nothing of his part in the murders, and told detectives that Roberts had bought a haversack, a primus stove and a sleeping bag from a second-hand shop and some tins of food from another shop.

This news suggested that Roberts was to seek refuge in the country. It was also in character. He had been a trained sniper with the Army in Malaya and was perfectly capable of fending for himself.

Every available policeman was rushed to Epping and a slow and thorough search began. Almost at the same time came the news that Duddy had been arrested in Glasgow by the local CID. Detective Chief Inspector Robert Brown had made several raids in Glasgow and had been tipped off that the wanted man was hiding in a tenement building. With two other armed detectives he broke down a door and found Duddy lying on a bed. He put up no resistance and Chief Inspector Hensley and Inspector Slipper flew up to arrest him. Until he was put in the aircraft Duddy denied having anything to do with the shooting, but admitted having been in the car on the day of the murders. But soon after the aircraft took off he said, 'I must tell you what happened.' He was immediately cautioned, then he said, 'It was Roberts who started the shooting. He shot the two who got out of the car and shouted to me to shoot. I just grabbed a gun and ran to the police car and shot the driver through the window. I must have been mad. I wish you could hang me now.'

The crowds, which had first collected at Shepherd's Bush police station on the day of the murders, were still there when the detectives arrived with their prisoner. The police were two up and one to go. Everything was concentrated now on Roberts. The hunt for him was to take another ninety days.

Only once in that time did Superintendent Chitty and Chief Inspector Hensley and the rest of the murder team take any time off. The first was when the police buried their dead in August; the second was when the nation paid tribute to those three policemen who had died while doing their duty.

Among the people who sent flowers to the funeral was Mrs Harry Roberts, who had not seen her wanted husband for seven years and who was working as a striptease dancer in the north of England. She had already been interviewed by detectives and was under constant watch in case her husband sought refuge with her. Roberts's mother had also been seen by police and she made a radio and television appeal for her son to give himself up.

Every day the armed squads of detectives hunted Roberts, not only in London, but all over the country. There were literally thousands of false alarms, but they were all answered. One night a garden square of faded Georgian houses in Islington was surrounded and searched, and on another occasion the Special Patrol Group, a mobile reserve of two hundred men, searched Sadler's Wells while a rehearsal of Offenbach's opera *Bluebeard* was in progress.

Chitty had 16,000 posters printed and displayed outside police stations throughout the country. The poster carried a photograph and description of Roberts with the lure of £1,000 reward offered by the Commissioner of the Metropolitan Police. Chitty asked all police forces to keep a special watch on fingerprints taken from arrested people, even those arrested for trivial offences. There was good reasoning behind this: if Roberts was on the run alone he might be forced to steal to live and, therefore, might be arrested as a petty thief.

By the end of September Roberts had been reported 'seen' more than 6,000 times, an unprecedented number for a wanted man. Ninety per cent of the calls were made in good faith, the rest were from cranks, drunks and practical jokers. At Shepherd's Bush the murder office was in a constant state of excitement. Despite all the disappointments, every ring on the telephone was greeted with enthusiasm and acted upon with speed. Every call was marked up on a giant map, which also showed the disposition of the hunters. There was still no sign of the three guns used in the shootings but dozens came into the hands of the police from the constant raids. They were all sent to the forensic laboratory for firing and comparison with the bullets found at the scene, but none of them matched.

Chitty flew to Eire to follow a strong tip and, at the same time, strengthened the checks on air and sea ports. He knew it was a forlorn chance, but the detectives had just about exhausted every theory except the one they had always most fancied – that Roberts was hiding in the country.

When the murders were committed it was high summer and detectives were wearing lightweight suits and open-necked sports shirts. Now they were muffled in heavy overcoats. In November Witney and Duddy were at the Old Bailey standing their trial and Chitty and Hensley were sitting in the well of the court, listening to the evidence. Soon after lunch on Thursday, 18 November, the court usher called Chitty to the telephone to talk to the Hertfordshire police who said they thought they had found Roberts's hideout. Chitty left the court and was driven to Bishop's Stortford. He was told that a gipsy farmhand, John Cunningham, aged twenty-one, had been out hunting for game in Thorley Wood when he had seen a light shining through the gap of a well camouflaged tent. From inside he had heard the rattling of a tin can. He crawled away and told his father what he had seen but Mr Thomas Cunningham told him not to worry about it.

The trial might have gone cold then, or even disappeared altogether, but for a police dog handler who was investigating local petty thefts and called at the Cunningham caravan to make routine inquiries. He was told about the concealed tent and at first light next morning he with other police officers made a stealthy reconnaissance. They found the tent with some difficulty. It had been carefully placed and superbly hidden in the thickest part of the wood.

Inside the tent was food in plenty, cooking utensils, two blankets and a fishing rod with bait. It was the complete survival kit. The policemen waited all that day and the next night in the bitter cold but the occupier of the tent did not return. Next morning the forensic men arrived and removed a number of articles, including a bottle of whisky and a gun holster, both bearing fingerprints. They were quickly identified as those of Harry Roberts.

Chitty called the Yard and asked for as many detectives as possible plus the Special Patrol Group to report to him at Bishop's Stortford at once. That night he had the whole area ringed with police, most of whom were armed. At intervals he had police dogs with their handlers and men with tear-gas guns in case of need. Again the night was bleakly cold, but the police were told to stay as still as possible and, at dawn, to make a thorough search. In the early hours of the morning Chitty returned to London and soon after ten o'clock was back at the Old Bailey, when the trial of Witney and Duddy was resumed.

The traditional atmosphere of calm in the famous court was somehow different. Everyone there had heard whispers of an imminent arrest and there was a suppressed air of excitement. A woman witness was telling the jury, 'When I was first seen by the police I was frightened that Roberts would come and shoot me,' when the news came through that Roberts had been captured. The news was not mentioned in open court but Chitty picked up his briefcase and left at once for Bishop's Stortford.

At dawn the police had closed in, moving quietly, and shortly before noon Sergeants Smith and Thorne searched a disused hangar full of bales of straw. Sergeant Smith noticed a bottle of methylated spirit and then, behind a pile of straw, he saw a small primus stove and a torch. He pulled down another bale and there was Roberts, right down inside a sleeping bag.

'When I poked the bag with my rifle,' said Smith, 'Roberts popped his head up and crawled out. Even with his ginger beard I recognized him at once. He said, "Please don't shoot. You won't get any trouble from me. I've had enough."'

Detectives searched the hangar and found a Luger pistol with a full magazine of bullets in the sleeping bag; a ·38 pistol was found in Roberts's rucksack. He had made no effort to use either of the guns.

In the afternoon Detective Superintendent Chitty walked into Roberts's cell. He looked for a long, silent moment at the man who had eluded him for so long, a man he had never seen before but whose face, through studying photographs, was engraved on his mind.

'You know who I am,' said Chitty. Roberts had never seen him before but there had been many newspapers in that hidden tent which carried pictures of the detective. Roberts nodded and then made a statement which was written down by Sergeant Fosbury. It read:

'Since I have been living rough I have lived by thieving either food or money to buy food. What you have found in the tent I have stolen, or bought with stolen money. I'll tell you the truth. I shot the policemen on that Friday afternoon and it was Duddy who shot the driver. I don't know what we were doing near the Scrubs. We were going to nick a car, but not that particular day.

'We had the plate [false index number] in Jack's [Witney's] van. We were going to rob the rent collector. When the police car pulled up I thought they were going to find the guns in the car and so I shot the officer who was talking to Jack, and then shot the one who was talking to Jock Duddy.

'Jock got out of the car and went to the police car and

241

shot the driver. We then got back into the car and Jack drove back to the arches at Vauxhall.

'We first decided to abandon the car and some of us decided to take it back to the arches. We were going to burn it later.'

He told the police that when their car was stopped by the police he had had three guns in a bag – an Army ·38 Colt, the Luger and another ·38 pistol. He and Duddy had buried the guns on Hampstead Heath but Roberts dug up the two that were found with him some days later. Chief Inspector Hensley found the third gun after Roberts told him where to look.

The Yard men had finished their colossal manhunt, which had lasted ninety-five days. At the Old Bailey the three killers were sentenced to life imprisonment with a recommendation that none of the three should be released on licence for a period of thirty years.

Since that time Witney and Duddy, still in prison, have not been heard of publicly. Roberts has made two daring but unsuccessful attempts to escape.

CHAPTER 23

The Shattering of Gangland

Gangs and gang warfare have never been more than a passing feature of crime in Britain, and this fact makes the Kray Gang's grip in the mid-Sixties all the more interesting. Even so their territory hardly extended outside the East End of London and by the time their sights had been set on broader pastures Scotland Yard had decided to call a halt.

It is difficult to do justice (if that is the word) in a single chapter to the range and brutality of the Gang's activities and more particularly to the twins who led it. But it was murder that finally drove a wedge between them and their 'friends' who were also potential witnesses; and murder which caused the Yard to step up its efforts.

With terrier-like tenacity Murder Squad detectives pursued the evidence to prove killings where sometimes no body could be found. In this kind of 'war' the police had to think like villains themselves, using every ruse, trick and disguise, and it is this aspect, still relatively rare in murder investigations in this country, that I have sketched.

Since 1965 Detective Chief Superintendent Du Rose had been working to bring about the downfall of the notorious Richardson Gang, a bunch of hoodlums terrorizing South London who specialized in fraud and protection rackets. The summer of 1966 found most of them in jail, awaiting trial on an assortment of charges ranging from robbery with violence to demanding money with menaces and common assault.

At the same time Du Rose, by now promoted to Commander, also set in motion an operation against the Kray 'Firm', then reigning in East London, who were trying to extend their empire to the West End, and even entertaining grandiose ideas of becoming Mafia bosses in Britain.

Earlier that year George Cornell, a bullnecked member of the South London Richardson Gang, had decided to venture on to Kray territory and visit the Blind Beggar, a pub in Bethnal Green. His visit was short – and ended with a bullet in the right side of his forehead, which killed him almost immediately. The police, led by local Detective Superintendent James Axon, rapidly found their investigation into the murder grinding to a halt. Mysteriously, it seemed that no one at all in the pub had seen anything. All the police had was rumour, and rumour had it that the Krays were involved, but no one was talking.

Du Rose had already selected Detective Superintendent Ferguson Walker from the Murder Squad with Detective

243

Sergeant Algernon Hemingway to tackle the matter of the Krays.

For some months Superintendent Walker and his team hunted for information and for people who were prepared to give evidence. They drew a blank. They were still trying when Ferguson Walker was promoted and transferred to another department. He was replaced by Superintendent Leonard Read, a shrewd choice since he had worked in the East End and knew the three Kray brothers extremely well. Indeed, he had arrested the twins, Ronnie and Reggie Kray, and a man called Edward Smith in January 1965, for demanding money with menaces or by force from Hew Cargill McGowan, a baronet's son who owned a Soho night club. At their first Old Bailey trial the jury had failed to agree. At the second trial the three men were acquitted.

Detective Superintendent Read was well known in East London both as a policeman and as a champion boxer. He was a lightweight, nicknamed 'Nipper' for his footwork in the ring which allowed him to get close to his opponent, land a punch and then dance away out of danger. The Krays, too, had boxed as lightweights but that was all the policeman and the two criminals had in common. Read, however, knew all about the Kray family – Charles, the eldest by seven years, and the thirty-one-year-old twins, Ronald and Reginald. They lived in Vallance Road, Bethnal Green, popularly known as Fort Vallance.

From boxing as amateurs the twins turned professional but, tired of losing, had recruited a number of local toughs to exact money from local publicans and bookmakers by threats of violence. The twins were called up for National Service, but were arrested for absenteeism and assaulting the police and jailed for a month, followed by nine months in Army detention. Once discharged, they turned again to crime, working as 'minders' in sleazy clubs. As new clubs opened the Krays demanded a percentage of the takings to ensure they would not be wrecked by gangsters. The Krays pretended to offer a genuine service of protection when in fact they were prepared to put in their own thugs to exact money or to destroy the club.

Their progress was swift as they took over club after club by the simple but effective method of saying 'Accept our offer or pay the consequences,' a system which worked so well that in time not only did they acquire clubs in the East End but two quite fashionable establishments in the West End. Despite their knowledge of the twins' activities, police had been able to nail one of them on only one occasion. In 1956 Ronnie had been sentenced to three years' jail for causing grievous bodily harm.

Now the mysterious murder of Cornell was added to the list of suspected crimes and was soon to be joined by two other rumours – the equally mysterious disappearance of a small-time gangster called Jack McVitie, known as Jack the Hat because of the small felt hat he always wore to cover his prematurely bald head, and later the disappearance of Frank Mitchell, known as the Mad Axeman, who had disappeared after a daring escape from Dartmoor Prison. Mitchell was mentally retarded but immensely strong. More rumours said the Krays had engineered his escape so that he could be a match for Frankie Fraser, the terror man of the Richardson Gang.

Faced with complete silence on the part of possible witnesses, Superintendent Read concentrated on some of the lesser crimes involved, trying to force a wedge which would persuade someone to talk. Eventually he found a businessman, Leslie Payne, who had had some dealings with the twins, had become disenchanted, and who said he was prepared to give information. That was the beginning and working with a brilliant investigator from the Fraud Squad, Detective Inspector Frank Cater, Read uncovered a multitude of frauds. However, there was one snag – the evidence depended on having witnesses who would be prepared to go to court, and none of them wanted to do that while the Krays were still at liberty.

So for months the patient work went on, with Read, a short man for a police officer, visiting many men serving prison sentences, always in the disguise of a prison visitor, parson or welfare officer, so that other prisoners would not recognize him and so alert the Gang. Day after day, night after night, the detectives talked to people, studied files and planned their next moves. It was inevitable that the Krays knew the Yard men were on their track, and they decided to try to find out how far the inquiry had reached by sending an informant to drop a few spurious facts. He was thanked and sent back with some equally spurious information to the effect that the Yard men were enjoying little success. The Krays relaxed and continued to walk into public houses and clubs with an entourage of ten to twenty people, ordering drinks and food without payment. The strong-arm threat was enough.

Slowly the team of detectives grew as it became imperative to watch more people. Men and women were shadowed round the clock. Policewomen dressed up one day as housewives, another as factory workers, calling on houses and making market surveys, finding out who lived where, who visited and why. Houses were watched and a record kept of the comings and goings. Normal police cars were not used except when the police wanted to be seen. Otherwise a host of old cars, shabby vans and lorries were put into use. Many officers used their own cars, but there was strict radio silence.

As the evidence began to pile up on the handling of forged five pound notes, selling of drugs, extorting of money, so the whispers about murder having been committed became louder, just as Read had hoped. Not only did the underworld say that one of the twins had killed George Cornell, but that Jack McVitie and Frank Mitchell had been murdered as well. Positive proof was still lacking but now there were many good leads and some people intimated that they would talk if they could be guaranteed safety. One particular relative of the Krays had carefully made it known that he would speak if the Krays were arrested. And so did a barmaid who had witnessed the murder of Cornell.

Inquiries had now been going on into the Kray affairs for

more than two years and Read's team, working from Tintagel House, a police office block at Lambeth, had been working non-stop for twelve months. At a conference there with Commander Du Rose, it was decided to take action. The detectives had done enough to disrupt the underworld and shake the legend of the omnipotence of the Krays.

On the afternoon of 7 May 1968 urgent calls went out from Tintagel House to officers of the Regional Crime Squad, calling them to a conference and briefing. They were told to arrive at intervals so that there should be no leak of a big operation, but to be there not later than 2.30 a.m.

At 3 a.m. Read began to address the sixty-eight assembled detectives. In an hour they all knew they were the raiding force which was to deliver a fatal blow to the Kray empire and cripple it for ever. Names, addresses and search warrants were given out. Some men were told to be armed and each raid was to be made at exactly 6 a.m. Watches were synchronized and the teams of detectives moved off to take their positions. There was strict radio silence and all communications to base were to be made by telephone to headquarters. No names were to be mentioned, only code words.

Soon after 7 a.m. the same morning seventeen men were sitting in interview rooms at West End Central police station. The last two to arrive were the Kray twins. They had been arrested personally by Read and Inspector Frank Cater at a ninth-floor flat in Braithwaite House, Bunhill Row, in Finsbury. Ronald Kray, who had long been a homosexual, was in bed with a young man; Reginald was sharing a bed with a young blonde. Later that day they were charged with a number of offences including murder.

The news hit the evening papers for the first edition and the telephones at Scotland Yard were inundated with volunteer witnesses – the people who for so long had been deaf, dumb and blind now found that, all fear of violent reprisal having been removed, their normal faculties had returned. Du Rose, and in particular Read and Cater, were assured that the witnesses to untold criminal offences would be ready and willing to make statements and give evidence.

One by one, as the people came forward, they were protected, moved to new addresses and remained anonymous.
The police knew that it would be a long time before those
witnesses could be taken to court and give their evidence on
oath.

John Du Rose wrote afterwards, 'We were well aware that
many people thought we had bitten off more than we could
chew in arresting a large number of known criminals without, at that time, having sufficient evidence to secure convictions. But we were convinced that once the Gang was in
custody evidence would be forthcoming. Events proved us
right but there was still a lot of work to be done verifying
statements and digging up fresh facts. Nothing was left to
chance and a vast team of detectives worked day and night.'

In this way it was possible to prove through eye witnesses
that Ronnie Kray had been responsible for the murder of
George Cornell. He was shot dead in the Blind Beggar public
house, in Mile End Road, on 9 March 1966. He had been a
member of a rival gang from South London and was killed
because he had strayed on to what the Krays considered was
their territory.

Witnesses, and forensic evidence found after information
had been given, enabled Read to charge Ronnie and Reggie
with the murder of Jack the Hat, although his body was
never found. McVitie was lured to his death from the Re-
gency Jazz Club in Amhurst Road, Hackney. The Krays
alleged they had paid him to kill a man and that he had
failed to fulfil the contract. From the club he was taken to a
'party' at a flat in Evering Road, Stoke Newington, and
there stabbed to death. A television set turned full on
drowned the screams of the victim. The disappearance of
Frank Mitchell remains a mystery.

The trial which finally opened at the Old Bailey in January 1969 lasted thirty-nine days. Ronald Kray and John
Barrie were sentenced to life imprisonment for the murder
of Cornell and Reggie Kray was given ten years for being
an accessory. For their part in the McVitie killing both
Reggie and Ronnie were sentenced to life imprisonment,

with a recommendation that they serve at least thirty years.

Brother Charles got ten years, various other members of the Kray Gang were given long sentences for their parts in the murders and some were given lesser sentences for less serious crimes.

It had taken many policemen years to smash the Kray empire and, in the end, it was the Murder Squad which put an end to organized crime in London. People who could have given evidence were terrified to come forward and the Yard men had to persuade them that it was safe to do so. The underworld appears to have learned the lesson, for since then no criminal gang of comparable size has reared its head.

Both John Du Rose and Leonard 'Nipper' Read have retired from the police but their success in ridding London of the menace of the Kray twins will be long remembered.

CHAPTER 24

The Scattered Body

Even experienced officers are sometimes appalled at the methods of killers, not only of taking away life but of trying to prevent identification. Detective Chief Superintendent Roy Yorke and his sergeant George Atterwill saw the remains of such a victim in the early hours of 5 April 1968. It was the mutilated upper torso of a young woman which had been packed in a locked olive green suitcase.

Their investigations were to take them into the comparatively new world of immigrant customs, yet, supported by a Scenes of Crime officer, a back-up team at Scotland Yard which co-ordinated the efforts of three police forces, and using textbook examples of simple inquiry techniques, they found the killer inside six weeks.

Detective Superintendent Sidney Seymour of the West Midlands police told the Murder Squad men that the suitcase had been taken off the 10.40 p.m. train from London when it had arrived at Wolverhampton station. Two drivers going off duty had spotted the case in an empty carriage and taken it to the left-luggage office where it was opened in the hope of tracing the owner. That was to take some time.

The body was that of an Asian woman aged, it was thought, between twenty-five and thirty. Her head, lower torso and legs had been removed; her upper torso, severed at the waist, was dressed in a pink cardigan, a blue pullover, a blue Indian-style dress with white embroidery, known as a *Kaniz*, a cotton vest and a white bra of Indian make. On her left arm were four white metal bangles, also of Indian design. The suitcase was fairly new and made in England. It was marked 'Spartan' and measured two feet by one foot ten inches. The upper torso and the clothing were wrapped in a square of green-coloured material.

Detective Sergeant Leslie Whitehouse, the Scenes of Crime officer at Wolverhampton, had taken photographs of the torso as it was found and of the suitcase. Then he had delivered them to Dr Richard Marshall, the Home Office pathologist attached to Wolverhampton Royal Hospital.

Chief Superintendent Yorke first went to Bushbury sidings, where the train had been shunted, and examined the compartment in which the suitcase had been left. All that week a team of experts combed through the train for any clues left by the person who had dumped it. Every carriage was fingerprinted – every piece of apparent rubbish taken away for close examination.

The train was a 100-mph electric express which had left Euston at 10.40 p.m., stopping at Rugby, Coventry and Birmingham, and it had arrived at Wolverhampton at 12.52 a.m. Yorke wanted to know who had travelled on that train, where they had boarded it and where they had left it. He organized detectives from the Murder Squad back-up team to go to Euston and men from the forces covering the route to make inquiries at the intermediate stations.

The passenger guard on the train was Terrance Proudman, who lived at Wolverhampton. He told the detectives that many people boarded the train at Euston before the lights were switched on at ten minutes past ten. The train consisted of six second-class carriages at the front, then a buffet car, followed by four first-class carriages and a goods car at the rear.

There had been a census on this train, and Mr Proudman had reported that one hundred and sixty people had travelled from Euston. At Coventry the train carried one hundred and twenty-nine passengers and from Birmingham to Wolverhampton only twelve.

Mr Thomas Rea of Warley, Staffordshire, was the ticket-collector, and he told the detectives that he had checked the tickets in the second-class carriage next to the buffet where the suitcase was found and that thirty people occupied seats but he had not noticed the suitcase.

The two drivers who had found the case had taken seats in that compartment next to the buffet car. It had a gangway down the middle flanked by tables. The case was under the second table on the left, looking towards the front of the train. They handed it in to Leslie Stevens of Wolverhampton, the left-luggage attendant who opened it and called the police.

It was important to the investigation that the movements of the case, once it was found, could be proved to be continuous from one person to another so that there could be no possibility of any interference, no missing minutes.

Originally the train had left Liverpool for Euston and there a team of cleaners had boarded the train, brushing the seats and wiping clean the tables. They had not seen the case, so it was reasonable to assume it had been placed in the train either at Euston or one of the other stations where the train had stopped on the way to Wolverhampton.

The Yard team who had gone to Euston had found the only ticket collector on duty that night at the barrier to Plat-

251

form Six, Mr William Faux. He said that the passenger traffic was light and that he was able to notice the passengers singly. He remembered seeing a coloured man carrying a suitcase who had arrived at the barrier before the train came in to Platform Six. It was, in fact, standing at Platform Seven, before being shunted round. The man asked if he could board it but was told he could not. He returned immediately the train arrived at its departure platform, still with the case, and walked along the length until he was lost to view. Between fifteen and thirty minutes later he came back through the barrier, still wearing his overcoat but without the case. Mr Faux recalled the man had presented a ticket for Wolverhampton which he had clipped, and he did not think the man returned to the platform because he would have seen the clipped ticket.

The ticket collector and a census officer on duty at the barrier at Wolverhampton were adamant that no coloured passenger had alighted from the train there.

Two more passengers were found who proved to Yorke that the case had been put on the train at Euston. One was Mr Frank Parkes of Cradley Heath, Staffordshire, who had travelled to Birmingham. When he boarded the train at Euston it was in darkness and he sat at the table beneath which the case was left. He felt something under the table when the lights came on and he saw it was a suitcase. Throughout his journey no one came near the case or sat in the adjoining seats, and it was still there when he left the train.

The other passenger, who had travelled with his wife to Birmingham in the same compartment, said they had noticed the case as they left the train. They were the last to get off and had discussed reporting it, but in the end had decided not to bother.

Meanwhile the Chief Superintendent had held a press conference and appealed for information about a missing young Asian woman who might recently have left home or disappeared from a boarding-house. He also asked for taxi-drivers or hire-car men or late bus drivers to report anyone catching late trains at Euston or any of the stopping points.

In the middle of that first day another sensational discovery was made. A second suitcase was found in the River Roding under a bridge in the Romford Road, Ilford. A woman had spotted it lying submerged in shallow water and had reported it to the police. A constable was called who opened the case and, on seeing a human foot, used his personal radio to call for help. Detective Sergeant Stephenson took charge and found the case contained the lower torso and legs of a woman. The legs, which had been severed at the knees were uppermost, and the body was wrapped in a green and black material. The case was a reddish-brown colour and there was lettering on the outside. Detective Superintendent Emlyn Howells, the CID chief of the area, took charge of the new development and kept a close liaison with Yorke in Wolverhampton.

Detective Sergeant Atterwill, who was working with Chief Superintendent Yorke at Wolverhampton, travelled to Ilford overnight and saw the lower torso. He then took it back to Dr Marshall who examined it on the same day. Yorke made another appeal for witnesses and several came forward to say they had seen the case in the river earlier than when it had been reported. The earliest sighting was by a traffic warden who said she had seen it at 11.15 a.m. on 5 April.

Dr Marshall reported to Yorke that in his opinion the two parts were from the same body. He based his findings on the texture of the skin, the fact that the severed parts roughly matched and that the internal organs were from one human being. The blood groups of all three sections of the body were identical and the pathologist said he thought the cuts through the body had been made with a knife or some sharp instrument.

Apart from dismemberment there were no marks of violence, but there were three distinguishing factors – a birthmark above the left breast, a half-grown nail on the right little finger and a scar on the inside of one of the legs just above the ankle. The scar had been the result of surgery and there were the marks of at least five sutures. Dr Marshall's view was that it was the type of cut made by a surgeon giving an intravenous infusion, or transfusion, common in cases where veins in the arms have collapsed following severe haemorrhage.

Superintendent Yorke was puzzled about discolouration of the skin in the areas of the cuts through the body – blue on one side and yellow on the other with odd spots of green. He posed the problem at his daily conference with his squad and a young constable supplied the answer. He said he knew a shop near Ilford police station where high tensile hacksaws were sold and that they were painted blue on one side of the blade and yellow on the other which, when mingled with blood, might result in the green spots.

The stomach contents and other organs had been examined at the Forensic Science Laboratory at Birmingham. In the stomach was found the equivalent of thirty half-grain tablets of phenobarbitone. Although there was little blood left in the body Dr Marshall was able to say that although the woman had taken a fatal dose it had not had time to be absorbed into the system, and as phenobarbitone is slow-acting, death would not have taken place from that cause for some hours at least.

His opinion was that the woman had died not less than twelve hours, or more than twenty-five hours previously. She was not pregnant, but was not a virgin. She had never had a child and he estimated her age between eighteen and thirty.

Dr H. J. Fisher, a consultant gynaecologist, confirmed the findings of Dr Marshall and added that the woman had never had a pregnancy of twenty-eight weeks' or more duration, but one of a shorter time would not necessarily have left any mark on her uterus.

There were good leads, but still the Chief Superintendent wanted to find the head, which he thought might be in another suitcase, so that he could positively identify the murder victim. He borrowed an RAF helicopter to fly over the railway line from Euston to Wolverhampton in case it had been thrown from a train window – the observer was a detective who had done that job in the RAF. Yorke got police frogmen to search the River Roding and other rivers and lakes in the Ilford district, and he sent a team of detectives to ride on the trains going to and from Euston and Wolverhampton with instructions to watch for anything which might contain a human head on the embankments and the permanent way. Another team walked the whole distance searching either side of the track.

A Photofit picture of the coloured man who was believed to have left the suitcase in the train was published in newspapers, together with pictures of the metal bangles and the dead woman's clothing. Yorke had visited many Asian communities and had found that the blue jumper was almost certainly hand-knitted. He had the same pictures printed on posters and the accompanying words were in the main three Indian dialects of Urdu, Punjabi and Gujerati. Thousands of those posters were circulated among the immigrant communities of the country.

Nine Indians from the Birmingham and Wolverhampton districts came forward to solve the knitting riddle, which had baffled detectives and garment experts. They identified the pattern as one which was handed down by tradition from mother to daughter in the remote villages of the Punjab, although it had never appeared in any knitting pattern book.

Dr Marshall had told Chief Superintendent Yorke that the pubic hairs of the dead woman had been cut short three or four months prior to death, but none of the hairs taken from under her arms or on her legs had been cut. Yorke learned from Indian sources that a Moslem, male or female, must shave all hair regularly except for the head. He was told that such shaving is a weekly ritual and also that Moslem women seldom wear underclothes under a sari or trousers.

The lower part of the body had cotton pants on and Yorke confirmed that it is the custom of Sikhs to wear such garments. In addition, one of the suitcases was of a cheap

255

variety manufactured in the Delhi district and not likely to be exported. The brassière was of the type and design worn by peasant women in the Punjab district, just north of Delhi.

Because of the shaved pubic hair and the surgical scar on the leg detectives were directed to look for Indian and Pakistani women who had received gynaecological treatment in areas where there was a concentration of immigrants. While that inquiry was going on the Yard men received an urgent call from police at Wanstead. The head had been found.

It was Tuesday, 8 May, more than a month after the first part of the torso had been found. A Mr Howard Perry had been cycling home from work and was held up in heavy traffic across Wanstead Flats when he saw a blue duffel bag lying about nine feet away. He thought it looked in better condition than his own so he had walked across to examine it and had tipped it up to see what it contained, if anything. A bundle wrapped in white linen had dropped to the ground. On closer inspection he had realized it was a human head and he telephoned the police. Again it was Detective Sergeant Stephenson who arrived on the scene and took the duffel bag and the head to Ilford Mortuary where later Dr Marshall examined them. Before he arrived Sergeant Stephenson had found that the wrapping round the head was of torn towelling, which had all been placed inside a cloth bag with the financial page of the *Daily Telegraph* dated 27 March 1968.

The doctor found that there were two large fractures of the skull, one on the left temple and the other on top of the head. He thought that both injuries had been made by a blunt instrument, probably a hammer.

The patient inquiries of the detectives trying to find women who had undergone gynaecological treatment had borne fruit in that one woman in the age group and possibly of the nationality had called at Barking Hospital, Upney Lane, Barking, on 20 November 1967. Her name had been recorded as Sarabjit Kaur with an address at Uphall Road, Ilford. She had been examined by Dr Joan Ellen Watts, a consultant gynaecologist, and had admitted sexual inter-

256

course in September 1967. The doctor was of the opinion that she had had previous sexual relations and her condition was consistent with a twenty-week pregnancy. A further appointment had been made for ante-natal treatment, but in spite of reminders she had not reappeared.

Chief Superintendent Yorke had by now had the whole body removed to the Anatomy Department at Guy's Hospital Medical School, where Professor Roger Warwick deduced that the age of the victim was probably between sixteen and eighteen. Photographs had been taken of the face and shown to Dr Watts at Barking Hospital, but she could not recognize it. She did, however, have a note of the general practitioner who had sent Sarabjit Kaur to her, Dr Gabriel Merriman. He had first examined the girl when he was practising in Ilford and it was he who had diagnozed her pregnancy. He was able to identify her, and told detectives that she had asked him to give her some tablets to get rid of the baby, but he said he had completely lost track of the girl because he had left the district.

The Chief Superintendent already knew that the dead girl was four feet eleven inches tall and weighed 6 stone $2\frac{1}{2}$ pounds – these figures compared exactly with the hospital records. Her address was recorded as a house in Uphall Road, Ilford. Detectives knew that her address in Uphall Road was near where the lower part of her body and her head had been found, and inquiries revealed that this same girl had been missing from the area for some weeks.

A call on the landlady at Uphall Road turned all the inquiries into something concrete. Sarabjit Kaur had lodged at that address for some weeks in November 1967 and the landlady knew she had visited a doctor in Ilford Lane. At one time, said the landlady, the girl had said that her family had returned to India, but later she had confided that she had left home because she wished to marry a boy in India. Her father had forbidden it and had beaten her and even tried to choke her. The landlady did not know where the family lived but Sarabjit had gone home and returned later with her mother and father to collect her belongings. At Easter-time the landlady had seen the father, who told her that he had sent for the boy from India, and that his daughter had married and was living at Southall. Before they parted he had admitted that he was happy his daughter had left home because they had not got on well together.

The landlady was also able to identify the green cloth in which the torso was wrapped, the cardigan and bangles found on the body. She had seen them all in Sarabjit's possession.

After a few more inquiries police learned that the father was a thirty-nine-year-old Punjab Sikh named Suchnam Singh Sandhu, a machine-minder and former schoolmaster. The family had been living at Sibley Grove, Bow, and from there they were traced to Fanshawe Avenue, Barking. On 11 May Detective Inspector Jim Smith and Detective Sergeant David Stephenson, who were on the local division but attached to the murder team, went to see Suchnam Singh who, at first, said he had only two daughters. But, when they pressed him, he agreed there was a third daughter, Sarabjit. She was the eldest, he said, but had left home and he did not know where she had gone. The detectives asked him if he had any photographs of her but he said he had not. When the detectives searched the house they found two photographs in an upstairs room and the officers considered they bore a striking resemblance to the head found on Wanstead Flats. They suggested he should accompany them to Ilford police station and he agreed.

Once there, they questioned Suchnam Singh further to establish that Sarabjit was the dead girl, but the father did not help. He admitted the photographs found in his house were a good likeness of his daughter but maintained that she had left home in February 1968, and that he did not know where she was. He firmly denied any knowledge that she had ever been pregnant and did not identify any of the clothing or the suitcases in which the body was found. He did agree, however, that he had told his daughter's previous landlady that Sarabjit was married and living in Southall.

On the following day Superintendent Yorke and Detective Chief Inspector Peter Amos interviewed Suchnam, but again it was stalemate. The father still refused to identify any of the dead girl's clothing or to admit to anything except that his daughter had left home in February. He did concede one thing – that his daughter might be dead, but he went no further than that. One day later, however, he asked to see Superintendent Yorke alone and made a full confession.

Suchnam Singh had an excellent command of English and a quiet voice, which made his story all the more horrific. He told the detective that on 4 April he was away from work, his wife was out and his younger children at school. Sarabjit had been staying there for a few days and they had had an argument about a married man in India whom she wished to marry. He said his daughter wanted the man to kill or divorce his wife to achieve marriage. She told him she had taken poison and had written a letter, saying that she was killing herself because her father would not let her marry the man of her choice.

Later that morning Sarabjit said again that she had written the note and he would be blamed for her suicide and would hang. He said he lost his temper, picked up a hammer used to break coal for the fire, struck her twice on the head and she fell to the floor.

Suchnam said he was wearing pyjamas, so he dressed and walked to Ilford, where he bought a hacksaw from the shop near Ilford police station. About half an hour after he had struck her he returned, changed back into his pyjamas and started to cut up the body. Sarabjit had tried to grasp the saw as he cut her neck, which explained a cut found on her thumb.

Suchnam went on to say that he covered the whole body in a large plastic bag to complete the dismemberment and later had emptied the blood into the bath. The bloodstained pyjamas and the hacksaw he put in the dustbin and the hammer he threw away in Barking.

Then he had packed the severed body into the suitcases and the duffel bag and taken the case with the upper torso to

Euston by public transport. He had seen the name Wolverhampton on an indicator board and bought a ticket, put the case on the train and returned home, after tearing up the ticket. He had then taken the second case and caught a bus to Ilford with the intention, he said, of going to the police. Then he had changed his mind, walked past the police station and thrown the case from the bridge into the river. The following day on his way to work, he strapped the duffel bag containing the head on his moped and left it near some bushes on Wanstead Flats.

Superintendent Yorke, now retired, still considers that confession the most horrible he ever heard. 'It was quiet, matter-of-fact and almost unbelievable,' he said, 'except that we had managed to prove most of it already. And, despite the cold-bloodedness of the dismemberment, I couldn't help feeling slightly sorry for the man for I had found out that Sarabjit was his favourite child. He had wanted her to be a doctor, but to a Sikh family disgrace is untenable and he had discovered she had been pregnant. It was an old custom among Sikh tribes to dismember a member of the family who disgraced the name, and send parcels of the body on trains going in different directions to evade discovery.' The police view, never proved, was that Sarabjit had been aborted by an Asian doctor, possibly something arranged by her parents. This would account for the suture scar on her leg.

Detectives never stop an investigation just because someone has confessed – there is always the chance that a statement may be retracted. So Yorke and his men continued to make checks.

They found that Suchnam Singh had worked in a manufacturing chemist's and that he had easy access to phenobarbitone tablets. Plastic bags, exactly similar to the one used in the murder, were readily available in the same factory. Traces of blood, of the same group as that of the dead girl, were found in the U-bend of the bath-pipe at Suchnam Singh's house and the fingerprints of Sarabjit were found on her clocking-in card at the factory where she worked.

Suchnam Singh was tried at the Old Bailey and pleaded not guilty. However, the evidence was overwhelming and the jury took only ninety minutes to find him guilty. He was sentenced to imprisonment for life.

CHAPTER 25

Three Hairs of a Dog

A child killing in 1968 involved a careful documenting of times combined with a new method of analysing hair to secure a conviction in the absence of a confession. Policemen combed, literally, 144 dogs, the canine population of an entire village, to provide back-up to this new style of evidence.

On 19 May 1968 the general pattern of life in the village of Buckden, Huntingdonshire, was normal for its population of 1,810 people. It was a Saturday in a mainly agricultural area and the farm work that day was concentrated on spraying the crops or thinning sugar beet. As on most Saturdays, many of the villagers visited the local town of Huntingdon, where they had their lunch, usually a snack meal or fish and chips bought from a mobile van.

On that particular day, however, two events made the day easier to remember. One was a local event, the Open Day at the United States Air Station at Alconbury, some four miles from Buckden, with a flying display of the Red Arrows aerobatic team. The other was the Football Association Cup Final at Wembley Stadium, which meant that many of the villagers planned their day to watch the match on television. Those two attractions meant that most people were off the streets in the afternoon and few were working.

One of the people who bought fish and chips for lunch on that day was eight-year-old Christopher Sabey, the youngest of a family of nine. He had last been seen by his parents, Mr George Sabey and his wife, Violet, when he cycled away from home, which was the near-by Falcon public house, kept by his father. He did not return.

At dawn on 20 May, after an all-night search, his body was found beside a sandpit, only two hundred yards from his home. He had been strangled.

That third event stunned the people of the picturesque village and prompted the local police to ask Scotland Yard for assistance. Early on Sunday Detective Chief Superintendent Kenneth Jones arrived in Buckden with his sergeant Reginald Brothers, and set up his mobile incident room on the village green.

The Yard man went to the Falcon to find out the events of the previous day. He learned that on the evening of the Saturday the public house had been busy and Christopher was not seriously missed until about 8.30 p.m. At first it gave no cause for alarm as it was thought he would be with his friend, David Ekins, who lived near by. His sister Pauline went to the Ekins's house but Christopher was not there and had not been there all day. She looked further around a building site, and visited some of his friends without finding either the boy or his red and white bicycle. At 10.55 p.m. she consulted her parents and then she went to the house of the resident policeman, Police Constable Dodman, and reported Christopher missing.

Dodman at once organized a search with the help of the local detective inspector. They had gathered a number of local residents and customers from the Falcon, and concentrated the search at Cracknell's building site and among the many gravel pits in the area, now mostly disused and full of water. At 11.40 p.m. PC Dodman had found the boy's bicycle leaning against a pile of bricks on the east side of Hoo Close, which was part of the Cracknell's building site. The bicycle was lifted into the boot of the police car and taken to the Falcon where it was identified by the boy's father. Then the search had continued until 3 a.m. when it was called off until daybreak. When it was renewed, the news of the boy's disappearance had spread through the village, and one of the men who had volunteered for the search, Brian Jolly, found Christopher's body lying on a grass-covered mound near a water-filled gravel pit.

He was lying on his back. Two policemen, PC Butcher and PC Wright, did not disturb the body but covered it with a blanket. The first medical officer called to the scene was Dr Daniel Connan who at 5.20 a.m. certified the boy was dead, probably from asphyxia. He was fully clothed with the exception of his left shoe, which was near the left foot. *Rigor mortis* had fully set in in all regions, and the doctor found multiple haemorrhages on the eyelids, forehead and scalp, and some bruising on the neck. Dr Connan considered the boy had been dead for about ten to twelve hours.

Detective Superintendent Davidson and other officers of the Mid-Anglia Constabulary had visited the scene and ordered a tent to be put up over the body to preserve any clues. The Scenes of Crime officer, Sergeant Hunt, found a number of footmarks close to the body and plaster casts were made of them. Dr William Bryan, Home Office pathologist and also consultant pathologist of the Northampton General Hospital, visited the scene with Jack Laurence Fish, a Principal Scientific Officer at the Home Office Forensic Science Laboratory at Nottingham. Only then was the body removed to the mortuary.

Dr Bryan, in the presence of Superintendent Jones, confirmed that death was caused by strangulation, probably by a two-handed grip on the throat from the front. That was supported by bruising on both sides of the chin and reddening on the front of the neck. There were also superficial marks on the back of both shoulders, leaving the pattern of the underclothes impressed on the skin and suggesting pressure on the front of the body.

People who live in small communities resent intrusion, and Jones and Brothers were strangers in a strange land. They therefore set out to cultivate the people of Buckden and the surrounding villages. The Murder Squad headquarters was set up under a chestnut tree on the village green, opposite Christopher's school. It was a shrewd move, for the Yard men needed the help of the school-children. Like all good detectives, they knew the value of their sharp eyes. And it had been under that same chestnut tree that the mobile fish and chip shop from Huntingdon had parked on the day of the murder and where Christopher had bought his lunch and then cycled away, somewhere, to meet his killer – the pathologist was of the opinion that he had died within about three to four hours of that time.

Superintendent Jones already had a suspect but no evidence. Within twenty-four hours of arriving in Buckden one man who had been seen by police had emerged as the possible killer, but facts were needed to substantiate a charge, and Jones knew that he had to rely on the villagers to provide the necessary knowledge. Only he and his immediate team knew the identity of the man, and the Superintendent determined to keep his suspicions quiet. He knew he needed the villagers' testimony, and he fancied their interest would flag if they knew he had a possible suspect.

Christopher's parents went on running their public house to take their minds off the tragedy, and when Superintendent Jones called on them they told him that Christopher had never gone far on his own. Even when he went out at night, if only to the backyard, he always took his dog with him.

Sixty extra policemen were drafted in to make a house-to-house inquiry and, in the main, they wanted the answers to two questions: 'Where have you been in the last forty-eight hours?' and 'Did you see Christopher Sabey alone or with any stranger after 1.30 p.m. on Saturday?'

Superintendent Jones spoke over a public address system from a car which toured the near-by villages. He said. 'It is vital that we solve this quickly because it could happen again. This is something the society of Buckden cannot tolerate, if only in protection of their children.'

He sent Inspector George Smith, a local policeman and

well known, to the village school to talk to Christopher's friends, and most of the children were escorted to and from their classes by their parents or friends, fearful that the killer might strike again.

However, in the first forty-eight hours the response from the villagers was poor, and Superintendent Jones decided to jolt them out of their apparent apathy. To pressmen he described the local inhabitants as 'rather secretive' and said, 'We must try to drive into the villagers that they must come forward. Little information has come voluntarily. We have been forced to go out and get it.'

Certainly none of the villagers could claim ignorance of the murder. Posters carrying a picture of the dead boy, his description and the two vital questions were plastered up everywhere.

The first tangible clue came after Jones's press statement. A six-year-old boy claimed that he had seen Christopher on the Saturday afternoon with a youth he did not know. The six-year-old was put under police guard while the police searched for the youth.

One of the biggest handicaps to the investigation was that, in the vital hours of Saturday afternoon when news of Christopher's movements was needed, almost the entire village had been glued to the television, watching the Cup Final. The wife of the vicar, Mrs Connie Davies, spoke in support of the villagers.

'We are sure it is not that people are withholding information but that they have no clues at all,' said Mrs Davies. 'When I walked down the main street on Saturday afternoon, while the Cup Final was being televized, there was literally nobody out of doors. Everyone in the village is very worried about this and I am sure if they knew anything they would come forward.'

A description of the youth said to have been seen with Christopher on the Saturday was circulated. He was described as aged about fourteen with slim build, five feet four inches tall with short fair hair, dressed in a black blazer and blue jeans. Jones said, 'We are anxious to trace this youth because the new information confirms that Christopher was alive throughout the afternoon. The young boy has said that he saw them talking in Park Field, which is off a road leading to the gravel pit.

'Do not shield him. It is your duty to bring him forward. His help could be vital. We do not know his name but this is the hottest tip we have had so far and we must find him.'

Jones admits now that he sounded like a Welsh evangelist, but he still thinks it was worth it at the time.

Christopher's father, fifty-four-year-old George Sabey, joined in the appeal: 'I implore anyone, parent or child, in this village or any other around who knows anything about Christopher's death, to come forward. If the strangler is being shielded, there is a threat to other children in the area. I do not believe Christopher would have gone voluntarily to the gravel pits with a stranger. He must either have been dragged or carried there.'

In fact, scientific tests had proved that the child had not been dragged to the spot where he was found and though it was possible he had been carried part of the way, the police were inclined to think that Christopher had died where he was found.

The scientists had also been putting the boy's bicycle under the microscope and had found some fingerprints. The Yard men let it be known that they might have to fingerprint all the people in the village, and the apathy began to erode.

Another twenty-five detectives were drafted in to bring up the squad to one hundred men, and the senior detectives talked at a meeting of the Buckden Parish Council. Superintendent Davidson, the local CID chief, stressed to them that no motive had been established and said, 'We might have someone in our midst who might be mental all the time, or a psychopath who might go away and commit a similar crime tonight. I urge you to impress upon the public, even your personal friends, that information given to the police will be treated in the strictest confidence.'

Then came a report of another schoolboy who had been seen on the night of the murder, between 8.20 p.m. and 9 p.m. He was said to be aged about ten and had been seen to fall off his bicycle in a road near the gravel pit.

Twelve police frogmen made underwater searches of all the gravel pits in the area, looking for anything the killer might have thrown away, or taken from his victim and discarded. The local parsons joined in the clamour for information, speaking from the pulpit after their sermons.

It was eleven days after the murder that Christopher Sabey was buried and after the detectives had attended the funeral service Superintendent Jones announced that he was satisfied that the murder took place between 3.16 p.m. and 5 p.m. He said he urgently wanted any sightings of the boy between those times, and also wanted to hear from anyone who had visited the gravel pits or the building site on that afternoon. Within hours he received information that a woman with a boy dressed in a cowboy outfit had been seen there but, as soon as that news was published, the two people came forward and were eliminated from the inquiry, for they had seen nobody else.

By now more than 4,000 statements had been taken and a total of 7,551 questionnaires had been completed. It was a long, weary task but it was done with great care. All the statements had been checked by detectives for their accuracy and some were suspect. Meanwhile the Yard team, still appealing for information, had received some electrifying news themselves. Mr Jack Fish, the scientist at Nottingham Laboratory, had found three dog hairs on the blue jersey of the murdered boy and now Jones was looking for someone with a dog or someone who had access to a dog.

Jones's prime suspect was in fact a nineteen-year-old youth called Richard Nilsson, who lived in Shooter's Hollow, Buckden. He had been interviewed several times, and had first been seen by police on the day after the murder along with other employees on the building site. Nilsson was a labourer there, and had said he had left the site on 19 May at about one o'clock. The officer who interviewed him was not particularly suspicious, but he had noticed Nilsson had sweated a lot while they were talking and was continually swallowing hard. His name went into the checking system and by the evening of 20 May police knew that Nilsson had made an attempt some months before to strangle a boy. He was taken to the murder headquarters and questioned by Superintendent Jones, Detective Inspector Smith and Detective Sergeant Brothers.

Nilsson admitted he had been officially cautioned by police for indecent assault on small boys and admitted he had attempted to strangle another boy. He also said that the boy he had tried to strangle had run away and jumped into a near-by moat and that he had thrown stones at him whilst he was in the water. He was asked to demonstrate how he had attempted to strangle the boy and, after some hesitation lasting a few minutes, got astride Detective Inspector Smith, who was lying on the floor, with his knees on either side of Smith's shoulders, and placed his thumbs at his throat.

Jones pointed out that according to the evidence he had Christopher Sabey had been murdered in exactly similar fashion, but Nilsson said he had not been near the gravel pits that day apart from a few minutes around one o'clock. He claimed he had been in Huntingdon all that afternoon, then in various local shops and was home at 4.15 p.m.

Next day his mother, Mrs Nilsson, was interviewed by the Superintendent and she said her son had arrived home on the Saturday at quarter to four and that he had not gone out again. There was a missing thirty minutes.

Nilsson was seen several more times by the detectives but, although he told several different stories which when checked were proved to be lies, there was no evidence to prove he had been on the building site after one o'clock. Part of his alibi was that on the afternoon of the murder day his moped had run out of petrol. He had pushed it a hundred yards down the High Street of Buckden to a garage to get petrol. Since every person in the village had been interviewed and not one of them had mentioned seeing him push his moped through the street Jones thought that was almost certainly another lie. From inquiries he knew that most happenings in the village were seen by somebody.

Each time Nilsson was allowed to go, but each time detectives were getting closer. And they were getting closer in other directions, although they were still appealing for information. The three dog hairs from Christopher's body, dog hairs found on Nilsson's clothing and samples taken from his golden Labrador dog, were sent to the Home Office Central Research Establishment at Aldermaston and passed over to Dr Eric Francis Pearson for analysis by neutron activation, the most recent and exacting method in the analysis of hair.

The analysis showed that the concentration of four chemical elements were similar, all being within a similar range in parts per million. The remaining three chemical elements were all present but in too small amounts to determine accurately. Dr Pearson reported that it was not possible to say how many dogs in the United Kingdom had hair with trace-element characteristics similar to those found on the dead boy, Nilsson and Nilsson's dog.

In order to strengthen the evidence Jones decided to take a sample of hairs from every dog in Buckden which, in the first place, showed any similarity in colour, that is, white tinged with fawn. Hairs from one hundred and forty-four dogs were taken to Nottingham Laboratory and microscopic examination revealed fifty-four with similarity in colour and structure. The hairs from the Sabeys' black dog were not the same and were eliminated.

Those fifty-four samples went to Aldermaston for analysis by neutron activation. At the end of the tests it was revealed that the hairs from Christopher Sabey's jersey could have come from only three dogs in the village and one was the golden Labrador owned by Nilsson and called Susan.

Collecting the hairs had taken ten detectives three days. They could not use the same comb twice for fear of contamination and Superintendent Jones now readily admits that his men had no relish for the chore! He pointed out to them that it had never been done before and that they were making a little history, but he never did think they were entirely convinced, though the evidence proved telling.

Although Nilsson progressively changed his story, he now admitted that he *had* seen Christopher on the day of the murder until 1.45 p.m. and that they had been together in a house under construction in Hoo Close, Buckden, a house where Nilsson had been working as a plasterer's labourer. He said he had been sweeping it out and that Christopher had helped him. Still the evidence was not strong enough for the determined and pugnacious Welsh detective.

He saw Nilsson again and told him that the three dog's hairs found on Christopher's clothing could have come from either Nilsson's clothing or from his dog. In an effort to explain this, Nilsson said that Christopher had taken some cigarettes from his pocket while they had been together in the house at Hoo Close. Again Jones had to let him go. But now he was sure Nilsson, a husky boy known as a bully in the village, was his man.

Detectives were sent out again on a house-to-house inquiry, this time with specific reference to Nilsson and his moped, for there were only two such machines in the village, and his was easily recognizable – it was the biggest. On this inquiry, the fact that the televized Cup Final, the event which had kept the villagers in their homes, was on the day of the murder, turned to the advantage of the police.

On that afternoon Mrs Colleen Harries of School Lane, Buckden, was at home while her husband had gone to Wembley. She remembered the day the more particularly because it was also her husband's birthday. She remembered being in her lounge and, turning on the radio, realized she had missed the four o'clock news. She walked to the window facing School Lane and saw a blue moped being driven towards the Hoo Close building site followed by a small boy on a bicycle. She called out to her son Neil, who was in the street, not to run across the road and that command was heard by another child. Mrs Harries asked her son to inquire next door, at the house of Mr Ivor Blackburn-Hunter, as to the score at Wembley and he told the boy there was no score and that the match was in the second half. A check proved that the second half of the game ended at 4.47 p.m.

Jones was, therefore, able to deduce that Nilsson went to the building site at some time between about 4.35 p.m. and when the match ended.

Mrs Harries was able to identify the man on the moped as Nilsson and the boy following on the bicycle as Christopher Sabey. She was also able to say she had seen Nilsson again later from the rear window of her lounge, walking alone near Hoo Close. That was about 5.30 p.m. Even more important, Mrs Harries made a sketch of the moped which corresponded with the actual machine, including the detail that the front mudguard was missing.

On 17 July Superintendent Jones saw Nilsson, when he admitted he had been on the building site with Christopher from 4.30 p.m. to 5.15 p.m. and that he had left Christopher there. He was reminded of what he had said at previous interviews but he was determined not to confess. However, he was charged with the murder on that day and later at Nottingham Assizes he was found guilty and sentenced to life imprisonment.

In the dock, as he had before the trial, Nilsson denied the murder. He told the court, 'I had nothing to do with Christopher Sabey. I did not kill him. I had nothing to do with his death at all.' But Superintendent Jones remembered all the other evidence they had uncovered, of the earlier attempted murder, his bullying, the fact that he had once said, 'I despise people smaller than me,' and his indecency with small boys, though in this case there was no evidence of indecent assault.

The policeman also remembered that there was a wreath among the floral tributes at the funeral of Christopher Sabey inscribed, 'To a little friend' and signed 'Mrs Nilsson and Richard'.

CHAPTER 26

Murders on Paradise Island

The most outstanding feature of present-day murder trends is undoubtedly the increasing use of guns. Its growth persuaded senior men at Scotland Yard some time ago to make sure that a percentage of all policemen were trained in the use of firearms. Twenty years ago it was almost unheard of for policemen to draw firearms from the local station armoury because they were going after an armed criminal. Today such a request is much more common-place, when it is almost a fashion among villains to carry guns.

Early in 1970 Detective Superintendent Donald Neesham, now Commander in charge of the Flying Squad, went to Oxford where a middle-aged man had been killed by a shot-gun blast in his bungalow on the outskirts of the city. The scene was so well preserved by the local policeman that Neesham congratulated him. It enabled him to find some good clues which led to four young men, and within a week they had been charged with the murder. Bernard Wheeler, the local bully, was sentenced to life imprisonment, the three others to smaller terms, but their youth – Wheeler was only twenty-two and the others twenty-one – pointed up the new menace.

The following year a local Blackpool Superintendent was shot dead by jewel thieves resisting arrest. The trail led to London and the Murder Squad. Superintendent Chitty and Chief Inspector Jack Moulder worked with the chief of the Lancashire CID, Superintendent Joe Mounsey. They established that the man they wanted was Frederick Sewell. Eventually underworld information led to his arrest and on that raid the police carried guns.

A year later a police constable on armed protection duty was called to a raid on a bank in Kensington. The bandit was armed but refused to obey the policeman's repeated command to stop. The constable shot him dead.

Investigators have left the Murder Room on countless occasions to travel to many different parts of the world where the murder of a British subject has been reported. Bermuda, sometimes called the Paradise Island and still a British colony, was the scene of six sensationally brutal murders over a period of five years, all investigated by Detective Chief Superintendent William Wright and Detective Sergeant Basil Haddrell.

On 5 July 1971 the Yard men were warned to stand by to fly out after the body of Mrs Jean Burrows, a twenty-four-year-old British journalist from Chatham, Kent, had been found floating in three feet of water at the edge of Hamilton Harbour, where millionaires' yachts bob at anchor. Bermuda's Police Commissioner, George Duckett, conducted the original inquiry and called for the Yard men to come to the island on 28 July.

When they arrived they were told that on the night of 3 July Mrs Burrows, her husband and two other journalists had dined at Hoppin' John's, a fashionable bar and restaurant in Hamilton's Front Street and had left at one in the morning to go back to the Burrows's home for coffee. They were all riding mopeds, but Mrs Burrows did not arrive at the house with the others.

At first light, about 4.30 a.m., her almost naked body had been found at the water's edge, her only clothing a dress around her waist. She had severe head injuries and an attempt had been made at strangulation. At the King Edward VII Hospital the local pathologist, Dr Wenwyon, had carried out a post-mortem and found the dead woman had been raped before being knocked unconscious by a heavy blow on the head. She had then been drowned by being held under the water. Dr Wenwyon had taken specimen slides of the skin at the points of injury and bruising and a brilliant sequence of photographs were taken by the local police.

Then the local detectives had searched the area around where the body was found. It was a search well made, for what was found, and where, later proved to be a vital factor in a quite remarkable investigation.

In a mangrove swamp near by were her wrist-watch and her shoulder-bag. On the opposite side of the road, and fifty yards away in the long grass were her earrings; her sunglasses and briefs were near the sea wall and her moped was hidden three hundred yards away in another patch of long grass.

Chief Superintendent Wright sent the slides and photographs collected by Dr Wenwyon to Professor Keith Simpson, the Home Office pathologist in London, and asked for his views on the sequence of events in the killing. Then he set up house-to-house inquiries in the area of the murder, working backwards to the Hoppin' John restaurant. He interviewed Mrs Burrows's husband and the two reporters who had dined with them, but they had seen nothing. Patient inquiries, however, did reveal the name of a man who, although he had not been seen on the night of the murder, had been frequently noticed in that area of the beach, watching young women bathing and sunning themselves. His name was Paul Augustus Belvin, a local man aged twenty-eight who drifted around with apparently little to do and with no fixed home.

Two witnesses remembered him from a competition held the previous year in the area when the entrants had been asked to find a hidden key for a cash prize. Paul Belvin had won the prize and there had been considerable publicity.

Belvin was not particularly intelligent, but he was sharp and cunning, and the two detectives from the Yard interviewed him gently about his general knowledge of the area. He appeared to know a great deal of the general comings and goings of people in the district and the veteran investigator, Bill Wright, suddenly astonished his sergeant by suggesting to the suspect that he might like to play detective and help Scotland Yard. Perhaps he would help to reconstruct the murder, suggested the detective. The young Bermudan, pleased with the idea, agreed.

The three men drove down to the harbour, the

fashionable end of Hamilton, got out and walked along beside the sea wall. After a while Wright stopped and suggested the amateur detective might like to say what he thought had happened. Belvin then went through in amazing detail how he thought the killer must have hidden behind a palm tree, near the side of the road, knocked Jean Burrows off her moped, then hit her and raped her, probably on the sea wall. He pointed out where he thought the murderer would have hidden the moped, and the place he indicated was exactly where it had been found. It was also where he had found the hidden key the previous year. He gestured with a throwing motion the direction where he thought the woman's briefs had been thrown, and that too approximated to where they were found. Questioned about the dead woman's watch and shoulder-bag, he said he thought they would have been thrown away on the opposite side of the road.

Chief Superintendent Wright described the injuries which had been inflicted on the victim and Belvin's view was that the murderer had used an iron pipe. Wright pointed out that no iron pipe had been found. 'What do you think the man would have done with that?' queried the detective.

'I think he would have thrown it into the sea,' said Belvin.

'Where do you think he would have thrown it?'

He pointed out to sea, to a spot some yards from the shore.

Finally he was asked how he thought Jean Burrows had died. He went and stood in the shallows and knelt down, his hand pressing down in the water. Then he put his left hand round his own throat, with the palm uppermost, leaving his thumb under the right side of his throat.

Chief Superintendent Wright took him to police headquarters, satisfied that he had the murderer, for only the police and the pathologist knew all those details and about the dead woman's injuries. Later that day US naval divers searched the sea where Belvin had indicated the iron pipe would be. It was there and brought to the police station.

275

Soon afterwards the report from Professor Simpson arrived and, based purely on the slides and the photographs, he had reconstructed the murder with uncanny accuracy. Detectives found Belvin's clothes in the suitcase he carried around from one lodging house to another, and they were sent to the Yard laboratory. Tests proved conclusively that he had been in close contact with the dead woman. There were more than one hundred fibres which exactly matched those from the dress Jean Burrows had been wearing when she died.

It had been a phenomenally fast investigation and Paul Augustus Belvin was charged with murder on 1 September 1971. He made a full statement, which was backed up by the scientific evidence given by Professor Simpson at the court in Bermuda. Belvin was found guilty and sentenced to death, commuted later to life imprisonment.

Throughout the investigation the Police Commissioner in Bermuda, George Duckett, OBE, had given invaluable help to the Yard men and when he visited London in the following year they met for dinner. It was the last time Bill Wright and Basil Haddrell were to see him alive, for on 9 September 1972 he was murdered at his home at Bleak House in the suburb of Devonshire, only half a mile from his police headquarters.

At the time Chief Superintendent Wright was working on a murder case in the Thames Valley. He was taken off that case and, with Haddrell, flown straight back to Bermuda. On the way he studied the police career of forty-one-year-old George Duckett. He joined the colonial police, served in Nigeria and Jamaica and was appointed to Bermuda as Commissioner in 1969. He was six feet five inches tall, a strict disciplinarian who took a hard line on criminals, particularly those who trafficked in drugs.

The officers went straight to Bleak House and met the local detectives who told them the details of the killing. Soon after 9 p.m., following dinner with his wife Jane and daughter Marcia, George Duckett had collected the plates and taken them to the kitchen. He had called to his wife to bring a new bulb because the security light at the back door was out. He had opened one door inwards and then opened a screen door and reached up to remove the bulb, when he was shot from the darkness at close range. He fell inside the house and the door closed and locked behind him. More shots were fired into the kitchen from the other side of the house and the seventeen-year-old Marcia fell, wounded in the chest. Jane Duckett went to the telephone but found the wires cut. She checked that Marcia was only slightly wounded and then ran to their official police car to try the radio. That, like the telephone, had been put out of action, so she drove to the police headquarters with the klaxon blaring and reported the murder.

Wright learned that nobody had been seen or heard and no alarm had been raised, probably because the family's Alsatian guard dog had died mysteriously some weeks before.

The bullets fired that night and recovered from the bodies of George Duckett and his daughter were fired from a ·22 revolver, although no gun had been found. There was no apparent motive, apart from the fact that George Duckett was a policeman. There had been no attempt at robbery. From the point of view of the killer it had been easy, for the family had regular habits and mostly dined at the same time each night.

This time the Yard men found the going very tough and for more than three months they had to make intensive inquiries in a very different world from their homeland. Local people were disinclined to talk, although they were friendly enough on the surface. Despite a reward of 24,000 dollars offered by the government for any information, there was little help forthcoming.

All detectives who travel abroad on foreign assignments experience similar basic difficulties. Even in English speaking countries terminology is different, particularly in the vernacular. That has to be learnt and so do the nicknames, which for many people are the only names they know or answer to. Wright and Haddrell got to know men with

277

names like Thick-Lip Smith and Pork Chop, and it was quite pointless asking for them by any other name. But slowly they managed to infiltrate the varying social scenes and as they became accepted, slowly the barriers came down.

In December 1972 they returned to London for a conference. At 33,000 feet above the Atlantic Sergeant Haddrell received a message that he had been promoted to Detective Inspector but was to stay on the inquiry. The two detectives returned to Bermuda in January for another six weeks of hard investigation, but still they failed to get the break they needed. In all investigations abroad there is a sticking point, and Chief Superintendent Wright decided in February to call a halt and he and Haddrell returned to Scotland Yard. Local detectives were given strict instructions to pursue the inquiry. With their local knowledge it was thought they would find information more easily, and they did, in fact, come up with much useful knowledge which was afterwards to prove valuable.

It was less than a month later when the call came to return. It was the night of 10 March, exactly six months after the murder of George Duckett. It happened to be Bill Wright's wedding anniversary and Basil Haddrell was the night duty officer on the Murder Squad. When he picked up the telephone he talked to a man he knew well. 'It's Nobby here,' said Bermuda's new Police Commissioner, Lefroy Maxwell Clark.

This time the summons was to investigate the double murder of Sir Richard Sharples, KCMG, OBE, MC, the Governor and Commander in Chief of Bermuda, and his ADC Captain Hugh Sayers of the Welsh Guards. The third casualty was Sir Richard's dog, a Great Dane called Horsa. The two men and the dog had been shot dead, apparently at the same time and by the same person.

Commissioner Clark asked for the same two officers to return. Haddrell found that there was a flight at 8 a.m. and he booked two seats on it. His chief was at home, having returned from his party at 5 a.m.! They met at Heathrow Airport at 7 a.m.

It had already been a busy week for Haddrell – a car packed with explosives had been defused outside the Yard and another car bomb had exploded outside the Old Bailey. As night duty reserve man he had had little rest.

Next morning they were back on a now familiar island, but at a different scene of murder. The same local detectives were there to help and they had adhered strictly to correct procedures, including preserving the place where the shootings had occurred. This was part of the garden at Government House where a balustraded stone staircase led down from a terrace to a lower lawn. Photographs showed that Sir Richard and Captain Sayers had been killed on the terrace quite close to the house. The dog had been found a few yards away at the end of a trail of blood.

The detectives learned that there had been a dinner party that night. About ten o'clock Lady Sharples had felt unwell and had retired to bed. The party had broken up about an hour later. At 11.30 p.m. Sir Richard had walked past the policeman on guard inside the foyer, to take the Great Dane for his customary walk. Sayers had followed a few minutes later, having first gone to collect his ·38 revolver which he stuck in his cummerbund. The two men were talking when they were shot at close range. Sir Richard received one bullet and Captain Sayers was shot twice. He fell, still with his hands in his pockets, as he had been standing seconds before. The dog was shot just once. Hearing the shots, the constable had raised the alarm and the house had been surrounded, but no trace of the gunman had been found.

An examination of the scene proved that the shots had been fired upwards through the stone balustrade. There were powder marks on the stone, indicating that the muzzle of the gun, believed to be a revolver, had been close to one of the stone pillars when it was fired. Local inquiries had revealed that two black men had been seen running away immediately after the shooting, but no one could identify them.

The Chief Superintendent was convinced there was a connection between the shooting of the Police Commissioner,

George Duckett, and the murders at Government House, but the investigation hit a wall of silence. He and his inspector went back over all the old ground and for six weeks they followed up the leads which together were beginning to prove useful but were not conclusive. Then came another double murder.

On 6 April two men were found shot dead in their shop in the shopping centre at Victoria Street, Hamilton, a multiple store run on supermarket lines. The victims were partners Victor Rego and Mark Doe. Chief Superintendent Wright and his inspector went to the scene to find that the two men had been shot at point-blank range, having first been tied hand and foot with blue cord. They were still lying face upwards and must have seen their executioners.

The detectives reconstructed the crime and discovered that Rego and Doe had closed the shop at 8 p.m. and locked it up. Then they had emptied the tills and counted the money which, according to the tills' addition sheets, amounted to about £6,000. There was no sign of any break-in and it appeared that the killers had hidden themselves on the premises before the shop closed. That was supported by the fact that two iron bars at the back of the premises had been sawn through from the inside to help their escape. The telephone wires had been cut and police took away the cut ends.

A post-mortem revealed that Rego had been shot twice and Doe once, both by a ·32 revolver. Some ·22 revolver bullets had also been fired at the scene, which suggested that at least two men had taken part in the murders and that one of them, with the ·22 gun, had fired at the shopkeepers and missed.

The Yard men were now investigating five murders and the government increased the reward to three million dollars, to be paid in any currency, for correct information. Because of the gravity of the murders the Commissioner of the Metropolitan Police decided to reinforce the Yard men in Bermuda. A team of detectives, led by Commander John Morrison, Chief of the Murder Squad, with a superintendent from Fingerprints, two teams of Scenes of Crime officers and four men from the Flying Squad arrived in Bermuda on 13 April. Morrison was not only a great detective but he was also something of a diplomat. Bill Wright and Basil Haddrell were his men and had been in Bermuda for some time, so he did not interfere in their investigation but he and the men he brought with him merely set out to help them as much as possible.

Intensive inquiries in the busy area of the last two murders produced some vital information. Witnesses said that three black men were seen to run away from the shop and jump into a waiting car which was driven away at high speed. More importantly, one of the fleeing men had been recognized as Larry Winfield Tacklyn, a local man. He was arrested and the investigation continued.

Tacklyn's arrest was the first blow and was clearly resented by the Bermuda underworld. On 5 May a man on a motorcycle fired a number of shots at police headquarters and broke the windows of the Murder Room. Soon afterwards, a man again fired into police headquarters with a pump-action shotgun, and a number of empty shells were found. Throughout September there was a series of armed robberies and shooting incidents, including one on the police officers' mess, where several shots were directed at the place where the Commissioner, 'Nobby' Clark, normally sat for his meals.

On the eve of the anniversary of the murder of George Duckett, the local newspaper recalled the fact, and next day shots were fired into the kitchen of Bleak House, the exact spot where the former Commissioner had been killed. A schoolteacher had taken over the house and he moved out next day.

All the shells and bullets from these incidents were carefully collected. Some were dug out of walls, others found in woodwork and some in trees and in the ground. They were all carefully labelled and sent to Brian Arnold, the ballistics officer at the Yard laboratory.

The Yard men were in full cry. One encouraging fact was

the fear they discovered among witnesses. It hindered their inquiries but it also meant they were getting nearer the killers.

On 25 September 1973 the Bank of Bermuda was raided by a man with a sawn-off shotgun and a ·32 pistol. He escaped on a Mobilette with 28,000 dollars. That man was seen and identified as Erskine Durrant Burrows, known as 'Buck', also a local man. Four days later there was an armed robbery at the Pigley Wigley Plaza, a shopping complex. Again the bandit had a shotgun and a ·32 pistol and again Burrows was identified. That time the police were quickly alerted and chased Burrows on his Mobilette through a tropical rainstorm. They lost him in the labyrinth of Hamilton's slums.

Burrows was now on the run and the evidence was piling up. Detectives found that telephone wires had been cut at the Bank of Bermuda. When Chief Superintendent Wright and Inspector Haddrell searched Burrows' room in a neglected street of derelict buildings they found a pair of wire-cutters which were sent to the Yard laboratory. There the scientists found the cutting blades of the instrument compared exactly with the striation marks on the cut ends of the telephone wires at Bleak House and the telephone wires at the shopping centre supermarket. The absence of any inconsistent detail suggested that both sets of wires had been severed by the same cutters.

Detectives were keeping observation round the clock on all the places Burrows was likely to go and on 18 October 1973 he was seen in the street carrying a sawn-off shotgun. Inspector Haddrell organized an ambush, hiding himself and his men in thick bushes under cover of darkness. As they waited there they heard the staccato stutter of what sounded like a Thompson machine-gun and wondered if Burrows had recruited some armed friends to help him. In fact the noise was the Fire Brigade's transmitter exploding its valves! Just then, as the explosions ceased, Burrows came riding down the road on his Mobilette. Detective Inspector John Donald of the Bermuda police jumped on his back and knocked him off his bike. Burrows was held and led, handcuffed, to a cell. The ·32 revolver and the sawn-off shotgun that he had had with him were both loaded and cocked.

The fact that both Tacklyn and Burrows were in custody meant that people who had previously been frightened to talk to the police now did so. Although it took a long time, a mass of fascinating evidence was uncovered. In the end all the guns used were found and the police were able to prove that they included not only the guns which were used in the murders by Tacklyn and Burrows but also those which were fired indiscriminately at buildings.

One was found buried in the garden of a house; another was found with two young men who had been arrested for robbery and shopbreaking; another was dug up from a garden, wrapped in an old newspaper, and a man in jail in the Bahamas agreed he had bought it from Burrows after the shopping centre murders.

Later two Bermudian subjects testified to conversations they had with Tacklyn and Burrows, some before and some after the various murders were committed. The conversations amounted to admissions of responsibility for the murders and corroboration of some of the detail, detail which could be known only by the perpetrators. Tacklyn admitted, for example, having killed the Governor and the ADC, and said the dog Horsa ran up to him and so he had shot it. The bullet that had killed the animal was found in the earth at the bottom of the steps, although a blood trail made by the dying Horsa finished at the top of the terrace steps. That proved knowledge only the assailants or the police could have known.

When Burrows was questioned about the Bank of Bermuda robbery, he admitted he had used the old military mortuary to bury the proceeds. Later, when Tacklyn and Burrows were standing trial for the shopping centre murders, an eleventh-hour witness came forward to say he had seen the two men, on the morning of the killings, digging up something from the old military mortuary which appeared to have previously been buried. He had noticed that one of the men had put a length of blue-coloured cord into a paper bag. Both the victims, Rego and Doe, had been bound hand and foot with blue-coloured cord. At the time of the murders the cord had been photographed and published in the press with requests for help in identifying it. The witness had tried to contact the police, but, because of a misunderstanding, had been unable to do so. However, although it was three and a half years later, when the witness was shown the cord used to tie up the victims he identified it as that he had seen in the hands of the two defendants.

Both Tacklyn and Burrows were charged with the murders of Sir Richard Sharples, Captain Sayers, and of Rego and Doe at the shopping centre, while Burrows alone was charged with the murder of George Duckett. Burrows was found guilty on all counts and Tacklyn guilty only of the murders in the shopping centre. They were both sentenced to death and were both hanged.

Tacklyn and Burrows were criminals who had had some connection with Black Power, but only in so far as it suited their purposes. Burrows, in fact, made a written confession. He did not indicate his reasons for killing George Duckett, but said he was not alone when he killed the Governor, whom he had shot because of the office he held, and not because of the man he was, to make black people aware of the evils of the colonial system in Bermuda.

For the better part of five years the two Yard men had been engaged on six murder cases in Bermuda and flown the Atlantic countless times. By the time the trials were held the senior detective was plain Mr Wright, because he had retired, but he crossed the Atlantic once more for the final stages of his investigation and was sworn in as a Special Constable. His co-investigator, Detective Inspector Basil Haddrell, returned to Scotland Yard to be promoted to Detective Chief Inspector.

CHAPTER 27

The Black Panther

The use of guns by the murderer, the use of mass publicity by the police, the liaison between police forces countrywide, car chases, security guards, tape recordings, kidnapping, and hundreds of smaller pointers tell us that the case of the Black Panther is a story of the Seventies. Yet in 1975 every fingerprint investigated during the long inquiry was checked by individual experts – computer checks came in only in 1977 – and the key to the whole operation lay in the massive card index, a system of cross-referencing developed long before and passed down the years as a totally reliable way of holding on to every scrap of information obtained by a Murder Squad team.

On 7 March 1975 seventeen-year-old Lesley Whittle was found dead sixty feet below ground level in a circular concrete shaft. The place was Bathpool Park, Kidsgrove, Staffordshire.

The girl had been kidnapped from her home in Highley, Shropshire, shortly after four o'clock on the morning of 14 January 1975, and held to ransom for £50,000. She had been asleep and was naked. When her mother found next morning that she was missing she told the police. Also missing from the bedroom was a nightdress, a dressing-gown and a pair of slippers. In the sitting-room she found a Dymo tape stuck to a vase. It read: 'Go to the Swan shopping centre, Kidderminster, today between 6.00 p.m. and 1.00 a.m. and wait for a call at one of the three telephone boxes. I want £50,000 – if police or tricks – death.'

Detective Chief Superintendent Robert Booth had been in charge while the case was being investigated as one of kidnapping by the West Mercia police force. But when the murder was discovered in Staffordshire responsibility shifted to that county and the Chief Constable of Staffordshire turned to Scotland Yard for help.

On the day that Lesley's body was found Scotland Yard's Murder Squad chief, Commander John Morrison, left his desk to take over the investigation. His assistant was Detective Inspector Walter Boreham. Commander Morrison had been in charge of the Squad since 1947 and, in this case, decided to take the unusual step of taking command himself. This quiet-voiced Scot from Stornoway had risen from constable to his present rank and built himself a reputation as a tough and remarkably thorough detective. Detective Inspector Boreham had been with the Murder Squad for some years and was an experienced officer.

Morrison's first move was to confer with Detective Chief Superintendent Booth. He then went to the shaft in Bathpool Park, less than half a mile from the village of Kidsgrove. Lesley was naked, her hands tied behind her, hanging by her neck on a thirty-foot length of quarter-inch galvanized wire which had a yellow plastic cord running through its centre.

The shaft had three small platforms between the top and the bottom, measuring five feet across. A steel ladder was cemented into the wall and the wire from which Lesley was hanging had been tightly wound around the rung of the ladder nearest to the lowest platform. On that platform was a red quilted sleeping-bag. Her dressing-gown was on the platform within reach but it was soaking wet.

Police suspected that Lesley Whittle had been taken to the shaft only a few hours after she had been snatched from her bed. The only light came from the open bottom of the shaft where it led into a sewer-like drain, which was running with water. The cause of death was said by Commander Morrison to be vagal inhibition – her heart stopped through sheer terror – not strangulation through hanging. Pathologists were unable to establish exactly when she died, but police suspected it was shortly after she had been brought to the tunnel.

The Yard men had brought with them their own fingerprint experts and officers trained in looking for clues at the scene of the crime, and they searched every inch of the shaft. They found a pair of Carl Zeiss binoculars and a notebook. They also took away the sleeping-bag and the wire which had held her. At the bottom of the shaft near the running water they found a pair of men's shoes, size seven.

Back at Kidsgrove Commander Morrison and his assistant studied reports, some of which went back to 1974. In late January 1975 a stolen car had been found with a positive treasure trove of clues, one of which was a tape recorder with Lesley's voice on the spool. The rest of the contents inextricably linked whoever had used the car and kidnapped Lesley with a series of brutal murders covering three counties and dating back to February 1974.

The first crime was at New Park, Harrogate, Yorkshire, when a hooded man shot fifty-four-year-old sub-postmaster Donald Skepper, who later died in his wife's arms. The gunman had woken Mr Skepper's eighteen-year-old son, prodded him with a shotgun, tied him up and demanded to be told where the post-office safe keys were. He had taped the boy's mouth and prodded him to his parents' bedroom. The only light came from the torch the intruder had strapped to the shotgun barrel. As Mr Skepper woke and shouted, there was a flash from the gun. The hooded man escaped empty-handed.

When the police arrived, the only clues they could find were two small holes bored beneath the catch on the window, a burglar's well-known method of entry.

Detective Superintendent William Dolby investigated that murder. While he was still no nearer a solution another, similar, murder occurred at a sub-post office at Higher Baxenden, Accrington, Lancashire. It was on 6 September 1974 and the victim was Derek Astin, aged forty-four. This time the killer had climbed into the bedroom of the daughter of the house, Susan, who had screamed for help. Her father had tackled the gunman and was first shot in the shoulder. A second shot took him in the back. Although dying from shotgun wounds, Mr Astin had flung the raider

287

down the stairs. The gunman had sprung to his feet and coolly shot again, this time using a ·22 automatic pistol attached to a lanyard round his neck.

Both raids were at four o'clock in the morning and the same method of entry was used. One month and five days later came murder number three.

On 12 November 1974 at Langley sub-post office, Oldbury, Worcestershire, the sub-postmaster, Sidney Grayland, answered a knock on the door in the late afternoon. On the step was a masked gunman who fired at point-blank range with a pistol. As Sidney Grayland collapsed and died, his wife Peggy ran out. The gunman pistol-whipped her round the head, tied her up and dumped her in a corner. The attack was so ferocious that she nearly died, but in that raid the gunman's mask was slightly dislodged and Mrs Grayland was able to help the police build a description of the killer.

She said he was a man in his late forties, of medium build, clean shaven with dark hair. The police of the three counties concerned had collected a few more interesting details about him. He spoke in monosyllables, possibly to hide his native accent; he had sometimes been compassionate in loosening a captive's bonds but he had an utterly ruthless triggerfinger when challenged by a man.

A reward of £25,000 was offered for any person who could give information leading to the killer, and police all over Britain were hunting him. Only three things were certain at that time. He was always dressed in black, he was cold-blooded and he had the agility of a panther.

Soon after Lesley Whittle's kidnapping in January police had found a stolen Morris 1300 saloon car abandoned in a public car park at Dudley, Worcestershire. The index number plates had been changed and it was eventually discovered that the car had, in fact, been stolen from West Bromwich, near Birmingham, on 22 October 1974.

When the detectives forced open the car they had found clues, some of which tied in closely with another crime which linked the person who had used the car with an incident on 15 January 1975, the night after Lesley had been kidnapped. On that night a freightliner depot security guard named Gerald Smith had been shot and left for dead by an intruder he had disturbed. However, he survived, critically injured, to give the police a description.

Smith had been told to keep a special watch for IRA men who were thought to be in the area. That evening he had seen a man lurking in the depot and had challenged him. The man had said nothing but shot Smith six times at close range and then disappeared. The scene of that shooting was only a few hundred yards from where the stolen car was found.

When Lesley Whittle's body was finally found, Commander Morrison and Inspector Boreham recruited an investigation team of more than two hundred men and they worked closely with Detective Chief Superintendent Harold Wright, the Staffordshire CID Chief. The murder team, which had been working in small rooms at Kidsgrove police station, now took over the whole building, while the local police moved into the Town Hall. All the clues which had been found over the country were moved to Kidsgrove so that Morrison could study the overall picture of the investigation which had begun in 1974.

From the inspection shaft where Lesley was found were the binoculars, the shoes, the sleeping-bag and the wire. From the car was half a foam-rubber mattress, a tape recorder, paper, envelopes, forty feet of strong rope, a petrol can, blankets, a puncture repair outfit, a black anorak, a torch, a bottle of Lucozade and some barley sugar. There was writing on an envelope, which appeared to be a list of years and opposite each one a number.

Commander Morrison knew he had the kidnapper's car. He also knew that if he could find out where all the articles had been bought he might get a lead to the man the press had nicknamed the Black Panther. It was a mammoth task and hundreds of detectives scoured the country, calling on shops, showing photographs, hoping that a shopkeeper would remember a sale and the man who made the purchase.

They had some astonishing successes.

The killer had bought the binoculars found near Lesley's body from a Manchester shop for £88.45 on Friday, 27 October 1972. For the guarantee he gave the false name of Turner but a genuine address in Wilmslow, Cheshire. The sleeping-bag found in the inspection shaft was bought from a store in Stafford on 12 April 1973. Some of the clothing found in the car he bought from a Leeds store on 20 November 1974. The nine-metre coil of strong wire found round Lesley's neck was bought from Pitcher's ironmonger's shop in Walsall. The purchaser paid for it in cash some time between September and November 1973. The shop originally had ten coils of the wire and six innocent buyers were traced.

But not one of these shopkeepers could remember what the man looked like.

The shoes had been manufactured by the Bata Shoe Company, one of a range of 30,000 pairs. Police managed to account for every single sale but for forty-two pairs which had been sold to a market trader in Leicester.

On the stolen Morris car police found an excise licence which was traced to an A55 van in Leicester from which it had been stolen early in January 1975. The thief had put the licence on the Morris but had not bothered to change the details.

Six days later he had kidnapped Lesley Whittle.

Commander Morrison went back over all the old evidence and listened to Lesley's voice on the tape recorder, hoping to hear something which would lead him to the kidnapper's hiding place. The voice said, 'Kidsgrove post office box. Find message behind the back board.' It was repeated three times. Police were sure this message was made by Lesley and dictated by her captor. It was to have been played over the telephone to Ronald Whittle at the Swan shopping centre, directing him to the British Railway freightliner depot at Dudley where he was to pay over the ransom. The tape was never played for the guard Smith intervened. The instructions were for Ronald to attach the bag containing the money to a rope hanging over a green gate in the boundary wall. Ronald would not have been able to see the kidnapper who had a prepared line of escape.

Morrison read the reports for nights on end, and then read them again. He got all his senior officers to read them, looking for the one clue that would lead him to the killer.

Morrison knew that Lesley Whittle's brother Ronald had been called and was present when the police read the original message, and it was agreed that he and the police would act together but would keep their liaison secret. Ronald Whittle drew £50,000 cash from his bank and it was carefully marked by Detective Chief Superintendent Booth and his men.

At 6.00 p.m. that night Ronald Whittle waited for the call by the three telephone boxes. A team of detectives waited in the shadows. There was no call, and looking at the assembled facts later it seemed to the Yard men that it was an interesting coincidence that it was on the same night that Gerald Smith had been shot. The man who had shot him had been in the dark but had not been masked, and it was close to where the kidnap car was found.

On the next day, 16 January, Mr Leonard Rudd, the transport manager of the Whittle bus company, the Whittle family business, took a telephone call and heard a voice he thought was Lesley Whittle's on a tape recorder. The voice said: 'Kidsgrove post office box. Find message behind the back board.' The message was repeated three times and then the line went dead.

Rudd passed the message to Ronald Whittle who passed it on to the police. At the telephone box Whittle found a Dymo tape, instructing him to go to Bathpool Park, Kidsgrove, at midnight with £50,000 and follow a flashing light.

Ronald Whittle was late in arriving because he did not know the way. He waited in the dark but since he saw no signals he went home with the ransom money and his bodyguard of policemen, not realizing that his sister was only eighty yards away, hidden in the inspection shaft.

From that time on, the trail of the Black Panther went cold. The police work continued, however. From the clothes found in the car and partial descriptions, they knew that the man they were hunting was aged between thirty and forty, five feet five inches to five feet eight inches tall, with dark hair, high cheek bones, and dark staring eyes. From the clothes they had they knew he had a 38-inch chest, a 32-inch waist, a 29-inch inside leg measurement and a size seven foot.

Morrison kept a close liaison with the press, with radio and television, and the Black Panther became the most wanted man in Britain. The dragnet was spread all over the country. Every drunk was picked up with more than cursory interest, every petty crook arrested was given a closer look. Every set of fingerprints was sent urgently to Scotland Yard for comparison with one tiny fragment of a fingerprint found on the page of a notebook left in the inspection shaft. In the course of the inquiry thirteen million prints of known criminals were checked by experts working in the Criminal Record Office.

A massive cross-index filing system had been installed at Kidsgrove police station. By the end of November 1975 there were 28,000 statements, 32,000 recorded telephone calls, 2,500,000 filed index cards and more than 60,000 people had been interviewed. More than half a million checks were made on driving licence application forms to compare the writing found on pieces of paper in the car.

Everyone on the murder team worked at least fourteen hours a day. The inspiration for this devotion to duty was Commander Morrison, who frequently did not see his hotel room for several days at a time, except for a bath and a shave.

During that summer Morrison, Detective Inspector Boreham, Chief Inspector Len Barnes and Detective Inspector Malcolm Bevington, both the latter of the local Staffordshire force, had toured the country, talking to policemen, telling them what to look for, impressing on them that 'the Panther' might easily kill again. They went over his description, the clothes he might wear, the fact that he might be carrying a holdall or a bag of some kind carrying a gun or implements of burglary, that he preferred to operate in the dark and that he walked like a physical training instructor – on the balls of his feet.

The tour of instruction paid off. At 11.00 p.m. on 11 December 1975, eleven months after Lesley was kidnapped, two police constables, Stuart McKenzie and Anthony White, cruising along in their Panda car outside the Four Ways public house in Mansfield, Nottinghamshire, became suspicious of a man carrying a bag. There was a sub-post office near by.

When they stopped to question him he told them he was a lorry driver, that his name was John Moxon, and he was on his way home to Chapel-en-le-Frith, in Derbyshire. They asked to see what was in his bag and he put it on the ground and bent over it. When he straightened up he had a shotgun in his hands, pointing at them. He motioned them to their car, ordered White into the back seat and got in beside the driver McKenzie. With the gun cradled in his arms he ordered McKenzie to drive to Blidworth, a village eight miles away.

For five and a half miles the Panda sped along, with Constable White in the back waiting for a chance to pounce. In the village of Rainworth, just by a queue of people outside a fish and chip shop, White grabbed the gun. It went off and the people from the queue ran to help. White had been shot in the hand, but the gun was wrested from the man and within minutes he was handcuffed to near-by railings.

White was not badly hurt and when more police arrived the man was searched. He had a knife in one of his boots and another in his cartridge belt. On top of that he answered the description of the Black Panther. Commander Morrison was in London for a conference at the time, and he raced north, saw the prisoner and had him transferred to Kidsgrove, where he gave his real name, Donald Neilson, and his address, Granefield Avenue, Thornbury, Bradford.

Having waited so long Morrison was in no hurry to hear Neilson's full story, but he sent Detective Inspector Malcolm Bevington and three other detectives to look at Neilson's home. They roused Mrs Neilson from bed and searched the house. When they came to a locked room in the attic Bevington asked Mrs Neilson for a key but she said she had never had one. He forced the door and found the Panther's lair.

There were eight hoods in black and red wool, black, dark blue and red track suits; three coils of wire, identical to the one used to hang Lesley Whittle; a Dymo tape dispenser, similar to the tapes used on the kidnap trail; combat jackets with extra pockets stitched in and transistor radios capable of picking up police frequencies.

The table was a home-made work bench and there were racks of carpentry and metal-work tools the Panther had used for making false car number plates; a brace and bit he had used for burglary; blankets, ropes, tents, heavy boots, gas lamps and groundsheets. There were similar envelopes to those found in the stolen car, specimens of handwriting which matched those found in the car, a number of books on crime, and books about the Commandos and the SAS and some military histories.

And underneath the floorboards were two shotguns and hundreds of rounds of ammunition.

Back at Kidsgrove, the interrogation of Neilson went on and, slowly, as he realized the Yard men had a mass of evidence, he 'put his hands up' – the Murder Squad term for the prisoner accepting defeat.

He told them that he had got the idea of the kidnap from a story he had read in a newspaper about the wealth of the Whittle family, and that he had laid the ransom trail at the freightliner depot on the night before he kidnapped Lesley. On the night afterwards, when he should have telephoned Ronald Whittle, he had gone to the depot to make sure his direction signs were still in place and had been disturbed by Gerald Smith.

Had he been able to telephone he would have directed Ronald Whittle to a green gate over which would have been hanging a rope. He planned to direct Whittle to tie the case containing the money to the rope and Neilson would have pulled it over the gate without having been seen. The inter-vention of the security guard forced him to change his plans and organize another ransom trail to lure Ronald Whittle to Bathpool Park, where he planned to escape with the money through the inspection shaft and out of the tunnel at the other end of the complex.

Then he told them the terrible story of the kidnapping. He said he had entered Lesley Whittle's bedroom wearing a black hood and carrying a sawn-off shotgun with a torch taped to the barrel with sticking tape. He had shone the torch into her eyes to waken her. Then he had tied her wrists and feet together with sticking tape, and taped sticking plas-ter across her mouth and eyes. He had carried her to the car, which was parked outside the house, and put her in the back with the foam-mattress on top of her so that she could not be seen. Then he had driven sixty-five miles to Kidsgrove, arriving at 7 a.m. He mentioned that it was a bitterly cold morning, that the ground was covered with white frost. She was still blindfolded as he walked her along the tunnels to the bottom of the inspection shaft. She had to walk 150 yards in six inches of freezing water and then climb the steel ladder to where he tethered her. There she had remained and no one knows to this day whether she fell from the ledge accidentally or whether Neilson pushed her off it to her death.

He then told them about his early days and about his life of crime which began seriously in 1971.

He was born on 1 August 1936 in Morley, Yorkshire, and christened Donald Nappey, the only son of a working-class family. His mother died when he was eleven and he was brought up by his father and other relatives. He hated his own name because it led to endless jokes. When he left school he was apprenticed to a local carpenter and, in 1955, began his National Service with the King's Own Yorkshire Light Infantry.

In his new Army uniform, he married his childhood sweetheart, Irene Tait. He was a lonely young man of eight-een. None of his family would come to his wedding and, on

295

the night before, he had to ask some former neighbours to act as witnesses.

His Army service took him to Cyprus, Kenya and Aden. He became a marksman and was trained to survive in rugged conditions, including action under fire.

Discharged from the Army, he returned to his wife, gave up his apprenticeship and bought a taxi from a man called Neilson. He kept the original log-book and changed his name to Neilson by deed-poll. His daughter Kathryn was born in 1959 and he spent his family holidays in disused Army camps, playing war games as though he were on active service.

In 1971 work was scarce and he broke into a house in Yorkshire and stole three shotguns and hundreds of rounds of ammunition. In three months he held up the three sub-post offices at gunpoint and stole £9,200. In his next raid a sub-postmaster in Lancashire tore off his mask and he fired his shotgun into the ceiling and escaped.

It was then that the killings began, ending with the kidnapping and murder of Lesley Whittle. He had read that the family was wealthy and he had already found the tunnels under Bathpool Park. To his organized mind he now had the ingredients for the perfect crime – a ransom of £50,000, a place to hide the victim and collect the money without being seen, and a ready-made escape route.

There was one more victim of this one-man wave of terrorism – Gerald Smith, the guard he had shot when laying the kidnap trail. It was his fifth killing for Gerald Smith died after Neilson's arrest.

At his trial at Oxford Assizes, in July 1976, Neilson pleaded not guilty, saying he had not meant to kill any of his victims, that the guns had gone off accidentally, and that Lesley Whittle had fallen by accident from the ledge. But he was found guilty of murder and jailed for life. By his demeanour it appeared that he still thought of himself as the supreme criminal, a man who could outwit the nation's police forces.

Only once before had the chief of the Murder Squad left

his office to go out on an investigation. On that occasion it was also Commander Morrison, when he went to Bermuda to help Superintendent William Wright and Detective Inspector Basil Haddrell.

CHAPTER 28

The Cartridge Clue to Murder

On 3 November 1977 Scotland Yard's Murder Squad had been operating for seventy years and on that day bank killer Michael George Hart, aged thirty, was found guilty of shooting dead at point-blank range twenty-year-old Angela Woolliscroft in a raid on Barclays Bank, Upper Ham Road, Richmond, Surrey.

At the Old Bailey, Judge Melford Stevenson addressed the court: 'This case has emphasized the experiences I have had in other cases of the magnificent work done by police in pursuing an investigation of very great difficulty and demands on personnel which it was difficult to meet.

'When one thinks that 5,000 people were interviewed and 15,000 house inquiries made, not to mention the steps taken by officers into another 125 cases which resulted in 65 arrests then one begins to appreciate the debt which the community owes to the police.'

The Hart case demonstrates how murder investigation has developed, and how all the experience gained over the years has been passed on and improved upon. All the scientific aids were at hand, there was ample transport, almost unlimited manpower and even the use of a helicopter.

The case had begun nearly a year before on 10 November

1976, when Hart walked into the bank and up to the counter where Miss Woolliscroft sat at her desk behind the safety-glass screen at Number Three till. He pointed a sawn-off shotgun at her and in a quiet voice said, 'Give me some money. Hurry up.'

The girl took the money from the till and pushed it across the counter – £2,500 in notes of different denominations. Then Hart raised the gun a little higher and fired, shattering the safety-glass and hitting the girl in the chest and hand. She fell from her stool, and as the gunman turned and walked away Mrs Sheila Reid, another cashier, pressed the alarm bell. An ambulance was called, but Angela Woolliscroft died on the way to hospital.

At Scotland Yard Detective Chief Superintendent James Sewell was the first Murder Squad man on call. He and his team of Detective Inspector Alan Wordsworth and Detective Sergeant Bob Hancock had been on the customary one hour's notice for days – a duty known as 'first in the frame', from the wooden frame in which the three detectives on call for a murder case are listed in order.

Sewell and Wordsworth immediately left for the scene of the crime and Hancock, who had just run on to the rugby field at Imber Court, the police sportsground, was sent for. He tore off his green shirt, got dressed and also drove to the bank.

The Yard team had worked together before and they moved smoothly into action. The eleven other bank staff were interviewed. Only five of them had noticed the murderer and none thought they would be able to identify him. Even so they were able to help the detectives put together a description. Sewell sent an urgent message to the Yard for immediate release which read: 'Wanted for murder: man aged about twenty-five, five feet eight inches tall, of slim build with black hair, well-styled and with a parting; thin face with hollow cheeks and tanned or dark complexion. Wearing blue jeans, a dark-blue knee-length raincoat and black plastic sunglasses with large round frames. May be armed.'

While the Home Office pathologist, Professor Keith Mant, examined the body of the victim the Chief Superintendent and his men began their hunt for clues. The glass and other debris from the shattered screen was carefully collected and a search made for fingerprints, although witnesses had said they thought the man had worn gloves. But gloves sometimes have holes in the finger-tips.

When the killer fled he had dropped a woman's yellow raincoat and an empty plastic bag which, according to its markings, had once contained one hundredweight of chemical fertilizer. Two screwed-up pieces of paper were also found in the pocket of the raincoat and were carefully preserved.

Sewell set up his incident room at Richmond police station and reinforced his squad with Detective Sergeants Robert Geggie, Constable Graham Forsyth and Detective Constable Michael Sands.

Forsyth was a local officer and he took charge of the incident room, which was to be the hub of the investigation. Police Sergeant Noel Fisher was given the job of organizing house-to-house inquiries and a young Detective Constable, Kenneth Mason, was put in charge of exhibits. He was inexperienced but, in Sewell's words, 'came good' and recorded 2,300 separate actions in the course of the investigation. Woman Detective Constable Brenda Regan helped organize the incident room and did the office work.

Sergeant Fisher's immediate inquiries produced some useful information. He found out from passers-by that the killer had arrived opposite the bank in a car and had left in the same vehicle. They said the car was dark in colour and the letter 'C' might have been on the number plate.

More importantly, he found two witnesses who had seen the killer. One was a greengrocer's boy, Steven Harry, aged sixteen. He told Sergeant Fisher: 'Most people in this area are in a hurry at that time of the day but this man walked slowly. He walked across the road diagonally. It seemed to me he was walking slowly deliberately. I got a good look at

299

his face and I would remember him and recognize him.' He said the gunman was wearing black sunglasses.

The second witness, Nigel Sayers, a milkman, told police that he thought the man had his face blackened and that he saw him carrying a shotgun.

Almost opposite the bank where the murder took place is the Hawker Siddeley factory. Their doors opened at 12.30 p.m., one minute before the shooting. Hundreds of workers had walked out for their lunch-break and every one of them was a potential witness.

The woman's raincoat was made of lightweight material with the St Michael trademark, size 16 (to fit a 38-inch bust), and was 44 inches long. A label inside bore the mark 'Tricel 2117/105A'. But there was no clue as to the owner.

The fertilizer bag was a pale orange colour. It bore the words 'Newgrain. 26 per cent N. calcium ammonium nitrate, 1 cwt gross foreign'.

Chief Superintendent Sewell wanted publicity and he got it. He appealed for any witnesses to come forward, and he set up a mobile police station outside the bank. He told reporters, 'This was a cold-blooded, callous, calculated killing.' Barclays echoed that sense of outrage by offering their biggest ever reward to catch a killer – £50,000. 'I would like to hear from anyone who saw the man leave the bank, who saw the car he left in,' said the detective.

No fingerprints were found in the bank other than those of the staff, which supported those witnesses who thought the man they had seen had been wearing gloves.

The father of the dead girl, Mr William Woolliscroft, made an appeal to the killer to surrender to the police, suggesting that 'he must be a sick man'. That was not Sewell's point of view. He was adamant that the man he wanted was sane and utterly ruthless but he also believed in keeping the story alive and that all publicity was useful.

He organized a posse of mounted police to search all the open spaces and the big parks in the area in an effort to find the shotgun, which, he believed, the killer would have abandoned.

At the Yard laboratory scientists had been examining and photographing the two scraps of paper which had been found screwed up in the pocket of the yellow raincoat. One piece was the bottom half of a photo-copied entry from a wine-making competition run by the Weybridge Wine Club. The entry was signed 'Grahame' in the bottom right-hand corner, and on the reverse side was a shopping list for food-stuffs.

The man who had signed that entry form, Mr Grahame James Marshall, heard this news on his car radio and went to the police. He identified the pieces of paper and was also to shed some light on the events leading up to the murder. It was the first breakthrough in the three-day-old investigation.

Not only was Mr Marshall able to identify the entry form, which he had filled in in 1974, but he could say that the person who had written the shopping list was his sister, Miss Marshall. She was able to tell the police that on the morning of the murder she had taken her sister-in-law shopping in her A40 car and had parked in Bentalls' store car-park in Kingston.

Her car, a faded maroon saloon, was now in the garage at her home in Mitcham and detectives searched it minutely. Meanwhile Miss Marshall told her story of the morning of 10 November. She had parked the car on the ninth floor of the car park and gone shopping, leaving the passenger door unlocked. When she returned, soon after two o'clock, she noticed the car was in a slightly different position but, since she had left a door open, she thought perhaps the staff had moved the car for convenience. She had noticed her yellow raincoat and her sunglasses were missing but had not thought to report so insignificant a loss to the police.

Sewell remembered that witnesses had said the killer had worn sunglasses with big frames and it began to look as though he had used the pair he had found in the car as part of his disguise.

Once the detectives started making inquiries at the car

park parts of the jigsaw began to fit. Sewell was now certain that the killer had parked his own car on the morning of the murder near to the A40, driven it out of the park to Barclays Bank, and stopped nearby. After the robbery and the murder he had driven it back to the car park and escaped. But now, with a description of the A40 car and its index number UJD 362F, the detectives went back to all their witnesses and got some positive sightings. They discovered that immediately after the raid the driver of that car had narrowly escaped collision with another car and that when he was attempting to re-enter the car park he had tried to overtake a line of cars in the queue and had hooted continuously to make other drivers give way to him.

Miss Marshall also noticed that there was a considerable amount of wet earth on the back of her car, a good deal of it still sticking to the rear index number plate. Sewell pondered about that mud. He wondered if the car had been driven to some rough ground en route to the murder. He called for a police helicopter and, because he knew exactly what he was looking for, he decided to act as observer himself. Armed with powerful binoculars, he was flown over all the open spaces around Richmond.

Although he thought the killer might have been seeking refuge in the open he also thought he might see some distinctive tyre tracks or a place where the A40 had been bogged down and had collected the mud which had stuck to the back of the car. And there was the possibility that the wanted man had abandoned his own car after his escape. In that case he might be trying to hide by himself, using the cover of the woods or other cover like sports pavilions, gardeners' sheds or greenhouses.

Every motorist who had used the Bentalls' car park on the day of the shooting was traced and interviewed. Another witness now remembered seeing a man emptying a plastic bag full of leaves on a small green opposite the bank. That bag was identified by part-time gardener and retired Royal Navy officer George Paske, who had used it to clear up wet leaves and had left it by a tree. Mr Paske told the police, 'I recognized the bag in a newspaper photo. It gave me a bad shock.'

On 15 November a police placard was put out. It read: 'Metropolitan Police – Appeal for witnesses to the murder of Angela Woolliscroft, aged twenty, on Wednesday 10 November 12.30 p.m. at Barclay's Bank, Upper Ham Road, Ham, Richmond. She was shot during a robbery in which £2,500 was stolen. DID YOU SEE ANYTHING? Please contact the Murder Squad at Richmond police station at Telephone 01–940–9595. All information treated as strictly confidential.'

The ballistics experts at the Yard laboratory had by then decided that the gun used to kill Angela was a twelve-bore shotgun. They had discovered that from careful examination of the lead pellets which had penetrated the safety-glass and killed the young cashier. Pellets taken from her body confirmed that only one gun was used.

In the meantime Sewell had had a report from an informant that he had seen a man he knew named Hart transferring what looked like a shotgun from one car to another, a Wolseley saloon. Like the hundreds of other tips that followed the offer of a reward, this was followed up, even though the informant said that he had seen Hart in Basingstoke, twenty-five miles away.

Hart was interviewed, but he did not answer to the description of the killer and had a perfectly good alibi for the day in question. His house was searched but nothing incriminating was found. In routine fashion, his name was put into the Murder Squad 'system', a method of cross reference which among other things established if a suspect had previous convictions or was wanted.

In fact Hart did have a criminal record. He was then on bail for burglary, but there was no evidence to connect him with this crime. Because he lived in Basingstoke, outside the Metropolitan Police district, arrangements were made for local police to watch his movements. He was a possible suspect but no more than that.

Sewell went back to the Hawker Siddeley factory, where

303

sixty people had come forward to say that they thought they had seen the murderer of Angela Woolliscroft. It occurred to him that any one of them might be mistaken, and have seen one of their workmates and described him as the murderer. So Sewell had each of the sixty photographed and asked them to look at all the pictures and compare them with the Photofit reconstruction of the suspect. He also held a tea party in the factory and asked all the people photographed to look at each other.

That unique exercise eliminated all sixty people, in that those among them who had seen the suspect had seen a stranger and not one of their colleagues.

Twelve days after the murder the crew of a Hampshire patrol car, Police Constables McIlwraith and Mycott, answered an emergency radio call to Jackson's Garage, Basingstoke, which had reported a car crash. The police were told the offending car was a Ford Consul, index number WLM 370M. They picked up the car outside Basingstoke and gave chase – they lost the car eventually but during the chase they recognized Hart, whom they both knew as a local criminal.

They found the car later, broken down. The driver had disappeared, but their search of the vehicle produced a bonanza. In the boot was a Hendal ·22 automatic pistol and seventy-two rounds of ammunition for it. At Hart's home address in St Peter's Road, Basingstoke, Detective Sergeant Geggie and Detective Constable Sands found a box containing fifteen 'Eley' trapshooting No. 7 cartridges. When the detectives checked up on property reported stolen they found that the ·22 automatic pistol, a ·32 Webley revolver, a double-barrelled Reilly shotgun and some ammunition had been taken by a burglar who had broken into a gun-shop at Whitley Street, Reading, on 4 November 1976.

Chief Superintendent Sewell had a strong suspect, but first he had to find him and, secondly, prove the murder. There was no Christmas leave for the Murder Squad. On Christmas Eve Sewell was again up in the helicopter, hoping to find the fugitive murderer, and traffic patrol crews and all other car crews were making spot checks in the hope that Hart had broken his cover during the holiday period.

While the hunt went on the detectives found out that Hart had been a self-employed builder before the murder, and in August 1976 had carried out some work at a petrol station. He was due to be paid but had not called for his money. Sewell thought he might call some time and notified the staff at the office of Station Supreme Ltd, Lampton Road, Hounslow, Middlesex, that if he called they were to inform the police.

Meanwhile Sewell re-examined the medical evidence. The shots and the wads (the compressed cardboard used to pack the shot) removed from the dead girl's body were found to be Eley No. 7 shot, which can be either game or trapshot, and the wadding was of a new type.

The shot found in the body was No. 7 gameshot but the cartridges found at Hart's home were labelled No. 7 trapshot, and that worried Sewell. Gameshot is softer than trapshot, having only half per cent, as opposed to one per cent, antimyzne content, antimyzne being the hardening factor. Sewell had to be sure that the shot found in the body of Angela Woolliscroft had come from the cartridges found hidden in Hart's home and from the gun he had fired.

Sewell split one of Hart's cartridges open and sent the contents to the Yard's laboratory. Two hours later he got the answer – the cartridge contained game pellets. The manufacturers, Eley Kynoch Ltd of Birmingham, explained what had happened when Detective Inspector Wordsworth went to see them. An expert there told the inspector that it sometimes happens, because of human error, that the wrong shot is put into the shells. The wad in the shot, a design unique to Eley Kynoch, was known as Thamesboard and had been used only since 1 March 1976. It is made from cardboard impregnated with paraffin wax. The make-up of the live cartridge was, therefore, identical to the shot and wads found in Miss Woolliscroft's body and identical to the cartridges found at Hart's address. There had been a million-to-one labelling error caused by a computer fault during manufacture. A batch of game cartridges had been wrongly labelled trap cartridges.

The batch had been supplied to a dealer. The dealer had been burgled and a shotgun and the ammunition stolen just before Angela was shot dead. The evidence was nearly complete.

On 20 January 1977, seventy-one days after the murder, Hart walked into the offices of Station Supreme Ltd, Lampton Road, Hounslow, Middlesex, to collect the money he was owed. While he was talking to the manager, Mr William Smith, another employee, Security Manager Mr Ernest Culver, telephoned the police. Police Constable Ronald Hines arrested Hart and took him to Hounslow police station and from there to the murder hunt headquarters at Richmond. Hart had been travelling in a white Fiat car, which had been stolen on 7 December 1976 from a garage at Kingsbury, in North London. He had substituted false index plates for the original ones to avoid being stopped by the police.

At 5.30 p.m. on the evening of the following day he was interviewed by Detective Inspector Geggie and Sergeant Hancock. It was a preliminary interview and lasted an hour. The officers arranged to return at 7.30 p.m. It was fortunate that the detectives were punctual, for when they returned to the cell, they found Hart hanging from his cell door with his trouser belt round his neck. He was unconscious and barely breathing but the two sergeants managed to revive him and he was rushed to the West Middlesex Hospital where, after treatment, he recovered.

On the following day he was returned to police custody at Richmond. After being examined by the police surgeon, Dr Foster, he was declared fit to be detained and interviewed.

At first Hart insisted he had bought the gun from another man, but inquiries proved that to be false, although it took three days to do so. During the late afternoon of 26 January 1977 Hart saw his wife and brother-in-law, who visited him in the presence of two detectives. When their visit ended Hart asked to see Detective Chief Superintendent Sewell.

Hunter and hunted faced each other, Sewell calm but tri-umphant, Hart ready to talk. In the presence of his wife and brother-in-law he admitted killing Angela Woolliscroft, but said, 'It was an accident.' Hart was then interviewed alone by Detective Inspector Wordsworth and Sergeants Geggie and Hancock.

He said that he had broken into a shop in Reading in November and stolen two pistols, a shotgun and the No. 7 cartridges. On the morning of 10 November, the day of the murder, he had borrowed a gold-coloured Wolseley car from a garage at Basingstoke, driven to Bentalls' car park at Kingston and had taken the A40. He had already rec-onnoitred Barclays Bank at Upper Ham Road, Richmond, and on his way to make the raid he had bought a similar ignition key to that of the Wolseley in case he had to aban-don the A40. He chose the A40 because his Wolseley key fitted it.

Then he had gone to the bank, parked opposite and buried the sawn-off part of the shotgun on a small green near by, called Parkleys. He had taken a plastic sack, which he had found full of leaves and which he had emptied, to carry the money, wrapped the gun in the yellow raincoat and walked into the bank. He was wearing gloves, a wig and his face was coloured black. He also wore the sunglasses he had found in the A40.

He said he demanded money from the cashier and when he banged the glass partition with the gun it went off. He went further and said that Miss Woolliscroft leant to her right to get the money from the case drawers and, as she was straightening up, the gun went off by accident. Scientific evi-dence proved that to be false because some shot had pene-trated Miss Woolliscroft's right hand and that could not have happened if she had been leaning to the right, because her right hand and arm would have been protected by the cash counter below the safety screen. Incredibly, before he left the scene, he made time to cover the rear number plate with mud and then it had taken him thirty minutes to return to Bentalls' car park. He had got lost in the one-way traffic system and could not find the entrance to the car park. Then he had driven to Basingstoke in the Wolseley, via Hampton Court, where he had thrown the gun into the Thames. Later the car had broken down and at Fleet he had asked for help from the RAC. Not being a member he had joined on the spot and he also made his wife a member and paid £14. Then he had motored on to Basingstoke where he had left the car.

That night he had burnt his clothing and the wig he had worn in his own back garden and put the ashes into the dustbin.

Hart was taken by detectives to Hampton and he pointed to the place where he had thrown the gun into the river. Two police frogmen, Constables Lawson and Wort, dived in and found it. One barrel had been fired and the other was fully loaded and cocked. He also showed where he had buried the sawn-off section, which fitted exactly with the gun found in the river.

Sewell and his men were still not satisfied. They discovered that a man answering Hart's description had bought a black wig from a hairdresser's shop in north London for £4.95 and Hart admitted that he had bought a tin of black boot polish from Woolworth's to smear on his face on the day of the murder. On that same morning he had sawn off the barrel of the shotgun in his garage. Detectives continued their tightening of the evidence to maintain meticulous care and fairness. Leaves found in the plastic bag were found to be the same type of poplar leaves emptied out by Hart at Parkleys, but leaves found in the A40 were not identical. A pair of gloves, which had been in the A40, were found to contain glass identical to glass from the shattered screen. Those gloves had not been worn by Hart but the glass could have been transferred from Hart's clothing to the gun when it was put on the floor and thence to the gloves.

Hart was already on burglary charges at Basingstoke court and on four occasions the magistrates had refused bail. At the fifth bail application the officer in charge of the case was absent and bail was granted. But the court had been told that Hart was wanted in France for shooting at five French police officers and that Interpol had said the French police wanted to charge Hart with attempted murder. On his behalf a lawyer said that he had a fixed address, a family, substantial sureties and was willing to report to the police twice daily.

On the morning of the murder Hart had reported to Basingstoke police station. At 5.50 p.m. he again went to Basingstoke police station and again signed a bail form. It is believed to be the only case on record where a murder has been committed between visits to a police station!

From the time of Angela Woolliscroft's killing Hart had lived by crime, fraud and burglary, theft and car-stealing, receiving stolen property and criminal damage, thirty-nine offences in all. Some of them, although not the murder, had been committed with his woman chauffeur, twenty-year-old brunette Sharon Stacey, and she was sentenced at the Old Bailey to three years' imprisonment for using worthless cheques in a £777 spending spree with Hart.

When Mr Justice Melford Stevenson sentenced Hart to life imprisonment with a recommendation that he should serve at least twenty-five years, he described him as a 'wicked and dangerous criminal'. When he praised the work of the Murder Squad he mentioned that during the investigation the detectives had cleared up another 125 cases which resulted in 65 arrests. Even defence lawyers complimented the Squad on its superb documentation and the gathering of the evidence.

Conclusion

There seems to be one inescapable conclusion in the pattern I have outlined – it is that regardless of scientific advances, the complexities and speed of life today, nothing is more important to a detective than the experience he brings to solve each puzzle, and the dependence on his sense of 'smell' for the vital clue. Jim Sewell in 1976 was no less convinced that the answer to the killing of Angela Woolliscroft lay in the pellets in a cartridge than was Fred Wensley whose hunch sixty years before had led to the conviction of Louis Voisin for the murder and dismembering of Emilienne Gerard.

If the man's dependence lies in expertise and 'nose' then the team depends on its individuals. And what a mixture of the extraordinary and ordinary they have turned out to be! So many of them, in the early days as now, have been country-born and bred, often from humble backgrounds, their shared characteristics being tenacity, loyalty, ferocious application to duty and with few exceptions dedication to their task to the exclusion of family life, wealth or private interests. Little of this has changed in seventy-odd years. The hours are just as killing, the demands are certainly greater. Retirement now comes at fifty-five for most senior detectives and they are thrust back into a world in which nothing can seem quite as real as the world of villainy they have left, and in which they have had precious little time to cultivate either garden or acquaintances outside 'The Job'.

Today, although murder figures stay more or less constant, the work of the Murder Squad has been reduced. So diligent have they been in passing on their expertise, that more and more murder inquiries are being successfully dealt with by local forces, whose men are now better educated and infinitely better trained than their counterparts of seventy years ago.

The Yard men for their part are reverting to the more generalized field which their formal but less popular title accurately describes – the Serious Crimes Squad. The Woolliscroft case was one of only seven murders in 1977 involving Yard detectives, but the Squad remains on call to any police force asking for help. There are still three names in the frame in the Murder Room, in turn ready to go to whatever crime turns up, and when the telephone rings a detective still answers 'Murder Room'.

Index

313

316

318